SHADOW OF THE LIONS

SHADOW

of the

LIONS

A NOVEL

CHRISTOPHER SWANN

ALGONQUIN BOOKS
OF CHAPEL HILL
2017

Published by
ALGONQUIN BOOKS OF CHAPEL HILL
Post Office Box 2225
Chapel Hill, North Carolina 27515-2225

a division of
WORKMAN PUBLISHING
225 Varick Street
New York, New York 10014

LIBRARY OF CONGRESS CATALOGING-IN-PUBLICATION DATA
Names: Swann, Christopher, 1970– author.
Title: Shadow of the lions / a novel by Christopher Swann.
Description: First edition. | Chapel Hill, North Carolina :
Algonquin Books of Chapel Hill, 2017.
Identifiers: LCCN 2017002940 | ISBN 9781616205003
Subjects: LCSH: English teachers—Fiction. | Missing children—Fiction. |
Preparatory school students—Fiction. | Preparatory schools—Faculty—Fiction.
Classification: LCC PS3619.W3557 S53 2017 | DDC 813.6—dc23
LC record available at https://lccn.loc.gov/2017002940

10 9 8 7 6 5 4 3 2 1
First Edition

This novel is dedicated
to my sons, Whitaker and Sullivan,
and to my wife, Kathy, for everything.

SHADOW OF THE LIONS

PROLOGUE

The two lions crouched on top of their pedestals, frozen in preparation to leap. One was snarling, its stone teeth menacing in the late-afternoon shadows, while the other stared out with disdain at the broad sweep of empty soybean fields that lay just across the state highway, a disdain made all the more pointed because the lion was missing its left eye.

The missing eye was their only major flaw. A myth of swift and terrible justice falling on those who harmed the lions had shielded them from further disfigurement over the years. Blackburne legend had it that the student who chiseled out the left eye as a class prank in 1947 died that same week, drowning in the Shenandoah Creek when his canoe tipped over. Since then, the lions had been revered by the students, and although time had worn away at these guardians of Blackburne's front entrance, the lions remained fixed to the spot where they had sat for more than a century. The columns of Raleigh Hall, the freshman dorm, might be painted pink; a faculty member's car might be placed inside the dining hall in the dead of night; the headmaster might open his office one morning to find every square inch filled with balloons. But the lions were left alone.

Jogging in place to keep from cooling down, I stared up at the lions, breath issuing from my open mouth like steam. It was half a mile back to the track, and the temperature was unusually cold for the middle of March. I didn't want to cramp up. But I didn't leave, either, just jogged in place and tried through sheer willpower to lower my heart rate and slow my breathing. Running from the track to the school gate and back was a typical warm-up, but I was alone. My teammates were running in the opposite direction, to the old closed bridge over the Shenandoah. I had asked Coach Meier if I could run to the gate, knowing he would say yes. I was a team captain and a senior—he had every reason to trust me. So when he nodded absently at me, I ran hard, sprinting away from the track and putting distance between myself and my team. Living at Blackburne, in close quarters with four hundred other boys in the Virginia countryside, could be claustrophobic. But that wasn't why I had run away from the others, feet pounding the road even after I reached the broad belt of trees that surrounded Blackburne's campus like a forest wall.

My father had told me the previous fall at the annual Blackburne–Manassas Prep game that in times of crisis, a man's instinct is to do one of two things: retreat to a place of safety, or gather up his strength and hurl himself headlong into the fray. We had been talking about football—Blackburne was down ten points in the third quarter—and I had been all for the headlong hurling into the fray, in this case a grand and sweeping gesture, a trick play like a flea flicker. My father had shaken his head gently—he was always gentle when he disagreed with me—and said that we needed to stick to basics, trust our defense and our running game instead of trying to be something we weren't. "Y'all keep throwing the ball and going nowhere, Matthias," he said. "Play to your strengths. It may be boring, but it works."

This had angered me, as my roommate was one of the wide receivers. Granted, he had uncharacteristically dropped one pass, but my father's words had sounded treasonous. "Fritz is doing his best," I told him sullenly. My irritation only deepened when Blackburne started running the ball and slowly but inexorably marched downfield, scored a touchdown with six minutes left, and then forced a turnover, running the ball back to win twenty-one to seventeen.

Looking from one lion to the other while I ran as if on an invisible treadmill, I did not know whether I was retreating to a place of safety to lick my wounds, or trying to gather myself together before heading back to school and facing what I had done.

The Blackburne School, like most boarding schools in America, has its own fiercely held traditions. Some are idiosyncratic, like the bonfire torches that freshmen—third formers in Blackburne parlance—must construct out of burlap, wire, and two-by-fours. Others are born out of a fundamental belief in certain core principles, a belief that borders on fervor. The honor code at Blackburne is rooted in such a belief. Its rules are stark as barbed wire against snow: you will not lie, or cheat, or steal, or tolerate those who do. The punishment for being found guilty of violating the honor code is expulsion. And I had violated the code.

Running in place between the two lions, I didn't hear Fritz coming down the drive. One moment, I was alone; the next, Fritz appeared from out of the trees that were beginning to soften with shade as the sun lowered to the horizon. He ran up, gasping, and stopped by the lion with the missing eye. "Ho, Matthias," he said, and then bent at the waist, sucking in air through his mouth, hands at his hips.

"Ho, Fritz," I said halfheartedly. It was our typical way of greeting each other, almost a call-and-response. Both of us had been teased about our Germanic first names when we started rooming together our fourth form year. The Huns, some of our classmates called us. At first we ignored the nickname, and then we gave in to it. Apart from being a rather mild joke at our expense, it was now an identifying label, another thread in the fabric of our class. Daryl Cooper was called Diamond, Jay Organ was Beef, and Fritz and I were the Huns. Such tags were a sign of acceptance, even approval, and they often had odd effects on those who bore them. One morning when the clock alarm went off and I was slow to hit the snooze button, Fritz looked over the rail of his upper bunk and stared blearily down at me. "Ho, Matthias," he said. I looked up at him. "Ho, Fritz," I said. And that was that. People outside of all-male boarding schools might snigger about the close relationships that develop between boys, imagining some sort of fervid buggery in the basements of the classroom buildings or the shower stalls of the dorms. While this wasn't true, at least in my experience, students at Blackburne did establish intense, long-lasting friendships with one another, something that on a platonic level was most likely not experienced again until marriage. Fritz and I had that bond. We weren't brothers; we were beyond that. He was perhaps the one person whose counsel and opinion I held higher than my own.

Facing Fritz at the lions, I realized with a soul-biting irony that I could tell him anything except what I had done, because aside from possibly being furious, he would also be ashamed for me, and I wouldn't be able to bear it.

"You really ran here," Fritz was saying. He was looking at me, waiting for a reply.

"Just needed to," I said, still jogging in place, hands flopping at the end of my arms. "Wanted to see how far I could push it, you know?"

Fritz wasn't buying it, I could tell, but he just looked off at the fields and gave a knowing nod. It was one of a hundred slight, deliberate gestures boys granted to one another at Blackburne. A warning shake of the head meant *Watch out*, as in *Watch out for Mr. Downing—he's on the warpath.* A one-shouldered shrug was a studied gesture of indifference. Cutting your eyes away from a classmate you passed in the hall could be as cruel as sneering in his face. Fritz's nod meant he didn't believe me, but he affected understanding—he knew I wasn't telling the truth but accepted my lie all the same. That nod about did me in. I had to blink away tears, which thankfully I could blame on the sharp weather. My emotions welled up and threatened to spill out of my throat, but I choked them down with an effort.

"Mail came," Fritz was saying.

I was taken aback, and then relaxed. This was familiar territory. "And?"

"Nothing."

"It's early yet."

"True."

"Look, you're gonna get in, Fritz. If not UVA, then Georgetown, or Washington and Lee, or William and Mary."

Fritz stared over the fields. They were brown and rutted—nothing had even been planted yet. "Okay, but . . . ," he began, and then sighed.

Since the start of the school year, Fritz's anxiety over getting accepted into college had grown until he was muttering to himself between classes, in the dining hall, and when he plodded to the bathroom to brush his teeth. At night he twisted and turned, so by morning his bedsheets were an absolute wreck. It didn't matter that his grades were excellent, that he was a shoo-in for the Latin medal, and that his family was rich and could trace its lineage back at least to the Jamestown colony. It didn't matter that included among his relatives were one grandfather who had been a Pacific combat veteran in WWII, another grandfather who had been a shipping magnate, and an uncle who knew everyone of importance in Washington, D.C. Despite all of this, whenever college was brought up, Fritz looked panicked, as if he couldn't get enough air.

That I had been accepted early to UVA didn't help. Fritz was not petty or shallow—not once did he openly express anything but congratulations for my early acceptance. And yet I knew it had to be eating away at him. At Blackburne, seniors taped their college acceptance letters to the doors of their rooms, icons of our devotion to academic achievement. When I got the UVA letter, my first thought, after experiencing a fierce pang of delight, was to look in Fritz's mailbox. It was empty—he hadn't gotten a letter. At the time, I didn't resent how his disappointment might cast an unwelcome shadow over my success; instead, I worried how I would break the news to him. I even considered hiding the letter. Of course, I ended up telling him that evening during study hall in our room. He gave me his typically lopsided grin and even hugged me, slapping me twice on the back, and then stood expectantly in the middle of the room. "Well?" he asked, and I got some tape out of my desk drawer and affixed the letter to the door, leaving room next to it for its twin when Fritz got his own letter. Every day, Fritz had to pass by that letter and the blank space next to it. Only once did I see him react to it. He was coming into the room—I was at my desk, working—and he paused in the doorway, a hand lifted in greeting, and glanced at the letter on the door. The look on his face was like watching the sun disappear behind a cloud. It passed and then Fritz entered, complaining loudly about a Latin test, but that momentary glance had been all I needed.

Standing by the one-eyed lion, Fritz looked out forlornly over the empty fields. He fingered the Saint Christopher medal he wore around his neck, a gift from his grandfather who'd fought in WWII. Watching him fiddle with that medal, I was annoyed. It was something of a shock to realize that. It felt like a betrayal, but it was also liberating. Tamping down my excitement about UVA had created a resentment that now swelled and threatened to burst. Fritz was being neurotic and self-indulgent and attention-seeking. I knew any minute he would sigh and talk in a defeated tone about college. And I couldn't take it. Not then, not while I was consumed by my own guilt, wrapped up in my own garbage.

Oblivious to all of this, Fritz shook his head. "It's stupid, but it's just— there are all these *expectations*," he said. "I mean, I go to Blackburne, so I'm supposed to be set, right? But what if I'm not? When I was a kid, I told my father I wanted to be a cowboy. He handed me a copy of *Lonesome Dove* and said that was as close as I'd get, that I was *meant* for things. But what? Granddad got a medal at Okinawa. Grandpa Joe built a shipping company out of nothing. My father is a defense contractor who minored in English. *He* built his own company from the ground up, and he can quote Shakespeare and Tennyson at the drop of a hat." He stopped, grimaced, and then shook his head again. "Jesus, listen to me," he said. "I'm sorry. After all you had to go through today with the J-Board and everything, here I am bitching about college and all the crap in my life."

The J-Board, or Judicial Board, was the school's organization of student-elected prefects, the students who embodied the honor code. When a student was accused of violating the honor code, the J-Board determined whether or not that student was guilty. Fritz was a prefect, and I had appeared before the J-Board that morning.

"It's okay," Fritz said, mistaking my silence for feeling awkward about the hearing, having had to sit across from a group of my peers, including my roommate, and be judged. Fritz shrugged with that half smile of his. "I knew you couldn't have done it."

The moment stretched and took on weight like a branch bowing under a load of snow. Long past the point when I should have affirmed my innocence, I said nothing. Fritz stared at me, his eyes widening. It must have been all over my face.

"Fritz," I said, and then stopped. What could I possibly say?

"Jesus Christ," Fritz said. His face was pale. "You fucking did it, didn't you?"

"Fritz, I—"

"I stood up for you. I said there was *no way* you would've—"

"I know," I said, rushing through my confession. "I know, I'm sorry—"

"Do you get what you've done? What kind of position you just put me in?" His voice rose, tightening like a screw biting into wood. "I have to turn you in, Matthias!"

"You can't do that!" I said. "Please, Fritz. It was an accident, I swear."

"You cheated by *accident*?" Fritz looked at me as if I were a stranger, someone contemptible. The pain I felt from his look was so bright and immediate that I was unable then to consider whether or not he was right to judge me that way. He was right, of course. But at the time, all I could see was a rejection of nearly four years of friendship. "Was it an accident when you lied to the Judicial Board?" he said. "When you lied to *me*?" He raised his hands to his head as if he would pull out his hair. "Jesus," he said. "It's too much. It's too goddamn much. I can't trust anyone."

Something in me gave way, a floodgate opening to vent my fear and self-loathing. "Don't give me that holier-than-thou crap," I said. "You're telling me you haven't ever made a mistake?"

He stared at me. "I've never cheated," he said. "Not once."

"Because you haven't had to," I said, warming to my ugliness as if I were holding my frozen hands over a fire, gathering comfort from its heat. "You're a fucking genius who's going to get into college. Yes, you are," I said as he opened his mouth. "You are. And so am I. But the difference is that you don't have to worry about paying for it, or even getting in. You've got the grades and the extracurriculars and all that shit. I mean, Jesus, look at your *family*. You think your father and your uncle won't pull strings for you if they have to? Stop being such a fucking drama queen about it. *God*."

For a few frozen seconds, we stared at each other, stunned and hurt, but only one of us in the wrong. A jay cried in its harsh voice from the darkening wood. Aside from that, we were alone, locked into a terrible moment at the edge of our friendship.

Fritz made the first move. He let the Saint Christopher medal drop from his fingers to dangle on the chain around his neck; then, without a word, he turned and began running up the drive, back to school. Within ten seconds, he was among the trees, and then the drive curved and Fritz curved with it, vanishing from my sight.

After a few more precious seconds passed, I, too, began running, trailing my roommate. My breathing was harsh in my ears as I ran down the drive, leaving the lions behind. I entered the trees, the air beneath the boughs dank and dim and slightly chill. There was a damp, organic smell to the oaks, an earthy scent like ground coffee. I glimpsed Fritz ahead, his tee shirt a white blur, and then he was gone again. I ran after him, my feet and legs registering each impact with the pavement. I felt uneasy, as if I were missing something, or about to. I couldn't see Fritz. Ahead of me, the drive straightened into a short stretch before the final curve, and after that curve, the trees would fall away before the playing fields. The road was empty—no Fritz, no anybody. An invisible hand threatened to squeeze my heart, my stomach. My lungs began to burn as I started sprinting. It wasn't just that I wanted to catch Fritz. I had the distinct feeling that I was chasing him, that I had to catch up with him, before something caught up with me. The trees loomed around me; the road seemed to buckle at my feet. I would have sworn something was behind me, but terror seized me at the thought of turning around to look. To say that I thought the lions had finally leapt off their perches and come bounding after me would sound insane. But I ran up the last hundred yards of that driveway as if I had to outrun whatever imagined thing was pursuing me, or be caught and suffer some horrific fate.

I burst out of the trees and into the wide, sheltered bowl of the playing fields, gasping like a man emerging from a forest fire. I stopped and bent over, trying to catch my breath, hands on my knees. My pulse sledgehammered in my temples. I looked up to see the drive stretch before me and up the Hill, a good quarter mile of asphalt bordered by the track, the golf course, and various dotted stands of trees. Fritz was nowhere to be seen. I turned back to face the wood, half afraid of what I might see, but it was simply a belt of trees that stood there, silent, unrewarding, a dark green forest wall shaded with black as the sun fell. "Fritz?" I called out. "I'm sorry. Where are you?" Nothing. There was no way he could have already made it up the Hill. I could see a few people at the track, but none of them was Fritz. Where the hell had he gone? Maybe he was in the trees behind me, hiding. Or maybe he had made it to the track and I just couldn't tell—the light was dim, fading moment by moment, except for the bright red bars of the clouds overhead, glowing like a grate in a forge with the light of the setting sun.

I gave up. Fritz was hiding, or he had run faster than I thought. I'd apologize to him later, somehow. We would fix this. It would be okay. So

I tried to convince myself as I began walking, slowly, up the Hill and to the dorms.

I DIDN'T APOLOGIZE TO Fritz that night. Not because I changed my mind or didn't need to. I still need to, all these years later. I didn't apologize to him because he wasn't there to apologize to. No Fritz at dinner; no Fritz at study period. He was gone.

By lights-out, the sheriff had been called. By the next morning, searchers were combing the campus—every building, every subbasement and attic, every shed and grove and hillside. We weren't allowed to join in the search. Dr. Simmons, the headmaster, insisted that we continue with classes, maintain our routine. I think the sheriff probably didn't want us involved, anyway, especially if—as the prevailing theory came to be at the time— Fritz had killed himself. No one wanted a student to stumble across a classmate's corpse.

It would have almost been better to find his body. Instead, Fritz ran into those woods and off the edge of the earth. Police and search-and-rescue groups descended on Blackburne, upending everything. In a way, it was almost exciting, except for the reason they were all there. I was questioned four separate times, including one painful time by Fritz's father, who was almost unhinged with rage and grief. And it was all useless. Every lead, every possible trace, went nowhere. It was like Fritz had been deleted, erased. We didn't even get the scant comfort of a funeral service. We grieved, sure. Boys cried; I was one of them. But at night, alone in my room—our room—for those last terrible weeks of school, it wasn't grief that kept me awake until the deep hours of the night. Two feelings, each contradicting the other, swept through me. First, I was afraid that, because of what I had done and could not confess to doing, whatever gods there were had taken Fritz as punishment. But more than that, I felt jealousy, a bitter jealousy mixed with anger at the fact that Fritz had gone, without me. He had left me behind.

CHAPTER ONE

Years later, I stood again in front of the lions, hands in my pockets as I looked up at them, one defiant, the other coldly reserved. My car—a red Porsche Boxster, my last personal asset of any value—sat parked before the entrance, its driver's side door flung open like an aimless wing. I could smell on the air the sharp tang of cow urine, like cider that has turned. The heat lay heavily on me, and my shirt clung to my back. Summers were always like this here, so warm and humid that you felt you would lie down and sleep forever come evening. But summer was ending, and it seemed as if everything—the trees, the fields, the sky itself—was pausing in anticipation, quietly gathering itself for the leap forward into autumn.

I reached out and ran my hand across the snarling lion's flank. It was rough and surprisingly cool to the touch. My fingers traced the lion's tail, ran up to its mane. I touched an ear, avoided its smooth, perfect eyes, and paused, my finger barely pressing against the tip of a tooth. The lion did not budge. I removed my hand, took a last look at it and its one-eyed partner, and returned to my car. It was getting late, and Sam Hodges was expecting me.

I drove between the lions and into the trees, winding my way slowly up the drive, and remembered something I'd learned as a student at

Blackburne. The school's founder, Colonel Harold "Harry" Blackburne, had planted these trees, mostly oaks, upon his resignation from the Army of Northern Virginia following Lee's surrender at Appomattox. As I drove, I noticed how pristine the ground was for fifty yards on either side of the road. No virgin wood ever looked like this one, with mown lawns at the feet of the trees. It was a minor detail, but it reminded me of how attentive Blackburne was to appearances.

Returning to a place from your past is unsettling. You expect to find the place altered somehow, different in some essential way. Many alumni who return to Blackburne say that the school hasn't changed a bit, and they find comfort in this, a constant in the rapidly shifting, twenty-first-century world. Some, however, return to campus and look disturbed, as if searching for something they cannot find. I'd always rolled my eyes when I'd seen older men gaze wistfully at the oak trees on the Lawn or at the empty football field. It had seemed somehow pathetic. But now I understood why they had looked the way they had. The unchanging school had reminded them of how they had changed, and conjured in them sorrow at the loss of intangible things, innocence and youth and time.

I'd lost all three in the nine years since I had graduated, and I'd lost more besides. Money, for one, a lot of it. A girl, too, Michele, a long-legged pouty blonde—a model, of course. She was poised to get her first magazine cover shoot, and I was a debut novelist with a starred review in *Publishers Weekly*. We careened through New York City like lost partygoers from one of Gatsby's soirées, occupied with getting reservations at the hottest restaurants and being seen at the newest nightclubs and searching for the perfect designer-casual blazer—all the things that I thought were important in my new life as a Young Urban American Novelist. And after the fancy cocktails and the empty brushes with celebrity and the mounting bills and festering insecurities and the small, petty arguments with Michele that turned us into small, petty people, the one thing I'd had and could depend on—a talent for writing, one that had led to a well-received novel, a big advance for book two, and an even bigger payment for the film rights, which were now languishing in some Hollywood studio office—well, that talent had dried up, gone, vanished. It seemed like the most important things in my life vanished.

Sam Hodges, the academic dean at Blackburne and my former advisor, had called me in New York a month before. I hadn't spoken to him since graduating. But when I heard him on the phone saying, "Matthias, my boy!" I could see him as if he were standing in my cramped apartment: prematurely white hair, upturned nose, and the beginnings of a potbelly, all combining to make him look like a spry elf who had his eye on the reindeer and sleigh when Santa retired. Many boys, myself among them, had made the mistake of thinking that Mr. Hodges, with his bow tie and suspenders and jolly smile, was some sort of dim, amiable hick. We hadn't made the same mistake twice.

I couldn't fathom why Sam Hodges would be calling me. And the reason was a genuine compliment. He told me the school had an unexpected opening in the English department—one teacher had gotten married and was moving to Atlanta, and the man they had hired to replace him had been diagnosed with cancer and had chosen to remain where he was in Milwaukee, leaving Blackburne with a spot to fill less than two months before the start of school. Sam Hodges said he'd read an interview with me in the Blackburne alumni magazine in which I was quoted as saying I would be taking some time off from writing. He asked me, if I was still taking time off, whether I would consider spending some of it teaching for a year at Blackburne.

I remembered the interview, which I'd given the previous January, just a couple of months before my agent had dropped me and things with Michele had really started falling apart. I'd been tentative about doing the interview in the first place. It would be my first real connection with Blackburne since graduation, for one thing. For another, I worried about what the interview could reveal, as if I would be submitting to an interrogation.

In the end, all it involved were some e-mail exchanges and one longish phone call with a woman in Blackburne's alumni office. It wasn't an investigative piece by any stretch of the imagination, but more of an overview of my writing career and a few standard questions about my novel and how I'd come to write it. And now Sam Hodges was offering me a job to teach at Blackburne. Jesus.

If I hadn't been desperate, I would have laughed at the irony. But there wasn't anything left for me in New York, except a propensity for accumulating debt, both financial and emotional. There was no new novel coming, Michele was most definitely out of the picture, and I needed to get my shit together. I actually had some teaching experience, too—a couple of comp and lit courses while I was in grad school, nothing extensive, but I hadn't been horrible at it. Also, at some level, I felt I owed Blackburne. I'd grown up there, written my first fiction there. And I had turned my back on the place. I had not been to my five-year reunion, nor had I seen any of my classmates since graduation except for the handful that had gone to UVA with me, and even then I'd consciously avoided them as much as I could without being openly rude. I'd cut Blackburne off like pruning a blighted branch from a tree. And now I, the product of that school so dedicated to rigorously training its students to achieve success, had soared out into the wider world, briefly scaled the empyrean heights, and then plummeted to Earth. In short, I had failed. Perhaps by returning to Blackburne I could start over.

Downshifting around the final turn before the edge of the wood, I almost didn't see it in the fading daylight. But as the fields beyond became visible through a glimmering arch in the trees, I glimpsed movement among the gray trunks to my left. It was as if someone had suddenly shouted in my ear. Everything else fell away. I slammed on my brakes, my seat belt locking across my chest. Something next to a tree raised its head and gazed at me. I registered a long neck, a black nose, ears wide and alert above a pair of dark, cool eyes. I stared at it for a few heartbeats, and even as I thought the word *deer* it turned and leapt gracefully between two trees, then bounded away into the woods, its tail flashing into the dark.

I let out a shuddering breath, and as I drew air into my lungs I felt a pang of anger so fierce that I had to squeeze my steering wheel. I told myself it was because I could have hit the deer, that I could have seriously damaged my car, or killed the deer, or me. After taking a couple of deep breaths and peering carefully into the trees on both sides of the drive, I drove on, finishing the final curve. I resisted the urge to glance in my rearview mirror.

My car burst out from the protective cover of the trees onto the hard, flat playing fields. I slowed to bump gently over a speed trap, stopped briefly at the new security booth to give my name to the guard, a polite and efficient stranger, and then rolled on when the gate lifted. I cruised past the soccer goals, skeletal without their nets, and then the newly re-furbished track that ringed the old football field. Next came the low field house with its roof proclaiming, in red and yellow paint, "Lions Number One!" While I had braced for it, seeing Blackburne after all that time was almost a physical shock, as if I were standing under a great bell that had just struck the hour. And then I saw up ahead, past the boxwood shrubs that lined the upper part of the drive, the gleaming white columns and Colonial brick of the Hill, and as I watched, the setting sun touched the front of the buildings with a departing glow, melting against the windows and setting them afire with a golden light.

CHAPTER TWO

lmost fourteen years earlier—half my life ago!—I'd stood in the center of my new room at Blackburne, holding a suitcase in each hand and staring around me in disbelief. The room was empty save for a bunk bed, two desks, a wooden dresser, a closet alcove with a single rail but no door, and a window that looked painted shut. The window was covered on the outside with mesh wire, presumably for security or to keep the glass from breaking. To me it looked like a cage.

My father, hands in his pockets, was doing much the same thing as I was, but I could tell, even without looking at him, what he was thinking. His first words confirmed it: he was going to look at the bright side, find the silver lining. "Well, your roommate's not here yet," he said. "Looks like you get to choose which bunk you want."

I just looked at him. My parents were going to leave me here, abandon me in this cell, and my father was cheerfully offering a choice of beds. "Doesn't matter," I muttered.

"Sure it does," Dad insisted. "Bottom bunk's easier—you don't have to climb in and out of bed—but then you've got somebody sleeping on top of you, and you're staring at the bottom of a mattress all night—"

I tuned him out and continued to stare miserably around me. I couldn't believe they'd talked me into this. "Blackburne will be a whole other world," my mother had said. "You'll have so many opportunities." Words like *opportunities* and *education* and *personal growth* had floated around my house for months. My teachers had been highly impressed that I was applying to Blackburne. Even my small group of friends, who I thought—with a tinge of desperation—would miss me if I went to boarding school out of state, had started looking at me the way I imagine people who wait tables in L.A. look at one of their waiter buddies who finally lands a small TV role: with a combination of amazement, suspicion, and mute respect. All this had been wrapped up in the kind of mumbled good wishes fourteen-year-old boys give to one another. When I'd gotten my acceptance letter from Blackburne, I had thought, like an idiot, that this was a good idea.

As my father listed the pros and cons of bunk beds, my mother unzipped my bags and started hanging shirts and pants in the closet. Dad was a pediatrician, much beloved by his patients back home in Asheville. Mom had been a nurse's assistant and now managed my father's practice. They were both good, decent people, obvious in their care and love for each other and for me, their only son. At fourteen, I thought they were completely mortifying. I even hated them a little, not just for threatening to drop me off here and drive away, but because, deep down, I loved them fiercely and was stunned to realize this as I stood in that room, imagining our good-byes.

I probably would have started weeping, maybe even thrown myself onto the floor at their feet, pleading to go home with them, if my roommate hadn't shown up just then. I was suddenly conscious of a tall, muscular boy standing in the doorway, his hair in cornrows and a tiny diamond stud in his left ear, a duffel bag slung over one arm. "Hey," he said to me, jerking his chin up in greeting. "'S'up."

"Hey," I said.

"Guess we're roomies, huh?"

"I guess. Yeah."

He grinned, a warm, bright smile that lit up his face and even made the room a little less barren. "I'm Daryl," he said.

"Matthias." We shook hands. I remembered my parents and introduced them. Then Daryl's parents came in, tall and slim and dressed as if for church, his dad in a three-piece suit and his mom in a dress and hat. We shook hands all around. I remember being astonished once again at how easily my parents, especially my father, could talk to anyone. Daryl took the opportunity to ask if I cared which bunk I got, and when I shrugged, he tossed his duffel onto the bottom bunk. "Got to get up early for football workouts," he explained. "Don't want to be climbing down out of bed and waking you up, shaking the bed frame."

Eventually, our parents left. Daryl shook his father's hand and then hugged his mother, telling them not to worry because he would be tearing up the place soon. He punched me on the arm when he said this, as if for emphasis, and I gave a sickly grin. I was too embarrassed to cry in front of Daryl, and a little in awe of him, so I screwed my face on tight and suffered my mother's tears and my father's proud smile. Daryl and I watched our parents drive off, their taillights flashing red as they neared a curve on the road around the Hill, and then their cars slipped around the curve and vanished. I cried into my pillow that night—fierce, silent, jagged sobs. If Daryl heard me, he didn't say anything, for which I was grateful.

It was our hall prefect, John Cole, who gave Daryl his nickname when he told him to take his diamond stud out. As a prefect, a member of the student-elected Judicial Board, John was in charge of our floor as a kind of resident advisor, or RA, making sure we woke up on time, made our beds, behaved somewhat better than caged animals, and went to sleep at lights-out. Our first week of school, he also talked to us about Blackburne's honor code, which had been in existence since Colonel Blackburne began his school in 1876. My parents had sung high praise for the wonders of such a code of conduct, which, to me, seemed only to offer more reasons for which I could be expelled.

That first week, John Cole took everyone on our floor outside onto the Lawn, where we sat in a ragged circle under one of the oak trees. John was from New Hampshire, and for that alone I held him in some respect, having never been farther north than Virginia. John was fair-skinned with bright blue eyes and straight brown hair neatly parted to one side. If he'd worn glasses, he might have been pegged as a geek, but he was self-assured in the way only high school seniors can be. A wrestler, he also displayed a kind of monastic discipline, an economy of movement and expression that made him seem older and wiser than seventeen.

When we had all sat down underneath the boughs of the oak tree, John asked us if we knew about the honor code. Dutifully, we murmured yes. We'd all been given a small white pamphlet outlining the honor code and the role of the Judicial Board. John nodded thoughtfully. "The honor code is the oldest institution here at Blackburne," he said. "Older than some of these trees, probably. It has not changed since it was first implemented. Think about that. Over a hundred and twenty years." He looked each of us in the eye as he said this last part. I glanced away, slightly embarrassed.

"It hasn't changed because it's simple and it's effective," John said. "Don't lie. Don't cheat. Don't steal. Don't permit others to do those things, either. Simple."

Miles Camak raised his hand. "So, you just get kicked out if you do one of those things?" he asked.

"Yep," John said.

Miles scratched his cheek. "Okay," he said, somewhat doubtfully.

John gave a little smile. "Hard to imagine, isn't it?"

"Harsh," murmured Roger Bloom.

"Yes," John said. "But it's the only way an honor code can work. Really work." He looked at us. "Imagine that you're taking a test and you see your neighbor cheat. Could you turn him in?" Silence. "Could you, Matthias?" he said, turning to me, and heat rose in my face and the back of my neck as everyone stared.

"I—I don't know," I managed.

John seemed to consider this, while I had the distinct impression that I had failed some sort of test. John didn't change his expression, though, so I couldn't be sure.

"Centuries ago, in Japan," John said, "the samurai followed a code of conduct known as *Bushido*. It means 'the way of the warrior.' One of the most important tenets of *Bushido* was a sense of honor. The samurai valued honor above life. If a samurai felt he had failed in his duty, he would commit *seppuku*, ritual suicide." He paused, lifting an eyebrow. "Now *that's* harsh," he said. Several people chuckled.

I glanced at Daryl, making a face like *Can you believe this guy*, but Daryl was staring at John, a bit wary but obviously engaged. Quickly I looked back over at John, too.

"The honor code seems cruel, I know," John said. "I thought the same thing at first. But it makes this place what it is. There are no locks on the doors to our dorm rooms. You can forget your backpack in the library and come back the next day and it will still be there. Your word takes on real meaning. Someone tells you something and you know it's the truth. There aren't many places on Earth where that happens. This is one of them."

Over the next few days, the guys on my floor would whisper "*Bushido*" to one another and we'd crack up, but we did it secretly, out of earshot of John Cole. And although we didn't want to admit it, his earnest speech about the honor code, instead of sounding corny, had struck home with most of us. We were now a part of this century-old tradition.

However, the most immediate impact John Cole made on us was telling Daryl to take his diamond stud out of his ear or he'd give him detention. Daryl did it grudgingly, and the next morning, John woke us up for breakfast by knocking loudly on the door, throwing it open, and proclaiming, "Morning, Matthias! Morning, Diamond! Rise and shine, boys!"

"Don't know what Diamond that motherfucker be talking about,"

Daryl muttered, but the nickname stuck, and pretty soon he was Diamond to everybody.

Being fourteen and hopelessly naive about most things, including myself, I was captivated by Diamond. I had known hardly any black kids at my predominantly white junior high. His forceful personality, his easy use of profanity out of earshot of teachers and prefects, and his casual acceptance of me as his roommate bowled me over. Combine that with a keen intelligence and the physique of a Greek statue, not to mention that he seemed destined to be a starting varsity running back, and Diamond was like a demigod who allowed me, a pitiful mortal, to enter his sphere. Within a week, I was infatuated with the guy.

That my infatuation could be considered in any way homosexual was my secret fear. To be labeled gay at an all-male school was the worst, most devastating blow that could be leveled at a student. Being called a pussy just made you weak, and cocksucker was just another, harsher word for asshole, but being called a faggot was to be cast into the outer darkness.

To say categorically that I was not and am not homosexual, and that I did not harbor any such inclinations toward Diamond or any other student at my school, must come across as me protesting a bit too much. I can only say that it's true. I didn't lust after Diamond—I lusted after his attributes. I wanted to be like him so I could shut down any potential bullies with an angry stare, and conquer girls with all the rough ease of a 007. As I was nothing like Diamond, I could only gaze at him and hope that somehow some of his Diamond-ness would rub off on me, transforming me overnight from an awkward, metal-mouthed beanpole into a cocksure Casanova.

This did not happen. Diamond, as I've said, was cut like ancient statuary, whereas I had a concave chest and arms like rubber bands. In the bathroom, where we showered four at a time, I'd glance surreptitiously between his legs, wondering if what I'd heard about black males being well endowed was true, but the truth was that Diamond seemed, like everyone else I showered with, pretty much adequate, while I would peer in disgust at the wilted carrot between my own legs. (Jay "Beef" Organ, whose massive organ swiftly became legend, was the exception. "Boy's hung like a cable car" was Diamond's own assessment.) Even the tight cornrows sweeping across Diamond's scalp seemed to mock my own limp brown hair.

Ever hopeful, I continued hanging out with Diamond. I tried to listen to his music, a funky mix of Tupac Shakur and Wu-Tang Clan and Digital Underground, but I secretly preferred my old classic rock CDs, putting on my headphones and surrounding myself in a sonic fume of Led Zeppelin, the Doors, and the Rolling Stones. Diamond's quick wit proved even harder to copy, and I usually just resorted to profanity whenever a clever response was called for. "Yeah, well, fuck that" became my stock phrase until one day Diamond told me that I was going to be tagged Fuckhead for the rest of my life unless I pulled my head out of my ass and got my motherfucking shit together, dig?

All of this took place in a whirlwind of classes and study halls and sports—I was on the "Cub" soccer team for third formers—so that we were often too busy for any real introspection. What free time we had, we spent trying to improve our position on the social ladder, or sleeping. So I didn't realize that my clinging to Diamond, eating with him at every meal, or trying to copy his every move, could be viewed as annoying, or that he might find my constant questions and assumptions about him offensive.

I remember asking him once about girls and making some inane comment about how I'm sure his dance moves would "floor the bitches," with an intended sexual pun on *floor*. He looked up at me from his desk. "What, I can dance 'cause I'm black?" he asked.

"What?" I said.

"You heard me," he said. "It's a black thing, right? I can dance, I can 'floor the bitches' because I've got a higher level of melanin than you do?"

I stared at him from my upper bunk. "What the fuck are you talking about?" I asked.

He pointed at me. "See, that's another thing," he said. "You got to cut out this cussing shit all the time. 'Cause it's old, and all it does is make you look desperate. I cuss 'cause it's who I am. You do it 'cause you think it'll make you look tougher. Which it doesn't."

I was stunned. No one had ever so openly laid bare my insecurities. So I went on the offensive. "I want to go back to the part where you called me a racist," I said.

Diamond's eyebrows went up. "Nobody called you a racist."

"Yes, you did," I said indignantly. "You said—"

"What I *said*"—Diamond leaned forward in his chair, stabbing his finger in the air for emphasis, as if he were impaling his words—"was that you were *suggesting* I can *dance* well because I'm *black*, which I was trying to point out is a racial *stereotype*. So happens I *can* dance well, but that don't make the stereotype less bad, is all I'm saying."

"So I try to give you a fucking compliment and now I'm, what, some kind of *bigot*?"

"Man, what the fuck is wrong with you?"

"Uh-oh, better watch your mouth, Diamond," I said. "Somebody'll think you're just trying to look big."

We went on for a bit, insulting each other and becoming loud enough that John Cole came down the hall—it was a few minutes before lights-out— and told us to knock it off or we'd get stuck with demerits. We went to bed, still pissed at each other. The next morning, Diamond got up early and went to the weight room. Then he came back and showered and went to breakfast, all without saying a word to me.

After he left, I sat in our room and realized with horror that I had made precious few friends other than him. There was Trip Alexander, a tall, reserved boy from Dallas who played Cub soccer and was in my English class, but we didn't socialize much outside of class or the soccer field.

Miles Camak was in my biology class and liked the same music I did, and we'd swapped a couple of CDs. Everyone else in our class was either a brief acquaintance, a stranger, an undesirable, or someone who was friends with Diamond and simply tolerant of me as Diamond's roommate. I determined to start making some new friends and marched to breakfast as if on a mission. I sat with Trip Alexander and spoke with some other kids in our class, and was surprised to find how easy it was.

Later that evening, Diamond apologized to me. "Didn't mean to come off so strong, man," he said. "It's just that the work's harder than I thought and football's kicking my ass. I mean, I'm kicking it right back," he added, with a grin, "but it's worn me down a little, got me frazzled. We cool?"

I nodded. "Sure," I said, "I'm sorry, too," and gave Diamond a fist bump. But deep down I was still angry at Diamond for how much influence he had on me. Looking back, I realize I was mad at the wrong person.

I became closer friends with Trip and Miles, playing Ping-Pong with one or the other of them in the attic of Raleigh, going with them on weekend afternoons to watch one of the thousand or so movies in the school's old A/V center on the top floor of the library. Diamond and I still hung out and ate together most of the time, but I was pulling away from him a little. And then I fucked up.

Fletcher Dupree was a kid in our class who was both popular and annoying as hell. Today he'd be diagnosed with ADHD and slapped on Adderall, but back then, he was probably described by adults as just "high-spirited." He had a knack for figuring out your most vulnerable area and then exploiting it publicly for laughs. At a packed lunch table, Fletcher had asked Roger Bloom, an oversized football center, why he liked listening to George Michael, and then looked on with disbelief and mock disgust as Roger, who obviously did like George Michael and was embarrassed at this public outing, tried to stammer a response while everyone else roared with laughter. One Saturday night when it was hotter than a boiler room in Hades—Raleigh Hall did not have air-conditioning, and so we all had floor fans blasting away constantly—I stripped down to my underwear under my single bedsheet, trying to fall asleep. Soon after I did, Fletcher snuck into our room and yanked the sheet off me. Then he burst out laughing and ran down the hall. Next morning at breakfast, I had to hear from Fletcher all about how I wore tighty-whities. Never mind the guy who was creeping around the dorm and pulling bedsheets off people— apparently I was the pervert for wearing only jockey shorts in bed when it was ninety-seven degrees. But Diamond had laughed at Fletcher's comments, too, which only fanned the coals of resentment I had stoked.

One night after study hall, as a bunch of us headed back to dorm, Fletcher's voice rose out of the dark. He was complaining about his roommate, Max Goren, who snored "like a goddamn elephant seal," which made a few of us chuckle. Then Fletcher asked, casually, "Hey, Matthias, what's it like rooming with Diamond?"

My first instinct was to say it was fine, that he was a good guy, which was true. I knew, however, that this would probably result in some sort of ridicule from Fletcher about how much I worshipped my roommate, which would crack everyone up. So, sensing an opportunity to dig safely at my roommate, I said, "Oh, he's cool. But, man, does he stink when he comes back from football practice. It's like a fucking water buffalo or something."

To my horror, from out of the dark I heard Diamond say, "Fuck you, Glass!" Fletcher brayed with laughter, as did everyone else. In vain I tried to apologize to Diamond, who just muttered, "Whatever," and then ignored me while everyone laughed at how Fletcher had set me up and how spectacularly I'd fallen for it.

All that evening before lights-out, I apologized to Diamond, begged him to forgive me, told him I was stupid and insensitive. I even told him I was scared of Fletcher and thought if I made him laugh, maybe he'd think I was all right and not tease me. "That just shows how fucking stupid you are," Diamond said, heading for the bathroom with his toothbrush. I stayed in my bunk, staring at the ceiling until Diamond came back in, hit the lights, and got into his bunk, causing the entire bed frame to shiver.

The next day at breakfast, Diamond carried his tray to the far side of the cafeteria, away from the area where we always sat. After a moment of standing indecisively with my tray, I slowly headed for our usual table. Fletcher Dupree was already there, along with a few other classmates, and my heart sank, but he didn't seem to notice me, so I sat down at the table as far away from him as possible. Then Fletcher seemed about to sneeze and held up his hand as if in warning, and when everyone had stopped eating to look at him, his eyes shut, nose crinkled, mouth open in a grimace, he threw his head forward in a fake sneeze and uttered "Water buffalo," throwing the table into an uproar. After a few seconds, I calmly picked up my tray and, ignoring the catcalls and pleas to return, went to sit alone at a window table, staring out at the brightening day. Trip Alexander and Miles Camak came over to sit with me, and we ate mostly in silence, but their gesture meant a lot.

It was a brief respite. By the time I got back to my room, I found Diamond staring at a sheet of paper tacked to our door. It was a list of all the varsity football players and their jersey numbers, with a note stating that we needed to have these numbers memorized by the end of study hall tonight, or else. "Motherfucking don't believe this shit," Diamond said, scowling. "I got a Latin test *and* a bio lab today."

"What does 'or else' mean?" I asked.

Diamond shot a sideways glance at me, and then looked back at the sheet. "It's Third Form Night tonight," he said.

Third Form Night was a time-honored ritual at Blackburne. Immediately after study hall, the varsity football players would corral the third formers in the auditorium in the Montbach Fine Arts Center and lead us through a program of school spirit. Unofficially, it was a hazing, but no one knew what that meant. Did we have to do push-ups? Run laps? Eat onions? Fourth formers rolled their eyes and laughed when we asked about it. All we knew was that some of us would be chosen at random and told to identify the jersey number of a given varsity player. If we failed to correctly identify the player's number . . . Well, it was understood that we needed to correctly identify the number. Period. Not knowing what would happen was worse than having the fatal knowledge.

Diamond ripped the sheet off our door and handed it to me. "You better start reading," he said. "I already got one from Coach last week. Motherfucking bullshit." Before I had the chance to do more than stammer a quick thanks, he retrieved his backpack from our room and headed to class.

All anyone could talk about at lunch was Third Form Night. "They make you eat a stick of butter if you screw up," Roger Bloom said in a low voice. "With Tabasco sauce."

"I heard they make you run around the Hill until you pass out," Miles said.

Trip protested this. "You can't run until you *pass out*," he said. "You'd have to run, like, a marathon. That's like torture."

"Think they care?" Miles said.

"Glad I've had a week to look at the list," Roger said.

"A *week*?" Miles was incredulous. "That's not fair!"

"Who's gonna run with you while you run around the Hill?" Trip insisted, still arguing against the run-until-you-pass-out theory. "What, they've got golf carts or something? It's a crock."

"Why'd you get an extra *week*?"

"I play JV football. They gave it to all of us. But if we screw it up, we're dead meat. Worse than you guys."

Classes passed in a blur, all of us sitting at our desks like men awaiting the long march to the gallows, praying for a reprieve. At soccer practice, we played with a frantic energy that impressed our coaches, who didn't realize we were scared half out of our wits. We trudged reluctantly up the Hill after practice, not wanting to turn our backs on the fading day. Dinner was miserable, and even though Trip still swore they couldn't really hurt us because the teachers wouldn't allow it, his was a lone voice. A trio of sixth formers walked past our table and slowed, grinning at us like cats surveying a rack of mice.

For the first six weeks of school, all third formers had to go to the large lecture hall in Stadler for the evening study period. We shuffled in, all of us carrying our rosters to hopefully memorize over the next two hours. Mr. Downing, an old bulldog of a Latin teacher who had taught at Black-burne for thirty years, sat behind a desk on a dais at the back of the room where he could oversee us. He barked at us to get seated, and we obeyed. When the bell rang for the start of study hall, I got out my English grammar book to complete an exercise on fragments and run-on sentences. I couldn't look at the football roster. I was too nervous, and so I reasoned that homework would calm me down. After about half an hour, I did feel a bit calmer, and spent the rest of the first study period looking over the roster of fifty-odd names.

When the bell rang for break, everybody got up to stretch and go to the bathroom. I put my head down on my desk to take a brief nap, but startled cries brought me and everyone else out of the room and into the hallway. Posted on every door to every classroom was a photocopy of a stylized, roaring lion's head drawn in black, red, and gold. They had not been on the doors when we had gone into Stadler. Even Trip Alexander was quiet now.

The second study period was essentially useless. No matter how hard I looked at the roster, names and jersey numbers slipped out of my mind like water through a clenched fist. I looked at the clock on the wall, watching the second hand slowly sweep its way around. How many times had I willed that clock to go faster! Now I wanted it to stop, or start winding backward, maybe all the way back to the day my parents had first uttered the word *Blackburne* so I could say no and end this nightmare.

With five minutes left in study hall, I heard Trip gasp. I looked over and saw, with a start, a face looking at us through the square window in the door. It was a monstrous face, red and yellow and black, the eyes leering, the mouth open in a fierce grin. The face vanished. From the low, astonished cries around me, I knew I hadn't been alone in seeing it.

Behind us, in a low, gravelly voice, Mr. Downing said, "They're gonna getcha."

A whoop from the hall was answered by half a dozen other whoops, as if a troop of crazed Indian braves were waiting outside. I shot a look at Diamond, sitting two aisles over. He turned to look at me, the first acknowledgment he'd made all evening that I existed, and my bowels turned to ice water. Diamond looked scared.

Slowly, from outside the room, came a vibrating sound that grew in intensity. Whoever was in the hallway was stomping their feet, slowly at first and then faster and faster. A rebel yell broke out, followed by whoops and cries. Eyes widened and sought desperately, frantically, for escape. We all cowered in the lecture hall, waiting for the stroke of doom.

The bell rang. Immediately, the door to the room burst open, and three enormous sixth formers, their shirts off, their faces and chests slathered with red and gold war paint, bounded in. "Run, boys!" one of them hollered at us. He waved us on like a paratrooper waving new recruits through the open door of an airplane. "Go! Go!" We bleated like sheep and ran through the doorway, leaving our books and backpacks behind. Older boys lined the hallway, shouting at us and waving us to the exit doors at the far end. We burst out into the night between another double cordon of football players, some with flashlights, all of them waving us down the walkway to the fine arts building. They shouted and screamed at us, and we yelled back incoherently as we stumbled down the path and then up the stairs and into the lobby of the building. I barely registered seeing two teachers in the lobby, standing to the side as if viewing an art gallery. Then we thundered into the auditorium, where upperclassmen in white football jerseys guided us into rows of seats and yelled at us to remain standing. I recognized John Cole as one of them, gleefully haranguing a new boy.

Onstage, the varsity football team was stomping and clapping and hooting at us, the noise threatening to crescendo to an almost painful level. Spotlights from the ceiling washed over them, bathing them in white-hot light. Suddenly one of them shouted, "L!"

"L!" the team shouted back.

"I!"

"I!" they shouted.

"O!"

Enough of us had gathered our wits to shout "O!" along with the team.

"N!"

"N!" we screamed, shaking the rafters.

"S!"

"S!" I screamed, so loud I thought my vocal cords would bleed.

"Go-o-o Lions! Fight team *fight!*" the team finished in unison. Pandemonium—hollers, fists thrust to the ceiling, veins taut in foreheads and necks. Everywhere I looked, I saw a screaming, exultant football player. We tried to match them, but we were like Girl Scouts trying to drown out the audience at a metal concert. Never in my life had I been subject to such raw, impassioned noise, and it both terrified and thrilled me.

We were led through a few more cheers, which we dutifully screamed as loud as we could. It proved cathartic—I was able to shed some of my earlier fear by yelling my head off. But then I realized that the football players were ushering someone onto the stage, where a lone, empty chair awaited under a spotlight. They brought the boy to the chair and made him sit down. To my dismay, it was Diamond.

"All right!" one of the varsity players onstage said, this one with a shaved head and no neck to speak of. "We're gonna see how well you boys know your varsity football players. Diamond! Who am I?"

Diamond, surrounded by a semicircle of varsity players, looked up at the boy addressing him and tried to smile, though it looked like a grimace. He licked his lips and cast a glance around. "Uh," he seemed to say.

"What?" No Neck said, incredulous. "You don't *know*?" He plucked his jersey front and shook it. "Number forty-eight! Come on, Diamond! Who am I?"

Someone next to me said, "Don't worry, they won't hurt him."

I turned to see a boy about my height, with brown hair grown a little long in front. He gave me a slight, lopsided smile.

"What?" I asked.

"They won't hurt him. Your roommate." He nodded at the stage. "Look."

I looked. Diamond had gotten No Neck's name wrong, so they were making him do push-ups, bellowing out the count. At twenty, they made him stop and hustled him offstage while they brought up the next third former.

"It's just a game," the boy said. "There's a teacher at every exit. Plus they don't want to hurt us, anyway. It's just a way to get everyone pumped up."

I checked the exits to confirm what he was saying about the teachers, and there they were, one or two at every exit, watching silently, arms folded. And Diamond was safely back in his seat several rows up, smiling with relief. I let out a breath I didn't even know I'd been holding in and then glanced at the boy next to me. I felt a bit foolish about having been so scared.

But the boy seemed to read my thoughts and just shook his head. "My father went here. That's the only reason I know. Otherwise I'd be pissing my pants."

Relief and gratitude swept over me. "Thanks," I said. "I'm Matthias."

He smiled. "I'm Fritz."

CHAPTER THREE

O n the Saturday before students arrived for orientation, we had an all-faculty meeting and subsequent department meetings, where I had met with Sam Hodges and my other English department colleagues. They were all earnest, low-key, pleasant men who seemed to enjoy their work and their place at Blackburne. Despite their kind welcome, I felt a bit like an imposter, especially as more than one of them had taught me as a student.

That afternoon, Sam hosted a faculty party at his house. I walked over from my apartment in Lawson-Parker, the double dormitory for fourth- and fifth formers. The sun flared out of a white sky, and a sultry heat lay on the Hill, broken only by the occasional dry rasp from a field cricket. The trees themselves looked hot and tired as they threw blurred shadows over the grass. One of the ever-present faculty dogs lying on the front porch of Huber Hall raised a shaggy head to sniff at me, and then, uninterested, went back to its nap.

Sam and his wife lived just down the Hill from Saint Matthew's Chapel, which was a plain, austere building, its spire rising to a modest height on one end of the Lawn opposite the vast, four-story Stilwell Hall with its massive white columns and portico, its two wings sweeping around to each side as if to claim that end of the Lawn as its own. Sam's house was more in the style of Saint Matthew's: a brick ranch, white trim and black shutters freshly painted, the hedges clipped and grass mown, the brass door knocker gleaming against the black door. A weeping willow drooped in the front yard, its leafy branches trailing over the ground. It reminded me of my parents' house, and the thought stirred something in me that rolled over uneasily.

Several people were already gathered on the patio in Sam's backyard, from which you could see the entire western half of campus, the football field, the nine-hole golf course, and the green wall of trees shimmering in the near distance. Most people seemed relaxed, although Sam, in an apron and chef's hat, looked hot and flushed from the open heat of a massive gas grill, where he stood skewering hot dogs and flipping hamburgers. I saw a few of my new colleagues, some holding beers. I hesitated at the edge of the patio. It was something of a minor shock to look at this group of mostly middle-aged men talking to one another more freely than they had in that morning's faculty meeting—a meeting run in a dry, efficient manner by Dr. Simmons, the headmaster of Blackburne. I had known many of these men to wear ties and blazers almost exclusively, unless they were coaching on the athletic field or in the gym. There had always been a thin but impervious membrane between masters and students. And now I was about to become a master. Yet instead of feeling a sense of accomplishment, I felt reluctance, almost an aversion. Blackburne already had me as an alumnus. Now it was about to claim me as an employee. This was a mistake. I had no business being here, doing this.

"Hey! Matthias!" Porter Deems waved me over from his position by an open cooler. He was a short, dark-haired man with the intent look of someone about to sell you something you didn't want. Grayden Smith stood next to him, frozen for a moment like a startled deer by Porter's voice; then he raised his hand and smiled at me. Both were new Blackburne teachers like me. The three of us had met that morning.

"Fellas," I said, strolling over. "What's up?"

"Getting Gray here a drink. Man's uptight, needs to relax." Porter brought up three dripping bottles of beer from the cooler.

"I'm relaxed," Gray said, twisting the cap off his bottle and flicking it into a nearby trash can. "Just ready for school to start."

We drank our beers, measuring one another silently. Gray had gone to Kentucky and Georgia Tech. He wore spectacles and was quiet without being shy, measured and deliberate in his speech. He would teach chemistry. Porter was a UConn grad with a master's in history from Columbia. He radiated self-assurance and energy, the kind of man who would always be white-water rafting or climbing a rock face.

"Hey, I read your book," Porter said. "Liked the protagonist, that O'Keefe guy. Badass journalist. Sorta Anderson Cooper meets Indiana Jones. But the whole rebel-freedom-fighter thing? I dunno—it was too Hollywood for me." Before I could formulate a response, he continued. "So you're an honest-to-God novelist. What's that like?"

"Like?"

"You get noticed in the street, laid a lot, what?"

At this, Gray nearly choked on his beer but managed to cough it up. Porter whacked him absently on the back as he waited for my reply.

"Women every night," I said. "They send me their underwear to autograph. It's embarrassing."

Porter smirked. Gray cleared his throat loudly and gave me a weak but approving smile. "So," I said, swirling my beer a bit in my bottle and intending to ask something generic about why they wanted to become teachers or what they thought of Blackburne, something to get away from the topic of my writing.

Then Porter said, nodding behind me, "There's that creepy dude in the wheelchair." I turned and saw the man he was referring to. Wearing a short-sleeved denim work shirt and jeans, he was rolling over to Sam at the grill, his forearms tanned and corded with muscle as he swiftly worked the wheels of his chair. He stopped to exchange a few words with Sam and then gazed out blankly at the crowd. "Snuck up on me outside of Stilwell Hall," Porter said. "I came around the corner and he was sitting there like he was waiting for me. Fucking jumped out of my skin. Told him I hadn't heard him, and he said he always comes from downwind." Porter drained his beer. "What's up with him?"

Gray shot a glance at Porter. "Besides that he's a paraplegic, you mean?" he asked, taking a measured sip of his beer.

"He's not a paraplegic," I said. They both looked at me. "Double amputee. Lost both his legs in the first Gulf War. He just wears long pants to hide it, tucks the pants into work boots he leaves on the footrests of his wheelchair. Name's Pelham Greer. He used to work here as a maintenance guy, and then he joined the army. When he was discharged, they gave him his old job back."

Gray gave a low whistle. Porter looked uncomfortable. "Well, shit," he said. "Now I feel like a tool."

I shook my head. "He *is* a little creepy. Used to scare us when we were students, rolling out from behind buildings, stuff like that. But he's all right."

Porter gazed over my shoulder and lowered his voice. "Now there's a guy who would scare me if I were a student."

I casually glanced in the direction Porter had indicated. Standing off in the side yard and talking with Dave Heidel, our science department chair, was a tall, heavy man, bald as a cucumber and wearing a white suit and vest with a navy-blue tie. He had a tanned, fleshy face with a wide mouth a bit like a frog's. "He was at the meeting this morning," I said. "Associate headmaster. What's his name, Ron something?"

"Ren Middleton," Porter said. "School disciplinarian. Travis Simmons's right-hand guy."

Ren Middleton looked our way, and although he was too far away to have heard Porter, I felt like he had caught us talking about him. Dave Heidel then turned and gestured toward us, nodding, and Middleton headed in our direction.

"Shit," Porter muttered.

Ren Middleton walked up. "Porter, Grayden, afternoon," he said. His voice was Charleston to the bone, deep and heavy over the vowels, falling with a soft thud on the consonants. "Getting along?"

"Yes, sir," Gray said. Porter nodded politely but said nothing.

"Good," Middleton said. "I've found that nothing gets a man more ready for a hard job than good food and good company." He rested his gaze on me. "You must be Matthias Glass."

"Yes, sir." I offered my hand, which he shook firmly.

"Ren Middleton," he said. Middleton's eyes were large and mud colored, and he looked at me the way a jeweler would inspect a diamond. "You were a Jefferson Scholar at Virginia, weren't you? I also attended the university, though a bit before your time. Travis told me you'd indicated an interest in coaching track and recommended you as my assistant. I coach the varsity team."

"Sure," I heard myself say. "Happy to help."

"And I'd be glad of it," he said. "Oh," he added deliberately, "my wife loved your book, sir. Perhaps we could get together sometime to talk about it? I've always wondered what it must be like to"—he cast about for a word—"*create* a novel." He smiled beneficently.

I could feel my own smile tighten. "I don't know how much writing I'll get done this year," I said. "I suspect I'll be busy enough with my classes."

Middleton nodded. "Good man," he said. "Jumping in with both feet. Exactly what we need here." Then he turned to Gray and Porter, talking with each of them about their thoughts on the upcoming school year. I stood and watched him. I've always been drawn to strong personalities, and Ren Middleton was as regal and charismatic as a Renaissance cardinal. He asked Gray what he thought about the school's chemistry labs and seemed genuinely curious about whether Gray found them adequate. With Porter he talked UConn basketball and then asked if Porter had read a recent book on Afghanistan. This led to a brief discussion of Western involvement in the Middle and Far East, an obvious source of passion for Porter, who grew animated and gestured with his hands while Ren Middleton nodded soberly and posed an occasional question. Clearly, Middleton knew how to read people and get them to talk about subjects that interested them. I wondered how he had read me.

"I hope you'll excuse me," Middleton said, consulting his watch, "but I'm afraid I have to be getting home. My wife is cooking dinner. Good to see you, gentlemen." Then, in a slightly more confidential register, he said to me, "Matthias, do you have a moment?"

I glanced at Porter and Gray, who were already moving toward the grill, and Porter shot me a look that registered somewhere between sympathy and relief. Following Middleton's lead, I strolled with him off the patio and across Sam Hodges's backyard, negotiating a hedge of boxwood to come upon the first tee of the golf course, which lay behind Saint Matthew's. The boxwood hedge effectively cut us off from the party so that we were alone.

We stopped at the top of the fairway. Wide and straight, it unrolled like a fresh carpet of grass down a gentle slope to the track and the football field. My shirt was beginning to cling to my back again from the oppressive heat. The distant trees hung silently at the edge of the fields.

"I'm sorry to seem mysterious," Ren Middleton said. "I just wanted a word in private."

"Sure," I said.

"You see, it's been a while since a former student has returned to Blackburne to teach," he said. "I wanted you to know how much we appreciate it."

"We?"

"Dr. Simmons and I." He smiled, his fleshy lips stretched wide across his face. "It's a singular position. A young man who can truly relate to these students, their troubles, give them guidance." He bent over and picked up a stained golf ball that had lain to one side of the tee. He rolled it between his thick fingers. "This ball is a perfect example," he said. "It was neglected, left behind by a careless owner. It was inert, if you want to see it that way."

He drew back his great arm and, in a smooth, powerful motion, he threw the ball down the length of the fairway. The ball, a white blur, skimmed over the green swath and then bounced twice into the shadows of the receding pine trees at the bottom of the hill.

He turned to me. "That's what we do here," he said. "We give boys direction, purpose. We send them into the world as better, stronger men." He grinned. "We kill their inertness." The grin dropped from his face, and he peered seriously at me. "I'll be counting on your help with some of these boys. I'm afraid a few of the fourth formers need a firm hand. And they ought to respond to, well, a younger authority figure, I suppose." He inclined his head to the left, as if to see whether I followed him.

"I'll help in any way I can," I said.

He clapped me once on the shoulder. "Good man," he said. He turned and walked back toward the party, leaving me alone on the hot hillside.

ON SUNDAY, SUVS CRAMMED full of luggage toiled up the Hill in steady succession to unload their bags along with their boys. Car doors slammed shut, and voices called out in greeting. The Hill seemed to sprout dozens of loud, cheerful teenagers in polos and baseball caps. Most grinned at one another and coolly directed their parents in furnishing their rooms. These were the old boys, the returning students inured to the idea of boarding school, their self-confidence almost palpable in comparison to the new boys, who were almost all third and fourth formers.

Each new student stood nervously by the family car, as if trying to keep in contact with something familiar for as long as possible before his parents abandoned him. Almost all of them had braces, or big feet, or skinny legs like toothpicks poking out of shorts that seemed three sizes too large. They had not yet grown into their bodies, which were racing along in the hormonal clutch of adolescence. They appeared both defiant and fragile as they slowly unloaded their cars, stubborn in the face of the long months ahead even as a night of frustrated tears and loneliness awaited them. They murmured rather than spoke, cowed by the brick buildings and the clean walkways that were filling with people who were obviously comfortable here.

The old boys, for the most part, succeeded in making the new boys feel more miserable, calling out excitedly to friends and playing trashcan lacrosse on the Lawn. Teary-eyed mothers did nothing to help the situation. I knew from experience that the new boys would be far too busy a week from now to feel homesick. And yet I couldn't help but feel some sympathy for every boy with a sad, swollen face who walked grimly into Raleigh Hall or Lawson-Parker as if marching off to a deadly fate.

BRENDSEL DINING HALL IS a vast carpeted room of long dinner tables under a high-beamed ceiling. The first night at Blackburne, and every following Sunday night, students eat a formal, sit-down dinner in Brendsel with their advisors. Each student has a faculty advisor who tracks his grades and offers advice and encouragement—at least in theory. Some advisors were better than others. Sam Hodges was famous for taking his advisees to the Charlottesville malls once a month or so, while Stuart Downing, the longtime Latin teacher, basically ignored his advisees except at Sunday meals, and sometimes even then.

I met my advisees for the first time that night. I had inherited them from Keith Aspinwall, the English teacher I had replaced. A slip of paper with my advisees' names lay on the stack of dinner plates at the head of the table, and when the dinner bell rang and students arrived at my table, I began counting off names. Soon all the places were filled, and I saw with a bright pop of recognition that one boy I had helped to move in that afternoon, Stephen Watterson, was in my advisory. He gave me an easy smile and waved as he sat down.

The loud hum of conversation dropped and then disappeared as the headmaster's voice came over the PA system. Travis Simmons preferred rather severe suits of banker's gray, and he seethed breeding and culture like an ancient, musty library. At the first all-faculty meeting, Dr. Simmons had shaken my hand with one as dry as chalk dust, inclining his head to me in a way that accentuated his stooped shoulders as he welcomed me back to Blackburne. But he could shine brightly in front of a group, speaking eloquently and waxing rhapsodic about the school and its mission. It was this unswerving, intensely personal loyalty to Blackburne that engendered widespread respect for him, even among the students. For some reason, though, I thought about Ren Middleton and his odd lesson about killing inertness and needing my help, the throwing of the golf ball down the fairway, and I glanced at my advisees, wondering how they would react to the headmaster's voice. They sat quietly, some heads slightly bowed; a few faces were tilted up toward a speaker mounted on the wall.

"Gentlemen," Dr. Simmons was saying, "I would like to formally welcome you to Blackburne. I trust today went well with moving into your rooms and getting settled. It's an exciting time, and a busy one. I look forward to an excellent year with you. Please make the effort to turn to your masters for help of any kind. We are here for you." A pause. "Let us pray." Four hundred heads bowed in unison. "Lord, thank you for this good meal and for the hands that prepared it. Please be with all those who are less fortunate than we are. Watch over these students and guide them, and help them to strive for excellence. In your name we pray. Amen."

At the final word, nearly forty new boys, clad in white waiters' jackets and holding battered serving trays, rushed from their tables for the cafeteria door to pick up platters of food. The senior masters had tables close to the cafeteria and thus got their food quickly. I was back in a recess of the dining hall known as Graveyard Alley and wouldn't get my dinner for a few minutes at least. I did note with a bit of wicked pleasure that Porter Deems was at the very back of Graveyard Alley, two tables farther away from the cafeteria than I was. I caught his eye and grinned. He scowled and flipped me the bird under the table.

The clanging of the serving trays, which rang through the dining hall as they were slapped down on the cafeteria counters or crashed into one another, seemed an appropriate, unofficial opening of Blackburne. It brought back memories of my own first year, when I had stood nervously in a starched white jacket, its collar scratching my jaw, as I waited to pick up the full tray and wondered how I would do it without spilling food everywhere. I smiled and shook my head. Then I looked at my advisees, a few of whom were looking at me as if waiting for me to speak. I nodded at a tall, dark-haired boy seated on my right. "All moved in okay?" I asked.

"Yes, sir," he said, brushing his hair out of his eyes with the back of his hand. "The room doesn't matter as long as I'm on the same dorm and keep my roommate, Mack." He gestured to a freckled redhead down the table.

I remembered then that there had been a mix-up with room assignments that morning and I'd had to ask this boy to move upstairs after he'd already started unpacking. The tall boy was named Hal Starr, and his roommate was the freckled redhead. "You're Mack Arnold?" I asked, trying to look casually at the list of names in my hand.

The redhead nodded. "Sure you can't move me out of Hal's room? The guy snores."

Hal rolled his eyes. "Better than what *you* do at night, pal."

Laughter ran around the table and then fell silent as the boys glanced at me. I was being tested, I knew, all of them waiting to see how the new teacher would react. Laughing with them would make me either a pushover or a buddy, both of which were fatal. Or I could frown and be the joyless martinet. Instead, I ignored the comment and asked Hal, "Do you play basketball?"

Stephen Watterson spoke up before Hal could say anything. "He's our starting center for varsity. We call him Rebound."

"Shut up, Watterson," Hal said shyly, looking in his lap.

"It's true! You ought to see him rip the ball off the backboard."

"Well, this guy ought to try out for football," Hal said, jerking his head at Stephen. "He can outrun anybody." Stephen received this praise with a silent glow of appreciation.

"No kidding?" I said. "Maybe you'd try out for track in the winter."

Stephen laughed. "No way. Too boring. Who wants to run around in circles all day?"

I smiled. "That's what I might help coach," I said good-naturedly, reaching for the iced tea. Stephen lapsed into an embarrassed silence. "Hey, no big deal, Stephen," I said. "No offense." Stephen smiled, relieved, and then started talking with Hal about this year's football team.

I had not realized how isolating it could be to sit at the head of a table of ten boys. Teachers had always seemed to float above such considerations. Now I found myself feeling like a new boy struggling for acceptance. *This is absurd*, I thought. *They're fourth formers, for God's sake. I don't need a bunch of fifteen-year-old friends.* I turned to the boy on my left, who had not said a word since quietly taking his seat several minutes ago. In fact, I hadn't noticed him at all until just before the prayer. "Hi," I said. "I'm Mr. Glass. What's your name?"

"Paul," the boy murmured. He had mousy-brown hair and a pale complexion. Dark shadows sat under his eyes like newsprint that had been smudged there.

"Right," I said brightly, glancing at my list. "Paul . . . Simmons, right?" He nodded faintly.

"No relation to our headmaster, are you?" I said, trying to get a smile out of him.

"I'm his son," he said. Stephen Watterson looked up. A couple of the other boys did, too.

"Well, that's great," I said lamely. "Your father is . . . a heck of a man."

"Yes," Paul said, picking up a fork and turning it over in his hands.

Thankfully our waiter arrived then, sweating with apologies and bringing enough food to halt conversation for the rest of dinner.

CHAPTER FOUR

A t the beginning of my fourth form year, when Fritz and I started rooming together, I met his twin sister, Abby. She was fifteen then, a girl in the process of growing into a young woman. Her hair was long and glossy black, her eyes a clear blue above a straight nose and a wide, generous mouth. Fritz and I were moving into Rhoads Hall, unloading our cars in the gravel parking lot in the back. Our parents had greeted one another, and Fritz's mom, a kind but preoccupied woman who always seemed to have to move on to the next thing, had absently introduced Abby to me. Abby smiled and said hello, and then added that her brother had told her a lot about me and that she went to Saint Margaret's and would start school the following week. I mumbled something in response, afraid to look at her, and was rescued by my father, who needed help with a trunk.

Fritz, of course, had noticed my discomfort. "My folks are coming next weekend," he said casually a few weeks later, and I grunted as I pretended to read my World History textbook. Fritz waited, letting me twist in agony as he scanned a copy of *Sports Illustrated*, and then said, still looking at his magazine, "Abby might be coming."

I couldn't help myself. "Really?" I said before retreating behind a look of indifference. "I mean, that's cool."

"Told me to tell you hi."

"Who did?"

"My sister."

"That was it?"

"What?"

"That's what she said? 'Hi'?"

Fritz considered this. "No, that wasn't all."

"Well, what else did she say?"

And Fritz looked at me, his eyes big and round and smiling, and said, "She wanted me to tell you that she dreams about you every night, that she wants you to rescue her from the prison nuns at Saint Margaret's"—he ducked as I threw my book at him—"and she can't wait until the two of you make the beast with two backs." He said this last bit while laughing out loud and running out of the room. I gave chase, swearing to beat the shit out of him if he didn't stop.

But nothing happened. Abby didn't come that weekend. In fact, we didn't see each other again until the end of the year when Fritz and I were moving out of our dorm room, by which time I was sort of seeing a girl from Oldfields. Vague plans to get together with Fritz over the summer never materialized—I had a job as a lifeguard at a local pool, and Fritz went backpacking in Europe—but the Oldfields girl, who lived in Tennessee, managed to visit Asheville with her parents, and I joined them for a tour of the Biltmore House. The girl, Dana, and I ended up making out behind a greenhouse while her parents were in one of the gift shops. We damn near had sex right there in a bed of tulips, except that I didn't have any condoms and didn't know what the hell I was doing anyway, not to mention that her parents were only twenty yards away. This was the equivalent of love, or so I thought, and Dana became the object of my romantic obsession for much of my fifth form year.

Twice that year, on separate weekends, I visited Fritz's home, a beautiful brick Colonial outside of Fairfax, Virginia. The lawn always looked as if a team of gardeners had tended to each blade of grass that morning. There was a swimming pool and a stone patio out back, and a home theater and foosball table in the basement, and Fritz and I enjoyed playing foosball and watching movies and lounging by the pool, gloriously wasting time. All of this was tempered some by Abby's not being present either weekend.

Mr. Davenport, Fritz's father, was barely present himself. He ran some sort of IT firm in Arlington, and my impression was that he was a thoroughly busy man who read people swiftly in order to determine whether he needed to bother with them. Apparently I had made the cut. On my first visit to Fritz's house, I saw Mr. Davenport use a Montblanc pen as he sat in his easy chair going over paperwork, and I made some comment about how I'd write a novel with a pen like that one day. It was a ridiculously vain and pompous thing to say, but he'd chuckled at it, not unkindly. Later that year, on my birthday in January, I received a gift box from the Davenports containing an identical Montblanc pen.

That first weekend, Fritz also took me to visit his horse, Ranger, at a nearby stable. Ranger was a beautiful chestnut Thoroughbred with a white blaze down his face. He would nod and stomp his front hoof once when he saw Fritz. Ranger was a show hunter—Fritz had ridden him in competitive events, jumping fences and presenting excellent riding form. "Basically his job is to look good without trying," Fritz told me, stroking Ranger on his muzzle. I was wary of Ranger, afraid he would step on my foot, but I petted him on the nose and he blew warm air on my hand. I watched Fritz as he rode Ranger in the training ring of the stable, gently putting him through his paces. Ranger was getting older, but when he and Fritz approached a fence, Ranger went over it like a dolphin arcing out of the water, a single smooth motion that hardly interrupted his canter.

Fletcher Dupree had snorted with delight at learning that Fritz rode English style on a horse named Ranger (Fritz had been reading Tolkien when he'd first gotten him). At first, Fritz just rolled his eyes and ignored his comments, but one day at lunch, when Fletcher was talking about how gay English riding looked, Fritz put down his glass of iced tea and patiently explained that he loved his horse, that he had recently won second place at the Southwest Virginia Hunter Jumper Association Finals, and that he had done it while also playing varsity football. "So suck it," Fritz added sweetly, causing the whole table to laugh, even Fletcher.

In truth, Fritz had several trophies that he had won with Ranger, but what he enjoyed far more was to just ride across the fields by the horse stable. He tried to get me to go riding with him once, but I demurred, uncomfortable with the sheer size of the horses. I regretted that later, because that summer, when I was working as a lifeguard at the country club pool in Biltmore Forest, Fritz sent me a letter saying that Ranger had contracted Potomac horse fever and that they had had to put him to sleep. Ranger had been old, Fritz wrote, and he had known his horse wouldn't be around forever, but it was a hard thing to lose him. *It's like he stamped a hole through my heart*, he wrote. I realized then that Fritz had loved riding Ranger, and I had been offered an opportunity to share that passion with him, and now that opportunity was gone forever.

IN THE FALL OF our sixth form year, Fritz harassed me to invite Abby to the Fall Dance, a semiformal in October. I'd still been seeing Dana, but things had unraveled some since fourth form year, and when I had asked her to the dance, she said she'd already made plans to be in D.C. that weekend, so I didn't have a date. Still, I resisted Fritz. "Oh, come on," Fritz said. "Abby's fun, I'm taking her roommate, and you like her. What's the problem?"

"I don't know. It's a little weird, you know? I mean, she's your sister."

He laid his hands on my shoulders and looked earnestly into my face. "I give you permission to date my sister, you dipshit," he said.

Oddly enough, that settled it, and I called Abby—this was before Blackburne allowed students to have cell phones—from one of the old house phones in the hallway of Walker. She spoke brightly into the phone when she realized it was me, and I stumbled through a nonchalant invitation, holding my breath and my heartbeat as I waited for a reply. When Abby said she would love to come, I thought I would lift out of my shoes.

The weekend was a lot of fun, not least because she and her roommate, Heather, were two of the most attractive girls at the dance, and Fritz and I enjoyed the complimentary stares of our classmates. Around most girls I was either tongue-tied or babbled like a fool. I did both with Abby, but only at first, and as the weekend progressed and Abby spoke easily with me, my discomfort melted away. I even told her I wanted to become a writer, something I hadn't told anyone at Blackburne except for Fritz. In turn, she told me her dreams about going to Juilliard and becoming a concert cello player like Yo-Yo Ma. I remember we were walking across the Lawn toward Mr. Hodges's house where she was staying, and she turned to me with a smile. "So we're both artists," she said. "How cool is that?" She linked her arm with mine as easily as if we had been doing so for years, and I thought in a haze of rapture that I wanted to keep walking with her on my arm forever.

I enjoyed the dance, but I don't remember much about the dinner beforehand, or the music, or the dancing. What I do remember is that Abby and I engaged in a few long, warm kisses with the promise of real heat behind them. The next morning, when she boarded the bus that would take her back to Saint Margaret's, I kissed her good-bye in front of Fritz and everybody, and then stayed to watch the bus leave, standing there long after its brake lights had winked one last time before it drove into the trees and out of sight.

After the dance, we exchanged a few desperately romantic letters and hoped to see each other over Christmas break, but her father announced a surprise family vacation to a dude ranch in Montana, and we had to settle for a couple of long and maudlin phone conversations. During one of them, a week before exams and Christmas vacation, I said, "Play something for me. On your cello."

She laughed. "What, over the phone?"

"Yeah," I said. "I've never heard you play. I'd like to hear you play."

Max Goren, who was walking down the hall, started making gagging noises as he passed me. I flipped him off and turned my back on him, hunched over the phone.

Abby snorted on the other end. "Do you know how big a cello is? It's not like a harmonica or something. You can't just pull it out of your pocket and *play*. I don't even keep it on dorm. It's in the music studio."

I grinned. "No problem," I said. "I'll wait for you to get it." I wasn't sure where this cocky bravado came from, or why I was pushing Abby on this, but I liked it and suspected she did, too.

Abby lowered her voice. "I am *not* going to play the cello over the phone in front of my whole hall."

I kept grinning. "I don't care. Play for me, Abby."

This went on for a bit until Abby hung up in exasperation. I almost called back to apologize, but somehow I knew that wasn't the right play, and so I decided to hang tight and wait.

In the meantime, I agonized over what to get her for Christmas, but eventually, with my mother's help, and spending a lot of the money I'd saved from my summer lifeguard job, I got her a pendant with a Tahitian pearl set in white gold. It was the first time I had bought jewelry for a girl, and I was nervous about how she would react. On Christmas Day, I woke up in my house in Asheville, wondering if Abby had opened my present yet. Downstairs, I found a wrapped present from Abby under the tree. She had mailed it to my house, and my mother had kept it hidden with the other Christmas presents. I opened it and pulled out a CD with nothing on it except, written in black Sharpie, *To Matthias. Christmas 2000. Love, Abby.* When I put the CD into the stereo, there were a few seconds of silence, followed by some indeterminate fumbling noises, and then Abby's voice came out of the speakers. "Okay, this is Bach's Cello Suite number one, in G Major," she said. Another pause. And then music began to pour out of the speakers, low, deep notes that spiraled steadily upward and then dipped back down into the lower ranges before resuming their climb, as if soaring on an updraft. I sat in my living room, transfixed by the music.

Dad, yawning, came in, dressed in a tee shirt and pajama bottoms. "Merry Christmas," he said. "What's this?"

I turned to look at him. "My girlfriend," I said. It was the first time I had uttered those words, and they sent a strong current through me. "She sent me this. She's playing the cello for me."

In January, Fritz returned to school gushing about Montana and fly-fishing and horseback riding in Yellowstone. He'd decided Western riding was much cooler than English riding and wondered if he could convince his parents to buy him a new horse. Just as I was about to make him eat his new Stetson hat, he invited me to spend the MLK long weekend at his house. That Friday, Mrs. Davenport picked Fritz and me up from Blackburne and drove us to Fairfax. On the way, she said from behind the wheel, "Oh, Fritz, your sister's going to be home, too. Wat's picking her up."

Immediately my face went to slow burn. Fritz eyed me and slowly began to grin. "Good," he said. "Matthias is looking forward to that, I'm sure."

"Shut up," I muttered, grinning myself. I thought Mrs. Davenport glanced at me in the rearview mirror, but I wasn't sure. "Who's Wat?" I asked in what I hoped was a not-too-obvious bid to change the subject.

"Fritz and Abby's uncle," Mrs. Davenport said. "My husband's brother."

Fritz rolled his eyes. "He thinks he's hysterical," he said to me, his mouth twisted into an odd smile.

I didn't pay much attention to this—I was too nervous about seeing Abby again after three months. All my bravado from the phone call when I'd told Abby to play the cello for me seemed to have evaporated. Immediately I wished I had worn something other than the yellow oxford I had chosen simply because it had been one of the few clean shirts in my closet.

When we arrived at Fritz's house, there was a Land Rover in the turnaround drive. "Good, Wat's here," Mrs. Davenport said.

"And Abby," Fritz said, nudging me in the ribs. I shot him a look and willed myself to walk normally up to the front door.

Mrs. Davenport was reaching for the doorknob when the door swung open and Abby stood there, looking at me. "Hi," she said brightly and a little breathlessly.

I stopped. "Hey," I said. We stood there for a second, and then Abby stepped forward and hugged me, her cheek against mine. "Good to see you," she whispered into my ear.

"Yeah, you, too," Fritz said loudly from behind my shoulder. "Do I get a hug or what?"

Abby pulled back from me and made a face at her twin brother. "Hello, Mother," she said, hugging Mrs. Davenport pointedly.

There was the usual confusion of carrying bags up to rooms, the Davenports' yellow lab, Maisy, panting and grinning and slapping her tail against everyone's legs, and Fritz and Abby sniping at each other. Then I found myself alone in an upstairs hall with Abby. Fritz was downstairs calling for his mother and asking about dinner. I opened my mouth to say something, but Abby reached for my hand and pulled me into another guest room. I registered a red floral bedspread and matching curtains before Abby pushed the door shut.

"Hi," she said, putting her arms around my neck and looking up at me, smiling.

"Hi," I managed. My hands had found their way onto her hips. They felt right there, like they were shaped for nothing else but holding on to her.

"I missed you," she said, still smiling.

I answered by leaning forward and putting my lips on hers. Her hands went to the back of my head, and we drank each other in for a few delicious moments.

The bathroom door opened, and we broke apart, whirling around. A tall man in a tie and suit, a drink in his hand, came through the doorway.

He stopped, his eyebrows raised, and we looked at each other for a moment, my hands still on Abby's waist.

"Ah," the man said, putting his drink down on a dresser. He stuck his hand out at me. "I'm Wat Davenport," he said, smiling.

"Uh, hello, sir," I said, quickly letting go of Abby and shaking his hand.

"Hi, Uncle Wat," Abby said breezily. "This is my boyfriend, Matthias."

Wat considered me, his eyebrows still slightly raised. "Well, I certainly hope so," he said.

The rest of the weekend was thankfully devoid of similar embarrassing moments. Mr. Davenport made his usual, brief appearance and then disappeared into his office. Wat popped in and out, helping Mrs. Davenport in the kitchen, wagging his eyebrows at me and occasionally singing songs like "She Loves You" and "I Want to Hold Your Hand" in a surprisingly good voice. Fritz, annoyingly, stuck around with me and Abby much of the time, declining to go out to dinner with his uncle—"All he does is talk about famous people he's met or how he's been to the Louvre or the Great Pyramid of Giza," Fritz said—but finally his mother took him to exchange some clothes from Christmas that hadn't fit him. Mr. Davenport was still working in his office, and Wat had a meeting in D.C., so Abby and I got a couple of hours together. We spent them sitting together in their home theater, watching *Say Anything*, Abby's choice. It felt good, just sitting in the dark, holding Abby's hand or putting my arm around her. But soon I became very conscious of Abby's breath, barely tickling my neck as she rested her head against my shoulder. I could see the outline of her bra underneath her tight pink sweater. Her thigh was pressed against mine. Suddenly I understood that it was actually possible that Abby and I could sleep together one day. From there it was a single, short step to thinking that I could close the door to the theater, turn the movie's volume up a little, and we could have sex right there in one of the leather reclining chairs. I had a condom in my wallet. That her father was in the house added a thrill of danger. And I wanted Abby, every inch of her. I was thrumming like a tuning fork.

Abby turned her head to look up at me. "What?" she said, a slightly puzzled smile on her lips.

I shook my head. I wanted her, but as she looked at me, I realized that I wanted all of her, not just some quick, furtive sex in the basement. "Nothing," I said, squeezing her gently with my arm. "Just thinking that we're gonna be like them one day." I nodded in the direction of the screen, where Lloyd Dobler was warning Diane Court to avoid stepping near some glass in a parking lot.

This is perhaps the single wisest decision I ever made in a relationship, not just because it led to more kissing and to our hands wandering. We didn't have sex, and I was left aching with desire, but we discovered that, on some deep, instinctual level, we both liked and trusted each other.

If perhaps I had trusted myself half as much as Abby did, things might have turned out better.

LESS THAN TWO MONTHS later, on the day before Fritz vanished, Mr. Summerfield, my physics teacher, gave us a take-home test to complete. Teachers occasionally did this at Blackburne, assigning tests for homework so they could use precious class time to conduct more labs, or force students through the subjunctive mood again, or squeeze in one more lecture about the effects of the Peloponnesian War. In our case, Mr. Summerfield wanted us to work on one more set of practice questions in preparation for the AP exam. So I took my test back to my dorm room and left it in my physics notebook while I went down to the track to run laps in the cold and practice baton handoffs with the relay team. After practice and a shower and dinner in the dining hall, I returned to my room. Fritz was studying in the library for a calculus test with two other classmates, so I had the room to myself. It was dark outside the two windows of our corner room in Walker House, and my lamp threw a golden, solitary cone of light over the desktop. I liked studying this way, the harsh overhead light switched off and the desk lamp radiating a soft, focused glow that just touched the darkened windows. I pulled my physics notebook out of my backpack and opened it; then I took out the test, laid it out on the desk, and peered at it.

It consisted of four practice questions, each with various parts. The first question was about converting mechanical energy into thermal energy, something we had recently reviewed. Easy. The second question was about sound wavelengths, a topic I had presented to the class for a project assignment. I wrote out my work on my own sheets of notebook paper, comforted by the sound of the pencil scratching against the paper. Then I read the third question. As was typical with such questions, the description of the scenario was both clinical and absurd. Two small blocks, each of mass m, are connected by a string of length $4h$. Block A is on a smooth tabletop, with block B dangling off the edge of the table. The tabletop is a distance of $2h$ from the floor. Given a couple of other variables, I was supposed to answer various questions about the acceleration of block B if it was released from height h, the time that B would hit the floor, the time that A would hit the floor, and the distance between the landing points of blocks A and B. I stared at the problem and then looked back at the brief list of equations that came with the test, the only extra help we were allowed to use—no notes or textbooks. It was an easy set of questions about acceleration and mass, but for some reason I was drawing a blank. I made a stab at part (a), silently cursing the entire premise as ridiculous. When would I need to know the speed at which a block falls off a table? I knew this wasn't the point, but it felt good to grumble.

Halfway through part (b), I wrote to the end of my last sheet. I reached down to pick my physics notebook off the floor and opened it for a piece of scrap paper. Instead of opening the notebook to a blank sheet, however, I inadvertently opened it to a scrawled page of notes. I frowned and then actually felt my eyes widen. The notes were from earlier that month, the day Mr. Summerfield had gone over acceleration. The answer to the test question I wasn't sure about was in those notes.

Mr. Summerfield was a short, bearded bear of a man. He looked as if he could twist open a fire hydrant with his bare hands. He smiled often and spoke in a soft rumble. I liked him, and I think he liked me, although he graded insanely hard like many of my teachers. I was earning a B+, could maybe raise it to an A- by graduation. This had no bearing on getting into college; I was already accepted to UVA and was going to visit the following week to meet one of the English professors. But just before Christmas, Mr. Hodges had told me that I was being considered for a Copen scholarship, a prestigious award granted by Blackburne to a graduate of high academic caliber who would attend a college or university in Virginia. I couldn't help but fantasize about what it would mean to win the Copen and to see my parents' reactions when I told them that they didn't need to pay my tuition. My GPA was strong, but most of my classmates had strong GPAs, and several of them were applying to Virginia schools as well.

I don't believe I consciously considered the Copen as I looked down at my physics notebook. And I'm not trying to justify my actions. I knew what the honor code was, and I had signed up to live under that system. After three years at Blackburne, it had become second nature to me. Fritz had been elected as a prefect by our classmates, and I had seen him after he had come back from the three Judicial Board hearings held that year, two of which resulted in guilty verdicts and student dismissals. Fritz had looked tired, pained, suddenly adultlike, and I was a little in awe of what he must have had to do in those hearings. It had brought home to me the seriousness of the honor code and the consequences of failing to live up to it. I would have said, up until that point, that the honor code was one of the defining factors of my life.

And it was, though not in the way I would have thought. Because after accidentally seeing my physics notes and realizing that I had made an error on my test, I erased my previous answer and wrote out the correct one with an easy deliberateness. Then I moved on to the rest of the test. Within fifteen minutes, I had finished. I closed the test, placed it in my physics notebook, and put the notebook in my backpack. Then I read the assigned chapters from *Light in August* until the bell rang and Fritz came back from his study session and we got ready for bed.

The next morning, I woke up, went to breakfast, and then walked down to the physics lab, high-fiving my lab partner, Jeb Tanner, before taking my seat. Mr. Summerfield came in just before the bell with his thick textbook under one arm. "Tests, gentlemen," he said in his soft, deep voice, and we were pulling our notebooks out of our backpacks when the enormity of what I had done hit me like a sheet of flame from the sky. I sat there, the test in my hand, my lips parted as if I were about to sip from a cup. I had cheated on my take-home test, the one we were about to turn in. Dazed, I looked around, noticed boys making sure their names were on their tests, one or two frantically scribbling. I put my test down on the desk and looked at it. The question I had cheated on was on the second page. *Change it,* I told myself, followed immediately by *Leave it alone—how could he tell?* My mind darted back and forth between the two thoughts like a herring trying to avoid a pair of sharks.

"Now, boys." The deep voice had an edge to it. Despair fell on me like a fog. It was too late now. Jeb, sitting in front of me, turned around, expecting me to hand him my test so he could pass it up. Slowly, I did. He turned away, and I looked at Mr. Summerfield at the front of the room, praying he wouldn't be able to detect my dishonesty. I felt like I had the word *cheater* branded on my forehead. I was violating everything I had pledged to believe in, and I was doing it easily. And for what? The Copen scholarship? Was I mercenary enough to do this for an extra hundredth of a point on my GPA? But behind these thoughts, in a dark, hidden corner of myself, a small voice muttered about the ridiculous stupidity of that test question. Was I going to potentially lose the Copen because of my inability to perfectly solve a problem about falling blocks? And my classmates—

Fritz included—didn't need a scholarship. Their families skied in Gstaad every winter and would purchase their sons brand-new BMWs upon graduation.

"Hey," Jeb said. I looked up, startled. Jeb was holding out my test. "You forgot to pledge it," he said.

Forcing a smile, I took the test back. The pledge—"I have neither given nor received any unacknowledged aid on this work"—was usually written on everything we turned in, a restatement of our contract with the honor code. Jeb was smiling patiently. I picked up my pencil, wrote out the pledge, and then hesitated. This was a second chance. But what could I do? Jeb was waiting, and Mr. Summerfield was pacing at the front of the room, collecting tests. *Change it! No time!*

"Boys!" Mr. Summerfield barked, and Jeb snapped his head around to look at him. As soon as Jeb turned around, I lowered the pencil to my test and signed the pledge. As I did, my pencil lead broke.

"Mr. Glass, we're waiting!" Mr. Summerfield said. Jeb turned back to stare at me. I handed him the test with a muttered, "Sorry!" Then I looked at Mr. Summerfield. "Sorry, sir," I said. "I'm sorry." Mr. Summerfield grunted and received my test; then he put the stack down on his desk and moved to the whiteboard to begin a new lesson.

I have no idea what Mr. Summerfield taught us that day. Instead, I remember sitting in my chair facing the board, stunned in the wake of my success at cheating, and terrified of what it might bring about.

CHAPTER FIVE

T he dew-beaded bricks muffled my footsteps as I walked to Huber Hall the morning of my first day of teaching. The Hill was shrouded in a wet fog from the river that made the walkways and the Lawn glisten in the dawning, pearl-gray light. A fertile odor hung in the air, wet grass and straw and muddy river combining to suggest that the day was not merely beginning but being born.

It was five minutes to seven as I pushed open the door to Huber. Twenty minutes remained until the bells would ring to awaken the students, but I wanted an hour to work alone in my classroom, and Gray Smith had offered to take my morning dorm duty. I'd spent a fitful night, and a little before six o'clock, when I had realized that I could no longer pretend to be asleep, I had risen from my bed to shower.

Huber was known as the Tower of Babel since all languages were taught there. If you sat in the hallway during the school day, you could hear Latin, German, French, Spanish, and English all vying for your attention. However, what most people noticed was its gallery of photographs. On either side of the main hallway hung black-and-white pictures of smiling young men, boys almost, standing in officers' caps and khaki uniforms or pilots' leather jackets. The captions underneath each cheerful face proclaimed them as Blackburne graduates who proudly entered the armed services during WWII and died in combat. Here was a lieutenant fresh out of the Naval Academy; there an army fighter pilot with a tidy crew cut and a wool-lined leather jacket. They were part of the background, faces that hung silently in the crowded halls during the day, unseen among the turmoil of school life. That morning, however, I was keenly aware of the frozen features of those young men gazing down upon me as I walked to the stairwell at the back of the building and went downstairs to my classroom.

I stepped into the classroom and flipped the heavy black light switches, which, with an audible *chunk* and hum, caused the overheads to flare on, washing the room with a hard fluorescent light. A table and two dozen chairs with desktops sprang into view. Two whiteboards, a bookshelf half-filled with old paperback classics, and an enormous, ragged poster of Ernest Hemingway in profile, seated at his typewriter, completed the room.

I had just put my briefcase down on the desk at the front of the room and realized I didn't have a whiteboard eraser, when there was a knock on the door and Sam Hodges looked in. He was dressed to the nines: blue shirt with cuff links, paisley tie knotted to perfection, blue blazer, and dress khakis.

"Hail, fellow, well met," he said, a slight smile at the corners of his mouth.

I raised a hand in welcome. "*Ave! Morituri te salutamus*," I said, quoting the ancient greeting of gladiators about to enter the arena. *Hail! Those of us who are about to die salute you.* As soon as I spoke the words, I regretted them. Not because of the content, but because Latin had been Fritz's specialty. I thought of the photos in the hall upstairs, all the dead young men, and a great sadness fisted me just below the heart.

Sam laughed, unaware of my discomfort. "*Aut disce aut discede*," he replied.

I smiled, feebly. "I used up most of my Latin with the first one."

"Means 'Either learn or leave.'"

"Fitting. You always up this early?"

"I get up around six every morning to grade and do paperwork."

"Sounds fun." I picked up a pen and tapped it on the surface of the table. "You ready for today?"

Sam crossed his arms and leaned against the door frame. "You know, I've been doing this for thirty years, and I still get a little nervous on the first day."

"That's reassuring. I'm still trying to figure out what to say to them."

"Well, you could be original and say, 'Welcome to English Ten. I'm Mr. Glass.'"

I shook my head. "Too boring. Ought to be a bit more dramatic."

"Says the novelist."

I grinned. "Can you tell me where I can find an eraser?"

"I'll bring one down after breakfast." He started to step out the door and then looked back. "Break a leg," he said, and gave me a thumbs-up sign before leaving.

I sat in my swivel chair and propped my feet up on my desk, surveying the rows of empty chairs. "Don't screw this up," I said to the empty room.

MY FIRST-PERIOD CLASS CONSISTED of fifteen fourth formers who sat in a sort of numb acceptance, as if they were on Novocain. Although it was early, their blank looks were largely an act. Before they unmasked themselves, they wanted to see whether I was going to be easy or hard, pleasant or difficult, forgiving or demanding. They were going to have to wait, because I hadn't figured out what I was going to be yet.

"Welcome to English, gentlemen," I said. All fifteen pairs of eyes turned dutifully toward me. I saw my advisee, Stephen Watterson, sitting at the back of the room. He grinned at me, and I smiled back. "Good to see you all. Hope you had a good summer. My name is Matthias Glass. I graduated from Blackburne in 2001 and went to the University of Virginia and then to NYU for grad school. I figured you might want to know the new guy's credentials before he tried to teach you something."

"He wrote a book, too," Stephen said approvingly. "A novel. My mom read it. It was about this reporter who gets kidnapped by a bunch of South American terrorists."

"Cool," said another student, a gangly kid with a halo of curly blond hair. "Was it like a fictional novel?"

"That would be the definition of a novel," I said. "A long, fictitious prose narrative. Let that be the first literary term we learn." I was bemused when most of the students dutifully opened their notebooks and began writing down the definition. Then I noticed Paul Simmons, the headmaster's son, sitting in the back and looking dully at his desk. His notebook wasn't open.

"Are we going to read your novel?" another student asked.

"No," I said.

"What's it called?" asked the kid with curly blond hair, whose name, according to my roster, was Russell Andrew Scarwood, but he went by Rusty.

"*The Unforgiving*," I said.

Now a small assemblage of students spoke up.

"Are you famous?"

"Was it like a best seller?"

"Can we be in your next book?"

"Gentlemen," I said, raising my hands. "Here's the deal. I wrote a novel, yes. It sold fairly well. I am not famous. I'm your English teacher, and I'm looking forward to this year, so let's get down to it, okay?"

They settled down as I passed out the course syllabus. A not-insignificant weight seemed to roll off my shoulders. I'd wondered, perhaps with some self-importance, how this issue of my novel would go. At some level, I had been hoping it wouldn't even come up. At another, more hidden level, I was thrilled that they were interested, which in turn made me feel slightly disgusted. In any event, now I could move on to the business of teaching.

LIVING IN A DORM of sixty boys, all fifteen- and sixteen-year-olds, became a constant exercise in self-control. The pranks, crude jokes, profanity, water fights, phone use after lights-out, shouts echoing in the stairwells, running showers, wrestling matches, drumming feet in the halls, and loud music were enough to try the patience of a nun. Mild-mannered Gray Smith, the dorm master on the Lawson side, swore he would kill someone before Christmas. Small episodes of dormitory insanity occurred throughout a very busy fall. A urinal on the third floor exploded for un-known reasons at six thirty one morning, flooding the bathroom for nearly two hours before the housekeeping staff showed up. Hal Starr got a half-full Coke and a bag of Doritos accidentally mixed up with his laundry, and the spilled Coke shorted out the dryer before blowing the entire circuit and plunging the Hill into darkness for an hour one Saturday evening. I made my way through the darkened dormitory and found Hal in his room, red faced and embarrassed in the beam of my flashlight as he shook soggy Doritos out of his half-dry laundry, most of which had been stained by the Coke. The following week, Brian Schue sucked his bedsheets into the hall vacuum cleaner "to see what it would do." David Barnes ate soap on a dare and threw up on Jim Powell as they were walking to chapel, ruining Jim's brand-new blazer.

But it was Ben Sipple, a blond-haired fourth former, who seemed des-tined to be my dormitory nemesis. He possessed the pale, amused face of a Flemish angel and the cunning of a demon from the ninth circle of hell. The analogy was not, in my opinion, all that extreme: Ben's roommate, Robert Cummings, came to my apartment one evening and accused Ben of satanic worship.

"Ben says he's going to call the devil into our room tonight, Mr. Glass. He's got this old black leather book that's huge—he calls it a demonomi-con or something—and he says he's going to conjure up the devil with it." Robert was a starter on varsity soccer and generally implacable, but his face was pale and he was obviously shaken.

I went upstairs to Ben's room. Ben was sitting at his desk, working out an algebra problem.

"Hello, Mr. Glass," he said pleasantly.

I figured a frontal assault was most appropriate. "Robert says you plan to scare him tonight with some sort of satanic worship. That true?"

Ben assumed a pious expression. "Mr. Glass, I don't worship the devil. And why would I want to scare Robert?"

"He says you plan to—to bring the devil into your room." I felt ridiculous under his placid gaze.

Ben smiled as if confused. "Mr. Glass, do I look like the type of person who would be able to conjure the devil?"

I told him to leave Robert alone and went back to my room to continue grading papers on Oedipus as a tragic hero. Early on, I had realized that assigning papers was one thing, but grading them another. What looked like a great assignment idea was complicated by the fact that it resulted in a stack of sixty-odd papers appearing on my desk, all needing to be graded. My fourth formers' first paper, a short essay on their summer reading assignment, had nearly killed me. I'd spent around twenty minutes on each paper, writing detailed comments in blue ink about organization, textual evidence, even basic grammar, and had worked several nights past eleven o'clock trying to get them graded. When I had returned them, almost every student had flipped casually past my comments to find the grade, and then shoved his paper into the purgatory of his backpack. Now I was spending five minutes at most on each paper and would require all of them to submit a revision. My former English teacher, Mr. Conkle, who had retired to Florida two years ago, had written concise and trenchant comments that looped across the backs of my essays, and I wondered how he had done it year after year.

Bitching about student papers is probably standard for English teachers, but there were compensations. Paul Simmons's paper showed signs of serious thought, although he had carelessly slapped the words onto the page and turned in what was clearly a first draft. It must have been difficult for him to attend the same school that his father ran, but I wished he had put in a bit more effort. By contrast, Stephen Watterson had again earned an A. The boy had a talent with words—his prose could be a bit flowery, perhaps, but it was always insightful and often clever. I wondered if Mr. Conkle had felt the same reading my papers. I shook my head at my own self-indulgence and bent back over Stephen's essay, pen in hand.

Suddenly a shriek rang through the dormitory. Screams, cries, yells were all part of the daily repertoire on Lawson-Parker, but this was a howl of fear. My scalp actually crawled. *What the hell?* I stood up and stepped out into the hall. The scream came again, from upstairs. I saw heads poke out from behind doors as I ran down the hall to the stairs, which I took three at a time.

When I came out of the stairwell, Robert Cummings was running down the third-floor hallway, his face contorted in horror. "He's here!" he screamed, and then threw himself at my feet. "He's here! He's in my room!"

A few students were milling uncomfortably in the hall. Rusty Scarwood came over and tried to calm Robert down. I walked down the hall to Robert's room and went in.

Ben Sipple and Terence Jarrar, another of my sophomore English students, were giggling uncontrollably on Ben's bed under a circle of weak yellow light from Ben's lamp. A large black leather-bound book sat on the floor, its pages open to a picture of a pentangle. The boys fell silent when they noticed me.

"Evening, gentlemen," I said. "Any success with the demon conjuring?"

Ben's face hung in the dim light. Terence looked at the floor.

"Terence, you're in your room for the rest of the night. Mr. Middleton will inform you about any other punishment he sees fit to give you. Go." Terence went, leaving me alone with Ben.

I stood over Ben, who sat motionless on his bed. "Why'd you do it, Ben?" I asked.

"It was just a joke," he said.

"Some joke. You freaked out the entire dorm by scaring your room-mate." I sighed. "My guess is, Robert will ask to move out. I'll recommend that he do so. And I'll suggest to Mr. Middleton that you do work details for a week and be placed on probation. One more stunt like this and you'll be packing to go home."

Ben snickered. "Which home, Mr. Glass? My mom's in Miami? Or my dad's in Boston with his new girlfriend?"

Taken aback by his brazenness, I said, "Look, this is a good school. You've got . . . opportunities here." Even as I spoke, I knew how clichéd that sounded.

Now Ben laughed aloud, an ugly, derisive sound. "Is this where you tell me all the things I have to learn here, Mr. Glass? How it'll change my life? How I *wasn't* dumped here by my parents like a bag of laundry?" He paused to let this sink in. "All the teachers here hate me," he said coolly. "Did you know that? And now you do, too."

Most counselors, I guess, would tell you that a kid who said these things was seeking attention and that the kid was hurting in a bad way. And they would be right, probably. But all Ben's accusation did was make me mad. He had terrified Robert Cummings as a joke, and his justification was that his own life was too painful for him to bother to act like a decent human being toward his classmates.

"Don't try to guilt me, Ben," I said. "Your life sucks? Join the club. If you can't change what makes your life suck, then figure out what you need to do to deal with it. If you need help, I'm here. Other teachers are here. So don't give me any of that victim crap." I stopped, shocked by my own words. Ben was, too, apparently; he stared at me, slack-jawed.

I turned. "Go to bed, now," I said, and left. Only later did I realize that I was angry in part because my own advice to Ben was exactly what I could have said to myself.

CHAPTER SIX

B y dinnertime, almost an hour after Fritz had lost me in the trees, I still hadn't seen him. I sat in a corner of the dining hall and picked at my plate of food while the few classmates who had joined me caught my mood and left me alone, talking among themselves about an upcoming mixer with Saint Catherine's. I ignored them, afraid of what I would say if they asked me how I was doing. *I'm great, thanks. I cheated on a physics test and lied to my roommate.*

No one, other than the prefects on the J-Board and their faculty sponsor, Dr. Booth, had seen me go into or out of my hearing earlier that day. My teacher, Mr. Summerfield, was the one who had reported me for a possible honor code violation. He had wondered why I hadn't just turned in the test when he had called for them, why it had taken me so long to write out the pledge. In my hearing, the J-Board asked me if I had cheated. The question assumed that, if I were guilty, I would feel ashamed and confess. Instead, facing ten of my classmates, including Fritz and his half smile, I had felt something cold brush my heart, and I had told them no, I hadn't cheated. Two minutes later, I left my hearing, knowing I would be found innocent, and the guilt I had managed to keep locked down earlier seeped into every cell of my body until I found myself at the lions, as if waiting for Fritz to arrive so I could ruin our friendship.

I got up from the table and put my tray of uneaten food on the con-
veyor belt to the dishwashers and headed back to my room. Outside in the
gloaming, third formers hurried across campus to the study halls in the
basement of Stadler Hall. I got to our room in Walker with five minutes
to spare before the start of study period. No Fritz. This was odd—Fritz
was rarely late for anything. And we weren't typically allowed to study off
dorm two nights in a row, so he probably wasn't in the library. *He must
really be pissed*, I thought. I made sure he wasn't in the bathroom down the
hall, and then sat at my desk, disheartened, as the bell rang.

Half an hour later, I was worried. One of the masters in charge—the
teachers who had the weekly duty of running study hall for the third
formers and making sure the rest of us were working in our rooms—could
come by any minute and see that Fritz wasn't in the room. If Fritz didn't
have a very good excuse, he'd get detention, which took place on Saturday
nights. He'd probably miss the mixer with Saint Catherine's. But beyond
that, a selfish thought began crawling out of a dark recess in my mind.
Fritz could be in Stilwell telling someone, maybe Mr. Hodges, that I had
cheated. *He wouldn't do that*, I thought, chewing my thumbnail. But if he
did? Various scenarios played out in my head: Mr. Summerfield scowling,
and then assuring me all was well; Dr. Simmons gazing coldly at me from
behind his desk; my classmates rallying to my defense, and then turning
away in rejection; my parents coming to pick me up in shame, my mother
bawling.

Finally the bell rang, ending the first study period. I had fifteen minutes before the next one. I ran out of Walker into the night and down the
lighted brick path to the library. I could see dim, shadowy figures crossing
the Lawn, some disappearing, others hanging around the lit porches of the
dorms, like spies skulking in alleyways in a Cold War novel. The air was
frosty, giving the illusion that everyone outside was exhaling smoke. I got
to the library, entered the main doors, and, off the main hall, I found Trip
Alexander in one of the study rooms reserved for sixth formers. He was

drinking a can of orange juice at a table covered with math textbooks and various papers. I tapped on the glass door, and Trip looked up from the desk, brushing back the straight blond hair that was constantly falling into his eyes. I opened the door and stepped inside the study room, which was little more than a glorified closet with dark wainscoting and a table and two chairs. "I hate Kimball," Trip said to me by way of greeting, referring to the calculus teacher. "The man will be the death of me. Three tests in three weeks. Total bullshit."

"Have you seen Fritz anywhere?" I asked.

Trip raised an eyebrow. "No, not since breakfast. Why?"

I hesitated. "Well, I figured you guys were studying for calc again, like last night, and I need to talk to Fritz."

Trip shook his head. "No, I've been studying with Diamond. He really needs to pass this test, but he said he'd had enough. He's heading back to his room." Trip frowned. "What did you say about last night?"

"I was . . . Nothing. I mean, just that you and Fritz were studying last night . . ." *While I was cheating on my physics test.*

Trip sat back in his chair. "Fritz and I weren't studying together last night."

I blinked. "What?"

"Fritz and I didn't study together last night. Did he tell you we did?"

I looked at Trip, who looked back evenly. The honor system, straight-forward and unequivocal as it was, did not bend. But there was a whole gray category of behavior that the honor system tended to ignore, such as telling white lies in order to maintain your privacy or spare someone's feelings. I understood that Trip was trying to figure out if this was that kind of gray area, if Fritz had allowed me to believe he'd been studying with Trip without actually telling me a lie, or if Fritz's behavior was something else. This was tricky ground, for both of us.

"He told me he was here, with you," I said. "And now I don't know where he is."

There was a knock on the open door, and in stepped Mr. Hodges. His white hair lay on his head and over his ears, looking for all the world like some sort of medieval skullcap. "Gentlemen," he said. "Mr. Glass, I don't recall your having permission to study off dorm tonight. You've got about six minutes until the bell."

Trip and I looked at each other. Mr. Hodges tilted his head slightly, arms folded across his chest as he leaned against the doorway. "What's wrong, Matthias?" he asked.

Trip continued to look at me. I opened my mouth and then closed it. My earlier fear, that Fritz might have gone to talk to Mr. Hodges about me, receded; if he had, Mr. Hodges would already be hauling me into his office. But that didn't solve the problem of where Fritz was. My choices were all bad. I could say nothing was wrong, which might fool Mr. Hodges but definitely wouldn't fool Trip. Or I could tell Mr. Hodges that Fritz had been absent from our room during study hall and get my roommate in serious trouble, which was the last thing I wanted to do right now.

In one stroke, Trip cut through my knot of anxiety. "He's looking for Fritz, sir," Trip said, his eyes still on me. For a moment, anger flared up in me. Then it passed almost immediately. Trip had forced me into the position of having to tell an administrator about Fritz being AWOL, but this shielded me from being a rat. Also, Trip hadn't told Mr. Hodges that Fritz had lied to me. I could even make up a story to cover Fritz if I wanted, knowing Trip wouldn't say anything. Absently I wondered if Trip had thought all this out in the few short seconds since Mr. Hodges had arrived.

Mr. Hodges considered me with polite interest. He continued looking at me with the same interested expression as I explained that I hadn't seen Fritz since track practice, and that I had thought he had been studying with Trip but was obviously wrong. Mr. Hodges asked us a few questions— when was the last time either of us had seen him, whom else might he be studying with—and kept us past the bell for the second study period. Then he told me we were going to head back to my room. If Fritz wasn't there, I was to stay in my room and wait. Trip raised a hand in farewell as we left, and Mr. Hodges and I walked through the library doors outside.

The night had grown darker, broken only by the soft glow of the footlights along the brick walkway and the brighter porch lights of the academic buildings and dormitories. It was cold, and I put my hands in my pockets. Mr. Hodges walked purposefully yet without haste. Following a step behind him, I knew that Mr. Hodges would find out where Fritz was. What I didn't know was what else he might discover. The idea that this man, whom I had long admired for his intellect and his kind way with the boys at our school, could potentially discover that I had cheated was so wrenching that I half wanted to step off the lit path into the night and disappear.

My room was empty—Fritz wasn't there, and it didn't appear that he had come back in my absence. Mr. Hodges reminded me to stay put. "He may be out moping by the golf course," he said. "Or studying calculus in someone else's room."

I just nodded. Somehow I knew Fritz wasn't in either place. He had lied to me about last night; that much was certain. So where had he been? I recalled the last time I had seen him, running through the darkening wood before he disappeared around a bend in the road.

Mr. Hodges tilted his head to the side like an inquisitive bird and peered at me. "Is there any reason you're worried, Matthias?" he asked gently. "About Fritz?"

I shrugged, not trusting my own voice. My throat threatened to squeeze shut. Suddenly my eyes were burning. "He's stressed about college," I managed. Then I put my hands over my face and sat down in our beat-up green recliner and wept. Shame, guilt, and disgust flooded over me. Soon I became aware of Mr. Hodges's hand on my shoulder, and I pulled myself together, shaking my head almost angrily as I took his proffered handkerchief. I blew my nose and then hesitated, not knowing what to do with the handkerchief. "Keep it," Mr. Hodges said with a little smile. "It's yours now."

Despite myself I laughed weakly. "Sorry about that, Mr. Hodges," I said. "I just . . . I wasn't nice to him this afternoon. He was freaking out about college again. I mean, he's *going* to get in. If not UVA, then plenty of other places. I just . . . I just got tired of him complaining about it, and told him that, and he just . . . He ran away." A few more tears fell from my eyes, but I was done crying, as if my grief had cast me on some rocky shore, spent but clearheaded. Never before had I appreciated the subtlety, the hairsplitting involved in lying. I had cried because of what I had said to Fritz, true, but that wasn't the only reason I had broken down in front of Mr. Hodges. I had violated the most important rule at Blackburne, and I'd betrayed Fritz, and there was no way I could tell anyone about any of it without being expelled. Then I masked my guilt by revealing another uncomfortable truth. Dimly I wondered how much self-deception one had to practice in order to live with a lie.

Mr. Hodges squeezed my shoulder once, firmly, and then withdrew. "I'm sure he knows you didn't mean to insult him," he said. "Even if his feelings were hurt. You'll be all right?" I nodded, and he headed for the door. "Just stay right here, Matthias," he said. "It'll all be fine."

IT WASN'T ALL FINE.

Study period ended at ten. Immediately, stereos powered on. The Red Hot Chili Peppers competed with Eminem, the music threatening to make the windows vibrate. Ten o'clock became ten thirty and still no sign of Fritz. This was getting ridiculous, I thought. Avoiding me because he was angry was one thing, but eventually he had to come back to our room, if only to keep from getting suspended. Where the hell was he? I went to the bathroom and found Jay "Beef" Organ staring at himself in the mirror, picking a zit on his nose. He asked why Mr. Hodges had been in the dorm earlier. I made some noncommittal remark, brushed my teeth, and went back to our room. Ten forty-one. Lights-out was at eleven. For the fifth or sixth time I looked in and around my desk to see if Fritz had left a note but found nothing. I finally gave up and decided to try reading. I leafed through *Light in August* but couldn't handle any more Faulkner; I picked up *The Catcher in the Rye*, a favorite book, but after reading the opening paragraph twice, I put the book back on the shelf and threw myself onto my bed. Someone upstairs, probably Max Goren, was playing the Beastie Boys' "Brass Monkey," a song I had always hated. I reached underneath my pillow to pull it over my head and shut out the noise, and my hand touched something small and metallic lying on the mattress beneath the pillow. I pulled it out to look at it. It was a thin silver chain, and attached to the chain was a round medal about the size of a nickel. It was Fritz's Saint Christopher medal. I sat up and stared at it. Fritz had been wearing it when I had last seen him that afternoon. And it had been placed under my pillow.

The Beastie Boys' song cut off in mid-rap, silence falling like a curtain interrupting a bad play. There was a knock on my door. Instinctively, I shoved the medal back under my pillow, just as the door opened. I jumped out of bed and saw Mr. Hodges. Behind him was a sheriff's deputy in a brown uniform shirt and khakis, the star on his chest shining faintly in the glare of the overhead lights.

"Matthias," Mr. Hodges said. "I'm sorry to startle you."

I was still staring at the deputy. "Is everything . . . ," I began, and then paused. Suddenly I was seized with terror. "What's going on?" *They found his body*, I thought. Fritz had killed himself. And he had left his Saint Christopher medal on my bed. I couldn't look away from the deputy, an impassive-looking man with gray hair who seemed to be looking at something just above my eyes.

"We cannot find Fritz," Mr. Hodges was saying. "He's not anywhere on campus. No one has reported seeing him since dinner. Dr. Simmons has contacted his parents. They are not aware of any reason why he shouldn't be here. His father is driving over from Fairfax." He turned to the deputy, who looked me in the eye for the first time. "This is Deputy Briggs from the county sheriff's office. He wants to ask you a few questions. Is that all right?"

I nodded, trying not to stare at the pistol holstered on Deputy Briggs's right hip. My heart had been tripping away in my chest ever since seeing the deputy, as if he were there to arrest me. I recalled seeing him before, directing traffic and parking on campus for big football games. "Yes, sir, that's fine," I said. Then something that Mr. Hodges had said hit me. "Since dinner?" I asked. "Did someone see Fritz around dinnertime? I—I haven't seen him since track practice."

"Mr. Greer saw Fritz walk out of this dorm around six forty-five this evening," Mr. Hodges said.

I must have stared. "Mr. Greer?" Our wheelchair-bound maintenance man was not the first person I would have expected to have news about Fritz. Pelham Greer was friendly in a gruff way, but aside from joking occasionally with students in the Brickhouse, the school snack bar, or passing us on the walkways, he lived in his own peculiar orbit that did not regularly include students. As Diamond had once put it, he was one weird motherfucker.

Mr. Hodges was nodding. "He's quite certain. Fritz had a backpack over one shoulder."

"A backpack?"

Mr. Hodges nodded. "He must have stopped back here while you were at dinner," he said. He turned to Deputy Briggs with a slightly embarrassed air, as if he were trespassing on the deputy's business.

Deputy Briggs gave a little nod and stepped forward, immediately in charge of the situation. "Just a few questions, Matthias," he said.

As Deputy Briggs pulled out a worn, black clasp notebook from his hip pocket, I noticed that Mr. Hodges wasn't going anywhere, but any relief I may have felt at that was engulfed by what was happening. *Fritz is gone*, I thought. *He's missing, vanished. Lost.*

SUICIDE WAS THE PREVAILING theory by lunch the next day. No one said this directly to me—I found that I was surrounded by an invisible bubble that caused people to keep their distance and lower their voices when they saw me. I didn't need to hear what they were saying. I was thinking the same thing.

After Deputy Briggs had questioned me, it had been pretty clear he didn't think I knew anything about where Fritz might be. I just told him about that afternoon by the lions, downplaying my argument with Fritz, and then recounted what I'd done that evening. Briggs wrote down everything I said and then departed, leaving Mr. Hodges behind. Mr. Hodges sat with me awhile, not saying much of anything, just sitting at Fritz's desk and jiggling his foot. He said I could stay with him and his wife in their house if I wanted. I thanked him and said I'd be fine where I was. We didn't say much after that. The dorm began to settle down—some last-minute toothbrushing and toilet flushing, some muffled footsteps from upstairs, and then quiet. A moth batted itself against the window screen. Water gurgled in the pipes. Mr. Hodges looked up at that. "These old dorms," he said, gazing at the ceiling. "Full of quirks, plumbing older than Versailles. But they'll never fall down." At that he stood. "He'll be all right, Matthias," he said. "Fritz is a smart boy. He isn't reckless."

I nodded, not wanting to risk another crying fit like earlier. I stood up, too. "Thanks, Mr. Hodges," I said.

He shrugged. "Haven't done much of anything," he said. "But if you like, I'd be happy to call your parents for you, let them know what's going on."

I hesitated and then shook my head. "No, thank you," I said. "I don't want them to worry." But the thought of my parents made me feel safer—I could talk to them later if I needed to. I thought of Mr. Davenport, Fritz's dad, driving through the dark right then, knowing that his son was missing, and I shivered.

Mr. Hodges shook my hand on the way out, clapped me on the

shoulder, and told me to get some rest. I spent the night staring at the bottom of Fritz's bunk, holding his Saint Christopher medal in my hand as I tried to fall asleep. I must have dozed off sometime before dawn, because suddenly I was aware that the light outside the windows had gone a milky blue and that there was a dog nearby, giving a single sharp yelp. It was a search-and-rescue dog.

I skipped breakfast and went to first-period class, AP English. Mr. Conkle seemed surprised to see me, as did the rest of my classmates, but everyone politely ignored me as Mr. Conkle had us analyze, or "unpack," as he called it, Dylan Thomas's "Do Not Go Gentle into That Good Night." Usually this was the kind of thing I excelled at, even enjoyed, taking a poem apart and examining it line by line. This included looking at the words the poet had chosen, the meter, the figurative language, the clever turns and descriptions and insights. But I was in no mood for schoolwork, and all I could think about was how the father in the poem was dying and how Fritz might be dying or dead somewhere. After English, I headed to my room and lay on my bed. No one came to tell me to go to class, so I stayed and dozed until lunch, when hunger drove me to the dining hall and I learned of my newfound powers of attracting the attention of everyone within a fifty-yard radius like some twisted sort of magnet.

When I walked back into my room, I stopped so abruptly, I nearly stumbled into my recliner. Fritz's father was sitting on my bed.

His tie was loosened and his shirtsleeves were rolled to the elbows, though his hands dangled between his knees, as if he had been prepared to dive into some difficult task only to find that he was incapable of doing anything. His eyes, round with sleeplessness and disbelief, seemed to bore a hole straight through me.

"Mr. Davenport," I stammered. I placed a hand on the nearest chair, needing to grip something solid.

He nodded absently and then wet his lips with his tongue. I realized, for the first time, that Fritz looked very little like his father, but he had the same habit of wetting his lips with the tip of his tongue. That realization seemed absurdly tragic, and I stood mute before it.

When Mr. Davenport spoke, his voice was hoarse. "Matthias," he said, and then dryly swallowed. "Do you know where he is?"

"Sir," I began. "I—I am so sorry that Fritz . . ." I stopped, confused as to how to end that sentence.

Mr. Davenport supplied the ending for me. "He's missing, Matthias. My son is missing. His mother is at home right now, crying. I had to call my brother to come over." He paused, shook his head as if he didn't approve, and started again. "They tell me you may be the last person who spoke to him. I need to know what he said."

I couldn't seem to concentrate—his eyes were absorbing everything. "Sir?"

"What did my son say, Matthias? You saw him, down by the school entrance, yesterday afternoon. What did he say to you?" Another pause. "What did you say to him?"

I willed myself not to stare at my pillow, under which lay Fritz's medal. Mr. Davenport was sitting right next to it. I wasn't sure that I could pretend surprise if he found it. And then he would wonder why I hadn't told him or anyone else about the medal, why I had kept it secret. I wasn't even sure myself, except that Fritz had placed it under my pillow for a reason—why, I didn't know, but to give it to someone else, even Fritz's father, when Fritz had given it specifically to me, seemed wrong, another kind of betrayal.

"Matthias?" Mr. Davenport's tone was sharper now, impatient.

"I . . ." I hesitated, trying to think of how much to say, and that did it. He was off the bed and up in my face. His speed and ferocity so completely unnerved me that I was left gaping.

"*Where is he?*" he shouted. His anger was volcanic. I had never seen an adult so furious. His face filled my vision. I could count the pores in his nose, see the silver hairs in the black, uneven stubble around his jaw. His eyes were enormous and blazed with rage. "Where is my son?"

"He started talking about college," I blurted out, my words stumbling over one another. "About not—not getting in. He w-worried about it—*worries* about it, all the time." Realizing that I had spoken about Fritz in the past tense made me start to cry again. "I told him . . . I told him to shut up about it, Mr. Davenport. I'm so sorry. I told him you would get him into school, you and his uncle. I said you'd get him in. I'm sorry. I'm so sorry." And I cried, standing there in my room, in front of Fritz's father. I turned away, my face hot and slick, and I covered my face with my hands.

When I heard a rustle of movement, I didn't know if he was stepping back, or reaching out a hand to touch my shoulder, or just picking up his suit jacket. All I know is that, after a moment, Mr. Davenport walked out of the room without a word, leaving the door open behind him.

THESE STORIES USUALLY HAVE a dramatic, definitive end. A member of the search party, taking a quick leak behind a tree, sees a hand protruding from a nearby bush, blood on the frozen fingers. Or someone in a diner in Pennsylvania realizes the boy sipping coffee in the next booth over looks an awful lot like the picture of the runaway on the news. Or the missing person shows up safe and sound, a miscommunication having led people to jump to conclusions.

This story did not end in any of those ways. Fritz Davenport ran into those woods and it was as if he never came back out. There was no body found, no evidence of foul play. No ransom note was ever delivered to Fritz's parents or the school. A thousand tips were called in, people claiming to have seen Fritz in West Virginia, Idaho, Texas, Maine. None of them panned out. The state police posited that Fritz may have run away, pointing to his having withdrawn several hundred dollars from an ATM at a mall in Charlottesville the previous weekend, when a van had taken Blackburne kids in for dinner and a movie. Seeing as students weren't allowed to have cars at Blackburne, they figured someone may have helped Fritz to get away. This led to several uncomfortable interviews with school employees, particularly the maintenance and kitchen staff. Fritz's disappearance spared no one.

And all of this came to nothing, a void that grew around the hole that Fritz had left behind him, a hole that exerts its pull on us still.

CHAPTER SEVEN

I did not intend to start looking into Fritz's disappearance. I'm not a detective or an investigative reporter; I'm a novelist, and novelists are given to flights of imagination, to what-ifs and conjecture and spinning tales. Writing stories is a game I play with myself, an enjoyable one. At least, it used to be. But it isn't real, not like Fritz's disappearance was real. Poking around the meager facts would be hard enough nearly a decade later. I had simply come to believe that many things in the world did not make sense. They happen and we are left in the aftermath to deal with the new reality in which we find ourselves.

In retrospect, dating Michele had been my aftermath, my deliberate decision to break with the past. I had tried to bury Fritz as I tried to bury any secret—sealed him off in my heart with a thousand distractions. In college and grad school, it was easier to erect a barricade of books and essays and novels to write than it was to forge relationships. And then Michele. She didn't know me before Fritz disappeared. She knew me only afterward, and so I could reinvent myself for her as a cool brooding author. The problem was, I couldn't entirely fool myself. I was attracted to Michele not just because she was gorgeous and good in bed, but because of what she represented: a life of drifting through New York, cocktail glasses in hand, with beautiful people who were all apparently famous in fashion and who all promised to read my novel. We thought we were in love—and maybe we were, but more with the idea of ourselves than the reality. The truth is that we were both damaged people incapable of sustaining each other. I had run away from Fritz, but I couldn't run away from my own dysfunction. That was my narrative, for better or worse. And now I had come full circle and returned to the start of my story, to Blackburne, which I had never really left behind after all.

AFTER MARCHING MY FOURTH formers through our first text, *Oedipus Rex*, I was about to start teaching a short poetry unit, and as an introduction I had assigned some Anna Akhmatova. It was clear that many of them had little to no experience with poetry, outside of waiting for the teacher to tell them what a poem meant, as if it were a secret code, and then writing that down and later regurgitating it on a test. I had suspected—and a subsequent conversation with Sam Hodges confirmed my suspicion—that it might be better for me to guide them toward figuring it out on their own. I had always enjoyed reading poetry, although it's a very different thing to teach others how to read it. My students felt that poets were weird, which had actually been true of some of the poets I had known at NYU. They had scared me a little, to be honest—at parties, the poets were the ones swinging from the light fixtures and trying to get the faculty, or their spouses, into bed, whereas we fiction writers leaned against walls, drank early, and snuck glances at our watches. That hadn't kept me from sleeping with two of the poets. Beth was blond and warm and wrote Whitmanesque verse about rivers; Giselle was dark haired and dark spirited, with fingernails bitten to the bone, and wrote tight, acidic poems about death and betrayal, as if she were the love child of Emily Dickinson and Edgar Allan Poe. Beth said I was a lost soul while Giselle called me a fucking asshole, both of which, when you think about it, are pretty much the same thing.

Now I arranged my class of fifteen boys into a circle, and they looked down dubiously at the photocopies of Akhmatova's "The Muse" as I read it aloud:

> *All that I am hangs by a thread tonight*
> *as I wait for her whom no one can command.*
> *Whatever I cherish most—youth, freedom, glory—*
> *fades before her who bears the flute in her hand.*
>
> *And look! she comes . . . she tosses back her veil,*
> *staring me down, serene and pitiless.*
> *"Are you the one," I ask, "whom Dante heard dictate*
> *the lines of his* Inferno*?" She answers: "Yes."*

After I finished reading, silence held for a few beats. Stephen Watterson seemed to be bowing his head over his photocopy out of respect. Paul Simmons blew his nose loudly into a tissue. I frowned at him and he raised his eyebrows—*who, me?*—before tossing his used tissue into the trash can.

"Okay," I said. "So what do you think?"

"Kinda crazy," Rusty Scarwood said, one hand in his curly yellow hair.

"I like the muse," Stephen Watterson said. "It just sort of shows up. Like the Greeks thought the Muses did."

Terence Jarrar looked at the poem like a man considering how to remove a stump. "What's a muse?" he asked.

Stephen answered. "It's like your own personal goddess who inspires you. The ancient Greeks thought the Muses were the source of knowledge."

Paul Simmons, who was slouched in his chair so his legs stuck far out underneath his desk, glanced at Terence as if he were about to say something, but he saw me looking his way and went back to staring out the window.

"Okay," I said, "so how does the speaker here seem to feel about the muse?"

Stephen raised his hand. Everyone else pretended I hadn't spoken. Terence continued to look at the poem, possibly waiting for his own source of inspiration. Ignoring Stephen's hand, I addressed Paul. "Any ideas, Paul?"

Paul looked at me, startled, and then reluctantly studied his copy of the poem. "She likes it?" he said.

Stephen raised his arm farther into the air.

"A little more than that," I said to Paul.

This time Paul looked at me coldly, as if I had just insulted him. I looked back with what I hoped was a warm smile and not a nervous grimace. What if *none* of them would answer my questions? I knew I would rush to fill the silence with my own words. And then what if they simply sat in their seats, inert as clay, as I talked on and on?

Then, ever so slowly, Paul cast his glance back down to the poem and reread it. "She's anxious," he said finally. "About the muse."

Thank you, baby Jesus, I thought. "Where do you see that?" I asked.

Stephen could no longer constrain himself. "She says everything is hanging by a thread," he said.

"He was asking me," Paul muttered, looking at Stephen with heavy-lidded eyes.

I had gotten Paul Simmons to participate in class, and I wasn't about to let him quit now, even for Stephen. "Thanks, Stephen, but I want to hear from Paul first," I said, and then turned to Paul expectantly.

Suspicious, as if I had tricked him into learning something, Paul gathered his thoughts. "The speaker's anxious about the muse coming because she can't command her," he said. "So maybe she wants to control her, but that's not how a muse works. It just comes."

"Good," I said. "That's good, Paul."

Rusty Scarwood raised a hand. "What's up with the flute?" he asked. "The muse has a flute. Why a flute?"

Stephen raised his hand again, and I nodded at him. "Poetry is a lot like music," Stephen said. "They both have rhythm, repetition, lots of emphasis on sound . . . If this is Akhmatova's muse, and Akhmatova is a poet, then it fits. The muse is going to inspire Akhmatova to make her own kind of music."

Paul shook his head. "But the speaker says her muse stared her down. She's pitiless, without pity. She's not playing some pretty song in the poet's ear."

"Not all inspiration has to be pretty," Stephen insisted.

Paul picked up the poem and waved it in the air. "Hello, she's talking about Dante and the *Inferno*. Going to hell and seeing people burning or being eaten alive. Is that the kind of inspiration you'd want to get? I think the muse terrifies her."

"This is great, guys," I said, immediately regretting it—I sounded like a cheerleader urging my students to fight—go team, win!—while they huddled up to argue over their next play.

Then Terence sat forward in his chair. "Hey," he said, and Paul stopped in midsentence to stare at Terence. Everyone else stirred in their seats, like an audience before a stage play begins. Terence rarely participated in class, and now he'd spoken twice in a space of five minutes. Slowly, unaware of the rest of the class looking at him, Terence said, "When the speaker asks the muse if she dictated the *Inferno* to Dante, the muse just says, 'Yes.' Which is weird."

"Exactly," Paul said. "She's not helpful. Her muse is a nightmare." Across from him, Stephen Watterson humphed and glared at his copy of the poem.

Terence looked at me. "Didn't you say that . . ." He trailed off.

"Go on, Terence," I said, encouraging him.

Terence hitched his shoulders nervously. "Well, didn't you say that Akhmatova had to visit her son in prison? And that she was under lots of surveillance?"

Rusty nodded in recognition. "Yeah, and her ex-husband was arrested and shot, right?"

"Yes," I said, in my best deadpan voice. It took them a second to get that

I was echoing Akhmatova's muse. Even Paul Simmons smiled, although he rolled his eyes as he did it. "Okay, Terence, so what are you thinking?" I said.

"Well," Terence said, "maybe she *wanted* the same muse that helped Dante. Maybe she thought she was living in a kind of . . . hell. And she needed help describing it." Terence picked up the poem and then laid it back down on his desk.

I nodded my head, smiling. "That's about as good an interpretation as I've read, Terence. What do the rest of you think?"

Rusty Scarwood leaned over and offered a fist bump to Terence, who blushed but returned it. "That's good," Stephen Watterson said. The others murmured similar comments, but I saw Terence glancing at Paul sitting next to him, as though waiting for his friend's approval. Paul remained slouched in his seat, but he saw Terence looking at him and smiled a little. "*Exemplum de simia, quae, quando plus ascendit, plus apparent posteriora eius*," Paul said to Terence.

It was as if someone had struck a large bell behind my head. Paul's Latin saying evoked a memory so strong, it seemed to physically manifest itself and threaten to overwhelm me. No one seemed to notice as they were focused on Paul, but the memory pulled at me like a powerful current, and for a brief moment, sitting in my classroom, I let it carry me back, to Fritz.

DR. JUSTINIAN BOOTH TAUGHT us European History in our fourth form year, one floor above the room where a decade later I would be teaching Anna Akhmatova. Dr. Booth was a short, dapper, dark-haired man who always wore a bow tie and a blazer, whether it was snowing or humid as a hothouse. He beat facts into our brains with the single-mindedness of a monk instructing us in catechism, and then with equal fervor he pressed us to find connections, patterns, links between historical events and figures. Aside from assigning stunning amounts of homework, Dr. Booth would deliver engaging lectures on a wide variety of topics—Martin

Luther, Henry VIII's "wife problem," the execution of the Romanovs, the tulip mania in seventeenth-century Holland, the fall of Constantinople.

One day Dr. Booth was holding forth on the rise of the European nation-state, emphasizing its reliance upon codes of law, when a pudgy kid with curly hair held up his hand. "Excuse me, sir?" the kid said with a placid smile. "Wasn't Justinian the Roman emperor who established an important code of law?"

"The *Byzantine* emperor," Dr. Booth said, though his tone was kind. "But you are correct—he is credited with commissioning the *Corpus Juris Civilis*, or the Code of Justinian as it is sometimes known. It serves as the basis for much of modern civil law."

Fritz glanced at me from one seat over and rolled his eyes. We all knew Dr. Booth had been named after Justinian the Great. It was one of the first things we had learned in European History. The kid who had asked the question was a third former named Kevin Kelly. Third formers took Ancient and Medieval History, but apparently Kevin Kelly had taken that course prior to attending Blackburne, so the school had allowed him to take European History with fourth formers. Some fourth formers, like Fletcher Dupree, treated third formers like dirt, but I was generally kind to them—after all, I had been in their shoes just one year earlier. However, I didn't like Kevin Kelly because he was smug and manipulative. Clearly he was sucking up to Dr. Booth by mentioning our teacher's namesake. He knew very well that Justinian had been a Byzantine emperor, but by purposely mistaking him as Roman, he had given Dr. Booth an opportunity to both correct a student and demonstrate his vast knowledge, something he enjoyed immensely.

"Douche bag," Fletcher Dupree hissed quietly at Kevin Kelly from two seats back. He wasn't above sucking up to teachers himself, but Fletcher felt Kevin Kelly was overstepping some boundary.

"Mr. Dupree," Dr. Booth said languidly, "that will earn you a detention, as well as a five-hundred-word monograph on the etymology and historical significance of the term *douche bag*, due to me by Monday." He raised an eyebrow until Fletcher mumbled an apology. I glanced at Kevin Kelly, who was looking down at his textbook as if engrossed by something he was reading, but then I saw him smile, briefly.

Later that day, Fritz and I were sitting in the Brickhouse drinking Cokes and sharing a large paper cup of fries when we saw Fletcher and Diamond, sitting about ten feet away at a corner table half-hidden by an ancient pinball machine. I avoided Fletcher the way you would avoid walking through a mud puddle, but Diamond was a different matter. He was in our history class, too, but we acted as if we didn't see each other. We had hardly spoken since the end of our third form year, never really getting past the water buffalo incident. I wanted to fix our friendship, but I was too awkward and clueless to know how. I felt an ache like a sour tooth whenever we saw each other and he cut his eyes away from me. Now he was sitting in the Brickhouse, talking with Fletcher. In a moment of paranoia, I wondered if they were talking about me.

"Well, if it isn't the Huns," someone said, and I turned to see Kevin Kelly leaning back against a nearby counter and smiling. Two other third formers were with him, grinning at us.

Fritz nodded in greeting, then turned to me. "Want to study tonight for the Euro test?" he asked. "Booth said it'd be easy, which means two essay questions instead of three."

"Sure," I said, popping a french fry into my mouth. "We oughtta—"

"So how'd you get a nickname like 'the Huns'?" Kevin Kelly asked.

In a sad tone, Fritz said, "By slaughtering those who interrupted us."

"Our fallen foes are many," I added, taking a sip of my Coke.

Kevin smirked. "How alliterative," he said. "Very *Beowulf.*" Next to him, one of his sidekicks chortled.

I looked at Fritz. "Methinks he is trying to impress us."

"With the emphasis on *trying*," Fritz said.

"As in trying too hard?"

"Or that he's *being* very trying." Fritz glanced over at Kevin's sidekicks, who were looking back and forth between him, me, and Kevin. "That means difficult to deal with, or severely straining the powers of endurance," Fritz told them.

I raised an eyebrow. "Impressive."

Fritz shrugged. "Latin class," he said, reaching for another fry.

Kevin wasn't so easily put off. "*Tum podem extulit horridulum,*" he said to Fritz.

"I get *horridulum,*" I said. "I mean, I guess it means 'horrible,' right? What?" I said as Fritz shook his head. "You know I take French."

Fritz grinned. "He just told me I'm talking shit," he said to me. Then Fritz raised his hand, fingers together as if he were a food connoisseur tasting an excellent dish, and said to Kevin, "*Exemplum de simia, quae, quando plus ascendit, plus apparent posteriora eius.*" This one I knew, if only because Fritz was fond of this saying of Saint Bonaventure and would repeat it often in our dorm room: *Just like an ape, the more one climbs, the more one shows one's ass.* I laughed when I saw Kevin's face darken as he translated the Latin in his head. He licked his lips.

"I don't think 'Huns' is really the right epithet for you two," he said, loudly enough for those at a few nearby tables to look our way.

I nodded. "It doesn't really capture our intellectual acumen, no."

Kevin said, "I was thinking more like 'the Nazis.'"

His sidekicks laughed at that, one of them high-fiving Kevin, who continued to look at us. There was something hard in his smirk, a cruel intelligence that took pleasure in scoring points off a target. And he had scored with the Nazi reference—Fritz was angry. "Watch who you're calling a Nazi," Fritz said, his tone brittle. "My grandfather fought in World War Two."

Kevin's eyebrows rose in mock admiration. "My grandfather was a swimming coach who liked little boys," he said. "Not all of us have rich daddies or war heroes in our families."

"What is your *problem?*" Fritz said, his voice rising on the final word so it nearly cracked.

"Oh, that stings," Kevin said softly, his eyes on Fritz. "Don't like that, do you?"

"Shut it, Kelly," I said, my voice sharp.

"Or what?" he asked in the same soft voice. "You're going to punch me in the face in front of all these people?" His eyes on me, Kevin gestured around the room at the students now openly staring at us. I realized Diamond and Fletcher were among them. Fletcher was turned around in his seat to face us, while Diamond looked on impassively.

"I don't like being made fun of," Kevin said. "Or having people look down on me."

"We don't look *down* on—" I started.

"Oh bullshit," Kevin said. "I'm a freshman—sorry, a *third former* who's got the balls to take *your* fourth form history class. Of course you look down on me, just like Fletcher Dupree does."

Made uncomfortable by this bald assertion of what was basically the truth, I glanced at Fletcher, who glared at me as if I were the one who had just accused him of being a snob. Loudly, Fletcher said, "The hell is wrong with you, Glass? You gonna let this pissant keep jerking you off?"

My general irritation with Fletcher flared at this, but then Kevin spoke. "Interesting choice of words, Fletcher," he said coolly, "considering how you jerk off every night in the upstairs bathroom in Rhoads."

The blood drained from Fletcher's face so quickly that I thought he might faint, and then it came rushing back so his entire head flushed brick red. "How do . . . what . . . the fuck is that?" he managed to say. I have to admit that a tiny part of me danced at seeing Fletcher Dupree reduced to choking, enraged impotence. Then Fletcher was standing and walking toward Kevin, his fists balled. *He's going to hit him*, I thought with a kind of wonder, but I couldn't seem to make my body move.

Fritz stood up, his chair squalling across the tiled floor, and then he was standing in front of Fletcher, arms out and palms raised like an umpire who had just called a runner safe at home. "Don't, Fletcher," Fritz said. "He's not worth it."

"Get out of my way," Fletcher sputtered, trying to step around Fritz.

"Yeah, Fritz, let him take a swing at me," Kevin said.

Fritz, his arms held wide to keep Fletcher at bay, looked over his shoulder at Kevin. "I'm not doing it for you," he said. "You might even like it, for all I know."

Kevin actually leered at Fritz. "Nazi," he crooned.

A hot, red rage flooded me. Insults were a time-honored art form at Blackburne, and while the line between cleverly one-upping a classmate and denigrating him beyond what was admissible could be hard to find, it existed, and calling someone a Nazi wasn't clever but offensive and stupid. Kevin Kelly had just stepped over the line, unzipped his fly, and pissed all over it. But before I could do anything, Diamond was standing in front of Kevin, seizing his upper arms and lifting him bodily off the counter. "Hey," Kevin managed, his glasses askew on his astonished face.

Diamond leaned his face close to Kevin's. "Leave it, douche bag," he growled, and with those words, it was as if a spell had broken. Fletcher gave a short bark of laughter, and Fritz grinned. I felt like laughing myself, especially at the sight of Diamond holding Kevin in the air as if he were a naughty child.

"Leave my friends alone," Diamond said.

"Fuck you," Kevin said, his voice quavering only a little.

"Boys!" Dr. Booth appeared, a Burberry scarf around his neck, and he stood in front of Diamond and Kevin, his eyes flashing. "What in God's name are you doing?"

"Having a little disagreement, sir," Diamond said, his eyes still on Kevin, who looked positively murderous.

"Put him down now, Mr. Cooper," Dr. Booth said. Diamond promptly let go of Kevin, who dropped to the floor and staggered but did not fall. Dr. Booth chastised both boys roundly and dragged them off to see Mr. Manning, then the assistant headmaster and disciplinarian, who would put both boys in detention for the next three weeks. But as Diamond left the Brickhouse, he glanced at me and winked. That single gesture was enough to bridge the gap that had yawned between us. And from that moment on, our classmates referred to Fritz and me as the Huns almost triumphantly, as if bestowing a hard-won title upon us.

CHAPTER EIGHT

The afternoon after I taught the Anna Akhmatova poem to my fourth formers, I walked to the gym to check out a minibus from the athletic director's office. Blackburne masters have various extracurricular activities they must chaperone, especially on the weekends. My weekend duty was coming up, and I had to drive students to a mixer at Saint Margaret's School that Saturday. I wasn't excited about driving a dozen or so boys halfway across the state to watch them bump and grind in the dark while I drank watery Sprite out of a paper cup, but I shrugged off my discontent and headed to the gym, the memory of Fritz and Diamond and Kevin Kelly still fresh in my mind.

Coach Gristina wasn't in his office, but his secretary, Mrs. Wrenn, a lady with her white hair in a bun who had been at Blackburne since the mastodons, let me sign out a minibus and gave me a set of keys, admonishing me to return it with a full tank of gas. Then, having nothing to do until dinner, I decided to walk around the gym and revisit a few other memories.

Farquhar Gym had the same red brick and white columns as the other buildings on the Hill, but it was bigger, with broad concrete steps down from the portico on the front and enormous vertical windows on both sides, allowing sunlight to shine through and onto the varnished basketball court within. A first-class wrestling arena was buried in the bowels of the gym, along with squash courts, a weight room, a trainer's room that was almost a well-stocked medical clinic, and the requisite locker rooms and showers.

It was also where Pelham Greer lived, although I hadn't known that. Or, more accurately, I had forgotten it. Everyone had known that Greer lived in the gym, but that Greer actually lived and slept somewhere on campus had seemed odd when I was a student—he was just *there*, like the oak trees on the Lawn and the spire rising above Saint Matthew's, a permanent and unchangeable part of the campus.

After walking across the basketball court, the sunlight pouring through the windows like honey onto the floor, I headed down a flight of stairs and walked past the locker rooms with their miasma of sweat and steam. I stopped to glance at the caged-off room where students had received their gym clothes and towels from the Slater brothers, Ned and Ted, two more Blackburne institutions. Ned, who had grizzled gray hair, was folding shirts at a table behind the counter and gave me a bored nod. I wondered how many Blackburne graduates wandered past him every week, finding him in the same position, folding yet another gray gym shirt.

After poking my head into the trainer's room—and seeing, with a slight tug of sadness, that the old hydrotherapy whirlpools had been replaced with brand-new stainless steel tubs—I headed back past the locker rooms to the stairwell, intending to return upstairs. Just then, I noticed a door tucked in the space back behind the stairs. I had never really noticed that door before, probably because it had always been closed. It was now ajar, with a weak light spilling out of the doorway, along with a strange sound—a breathless, inarticulate grunt, like the sound you make when lifting something heavy. This was accompanied by an almost indecipherable noise, a shifting of leather, perhaps, or the kind of release a chair makes when you stand up out of it. The sounds repeated themselves, and then again.

I must have stood in the stairwell, head bowed, listening for about thirty seconds. I wasn't intending to spy on anyone, but I couldn't quite understand what I was hearing. *This is none of your business*, I thought as I walked toward the door, drawn by a powerful curiosity. I crept up to the door and then peered through the narrow opening between the door and the frame.

The room beyond, from the narrow slice of it that I could see, had a high ceiling from which hung a tangle of pipes snaking in various directions. The walls were a dull mustard yellow, though clean and lit by lamps and sunlight filtering through what looked like narrow skylights at the top of the back wall. About ten feet from the door, in the middle of the room, sat Pelham Greer in his wheelchair. He was turned about three-quarters away from me so that I mostly saw his back and the side of his long, lean jaw, but I could see that he was shirtless and glistening with sweat. Hair sprouted from the tops of his shoulders in ragged patches. He was curling dumbbells, one in each hand, releasing a grunt each time a dumbbell passed the apex of its curl. The right bicep would swell into a round, compact mass beneath the skin and then relax. Each time he lifted a dumbbell, he rocked slightly in his wheelchair, which creaked.

Then, just as he started curling his right arm again, something happened—the dumbbell fell out of his hand, causing his rising arm, which had been straining to lift the dumbbell, to jerk upright so that he barked his hand across the spokes of the right-hand wheel of his chair. "Fuck!" he said aloud, and he turned to examine his hand. As he turned, he faced toward the partly open door, and for an instant his eyes swept the doorway. I jerked back so he couldn't see me. I thought I heard a slight hiss, a sharp intake of breath. Was he in pain? Or had he seen me? I swallowed and waited a beat, and then called out. "Hey, everything okay in there?" I reached for the door, knocked on it twice, and slowly pulled it open. "Hello?"

When I stepped into the room, Greer looked up at me, startled. "What do you want?" he asked. I relaxed slightly—it seemed that he had not seen me spying at the door.

"Sorry, Mr. Greer," I said. "I was walking by and heard you cry out . . ." I paused, staring at his hand. It was bleeding from the knuckles, blood tracing the back of his hand to his wrist and forearm.

He shook his head in disgust. "Doing some curls and the fucking dumbbell slips out of my hand," he said. "Smashed it on the side of the goddamn wheel—" He stopped abruptly, as if he had just revealed a secret, and then sighed. "Get me a rag over there, by the sink. Please."

There was an efficiency kitchen on the wall behind me, next to the door, and a stack of dishcloths sat on the counter. I ran some cold water over a cloth and brought it and a dry one to Greer, who dabbed at his knuckles with the wet one, wincing once, and then wiped up the trickles of blood before awkwardly wrapping the dry dishcloth around his hand. I didn't offer to help—he hadn't asked, and I got the sense that he would resent such an offer—so I glanced around what was obviously his apartment. Aside from the kitchen, there was a bed, a workbench, a card table with a single chair, a small television on top of a trunk, two white fiberboard cabinets, and a large footlocker at the foot of the bed, and not much else. At the far end of the room was a slight ramp leading up to a door that led outside. As bare as the room looked, especially under the exposed pipes overhead, everything was neat and orderly, including the made bed.

Greer used his teeth to finish tying the dishcloth around his right hand, flexed his fingers, and seemed to think it would do. Then he turned his eyes on me. "Thank you," he said. "Like a beer?"

I hesitated. It was hot outside and a beer would have tasted really good right then, but I already felt guilty for having spied on the man; more practically, I also thought about running into students with beer on my breath.

As if anticipating this last thought, Greer said, not unkindly, "Kids are going to be at practice for another hour or so. If you don't have to go coach . . ." He paused, waiting.

"Okay," I said. "Sure."

He rolled himself to the kitchen, easily maneuvering around the two dumbbells on the floor. He got two bottles out of the refrigerator and returned, handing me one. I couldn't help but notice how deftly he handled the wheelchair. "Nice moves," I said, twisting off the bottle cap, and then I froze, unable to believe I had just said that aloud. But Greer just nodded, gave me a strange little smile, and raised his beer, and I gladly drank along with him. I could smell his sweat, hot and a little rank. It suddenly struck me that Greer was wearing soccer shorts, with what was left of his legs sticking out from the shorts and rounded off near the knees, like a battered pair of baseball bats.

"You like teaching so far?" Greer asked me.

I tore my eyes away from his legs and shrugged. "Yeah," I said. "I like it. Working with kids is fun. Sometimes." I said this last word ruefully.

Greer gave a short chuckle. "When they aren't yanking your chain?"

I smiled. "Something like that."

"Different than when you were first here."

"Yes." I couldn't help thinking that Greer must feel the same way. Aside from the passage of time, both of us had experienced loss, and we had both returned to Blackburne irrevocably changed. It must have been that thought that prompted me to put my beer down on the card table and say what I said. "I actually wanted to ask you a question about . . . Fritz."

Greer looked at me blankly.

"Fritz Davenport," I said. "He was my—"

"I know who he was," Greer said. His blank look had been replaced by one of wariness. "He went missing. Ran off and nobody's seen him since."

Something had changed in the room, a tension that displaced the earlier geniality. I plowed forward. "I heard that you saw him, coming out of our dorm that night."

He nodded slowly. "I did. He had a backpack over one shoulder."

"What—what was he wearing? His track uniform?"

"No. Jeans and a sweater. A dark blue sweater." His eyes narrowed slightly. "Told the police that."

And then I remembered. The Virginia state police had interviewed several faculty and staff members in the days after Fritz's disappearance. The rumor was that the state police suspected Fritz had disappeared of his own volition because of all the money he had taken out of the ATM the previous weekend, and that meant that he might have had help from a faculty or staff member. The police had grilled several Blackburne employees, including Pelham Greer. One of the cooks, a black man named Tofer, had grown upset, even belligerent during his interrogation. He'd had a legitimate alibi of some sort and felt the cops were questioning him because he was black and because he had a record, shoplifting or some other petty theft. Even though the police cleared him, he eventually quit, aggravated by the discreet glances and open stares that students and faculty alike had turned his way. Others, too, had resented the questioning, and for Pelham Greer, the memory still seemed to be fresh. I could imagine a proud ex-soldier resenting any implications that he could have been involved in Fritz's disappearance.

Greer ran his hand back and forth over the top of his right-side wheel. He didn't look upset, just preoccupied, as if he were considering how to get rid of me politely. I cleared my throat. "Look, Mr. Greer—"

"Pelham," he said.

I smiled weakly. "Okay, Pelham. Thanks. I don't mean to imply anything. I just . . ." I sighed. This was far harder than I had thought. "He was my best friend," I said simply. The words hurt to say, as if they confirmed that I had failed as a friend. Which I had.

Greer's jaw shifted. He drummed his fingers on the wheel, twice. "I wish I'd said something to him," he said finally. "Something about him made me think he wasn't okay." At the look on my face, he added, "He didn't look panicked or nothing. Just . . . *bothered*, like something was nagging at him. But I was busy trying to fix some landscape lights out in front of Stilwell, so I didn't. Wish I had. Maybe—" He shook his head.

I realized my mouth was open, as if I were a kid at camp hearing a ghost story. In a strange kind of way, I thought, that wasn't far from the truth. "What made him look like something was nagging him?"

Greer shrugged. "He was playing with that chain around his neck, that medal he wore," he said. He looked almost bashful. "I don't mean to sound like I spy on you all or anything, but . . . I *notice* things. And whenever I saw that boy when he looked upset or troubled about something, he was always messing with that medal. What was it?"

I couldn't answer him. I was trying to reconcile what he'd said with what I knew to be true. Fritz had left his Saint Christopher medal under my pillow, where I'd found it later that night, just before Sam Hodges and Deputy Briggs had come in. I'd assumed Fritz had placed the medal under my pillow before he had left with his backpack, which was when I was in the dining hall in Stilwell, pushing my dinner around on my plate. Now Pelham Greer said Fritz had still been wearing it when he'd left Walker House. He had worn only the one medal. So when had the medal been placed under my pillow? And who had put it there?

It took me a few moments to realize Pelham Greer had asked me a question. He was looking up at me, head cocked to one side as if to get a better read on me. "Sorry," I said. "It was a Saint Christopher medal."

Greer nodded thoughtfully. "I read somewhere that Saint Christopher would protect people when they had to travel, 'cause he carried baby Jesus across a stream and all." He glanced down at his injured hand, as if noticing it for the first time. Still looking at his hand, he said, "I hope for your roommate's sake that the story's true."

I SAID MY GOOD-BYES and left Pelham Greer's apartment, climbed back up the stairs, and headed outside to walk around the Hill for a while to let my thoughts settle. If what Greer said was true, Fritz had not left his medal under my pillow before leaving Walker House around six forty-five. That meant that Fritz had returned even later that evening, still unnoticed, and placed the medal under my pillow, or that someone else had put the medal there. Or that I did not have Fritz's actual medal but a clever fake. I didn't think this last theory could be right—Fritz had shown me the medal more than once, and on the back was stamped "1939," the year Fritz's grandfather received the medal from his own father. That someone could replicate the same medal with the same date on the back seemed ridiculous.

But what if Fritz had returned later, snuck into our dorm, put the medal under my pillow, and vanished into the night again? I had been in our room the entire evening, except when I had gone to the library to look for Fritz. I imagined Fritz crouching behind the boxwoods outside, watching me come out the front door and hurry toward the library, and then slipping inside to put the medal under my pillow.

I still didn't know, after all these years, why he had left the medal for me. Maybe it was a gesture of farewell. Or a sign that he was giving up whatever nominal protection the medal could afford him. Or there was an implied message in the medal itself, something hidden in plain sight that I could not see. This seemed too *Da Vinci Code*, and I wasn't a Harvard symbologist.

What's strange is how little I had considered the question of *why* Fritz had disappeared. At first, everyone leaned toward the scenario of a pedophile in a serial killer van abducting Fritz and driving away. Then, when the police learned about the ATM withdrawal Fritz had apparently made, coupled with his lie about where he had been the night before, it looked more and more like he had arranged his own disappearance. I had even supplied everyone with a possible reason for his disappearance: stress over college. Unable to handle the idea of not living up to his own ridiculously high expectations, he had stepped off the grid and left it all behind. My own dark secret, that I had betrayed Fritz and possibly driven him away, was one I could never share. But—and how ghoulish it is to say this—the more typical response to such stress is to shuffle off this mortal coil and head into what Hamlet calls the undiscovered country of death. It was possible Fritz had committed suicide after leaving campus; perhaps he hadn't wanted anyone on campus to find his body. But the fact that *no one* had found his body argued against this.

In the end, I didn't know with certainty why Fritz had disappeared any more than I had a decade earlier. His disappearance was an immutable fact, a stark iron signpost planted deeply and firmly in the middle of my life, compelling me to detour this way and that. I had come to think of it the way I think of natural disasters. *Why* the hurricane struck your coastal town isn't as significant as the fact that it *did*, resulting in a complete upheaval of your life.

Pelham Greer's story reawakened a fierce desire to know what had happened to Fritz. Because now I had a clue that no one else had: Fritz had come back to the dorm. I couldn't reveal this to anyone without revealing that I had the medal, that I'd had it all along and kept it secret. But this goad, this inconsistency, prodded me to explain it. I needed to find the narrative that made sense of the facts I had. And so, walking among the giant oak trees of the Lawn in the shadow of Stilwell Hall, I decided that I would do just that.

CHAPTER NINE

T he following Saturday afternoon at three o'clock, a dozen boys clambered onto the minibus I would be driving to the mixer at Saint Margaret's. Despite the three-hour drive, the boys were eager for a chance to escape school and even more so for the promise of girls. Clothing had been chosen for its cleanliness and bold colors, and as such the resulting outfits ranged somewhere between sharp and ludicrous. Aftershave stung the air, sharp as lemon juice. When every student on my roster had boarded the bus, I started her up, swung the door shut with a pneumatic *thump*, and slowly drove down the Hill.

The drive was long but comfortable, a series of short stretches on two-lane roads before we got on the interstate and headed over the mountains toward Charlottesville and then Richmond. The sky burned blue above us, and the dogwoods and sumac were starting to blush red.

I spent the time behind the wheel doing a good deal of thinking. Surprisingly, perhaps, I didn't think much about Fritz. I had been thinking about him over the past two days and replaying the conversation with Pelham Greer in my head. I'd spent enough time on it to fall behind on my class planning, so between Blackburne and Richmond, I thought mostly about the upcoming *Beowulf* unit and how I would teach it. Next week

I would try to find Deputy Briggs, the one who had questioned me the night of Fritz's disappearance, and see if he could—or would—tell me anything. For now, I was content to think about the Anglo-Saxons and *Beowulf* and its rude, majestic violence. My students would love the whole bit about Beowulf ripping off the monster Grendel's arm.

Aside from a brief food stop, we drove into the early evening, and by seven o'clock our bus rolled into Tappahannock. The boys shook their heads like young dogs newly awakened and were talking in loud, nervous bursts as I steered the bus onto Saint Margaret's campus. A series of long, low white buildings spread out on the banks of the Rappahannock River, which hung in the air in scents of mud, marsh, and grass that drifted through the open bus windows. A group of girls in dresses walked across the lawn, talking to one another, their hair long and swinging gently at their backs. One of the girls glanced at our bus and said something to her companions, who all turned to look as we drove past. Then Rusty Scarwood stuck his head out a window and shouted, "Evening, ladies!" which caused a few of them to laugh.

The dance was held in the gym, the walls and ceiling of which were swathed in white sheets contrived to look like a giant tent while softly glowing lights were strategically placed around its edges. Music—a heavy-thumping Gwen Stefani song—played too loudly through hidden speakers, although the small stage up front, apparently for the DJ, was empty save for a stack of stereo equipment and an unmanned mike on a stand. Several Saint Margaret's girls and boys from other boarding schools had already gathered, mostly clumped together by gender, although a few couples were scattered here and there. I checked in with a white-haired matron by the entrance and made sure the boys heard that the dance was over at ten thirty and that we would be heading out immediately afterward. They nodded dutifully and then gazed over the dance floor, some nervous, others like captains scanning a field of battle.

Terence Jarrar was standing near the wall, chewing a thumbnail and looking morosely at a group of girls nearby. I grinned at him, and then indicated the girls with a nod. "Ask one of them to dance," I said.

He frowned. "What?" he said, raising his voice over the music.

"Ask one of them to dance," I said loudly just as two of the girls glanced in our direction. Terence blanched and ducked his head. One of the girls raised her eyebrows at me in an expression somewhere between amusement and horror. I waved at her and turned to Terence, intending to tell him to give it the old college try, but he was examining the tops of his shoes, clearly embarrassed. "Hey," I said. "Sorry about that."

He shrugged, still looking at his shoes. "It's okay."

"Terence," I said, and he looked up at me. "Really. I'm sorry. Girls are . . ." I paused. Who was I to give anyone advice about girls? The last relationship I'd been in had been a mutual exercise in self-involvement, and after six months it had spiraled into public displays of heartbreak, rage, and reconcilement. I vividly recalled a very public argument in a restaurant, two or three bottles of wine into dinner, with Michele demanding to know when my next book would be finished and me telling her that writing a novel wasn't like smiling into a camera.

"Mr. Glass?" Terence was looking at me.

"Sorry," I said, shaking my head clear of the memory. "I just—well, girls are hard enough without your teacher making you feel like a jackass, is all I'm saying."

He smiled at that. "Okay," he said. "Thanks, Mr. Glass." He shook his head. "Girls are . . . well, yeah."

I laughed and was about to reply when I saw, across the room, two women talking to each other. One of them was short and round, with glasses and a cheerful face framed by straight red hair. The other was Abby Davenport.

AT HER HOUSE THAT January of my senior year, I had asked Abby to the Spring Formal and she'd said yes. Then we realized that my track meets and her concert schedule meant that we would not have a free weekend to see each other until the dance, which wasn't until the beginning of April. We moaned about such an unfair and empty stretch of time. Maybe spring break? But my parents had planned a trip to Atlanta to visit family over the break, and though I snarled and pleaded and basically acted like an ass, my parents were implacable. Truth to tell, I had been pretty close with my Atlanta cousins when we were younger, and we usually had fun together, but on that trip, I played the romantic martyr to the hilt, sighing and staring outside at the rain that I thought mirrored my soul. My mother said wryly that all I needed was a blindfold and a cigarette to complete the image of a man facing a firing squad.

And then Fritz had disappeared, two weeks before the Spring Formal.

I didn't see Abby in the terrible days that followed, didn't call her. I couldn't. Her brother was missing, and what could I offer her? Faint hope that he was okay? Part of my failure to call was because I was terrified of her father. But I was also numb, disengaging from everyone else as a kind of self-preservation tactic. It's not a good excuse for how I treated Abby, but it has the relative merit of being honest.

Three days before the dance, Miles Camak knocked on my door after study hall and told me I had a phone call. When he saw the hopeful look on my face—*Fritz?*—he shook his head sadly. I picked up the phone and heard Abby's voice on the other end. We spoke awkwardly, perfunctorily. I realized she was calling to say she would not be coming to the Spring Formal. I told her I understood, that I didn't want to go to the dance anyway. I meant, I would go with *her*, of course, but— "Yes, yes, of course," she said. "It just isn't the right—"

This went on for a little while. I felt both frantic and detached. It was as if, far up in some ivory tower in my mind, somebody else was feverishly planning what I should say next. Whoever it was did a poor job of it, because eventually I realized I was listening to a hollow dial tone. I hung up the phone and looked at it. Then I went back to my room and lay down on my bed.

Ten minutes before lights-out, I started awake from a light sleep, gasping. I had been in the woods again, Fritz ahead of me. The sky overhead was afire with sunset. Someone was chasing me in the dream, but when I turned around, I saw only Abby, walking away from me toward the lions, just as ahead of me Fritz turned a corner and vanished behind a screen of trees. "Abby," I had called out, but as I had turned around and taken a step toward her, the ground had opened beneath me and I had fallen into an abyss, waking up just before I was swallowed whole.

I jumped out of bed and went to the hall phone, which was thankfully free, and dialed Saint Margaret's. After an interminable two minutes, Abby had come to the phone. "Hello?" she said, her voice far away.

"Abby," I said. "Listen to me, okay? I love you. Do you hear me? I love you. I'm sorry I didn't say it earlier, I don't know why I didn't. And I'm sorry about earlier, on the phone, I—"

"Matthias?"

"And I want to make it work, seriously. I mean, I'll be at UVA, but we can visit, I can take a bus up to New York, or you can come to Charlottesville—"

"Matthias," she said again, and I stopped at the sound in her voice. "I'm not going to Juilliard."

"You—what? You mean, they didn't . . . You didn't get—"

"I deferred," she said, her voice still far away but determined. "I can't go away to school now. Not like this. Mother is—she's bad, Matthias. She's really bad." Abby started crying softly, almost as if she were hiccupping into the phone. "I can't leave her, too," she managed.

"Shhh," I said, sliding down the wall to sit on the floor. "It'll be okay. It'll be okay. Don't worry. I can help. If you stay at home, I can help. I can come over from school—it's no big deal. Whatever you need, Abby. You want me to come over and cook breakfast, I can do that. Okay? Whatever you want. Fresh fruit. Hot chocolate. Big stacks of pancakes."

There was another hiccup on the line. It sounded like she was laughing a little. "I hate pancakes," she said.

"Who hates pancakes?" I said. "You seriously hate pancakes? Okay, no pancakes."

She said something as I was talking. "What?" I said. "I couldn't hear you. I'm sorry. What?"

"I said," she managed, with a teary sigh, "that I love you, too."

"That's the best thing I've ever heard. Say it again."

"Ha."

"I'm serious. Say it again. Please."

"It." I swore I could hear her smiling.

"Fine. Pancakes for you, then. Every stinking day I'm driving over there and making you eat pancakes."

"Oh, shut up," she said. "I love you, okay?"

I held the receiver, my eyes closed. "It's more than okay."

And it was, for a time. That summer, I went to Fairfax twice to see Abby. My parents offered to put me up in a nearby hotel, but Wat Davenport, who had by now become a sort of majordomo of the Davenport household, handling much of their day-to-day business, wouldn't hear of it and had me stay in a guest room, which was down the hall from Abby and next to Fritz's old room. Mrs. Davenport remained cloistered in her bedroom both times I was there. Mr. Davenport seemed to be living out of his office, which was fine by me—the memory of his rage as he screamed in my face was still raw.

This left Wat to chaperone me and Abby. He made excellent dinners for us, risottos and steak au poivre and a chicken stir-fry in ponzu sauce that was to die for. He even gave us each a glass of wine with dinner. "Don't drive anywhere tonight," he would say, lifting an eyebrow at me.

On both of those visits, Abby and I didn't go anywhere much, didn't even talk much, really. We were simply content to be in the other's presence. We hugged a lot, or we sat pressed next to each other on the couch as if trying to permanently affix ourselves to each other, create an indelible mark. When we did talk, we were tentative, exploring neutral topics—

books we had read, movies, music. We did not talk about college, or her parents, or Fritz. And yet they all hung about us like ghosts, refusing to leave the premises.

Near the end of my first visit, Abby was downstairs, making popcorn, while I was changing out of my swimsuit. When I dressed and stepped into the hallway, I found myself looking at the door to Fritz's room, as solid and closed as it had been all week. I hesitated, glanced down the empty hallway, and then crossed to his door. After another moment of hesitation, I placed my hand on the doorknob.

I had been in here before, on my first visit to Fritz's house. Still, my breath caught in my chest when I swung the door open and saw the same bed with the cream-colored comforter and pillows, a watercolor of a beach in Bermuda over the headboard, a dark fan hanging motionless from the ceiling, Fritz's blond-wood desk tucked into the front dormer window. Slowly I walked into the room. I kept glancing at the bed as if Fritz were there, just about to pull the covers off his head and sit up, grinning. *Fooled you!* he would have said. There was nothing on Fritz's desk except a ball-point pen with a chewed cap, a first-place trophy for riding, and a set of Harry Potter books lined up neatly at the back. The books were what got me first. There were only the four of them at the time, *Sorcerer's Stone* through *Goblet of Fire*. Fritz had loved those books, as I did. Now he would never read the next ones in the series, or learn what happened to Harry and Ron and Hermione. I stopped, shocked at my own train of thought, thinking of Fritz as if he had died. I had attached myself to the idea that Fritz had run away, because I just couldn't stand the alternative, but now, standing in his abandoned room, I was struck by the morbid thought that I would never see him again. "No," I said, low but aloud. He wasn't dead. I refused to believe it. To the left of his desk, his closet door was open enough to reveal shirts and pants hanging neatly. *They're waiting to be worn again*, I thought firmly. Then I saw the poster tape on the walls, left over from all those movie posters Fritz had had up in his room and then taken to Blackburne and put up in our room: *Unforgiven, Tombstone, The Usual Suspects.* I had no idea where those posters were, now. The Davenports must have thrown them away. Suddenly terrified that Abby would find me in here, I tiptoed to the door and shut it behind me.

The whole first week I visited Abby, we barely kissed out of some sense that it would be indecent. On the last day, two hours before Uncle Wat was supposed to drive me to the airport, Abby was helping me gather my clothes and pack when we both bent over my suitcase at the same time, almost bumping heads. We stopped just in time and looked up, our faces three inches apart, Abby's mouth slightly open as if she were dazed. Without thinking, I kissed her, and then we were kissing frantically, as if trying to reach something deep within the other. Her hands were clumsy around my belt buckle; my hands were under her shirt, clawing at her bra. She pulled back suddenly, gasping. "Wait," she managed, and she left me with my pants half-unzipped to cross the room to a linen closet and grab a faded beach towel, which she threw over the bedcover. "Lock the door," she said as she began pulling her shirt off. We had sex for the first time on top of that guest bed, me fumbling with the condom wrapper, Abby whimpering into my shoulder even as she clutched me to her and crossed her calves over the back of mine, me managing half a dozen awkward thrusts before I came, and both of us lying stunned in the aftermath.

Leaving was awkward. We were both silent as Wat chatted away from behind the wheel of the car. I couldn't look Abby in the eye. It wasn't that I felt I had done something wrong, but more that I had not done it right. I'd had vague notions of getting a hotel room with Abby one day, a bottle of champagne in a bucket, a Do Not Disturb sign on the door. Now that first time—*our* first time—was gone. I stared out the window until Abby tapped my knee. I turned to see her looking at me, her eyebrows quirked together in a question, until a slow smile played at the corners of her mouth. Something eased and opened in my chest, and I smiled back. We were okay. Of course we were. We loved each other.

The next time I visited, we were able to plan ahead to when Wat would be attending some business function in D.C. We went down to the home theater armed with pillows and blankets, put on a Dave Matthews CD and turned down the lights, locked the door, and slowly explored each other. The second time we had sex that night, Abby was on top. Suddenly her breath grew ragged and her movement faster until she orgasmed with a loud, gasped "Oh!" In my shock at what I had helped to bring about, I felt like I had just discovered the answer to a mystery other men had died for.

Love can be a hell of a draw, the emotional holy grail. But love also exposes our flaws, can even draw out the worst in us. People want to perform heroic deeds, commit flagrantly dramatic acts for love. What they don't realize is that the daily grind is what is required. Instead of a single extraordinary act—slaying the dragon, throwing yourself in front of a bus—it is the repetition of small gestures over a course of years that makes love work. And if I am terrible at anything, it is that sort of consistency.

The problem wasn't that I became too used to Abby, too easily persuaded that there might be something better. The problem wasn't her. It was the person who was supposed to be there, who had been swallowed up by that belt of trees surrounding Blackburne, who in his absence had become the dark matter in my personal universe, mysteriously exerting his effect on me in ways I hadn't thought possible.

My first year at UVA, I roomed alone. It seemed wrong to share a dorm room with anyone else. It also seemed to me to be a perfect refuge for Abby when she needed to get away from home. But it was also the beginning of my semiconscious efforts to wall myself off from others. I didn't want to be a hermit; I tried to join a fraternity, for instance, but it didn't take. *More time for my writing*, I told myself, and that was honest, at least. I began a novel that I would eventually burn in a mall parking lot outside of Charlottesville before starting *The Unforgiving*. But there was a calculated pleasure in staying in my room on the weekends when Abby couldn't come up, typing on my desktop while my classmates were out partying. It was also, I see now, a self-imposed exile for the crime of making Fritz disappear.

It was hard enough dating Abby long distance, but to be attending classes where I felt Fritz was supposed to be, to walk past the Rotunda or cross UVA's own Lawn, felt like I had cheated all over again somehow, that I had wrongfully taken Fritz's place. Part of me, the same part that dimly perceived that, in some eventual future, I might be able to accept that my friend was gone, realized this wasn't true. But a larger, or at least louder, part of me had the sudden expectation that Fritz would be found, and soon. It had been six months since he had disappeared, and I was having the strangest premonitions. Three crows flew across my path, one after the other, as I walked to class; my dorm bathroom was clean three days in a row; I aced all three tests that I had in the same week. I took it as a sign from the gods, a portent of good news. I kept waiting for my phone to ring, for Abby to tell me tearfully that Fritz had been located, that he was coming home.

Magical thinking is nothing new. But it was all I had. Hitting a series of green lights on the way out of Charlottesville, finding a dollar bill on the hall floor outside my room—everything was a sign that the universe was conspiring to return my friend to me. That I received no phone call from Abby about Fritz did not matter. It was merely a test of patience, of will— of belief that my friend would be found. Abby did call to tell me that her mother was slowly improving, getting out of bed, even seeing visitors one at a time, but I half listened to such news, keeping my ear cocked and ready to hear approaching footsteps, the creak of a door, a sound of greeting.

Christmas break came and went. I had wanted to spend it with Abby but couldn't because her family had gone to the Keys. I called her the day she got back. I had a plan. "Listen," I said. "I've got a crazy idea. Something we could do this summer."

Abby yawned. "Sure," she said. "As long as it doesn't involve a lot of driving. Mother wouldn't fly to Florida, so we drove."

"I was thinking we could go look for Fritz."

I waited five very long seconds, holding the phone and listening to Abby hold her breath.

"What are you saying?" Abby managed.

"Look, I know it's crazy, but I've got it figured out," I said, plowing forward. "The police are idiots. They don't know your brother. You know all the places you've gone. On vacation. We go to all the places where Fritz went on vacation. That's probably where he ran off to, someplace he knows. I know we'll pick up his trail. I've saved up some money—"

"This is insane."

"It is not. I got a job in a restaurant, and I've saved some money."

"Matthias, we don't even know that he ran away."

"Sure we do. Sure we do. He took out all that money, right? And I told you about the argument we had, how stressed out he was about college. He *ran*, Abby. We could do this. I know you don't want to drive, but listen, I could borrow my mother's—"

Deliberately, Abby said, "I am not going with you to hunt for Fritz."

"What?"

"Matthias . . . I'm going to go to Juilliard. This summer."

Now I held my breath, staring at the water stains on my wall. "What?" I said again.

"I was going to tell you," Abby was saying. "This weekend, when I came up to visit—"

"You can't go to Juilliard," I said. "We—we have to find your brother. He's your brother, Abby."

Her voice was frosty. "I know who he is, Matthias. And don't tell me what I can and can't do. I need to play the cello again, I—" Her voice softened. "Look, my mother is doing better. She doesn't talk anymore about wanting to die. This past year—it's been awful. And now it's time for me to do what I need to do, to move on."

"Move on?" I said. "Move *on*?"

In a low voice, she said, "He's gone, Matthias."

"He's *missing*."

"And we're going to go find him? This isn't a Hardy Boys mystery, Matthias. He's gone. He's my brother and I love him, I always will, but it's been almost a year—"

"Ten months." Even as I said it, I knew it was stupid, but I was angry.

"And I hope he comes back," Abby continued, ignoring me. "But—I can't do this. I have my life to live, too. Juilliard has a spot for me. It's not like I'm going out of the country. It's New York City. I can take a train—"

"I can't believe this," I said. "It's like you don't even love your own brother."

A longer pause, like the empty space between peals of thunder. And then a decisive *click*, another pause, and then a dial tone.

I had not spoken to Abby Davenport since.

NOW, STANDING IN SAINT Margaret's gym, listening to Gwen Stefani insist she wasn't no hollaback girl, my first instinct upon seeing Abby was to drop my Coke and run for the door. But then Abby saw me. I stood there, ignoring Terence Jarrar as I watched Abby walking toward me, a neutral smile on her face. Her hair was cropped in a sort of pageboy bob, but aside from that and something a bit more adultlike in her stride, she looked remarkably like she had all those years before. She stopped just outside of hugging range.

"Hi," she said.

I smiled, my throat dry as sandpaper. "Abby, hey," I said. "Wow. You look great."

"What are you doing here?" she asked. Her tone wasn't challenging or defensive. Her words were a simple question.

"Well, I'm teaching at Blackburne now," I said, still keeping a smile on my face. "I got weekend duty, so I'm officially chaperoning for the dance tonight. How about you? Are you here for a reunion or something?"

Abby's red-headed companion from earlier stepped up, holding two cups. "She's a faculty member here," she said brightly, handing one cup to Abby. Then she smiled at me, a cherubic pixie. "Hi, I'm Kerry."

"Matthias," I said. We shook hands. Then I turned to Abby. "You teach here?"

She nodded. "Yep," she said. "Started last year. French."

Kerry looked from me to Abby. "So how do you kids know each other?"

I looked at Abby as if for permission. She brushed a strand of hair off her face and said to Kerry, "We knew each other in high school." She turned back to me. "You're teaching English, I guess, right?"

She was being polite and cold at the same time. "Yeah, fourth formers," I said. "Are you still playing the cello?"

For a moment Abby's composure slipped, and she glanced down at the floor. Kerry laughed. "The cello?" she said, disbelieving. "But Abby hates music. I'm the chorus director, and Abby can't *stand* to listen to recitals."

Abby stood stock-still for a moment and then looked up at me, her eyes registering a brief flare of panic. At that moment, the overhead lights cut out, and the students all cheered as the DJ took to the stage. A Katy Perry song played from the speakers, so loud it was almost percussive, and the students all began dancing in circles around us, waving their hands and arms and jerking their heads to the beat. Abby took the opportunity to step back into the crowd and walk away. I would have gone after her if Rusty Scarwood hadn't walked past at that moment and tripped, accidentally spilling his Coke onto Kerry's feet. By the time I gathered some napkins to wipe off her shoes and had Rusty stammer an apology, Abby had completely vanished.

CHAPTER TEN

T he late drive home from Saint Margaret's was quiet, most of the boys flattened by the disappointment of high expectations. Terence stared out the window into the night, his blurry reflection—two holes for eyes, a slack, round mouth—the face of a befuddled ghost. I hadn't seen him dance with anyone, which saddened me. Only Rusty Scarwood claimed to have had a good time, and judging by the lipstick at the corner of his mouth, I suspected he was telling the truth. He held court at the back of the minibus, talking in a low voice as a few boys listened with mingled awe and regret about how he had gotten a girl's phone number.

I tried to focus on the road, my head filled with Abby Davenport. Seeing her had shaken me, almost more than what Pelham Greer had told me about Fritz. How had she ended up teaching French at Saint Margaret's? What had her friend Kerry meant about Abby hating music? Was she seeing anybody? I hadn't noticed a wedding ring, but had I really looked? She walked away from me so quickly. Had she walked away because I brought up painful memories, or because she hated me? Did she know anything about Fritz? And if she did, how was I going to find out? These thoughts played in my head like a feedback loop, amplifying one another without providing an answer. But on that long drive back to Blackburne, I did reach one conclusion: seeing Abby only confirmed my resolve to find out what I could about Fritz.

LATER THAT WEEK, I drove to the sheriff's office outside of Staunton. It was a whitewashed cinder-block bunker with small windows and glass double doors in a heavy steel frame, all offset by a dusting of red and white flowers and low scrub bushes for landscaping. As I sat in the parking lot behind the wheel of my car and looked at the front doors with the sheriff's logo on them, I wondered what the hell I was going to say to Sheriff Townsend. I'd called his office the day before, hoping to schedule a phone meeting, but as soon as a receptionist had answered, I had abruptly hung up. My thought at that moment was that I would be more likely to get a response, maybe even some answers, if I spoke with the sheriff in person about Fritz's case. My experience with agents and editors in New York was that it was harder for someone to bullshit you to your face than over the phone.

Now that I was here, however, I was having second thoughts. Why would he speak to me in the first place? I wasn't a family member, I had no new information to contribute—Pelham Greer's info notwithstanding—and he had no obligation to tell me anything about Fritz's case. I was also suffering from an irrational fear that by going into the sheriff's office, I would run the risk of getting into some kind of trouble. I had always had a healthy respect for cops, but I had also been slightly afraid of their ability to put people in jail. Once in college, I had been pulled over for suspicion of DUI—the officer told me he thought I'd been weaving. I hadn't been, but I humbly submitted to the field sobriety tests while three of my classmates sat in the car. When I was done, one of them, Dax Mullen, angrily muttered, "Town and gown, man. He just did that shit 'cause he saw the UVA parking sticker on your car." He had urged me to go to police headquarters in Charlottesville to file a complaint, but I had declined. When it comes to the police, I am the kind of guy who hopes I never get stuck in a lineup, because I know I would look guilty enough to be mistakenly picked as the drug dealer or the hit-and-run driver or the child molester.

As I sat in the car, squeezing the steering wheel until my knuckles started to ache, two uniformed deputies came out the front door and walked past me to their cruiser. One of them swiveled his head to look at me, as if he were wondering why I was casing the building. That was enough to get me out of the car and headed for the glass doors, my heart thudding furiously.

As luck would have it, Sheriff Townsend was in, and I had to wait no more than ten minutes on a bench in the tiny waiting room before a female deputy waved me back to his office. Townsend was around fifty, with a suggestion of roundness in his features—his face, shoulders, even his hands. He wasn't fat, exactly; he looked like he knew his way around a buffet, but his handshake was firm, and he sat easily enough in his leather chair behind a massive wooden rampart of a desk.

I started by introducing myself as a Blackburne grad and said that I was interested in the Fritz Davenport case from 2001. His eyebrows lifted slightly at that, but he said nothing, so I explained how I had been Fritz's roommate and very close to his family and, now that I had returned to Blackburne as a teacher, my interest in Fritz's disappearance was sharper than it had been in a long time. Sheriff Townsend was sympathetic. "No one wants to lose a friend," he said. "But to lose a friend like that, just *vanishing* . . ." He shook his head. "I sympathize, Mr. Glass. How can I help? Please understand," he added, waving a hand over his desk, as if dispelling an unpleasant truth, "there's not much to tell."

"Is there *anything* to tell?"

He smiled briefly, creases appearing and then disappearing in his round face. "Well, we never found him, obviously. And not for lack of trying. Local and state police in Virginia, West Virginia, North Carolina, Tennessee, Maryland, Pennsylvania, D.C.—all involved. Of course, we helped spearhead the initial search efforts. No evidence of foul play. No physical evidence of any kind, really. In this type of situation, it's the *lack* of physical evidence of a person that's the problem." He gave another brief, sympathetic smile, and then his face smoothed over, becoming professional again. "No eyewitnesses actually saw him *leave* campus. There was no ransom note, no letter home from Fritz saying he was fine, no nothing."

I looked at Sheriff Townsend's desk. Aside from two neatly stacked-and-squared wire in- and out-boxes, a phone, and a blotter, the desk was immaculate. "I'm sorry, Sheriff, but . . . have you been reviewing this case recently?" I asked.

He looked at me, his smooth face fractionally more serious. "Why do you ask?"

"Well, you seem to remember quite a lot about it. You don't have the file in front of you, and it was nine years ago . . ."

Townsend's features relaxed, and he gave me a rueful smile. I was beginning to realize that Sheriff Townsend had several smiles in his repertoire. "Not the kind of case you forget," he said, almost apologetically. "I was a deputy at the time, running our criminal investigations division. We were the guys on point for this case."

"Do you have any idea what could have happened to him?"

Townsend exhaled and leaned back in his swivel chair, the leather creaking beneath him. "You've got eight hundred thousand people reported missing each year in the United States," he said. "More than half of them are eighteen or younger. Most are runaways, and lots of them come back within three days. Some are kidnapped, usually in some sort of parental custody issue. Some are victims of violent crime. But some just go right off the radar. You never find them. Never. It's horrible for the families. They just want to *know*." He sighed. "I can't imagine how hard it was for the Davenports to do what they did."

"What do you mean?"

He glanced at me. "That's the other reason I remember the case pretty well," he said softly. "They had him declared legally dead, just last year. Got a copy of the death certificate for our files."

I stared at him. "What . . . How did they do that?"

"Law says someone can be declared legally dead if he's been missing for seven years with no sign. The Davenports held on for eight, but they finally went to a judge and got him to declare his death in absentia. It's terrible, but a family can go through that kind of thing for only so long. It's a way to come to terms, awful as it sounds."

I'm sure Townsend said something else, but it didn't register as I just sat there, staring blankly at him. The Davenports had declared Fritz legally dead. The news was like a heavy door swung shut with a *boom* that sent dust flying. No wonder Abby had reacted oddly when I'd shown up at the dance at Saint Margaret's.

Walking down the hall with Townsend toward the front door, the sheriff apologizing again for not having more to tell me, I gazed blankly at the flyers pinned to bulletin boards on the walls. A Most Wanted poster for a suspected bank robber. Public service announcements about seat belt use. A picture of a child—a little girl, age seven—missing since last month. And then I found myself in front of what looked like an invitation to an office party. It was in honor of Deputy Lester Briggs, who was retiring.

"Something wrong, Mr. Glass?" Sheriff Townsend asked.

"I . . . no." Briggs was the deputy who had come to my room with Sam Hodges the night Fritz had disappeared. The flyer for his retirement party was dated more than a month ago. "I just saw this flyer here and remembered that Deputy Briggs was one of the first officers out at Blackburne after Fritz disappeared."

Sheriff Townsend kept his face neutral, although I thought I saw his eyes tighten just a bit. "He was a good officer," he said. "Retired just last month."

I nodded. "I'd like to thank him, for everything he did with Fritz's case and all," I said. "Does he live around here?"

He pondered this. "I believe he said he was moving to Florida," he said. "Wanted to go fishing and live near a beach." He held out his hand and we shook. "Good luck, Mr. Glass," he said. He watched me through the glass doors as I walked to my car, his expression obscured by the sunlight glaring off the glass, transforming him into a shadowy apparition in the doorway.

CHAPTER ELEVEN

The day that Terence Jarrar shot himself was a beautiful fall day: crisp, about sixty degrees, boundless azure sky. It was three weeks before Thanksgiving break, the height of autumn when the trees refuse to surrender their colors to the gray chill of winter lurking around the corner. The air that day was so raw and clear, it was as if it had been created mere minutes before. The low mountains to the west stood in stark contrast against the bright, open sky, and everything was both vast and close at hand in that strange light. Cheeks burned and hearts quickened at the sudden gusts of wind that blew over the playing fields and against the brick walls. More and more students had been gathering in the Brickhouse for french fries and hot chocolate during breaks. Teachers had begun wearing turtlenecks and the occasional tweed jacket, while students wore baggy sweaters and college sweatshirts. Expectations of going home hung almost palpably in the classroom, and everyone seemed to step with a little more bounce than usual.

To add to the general sense of excitement, the Game was one week away. Since mid-August, our JV and varsity football teams had been lumbering around campus in shoulder pads and cleats, looking for all the world like large stuffed dolls. The helmets, painted in Blackburne's red and gold, were absurdly big. No one seeing those boys stumble to the dorms after practice could imagine them walking straight, much less running downfield. And yet their weariness would slough off when, limned in mud and sweat and occasionally blood, they crouched down in formation, leaping forward at the snap of the ball.

For parents, who returned to campus for Parents' Weekend and the November Blackburne–Manassas Prep game, a century-old contest known simply as "the Game," football was a metaphor for watching their sons grow into men. Each time those boys left the field, clotted with mud and torn grass, they left a part of their boyhood behind them, and it was a bittersweet thing to see that disappear into the wet earth.

It was a Saturday and I was on weekend duty, which meant I was responsible for any recreational activities, the checking out of equipment, locking up the gymnasium, and making sure students signed out before going off campus. It wasn't too much trouble, but it kept me busy until late afternoon. The majority of the kids were either shooting basketballs in the gym or getting ready for a mixer at Chatham Hall. Laughter spread from the showers as boys scrutinized themselves in the mirrors and boasted about their prowess with girls. I walked the hallways, urging the boys to hurry up. Finally all my charges trooped out of the dorm and headed to the bus with much fanfare and whooping. Off duty until dinner, I couldn't bring myself to face the stack of ungraded tests waiting in my apartment, and so I walked over to the infirmary, where Porter Deems sometimes hung out, sitting on the building's wraparound porch and grading papers. As I walked across the Lawn past the chapel, shadows stretched long across the Hill as the sun dipped westward. The trees on the Lawn were just starting to go bare, their leaves beginning to blanket the grass below.

I found Porter on the porch. Wearing sunglasses and sitting comfortably in a rocking chair, he was reading and sipping out of a mug. He looked up as I mounted the steps. "Kids gone?" he asked.

"Just got them on the bus," I said, and collapsed into another rocking chair. "I've been on duty since this morning."

"Want some tea?" Porter gestured at me with his mug.

"My, how civilized. Are there scones, too?"

"Nice. I offer you tea and you make fun of me."

"Okay, I'm an asshole. I'm sorry. Yes, I'd love some tea. Please."

"Bite me," he said, but he got up and went inside, the screen door banging shut behind him, and he came back with a steaming mug.

We sat on the porch and watched as the sun seemed to melt behind the mountains, spreading red and gold behind the darkening hills.

"Where'd you get the tea?" I asked.

"Betty lets me make tea in her kitchen sometimes," Porter said. He took a sip.

"Betty?" I drew a blank at first. "Wait, Mrs. *Yowell?* The nurse?" Betty Yowell was a formidable, matronly woman who had been the school nurse when I had been at Blackburne. She did not come across as the kind of person who would let someone like Porter make tea in her kitchen.

"I just asked nicely," Porter said. "Women love that shit. Butter up to Betty and she's like a big teddy bear."

"Dude, she's like sixty."

"Get your mind out of the gutter." He whacked me on the back of the head with his paperback. "I'm talking about being fucking polite, is all." He made to whack me again.

"Okay, Jesus." I swatted the book away. "What are you reading, anyway?"

Frowning, he took a moment to decide I wasn't worth smacking with the book anymore, and he held it up so I could see the cover. "*The Killer Angels,*" I read aloud. "I remember that."

"My U.S. History class finishes studying the Constitutional Convention next week. Thank God," Porter added, laying the book down in his lap. "I'm sick of explaining the Bill of Rights. Thought I'd get a jump start on next semester."

"I read that when I was here," I said. "*The Killer Angels.* My AP U.S. History teacher had us read it for class."

"Great fucking book," Porter said. "Everything hinged on Gettysburg. We'll get to it in January."

"Good time for it," I said. "Weather's lousy and everyone's stuck inside. I remember Mr. Conkle reading *Hamlet* out loud to us in February on a real nasty day, with dark, heavy clouds and this moaning wind. Perfect setting for a ghost story." I sipped some tea, welcoming the warmth of it. "I like the fall, though. It's more mysterious, you know? More . . . melancholy, I guess, but beautiful at the same time."

"There's nothing like fall, is there?" Porter said. "Kind of—"

That was when we heard the gunshot, a loud, flat explosion. We both turned and looked east toward the river. From the ring of trees at the foot of the Hill, three quail burst out of hiding, their flight low and fast toward the infirmary. Fifty yards out, they cut to our right and vanished behind the dogwoods lining the driveway.

Porter looked at me. "The hell was that?"

"Nobody signed out to go shooting today," I said. There was a sheet in the front office for students who wanted to go shoot in pairs at the skeet range on campus. It had been blank all day—I had checked before and after lunch. No one was supposed to have access to guns without signing them out from a locked cabinet in Stilwell Hall.

"That was close by," I added.

Porter looked steadily at me, his eyes hidden behind his sunglasses, which shone in the dull red glare from the setting sun. Then he put his mug and his book down, and he stood. "We have to go see," he said.

PORTER'S CAR WAS AN older Honda Civic, and we drove down the rear-entrance road in a brittle silence. I was afraid to say anything out of an irrational belief that doing so would bring about some terrible disaster. Porter merely drove, concentrating on the road and glancing out at the trees that began to pass us by.

When we reached the river and the bridge that spanned it, we were deep in the woods that encircled the school. Twilight had already settled on the forest floor. The last rays of sunlight touched the very tops of the poplars and oaks that stood by the river. Porter stopped the car just before rolling onto the bridge. I frowned. "What are you doing?" I asked. "The skeet range is over there, on the other side."

"Thought we'd check out the river first," Porter said. "You can see a ways from both sides of the bridge. Maybe it's a hunter, wandered onto school property." He opened his door and got out, and shortly I followed.

As we walked onto the bridge, I was conscious of the open space beneath us, the gurgling river twenty feet below. Porter looked downstream, and I crossed to the other side, leaned on the railing, and peered out into the gloom. Upriver, I could see a corner of the ancient outing cabin about fifty yards away at a bend in the river. The Outing Club sometimes camped there overnight. When I was a student, some of my classmates would sneak out to that cabin to smoke illegally, but now the cabin was as dark and cold as the forest around it. With a sudden passion, I realized how much I hated that forest, the circle of trees enclosing Blackburne like some enchanted wood from a medieval fairy tale. Those woods were haunted, even if only by memories. An image flitted across my mind like a sparrow crossing a room through open windows: Fritz running away from me into the trees, his white shirt gleaming in the shadows for a moment before he turned a corner and vanished forever.

"Matthias," Porter called, jarring me back. I crossed the bridge to his side and looked where he was pointing downstream. It took me a moment to see it. Something was lying on a large flat rock in the middle of the river, about a hundred yards away. It was too big to be a dog.

"Hey!" I shouted, but the form did not move. Porter and I looked at each other for a heartbeat, and then we ran back to the end of the bridge and scrambled down the riverbank. We hurried through the darkening wood, branches slapping at our faces. I tripped over a root and fell to the ground, catching myself on the palms of my hands. I got up and lumbered on. Porter crashed through the underbrush just ahead. We lurched out of the trees and came upon the form sprawled on the rock only ten feet from shore. One arm was flung out, its hand trailing in the cold stream, and the feet were turned outward. I could just make out the shape of a rifle or shotgun lying half in the shallow water next to the body.

"Go get help," I said to Porter, and as he crashed back up through the trees toward the bridge and the car, I approached the still form. Everything I saw took on equal weight in my mind: the watch on the arm, the fingers of which dangled in the water; the red Blackburne sweatshirt; the untied shoelace; the jeans that were water-darkened up to the knees. Memories of CPR classes flashed up on my internal screen—keep calm, ask questions, raise the feet, keep warm. Then, as I splashed through the water and reached the body, I saw the puddle of blood, slick and black as ink in the failing light, spreading across the rock and dripping ever so slowly into the gurgling river.

I SHIVERED IN THE flashing red-and-blue lights of the sheriff's patrol car. Floodlights were trained on the river, white shafts cutting through the night that had descended like some monstrous shadow. Two people dressed in yellow slickers lifted a stretcher and carried the body, now zipped into a black body bag, out of the river.

A deputy named Smalls stood nearby with an open notepad and pen. He was tall, maybe six foot three, hefty like a linebacker who's gone off his training, with an open round face and a pug nose. His nightstick and revolver hung like afterthoughts around an ample waist. As if he knew I was watching him, Smalls glanced over at me, and then approached with a grave look on his face.

"Mr. Glass?" Smalls asked. "I have to ask you some questions. You up to it?" I nodded, and Smalls flipped back a sheet of paper on his notepad.

"You were the faculty member on duty this afternoon, that correct?" Smalls asked.

"Yes," I said. "I was off duty when I heard the gunshot."

"What time was it when you heard the gunshot?"

"I'm not exactly sure. About six, I think."

"And you were with another person when you heard the gunshot?"

"Porter Deems. You already spoke with him."

"Yessir. And then you drove down to the river?"

"Yes. Porter drove the car."

"Why did you go to the river?"

I watched as one of the men in slickers slipped in the mud and nearly dropped the stretcher. "The shot seemed to have come from down this way. Then Porter stopped the car on the bridge, said we should look around. He thought . . ." I stopped, frowning. I couldn't remember what he'd said.

Deputy Smalls consulted another page on his notepad. "He thought maybe it was a hunter?"

"That's it," I said. "A hunter. So we got out and looked over the railings."

"And who saw the body first?"

The body. Just those words struck me—the finality of it. Not the person, but the body. My lips tasted like salt. "Porter did," I said. "I called out, but . . . it . . . didn't move."

"And you went down to see if you could help, that right?"

I stared down at the river. The floodlight illuminated the flat rock where the body had lain. "Yes."

"Could you identify the victim?"

I turned to look at him. "He blew his head off with a shotgun, Deputy. I'm not even sure it's a he." My voice had ratcheted up a few notches. I was on the verge of either sobbing aloud or screaming to the treetops.

Deputy Smalls clicked the top of his ballpoint pen. He tilted his head slightly to the side, as if trying a different angle of view. "Why do you say he blew his own head off, Mr. Glass?" he asked.

I stared at the deputy, who clicked his pen again, waiting patiently. "I don't know," I said. "I mean, I just assumed—"

In my mind, I saw the body on the flat rock: the shattered wreck of a head above the mouth, the chin and lower lip flawless, except for a sliver of gore lying across the lower front teeth.

I managed to turn to the side so I didn't vomit on Deputy Smalls's feet. A hand seemed to squeeze my gut like a child squeezes a balloon, and with an acid rush I emptied my stomach onto the bridge pavement. Dimly I realized that Deputy Smalls had crouched down beside me. When the retching stopped and I was able to spit, Smalls produced a handful of napkins. I feebly protested and then took them to wipe my mouth. "Sorry," I managed.

"That's all right," he said. "It was an ugly thing, to see a body like that." He stood up. "You feeling any better? I can get you some water if you like."

I ended up walking past the ambulance and police cars and off the bridge to sit on the ground, leaning back against an oak tree and taking tiny sips of water from a bottle Smalls brought me. I spat again, trying to get rid of the taste in my mouth. After a few moments, I cleared my throat. "Do you . . . Was it an accident, you think?"

"That's up to the county medical examiner," Smalls said. "Right now, we're just trying to ID the body."

I nodded. "You guys have always been helpful." When Smalls looked quizzically at me, I shook my head. "I—sorry, it's . . . I went here to school, and my old roommate, Fritz Davenport, he went missing. About ten years ago." I took a deep breath, released. "You guys did everything you could, looking for him."

Smalls nodded. "I remember," he said. "Lester Briggs was on that case."

"Yeah," I said. "I heard he just retired. It's too bad. I wanted to call him up and thank him."

"I can pass that message along, if you like," Smalls said. "I'll see him this weekend."

"Please, thanks," I said. This felt normal, having a mundane conversation with another adult, and I was afraid to end it and face what would come next. "Are you heading down to Florida?"

Smalls frowned. "Florida? No, we're going fishing up at Sherando Lakes," he said. He seemed about to say more, when the radio clipped to his shoulder squawked with static and a voice. He stepped away and spoke into the radio, leaving me confused. The Sherando Lakes were just a few miles away. Sheriff Townsend had told me Deputy Briggs had moved to Florida after retirement. Why had he said that? Or had I misunderstood?

Smalls returned, his face grim. "They think they've identified the victim, Mr. Glass. There's a name written on the tag of his sweatshirt." He glanced down at his open notepad. "Terence Jarrar," he said. He looked up at me.

The news sank into me like a cold blade. "He's one of my students," I said. "He . . . lives in my dorm."

"Your friend Mr. Deems just spoke with your associate head, Mr. Middleton," Smalls was saying. "They've checked, and Terence Jarrar is unaccounted for—he's not in his room or in study hall."

"I need to get back up to school," I heard myself saying as if from far away.

Smalls nodded. "Yessir. I'm sorry."

PORTER WAS SITTING MOTIONLESS behind the wheel of his car, which he had turned around so it sat at the end of the bridge, facing back toward the Hill. My breath visibly crystallized in the cold night air as I walked up to the passenger-side window, tapped on it, and then opened the door. "Sorry you had to wait," I said. Porter didn't respond as I got in and closed the door.

"It's Terence?" I asked.

Porter nodded, still gazing out the windshield.

"You okay?" I asked.

Porter sat still. "Yeah," he said slowly. He rubbed his face with his hands.

We sat there for a moment, saying nothing. A patrol car's lights pulsed red and blue in the rear window, casting a dim, hellish light on the back of Porter's head. Without another word, Porter started the car and we drove away, leaving the lights, and the body, behind.

CHAPTER TWELVE

News of the incident spread quickly. Travis Simmons was in Atlanta at a fund-raising event, so it was Ren Middleton who called the student body together that evening in the Fine Arts Center and informed them that Terence Jarrar had died in a shooting accident by the river that afternoon. Faculty advisors and Chaplain Joyner would be available for anyone who needed them. Terence's parents had been called and would arrive shortly, and they would need our courtesy and sympathy. Afterward, the boys, blank faced, quit the auditorium and filed slowly back toward the dorms. An hour earlier, they had been joking about girls and Thanksgiving break and the Game. Now they were like old men leaving a funeral. I'd seen the same reaction in students the day after Fritz vanished.

I had just stepped outside when Sam Hodges collared me. "We're having a meeting in Ren's office," he said. His face, lit from below by the footlights lining the walkway, looked haggard, with dark shadows smudged beneath his eyes. I followed him up the brick walk toward Stilwell Hall, and the wind blew against us as we crossed the empty Lawn.

By the time we arrived, Porter was already there, slouched in a chair and looking exhausted. Next to him was James Joyner, the school chaplain, a tall, freckled redhead with watery eyes. Ren sat behind his desk, gazing out the blackened window, the overhead light gleaming off his tanned, bald head. Porter looked stricken, and a little ill, and then I remembered with a sickening lurch that he was Terence's advisor. Sam walked over to the desk and murmured something to Ren, who sat up in his chair.

"Gentlemen," he said, indicating with a wave and a nod that Sam and I should sit, and I sat down on a sofa by the door.

"This has been a terrible calamity," Ren began. "It's unbelievably hard to deal with the death of a student here. Frankly, I don't think we've encountered this sort of thing since, well . . ." His voice trailed off, and he flicked a glance in my direction. Then he turned to Chaplain Joyner, who blinked as though someone had just shined a flashlight on his face.

"Well now, that would be, ah . . . yes, nearly ten years ago," he said. "Before my time. Although it wasn't . . . That is, there wasn't a death. That we know of," he finished lamely.

"This is better," I heard myself say aloud.

Joyner frowned, as if he thought he had misheard. Sam looked astonished. Porter let out a short, single bark, a bitter *ha!* without mirth.

Ren's reaction was to stare at me just long enough to be unnerving. "I don't follow, Matthias," he said calmly. "Better than what?"

I shook my head. "I'm sorry," I said. "I didn't mean to sound . . . I'm sorry."

Ren gave a faint smile that must have terrified boys on the receiving end of it. "Better than what?" he repeated.

I took a breath and forged ahead. "Better than not knowing if—" I stopped. I'd almost said Fritz's name aloud. "Better than not knowing if a *student* is dead or alive," I said.

Ren considered me. "I don't think the Jarrars could appreciate that right now," he said.

Sam stirred and leaned forward. "Ren, what's Travis have to say about all this?" he asked.

Ren reluctantly shifted his attention away from me and eyed Sam. *Thank you, Sam,* I thought. "He's flying back tomorrow morning," Ren said. "He doesn't think we should do anything else until then regarding the students."

Sam raised his eyebrows. "One of their friends just died, Ren," he said. "They're going to be upset."

"*I'm* upset." Ren brought his hand flat down on the desktop, smacking it hard enough to make all of us jump. "How careless are we?" he asked the room. "How utterly, criminally careless? How in God's name did that boy get hold of a shotgun?" He swiveled in his chair so that he looked directly at me. "Matthias, you were on duty this afternoon. Where were you when this happened?"

I stared blankly at him for a moment, feeling as if we were all riding together in a car and Ren had just spun the wheel and veered onto the wrong exit ramp. "Uh," I said, instantly regretting it—Ren was the kind of man who would hate people who said *uh* and *um.* "I was on the infirmary porch, talking with Porter. We were talking about—a book," I finished rather lamely.

"And while you were talking about a book, Terence Jarrar was shot."

"Ren," Sam said.

"How did that boy get a shotgun?" Ren asked. The question was asked of the entire room, but he was looking directly at me.

"No one signed it out—" I managed to say.

"*Signed it out?*" Ren looked at me incredulously. "Do you think I give a damn about a piece of paper? Where's your key?"

I reached into my pocket and took out the master key—it was a single key on an old plastic Blackburne Lions key chain that would get passed to whoever was on duty. I held the key out to Ren, who took it and shut it in a drawer. "Who else used the key today?" he asked. "Did you give it to another faculty member? A student?"

Realization and fear shot through me, lighting up my spine like a phosphorescent tube. Ren thought Terence had gotten the shotgun because of me, because of a mistake I had made. Some students brought their own shotguns to school to use when skeet shooting or bird hunting, both under close supervision. The few student-owned shotguns we had were kept in a gun cabinet in a locked closet in Stilwell Hall, at the bottom of the stairs that led from the admin hall down to the bottom floor, where the game rooms and mailboxes and the Brickhouse were. My master key would unlock that closet. I hadn't given the key to anyone—it had been in my pocket all day—but Ren's accusations threw me off and made me look guilty, which was a wicked sort of self-perpetuating cycle: I thought I looked guilty, which made me act as if I were, which further increased my fear of how guilty I looked.

"Matthias," Sam said, not unkindly, "could anyone have gotten your key? Either they borrowed it or maybe they knew where you kept it?"

I shook my head. "It was in my pocket all day. Plus there's a padlock on the gun cabinet, right?"

Ren leaned forward to rest his elbows on his desk, steepling his fingers like a judge in a courtroom drama. "There is," he said. "A combination lock. It's still on the cabinet. I checked it myself. And there's a shotgun missing from the cabinet."

After a pause, Sam asked, "Is it Terence's?"

"We'll have to confirm with the sheriff," Ren said, folding his steepled fingers together. "He kept the shotgun they found next to Terence for evidence. But for now, yes, it looks like the same gun."

I was about to protest my innocence again—and likely dig an even larger hole for myself—when Porter spoke for the first time. "I have a question." He looked terrible, pale and almost sallow, as if he'd become physically ill from what had happened. "The police are treating his death as an accident, right? That he slipped or something and the gun went off?"

Ren nodded slowly—his radar was up. "That's correct," he said evenly. Sam frowned. "What are you thinking, Porter?"

"I'm wondering if Terence might have killed himself," Porter said. "Purposefully."

Joyner's eyes fluttered. "Suicide?" he asked, his voice rising a notch.

Ren spread his hands and placed them flat upon the desk, as if he were about to push himself up. "That's speculation, Porter. We don't know what happened out there. We need to let the police conduct their investigation. Until then"—his eyes swept the room—"I don't want anyone spreading rumors. The Jarrars are coming tomorrow. God knows they don't need to hear something like that." He leaned back in his chair and sighed, then turned to the chaplain. "Jim, you might get a few calls tonight and to-morrow. Please minister to the boys as needed." Joyner jerked his head in a nod. "Porter," Ren continued, and I saw Porter look up from his lap, "you'll need to keep an eye on the rest of your advisory."

Porter said nothing for a moment, and then nodded. "Of course," he said. His earlier determination seemed to have been snuffed out, and now he looked like a mournful, washed-up coach. "Poor kid," he murmured. "I just took him to Charlottesville last week."

Gently, Sam asked, "Matthias, could you gather all of his personal things in his room? I think that if we packed all that up for the parents, it would be easier for them. And for his roommate, too."

"Of course," I said. Something sticky and solid had formed in my throat, and I coughed to try to clear it. "I'll do it first thing tomorrow."

As I walked out of Ren Middleton's office, I realized there must have been a very similar meeting the night Fritz disappeared, perhaps even in that same room. It wasn't a reassuring thought. As children, we assume adults will take charge when calamity strikes, that they will redress wrongs and make things right in the world. What I had just witnessed seemed more like a dutiful but resigned prayer that all would be well.

I left Stilwell Hall and crossed the darkened Lawn to Lawson-Parker, wanting nothing more than to collapse into my bed. Then I thought of the boys in their rooms, Terence's friends, grieving privately, and I recalled Sam Hodges's kindness to me when Fritz vanished. I felt a sudden tidal pull. I needed to check on them.

When I reached the dorm, I caught a glimpse of something moving out of the corner of my eye. I turned and saw, in the distance at the far end of the Lawn, a small, dark figure, barely registering in the faint light from the footlights, outside the chapel. It paused and then disappeared—I blinked and the apparition was gone. Gooseflesh broke out across my arms and shoulders. I shook my head, angry at myself; this wasn't a ghost, but someone sneaking into the chapel after hours. I stood outside the dorm, my hand on the door handle, and then I turned my back on the dorm and struck out across the Lawn for Saint Matthew's.

The front door of the chapel was shut tight, and there was no sign of the figure I had seen there just moments before. The door, however, was unlocked, and I slipped inside, closing the door behind me. Within, the air was stale, smelling of old books. Beyond the foyer, the rows of wooden pews stretched toward the marble altar at the far end of the nave. There was somebody in front of the altar. In the blue moonlight that streamed in through the stained-glass windows, I could barely make out the shape of a boy. He was saying something or making a noise of some kind. Then I heard it more clearly: laughter.

I clenched my teeth. "Who's there?" I called out, my voice falling flat in the dead air, and the figure jumped as if shot. It turned, and I saw it was Ben Sipple, his eyes impossibly huge even at that distance.

"Are you all right?" I asked, approaching him. He kept his eyes locked on mine. As I drew closer, I could see his eyes were swollen and red, and tears shone on his cheeks. He had not been laughing—he had been sobbing.

"Mr. Glass?" he asked in a small voice.

"Ben?"

"Terence died," he said. His voice nearly broke on *died*.

Slowly I nodded.

"He was my friend," Ben said. He was shivering. I couldn't look away from his eyes. There was something grief stricken and mad about them, something dangerous.

"I'm sorry," I said.

Ben let out a sob of laughter. "Everyone's *sorry*," he said. "They're so *sorry* about Terence. Well, fuck them."

"Okay," I said. I was still moving slowly toward him, like a negotiator approaching an armed hostage-taker.

"And fuck you, too, Mr. Glass."

I nodded. "Fuck me, too." For a second, Ben's angry mask slipped, and he looked confused, even frightened. I bore down on him before he could raise that mask again. "Fuck all of them. I know. I know exactly what you mean, Ben. I do. I understand. I wish I didn't, but I do." I realized my eyes were wet with tears and wondered when that had happened.

Then I was standing directly in front of Ben, still holding his gaze. He didn't move, just stared in helpless frustration and anger. I thought if I reached out and touched him, the shock would hurl me back as if I'd touched a live cable. Gently, I said, "Why did you come here, Ben? Did you . . . Do you want to pray?"

Ben's lip trembled. "I don't believe in God," he said in a low voice. Then, as if taking courage from his own words, he said firmly, "I don't believe in God." His face hardened. He spun around and, with a sweep of his arm, knocked the candlesticks with their unlit candles off the altar. I fumbled for him, tried to grab him around the chest, but he dodged out of my reach and with both hands grasped the white cloth covering the altar, yanking it off so it belled into the air like a sail. He would have gone for the crucifix next, carved out of mahogany and fixed to the front of the pulpit, if I hadn't finally gotten him into an awkward bear hug. For a few seconds he thrashed and kicked, screaming horribly and cursing. Then he collapsed into sobs, leaning back against me so that I had to brace myself with my legs to hold his weight. I squatted, my hands on Ben's arms as I guided him to sit on the floor. We sat there for a long time, saying nothing, Ben crying into his hands as I sat beside him, my hand on his shoulder in the darkened chapel.

CHAPTER THIRTEEN

Terence Jarrar's room was depressing even without the knowledge that he was dead. The bottom bunk held a sagging mattress draped with a brown comforter. A tattered composition notebook and chewed pencil lay on the desk. A lava lamp sat unlit and dormant in the corner. Presiding over everything was a poster of a glowering Snoop Dogg wreathed in smoke and gold chains. Terence's roommate, Brian Schue, was gone for the weekend with his parents in Charlottesville. I wondered if the news had reached him yet. The dorm was still, even for early Sunday morning. Usually someone was taking a shower or playing music or holding loud echoing conversations in the stairwell, but today it was eerily quiet, everyone huddled in their rooms. I hadn't been able to sleep, so a little after dawn I had gotten out of bed, washed my face, and climbed the stairs up to Terence's dorm room to gather his things for his parents as Sam had asked me to do.

It occurred to me, as I stood in his room, that collecting his things would be harder than it sounded. Dirty laundry vomited forth from the open closet and lay in a funky reek on the floor, and while I could guess that Terence's dresser was the one beneath the Snoop Dogg poster, I couldn't be sure whose clothes were whose in the heap of laundry. Maybe Terence's mother had ironed his name into his shirts like so many mothers still did, and like my own mother had. Then I remembered how Terence's body had been identified—just yesterday—by his name on the sweatshirt label. At that thought, I actually had to sit down on Terence's bed and wait out the moment. I didn't sob or tear out my hair—I was too drained for melodrama. It was more like enduring some sort of gut cramp, waiting it out until it decided to stop. The moment passed, and I got back up, wiped the back of my hand across my eyes, and looked in the closet for a duffel bag or suitcase in which to put Terence's belongings.

Once I started, I fell into a grim, methodical rhythm. The dresser seemed to empty out itself, one drawer at a time, into the blue duffel I had found under the bed. The pile of laundry in the closet was daunting, but it turned out that Terence's mother had, in fact, ironed in name labels, so I sorted his clothes and put them into the duffel as well. The composition notebook on the desk was stacked next to his schoolbooks—perhaps I could find a cardboard box to put them in. I took the Snoop Dogg poster down, rolled it up, and placed it on the desk next to the books. All the while the sunlight grew brighter outside the window until it seemed to take almost physical form, its warmth washing over the room.

With the clothes packed, I felt weirdly inert, my earlier sense of purpose having evaporated. Idly I glanced at Terence's composition notebook on the desk. It was the same kind of notebook I had written in during my student days, a journal in which students wrote their responses to reading assignments by hand—a throwback in an age of laptops and blog posts. It occurred to me that I had no memory of Terence's written work. I remembered him getting the Akhmatova poem in class a few weeks earlier, but I couldn't remember a single thing he had written for my class. This seemed wrong, a crime against his memory. Had I not read Terence's notebook? I had spent several nights going through my students' notebooks, poring over them as if I were reading their souls, writing comments and responses in the belief that I would be opening up a valuable communication with them. Instead, I had drowned under the sheer number of their words, their thoughts about the works we had read, the observations they made about school, movies they had seen, their own lives. Eventually I had skimmed the notebooks, just adding a check mark or a brief *Good work* in the margins. It was entirely possible I had read Terence's notebook the way I read tweets or Facebook status updates, like glancing at the sky to see what the weather was like. Good writing had mattered to me—*still* mattered—and it was highly probable that my own teachers' comments and encouraging words had helped propel aloft my own dreams of being a writer. How hard was it to take two or three more minutes to read what a student had dutifully written? I had been his English teacher, for God's sake; the least I could do was make sure I had read what he'd written for class. So, writhing with guilt and self-loathing, and not a little self-righteousness, I opened Terence's notebook and began reading the pages, slowly turning them over one by one.

It soon became apparent—and this caused yet another spasm of guilt—that Terence was not some adolescent Montaigne. He had written perfunctorily about his reading assignments, employing the same style used by veteran texters who cared less about syntax or spelling than they did about getting to the final period, shedding grammatical rules like a marathoner tossing away a water bottle as he nears the finish line: *I didnt care to much about Oddysseus, he was hard to understand sometimes but the gods and the Cyclops were cool.* Most of the notebook's pages were blank. But then I turned a page and read this:

> *The steel wheels*
> *Turn and turn and turn*
> *In the night*
> *Shining with light*
> *As if they burn*

There was more, all in cryptic fragments of verse as if Terence had tried out an idea and then abandoned it to try another:

Floating away
On a hazy day
Above the plain
Above the pain

Guitar solo like a loud laugh

summer smoke sounds

The crows fly overhead like black clouds

burning wheels light up the bricks
as fate rolls down the path toward me

Unsettled, I closed his notebook and stuck it on top of the other books stacked on the desk. I wasn't sure what the poems meant, but I felt like I shouldn't be reading them.

I roamed around the room, looking for anything else that may have been Terence's, and I came across the lava lamp shoved in the corner. The wax in the lamp had formed a single purple mass on the bottom. I picked up the lamp and peered at the base to see if Terence's name was on it, too. I'd forgotten how heavy lava lamps were. The liquid stirred sluggishly inside. There was no name on the base, but the bottom was covered in gray duct tape. As I looked at it, the duct-taped bottom fell to the floor, surprising me so that I almost dropped the lamp. I clenched it with both hands, imagining Terence's parents finding me in their son's dorm room, frantically trying to clean up his broken lava lamp. "That was a gift from me!" his father would say, balling his fists.

I knelt to pick up the bottom of the lava lamp, and then I noticed the plastic bag shoved into the lamp's base. When I pulled it out, I saw that the bag contained clumps of what looked like leafy moss. It wasn't moss. I opened the bag, and a potent, organic smell a little like fresh dung wafted out. Now I understood why the lava lamp didn't work. Someone had removed the heating bulb inside the base to make a crude storage place for what looked like some very dank pot. I knelt there, staring for a long time at the three marijuana buds in their plastic bag.

THE SMART THING TO DO, of course, would be to go to Ren Middleton or Sam Hodges, immediately, and show them what I'd found in the lava lamp. Then they could talk with Brian Schue, Terence's roommate, to learn what he knew and find out who else was smoking or holding or dealing, and I would go back to my English essays and writer's block.

Of course, it didn't work out that way.

I did go to Ren's office that morning, carrying the duffel and a box of Terence's belongings, with the buds safely stowed in my pants pocket. My plan was to show Ren what I'd found, answer whatever questions he might have, and then leave the whole business in his capable hands. I'd just like the record to show that.

What happened instead was that, when I knocked on Ren's office door in Stilwell, I heard Ren call, "Come in!" and I opened the door to find him sitting with Terence's parents. They turned to look at me as I stood, gawking, in the doorway, a cardboard box in my hands and a duffel bag full of their dead son's clothes slung over my shoulder. The Jarrars were Lebanese, with dark hair and pale olive complexions. Mrs. Jarrar was one of those women whose obvious grief simply made her more beautiful. She seemed far too young to have a teenage son. Mr. Jarrar was balding and wore a dark suit and, aside from a stiff nod and a weak handshake, did not look at me the rest of the brief time I was in Ren's office; the tragedy of his son's death had apparently struck him mute.

Ren murmured introductions, and I put the duffel and box down before greeting the Jarrars. Unlike her husband, Mrs. Jarrar clasped my hand firmly and looked me full in the face. Her tearful eyes were a deep amber, and they held me suspended, as if I were holding my breath. "Thank you for your kindness, Mr. Glass," she said. "We appreciate all that you and the school have done for us."

For a couple of seconds I was unable to speak. This woman had just lost her son, and she was thanking me for bringing his belongings to her. Lies are potent things—as I have come to know so well—but so is honesty, and this woman's straightforward thanks nearly undid me. By contrast, Mr. Jarrar's silence was almost worse than his wife's sincere candor. He stared into some middle distance, and I could read in his face how he struggled to hide the deep, terrible grief that threatened to consume him. The idea of pulling Ren aside at that moment to let him know that I had found weed in Terence's room was ludicrous. "Thank you," I finally managed to say. "And I'm so sorry." I glanced at Ren, who nodded at me, which was enough of a signal for me to retreat, leaving Terence's things, his sadly smiling mother, and his grim, silent father behind.

SUNDAY WAS MISERABLE. IT would have been better, perhaps, for Terence's death to have occurred during the week, because then students would have had classes and the regular school-day routine to see them through. I spent most of Sunday grading papers and rereading *Beowulf,* which I would start on Monday. I ate a quick lunch of rubbery chicken drumsticks with Gray and Porter. Gray and I murmured at each other about how we thought the boys were doing while Porter stared at his plate and pushed his food around with his fork.

The pot I had found in Terence's room lay in its plastic bag in the top drawer of my dresser. I knew I needed to tell Ren about it, or Sam, but something kept me from going to talk to them. I'd like to say it was out of some misguided sense of respect for Terence or his family, but it was more that I wanted to avoid being a narc and getting involved in what would undoubtedly be a messy situation. At the same time, I knew I couldn't just keep the pot. I even ridiculously considered smoking it just to get rid of it, which gave rise to all sorts of imagined scenarios with students, or Sam Hodges, or even Ren Middleton stumbling across me as I toked on a fatty. As absurd as that image was, it stirred up memories of my time in New York that I wanted to keep buried—Michele doing lines of cocaine on a bathroom counter and then handing me a silver coke straw—which may also be a reason why I was ambivalent about the pot. Even stashing the pot in my top drawer showed my ambivalence, not to mention a certain sense of paranoia or conspiracy-theory thinking; I didn't want to leave it lying around in plain view, yet if someone searched my apartment and found it, I could claim that I wasn't trying to hide it at all, because really, who hides three good buds of pot in an unlocked drawer next to his boxers? In the end, I decided to wait for Terence's roommate, Brian, to return from his weekend out with his parents; when he came back, I would go talk to Ren, hand over the pot, and let him talk with Brian about whose pot it was and whether he had known about it. So I left the pot in the drawer.

Later that afternoon, as I ironed a dress shirt for the formal sit-down dinner and the following chapel service, I realized with forehead-smacking clarity that Chaplain Joyner would undoubtedly turn chapel into a memorial service for Terence. The idea of this made me pause, hot iron in hand, and close my eyes. Chapel service was mandatory for all faculty and students, but at that moment I would rather have eaten a handful of cigarette butts than attend. I could picture it quite clearly: the solemn hymns, the pious dogma about Terence having gone to a better place, the personal testimonies and vignettes about Terence on dorm or in the classroom. It would be ripping a barely formed scab off a recent wound. Jim Joyner was a good-enough guy, and his sermons were usually short and occasionally relevant or even faintly amusing, but he was one of those people who blink with surprise at the evils of the world and fall back on oft-repeated bromides that a teenager would dismiss out of hand. Looking back, I realize that the students might actually have appreciated some sort of formal ceremony for Terence that could give them a kind of closure.

Dinner was a forced, awkward affair in which everything, even the clash of the serving trays, was muted. The boys were tense; when Hal Starr in an overly loud voice asked Paul Simmons to pass the biscuits, Paul literally jumped in his seat, knocking over his water glass. Stephen Watterson's halfhearted teasing of Paul, who dabbed at the spilled water with his napkin, seemed worse than if the entire table had roared with laughter. As I helped Paul wipe up the spilled water, I glanced down Graveyard Alley at Porter Deems. He was gesticulating at his advisees as he told a story, as if trying to animate them like some sort of demented puppeteer. His advisees looked blankly at him, an unappreciative audience.

After dinner, walking out of Stilwell with the students to chapel, I moved to catch up with Porter. "Nice story you were telling to your table," I said. "You looked like you were conjuring something."

"Ungrateful bastards," he said. "I'm telling them about climbing Grand Teton and rescuing this gorgeous girl and her dumbass boyfriend—they had the wrong gear, started too late up the mountain, all sorts of idiotic shit. I mean this is a great fucking story. And they just stare at me like a bunch of goddamn cows looking at a new gate."

I was relieved. Porter sounded more like his profane, funny self. "They're just thinking about chapel, probably," I said. "Terence and everything."

Porter stopped in his tracks. A pair of students behind us bumped into him and apologized as they stepped around. He didn't even notice. "Oh God," Porter said. He looked stunned. "I didn't even . . . aw, shit."

Guilt washed greasily over me. "Hell, I'm sorry," I said. "I didn't think about it until just before dinner." I paused. Porter's face—it was hard to tell in the dimming light—looked pale and drawn. "Are you all right?"

He shook his head, more like shaking off an irritating thought than saying no, and then looked directly at me. "Look, you didn't do anything wrong that day," he said. "You know that, right?"

I stared at him. "Yeah, okay," I said. "Thanks."

He nodded and clapped me on the shoulder, and then hurried on across the Lawn toward the chapel. I stood for a moment, pondering his words. Why would he tell me that? I knew Ren had been upset with me, but I'd put that down to frayed nerves at the end of a horrible day. Was Porter trying to give me some sort of support in advance of trouble? Were other people talking about me, affixing blame? I brooded over this until, with a start, I realized that almost all the students had entered the chapel, and I hurried in to get a seat before the service started.

My advisory group sat in a pew near the back, and my advisees had all preceded me into the chapel, so they scooted over to let me in at the aisle seat next to Stephen Watterson just as the organ music started. Slowly and with dignity, the crucifer, acolyte, and Bible bearer, all followed by Chaplain Joyner, processed down the aisle to the strains of "O God, Our Help in Ages Past."

The service, as I had feared, addressed Terence's death. My face grew hot as I sat through the readings—a passage from Isaiah about how the ransomed of the Lord shall return and sorrow and sighing shall flee away, followed by a reading from Paul's letter to the Romans. At Paul's reference to how we face death all day long and are as sheep to be slaughtered, I looked at the altar and thought of Ben Sipple, pulling the altar cloth off in a rage. I wasn't sure he would be able to make it the rest of the year and wondered where he would go, to his mother in Miami or his father in Boston. Or maybe just a different boarding school. *Another lost soul,* I thought.

When Chaplain Joyner ascended to the modest pulpit and began speaking about Terence Jarrar, about his life at Blackburne and the horrible pain we felt at his being taken away, I shut my eyes. His words echoed some of the platitudes served up after Fritz's disappearance. Mr. Hollis, the chaplain when I was a student, had been a rather meek and unassuming man who had often seemed perplexed at finding himself chaplain to nearly four hundred boys, but he had been a good guy. At the first chapel service after Fritz had disappeared, Hollis had done his best to comfort us. His best efforts had been lost on me at the time—I had sat in the pew, despising Hollis and seething as if he had caused Fritz to vanish. I had wanted him to stop talking in his easy, prayerful voice, to be struck dumb, to have a stroke. Now, I found myself sitting again in Saint Matthew's, the school having experienced another shocking loss, and I could see, at a remove, how my own pain and bitterness and anger had seeped out of me like radioactive waste, contaminating everything around me. I had suffered, true, but I had wrapped myself in my own suffering, displaying it like a flag worn by a patriot. I had cut everyone off and chosen to suffer alone. I looked now at the rows of blazered boys around me, their faces blank or sad or stunned, but they were together, joined by a bond made evident by their grief but stronger for it. And with a kind of shock, I realized that I was one of them, too.

A low, wet gasp caused me to glance at Stephen Watterson next to me. He was crying, his face red and shoulders hunched forward as he tried to hold in his grief. On his other side, Paul Simmons stared at the far wall, oblivious to his classmate. Stephen looked as if he were trying to silently give birth, his mouth open and his nose and forehead contorted, eyes screwed shut to deny his tears. For a second I just stared at him, unable to do anything. Then Stephen took in another quiet, shuddering breath and opened his eyes, looking directly at me. The pain and the loss and the sheer need in his look were so bald that I flinched. He looked as if he had just witnessed an atrocity. Dimly I realized that, in fact, he had. I fumbled in my jacket pocket and found a single tissue, which I handed to Stephen. He took it and tried to mop up his face. I hesitated—I didn't know how to do this, how to be the adult. Part of me wanted to run out of the chapel and hide in the dark. But then, with just a bit of awkwardness, I reached out and put my arm over his shoulders so he could lean into me. He did, uttering a few more strangled gasps. Chaplain Joyner continued to speak from the pulpit, handling his words as if they would be offended by being spoken too loudly.

"I don't understand," Stephen said. He was still leaning against me and wiping his eyes, but he seemed to be under more control.

"I know," I murmured.

"It sucks," he said, sniffling. "Sorry."

"It's okay," I said. "I lost a classmate, too. When I was here. It still sucks."

"Yeah," he said, and then we both wept silently as Chaplain Joyner began reading the Prayers of the People and the congregation responded, "Hear our prayer," the words rolling over us like a white summer fog.

I WALKED STEPHEN BACK from chapel to his room before study period. His roommate, Rusty Scarwood, didn't ask anything when we walked through the door. Stephen's eyes were still red and swollen, and that said enough. But when I left the room, Rusty reached out to put a hand on Stephen's back, a gesture so simple and heartfelt, I fought the urge to start crying again.

After study period, I wandered the dorm to check in with my boys. Many were listening to music, though at low volume, and they greeted me easily enough. Nevertheless, I could see a new wariness in their eyes, an uncertainty that had not been there before. I found several students in the commons watching a rerun of *Jurassic Park* on TV. They eyed me as I came in, and I nearly left, feeling I might be intruding. But Hal Starr and Mack Arnold spotted me and waved me over to their seats at the back of the room, where we immediately began a half-whispered conversation about our favorite movies, arguing agreeably about the old *Star Wars* films versus the prequels. After the T. rex in *Jurassic Park* made its appearance and devoured the lawyer on the toilet to a chorus of cheers from the boys, I turned to Hal and Mack. "You guys doing okay?" I asked.

Both of them nodded, their faces a faint blue from the light on the TV screen. "Yeah, we're okay," Hal said, brushing the hair out of his eyes. "Thanks, Mr. Glass." He smiled at me, more a genuine smile than a polite one.

At that moment, my cell phone vibrated. I thought it might be Sam Hodges or Ren Middleton, so I gave Hal and Mack a thumbs-up and walked out of the commons, pushing through the glass doors and out into the cool evening air. In fact, I took a deep breath like a diver surfacing before I looked at my cell. The number had a local area code, but I didn't recognize it. I answered. "Hello?"

"Mr. Glass?" the caller said. It was a deep voice, male. "This is Lester Briggs. I . . ." He hesitated. "I used to work in the sheriff's office. We met your senior year of high school?"

"Deputy Briggs," I said. "Uh, yeah, sure. Yes, I remember you. Uh-huh."

"I'm sorry it's late. Am I calling you at a bad time?"

I glanced back through the commons window. Hal and Mack were watching the movie, leaning back in their chairs. "No, it's fine," I said. "I, ah . . . How did you get my number?"

"Jimmy Smalls gave it to me. The deputy you spoke with during . . ." He paused again, and then continued. "During the incident yesterday. I'm terribly sorry for you all."

"Thank you," I managed. I moved away from the dorm and paced in a circle underneath the spreading branches of an oak. The leaves rustled in the near darkness above me.

Briggs's voice still sounded like honeyed-over gravel. "I'd like to meet with you, Mr. Glass," he said, no hesitation in his voice now. "I have some information I'd like to share."

I stopped pacing. "Information?"

I could almost hear him nod. "Information about Fritz Davenport. About the investigation into his disappearance. I don't know where he is or anything like that, but—"

"Yes," I said. Something shot through me, bright and red and pulsating. My nerves lit up like a dashboard's warning lights. "Yes. Let's meet. Where would you—?"

"I'd rather not meet out at the school, if you can get away."

I looked up at the tree, its branches dark against the deepening sky above, and willed myself to be still despite the hope and expectation and fear rising in me. "How about tomorrow night? Around eight?"

"There's a diner on Route Eleven just south of Staunton, the Fir Tree."

"I know it."

"All right. I'll see you there tomorrow night at eight, Mr. Glass." Briggs hung up.

I pocketed my cell and leaned back against the oak for support, trying to calm my heart. I was still there when the first bell rang for lights-out and the students in the commons stood, someone switching off the TV. I waited a few beats and then stepped inside as the boys came out of the commons. The solemn, set faces around me brought me back to where I was, and why. Lester Briggs could wait until tomorrow. For now, as the boys trudged back to their rooms like wounded veterans of an unwanted war, I wondered how I could possibly provide them any comfort.

CHAPTER FOURTEEN

onday's classes were not disastrous, which was about the best thing I could say about them. I had been worried about how the class would go as I was starting a unit on *Beowulf*, which is among many other things a violent work in which death seems to lurk just outside the brightly lit mead halls. I had been concerned that the topic might be disturbing, given Terence's death, but in the end it didn't matter. My students were listless, and many obviously hadn't slept very well. Stephen Watterson, to his credit, dutifully responded to my lame attempts to start a discussion on the monster Grendel and medieval Christianity, but our words sank to the floor like so many dying balloons. I think I was more relieved than the students when the bell rang and they filed out. I endured the rest of the day impatiently, hurried through dinner, and then drove off campus to meet Lester Briggs.

The Fir Tree was a piece of 1950s Americana, down to the mint-green vinyl booths and chrome-banded countertops. I'd been only once before—my parents had taken me there one weekend when I was a student—but I remembered the pecan pie was to die for. Now, I could barely manage a cup of coffee as I sat in a booth, waiting for Lester Briggs to arrive. Gray Smith once again agreed to cover my dorm duty that night, although I'd had to promise to cover him for the rest of the week while he caught up on his lab grades.

I had rearranged the salt and pepper shakers several times and managed to shred a paper napkin into confetti by the time Briggs walked in. He wore jeans and a plaid button-down shirt instead of a khaki uniform, and he looked a bit heavier and had less hair, but he carried himself with the same quiet authority I remembered from a decade earlier. We shook hands, his grip firm and dry, and he sat down across from me, turning his head to order coffee from the lone, bored waitress in the corner before returning his attention to me.

"Thanks for meeting me, Mr. Glass," he said.

"Of course." I raised my coffee cup and then put it back down on the table with a flat *clack*. "I have to say I was surprised to get your call."

He nodded. "I can imagine," he said politely. "It was out of the blue. Just to be clear, again, please understand that I don't have anything to tell you about where your friend might be."

I frowned. "You told me that earlier, but then why did you call? Are there any new leads or—" I paused as the waitress brought Briggs his coffee, smiled limply at me, and returned to her corner by the cash register.

Briggs shifted his weight comfortably, as if settling in. "There aren't any new leads," he said. "As far as I know. I retired earlier this fall."

"I heard. Sheriff Townsend told me you'd moved to Florida."

What might have been the beginning of a smile softened the corner of Briggs's mouth. "He did? When did he tell you that?"

"I met him last month to ask him about Fritz, see if there was anything he could tell me. He told me the Davenports . . ." I paused, as if at a speed bump, and then pushed forward. "He said they had him declared legally dead. I saw a notice on a bulletin board about your retirement, and the sheriff said he thought you'd moved down to Florida. Then when I met Deputy Smalls, he told me he was going fishing with you this weekend."

Now Briggs did smile, a full, beaming smile. He had a rather plain, stolid face, but the smile transformed it, like a lamp that shone briefly but to great effect. "We did," he said. "Yesterday. Caught some good trout, too."

"Why would the sheriff tell me you lived in Florida?" I asked.

The smile went out across Briggs's face. "Because that's where he'd like me to be," he said. "Somewhere other than here." He looked down at his cup and pursed his lips, and then looked back up at me. I was aware that he was sizing me up, weighing what he could tell me. "Do you mind telling me, Mr. Glass, why you're suddenly interested in Fritz Davenport?"

My face grew warm, lit by a slow-rising anger that masked a core of guilt. "He was my friend," I said tersely, and then corrected myself. "He *is* my friend."

"But you haven't been looking for him. Why now?"

"What do you know about what I've been doing?" I said sharply. Beneath the anger in my voice, I could detect my own fear. Briggs was asking me questions I didn't want to ask myself.

He sat there, calm as an ice floe. I couldn't read his expression. Absently I realized this must have been a useful skill for a cop. When he spoke, it was with the same even tone. "I know you became an author. You wrote a novel. So I wondered if you were doing some sort of research here, for another book."

Then I understood. Briggs was checking to see if I was exploiting Fritz's disappearance as material for a book. The idea was so ludicrous, I had to laugh, more of a short, rueful bark than actual laughter. "I'm sorry," I said after a moment. "I . . . It just struck me as funny. It's . . ." I sighed. "I'm sorry I bit your head off. Look, the last thing I'm interested in doing is writing a book about this. I just . . . I've spent years avoiding this, and now I've . . . *come back* to the place where it happened. I need to put it to rest." I briefly thought about telling him what I'd learned from Pelham Greer—that Fritz had come back to our dorm room that night while I was in the library talking with Trip Alexander—but that was my secret, and I was reluctant to give it up just yet, especially to someone I barely knew.

Plus, he was a former cop who might not look kindly on how I had kept Fritz's medal to myself for almost a decade. So I held back even as I leaned forward in my seat toward Briggs. "If you know anything about Fritz, anything that could help find him, or help me understand what happened to him . . . please," I said, "please tell me."

Briggs thought for a moment, looking out the window at the night, and then exhaled sharply through his nose. As he spoke, I felt a growing excitement. This was one of those key moments in life, when everything gets reduced to what is said and what is heard in the next few minutes.

"The night your roommate disappeared," he said, "I was the officer on duty. We got a call from Blackburne, from Sam Hodges, saying that a student was missing. I drove out there, thinking that it was probably a homesick boy who was just hiding somewhere, or at most that he'd run away and someone would pick him up in Staunton or Waynesboro. Wouldn't be the first time that's happened. But after talking with Mr. Hodges, I got the sense that it was more serious than that, and then I met with you and that settled it for me. You all were worried and frightened. I called in and requested a search party." He paused and quirked his mouth. "I was in CID then, our criminal investigations division, and I wanted to handle this quickly and quietly. Sam Hodges had told me about the boy's parents. Anytime you have a prominent family involved, you have to be careful about investigations getting too public. But Ricky Townsend—he wasn't sheriff yet, though he was on his way—he was in charge of my division, and he wanted a press conference and media coverage. He thought Fritz might have been abducted. He wanted this all out on the news to get the public involved in the search."

My throat was dry. "You didn't agree," I said.

Briggs shook his head. "Ricky was a good deputy, but he was slick. He *is* slick. He likes talking to the press, getting on television. Me, I like keeping my head down and doing my job. We'd butted heads more than once, but this was different, with a lot more at stake. Fritz was eighteen, which meant we couldn't treat this as a child abduction. Heck, we didn't have any *evidence* to suggest that a crime of any kind had taken place. I can't tell you how much I hoped we'd just find him out in the woods somewhere, with maybe a broken leg at worst. But after the search party didn't find Fritz, Ricky and I argued about what to do next. That ATM receipt in Charlottesville the weekend before, when Fritz had obviously taken a lot of cash out of his account, made me wonder if Fritz had planned this. But Ricky figured someone had taken Fritz, grabbed him off the road, and was holding him in a basement somewhere." He saw the look on my face and raised a hand as if to ward off my reaction. "I'm sorry the way this sounds. I don't mean to upset you. But you need to know how we were thinking. Fritz didn't own a car, and none were missing from Blackburne, or the whole county for that matter, so he must have walked away without anyone seeing him, had a car we didn't know about, or was picked up by someone, either a stranger or somebody willing to help him run away. Ricky even had a suspect, a guy named Tofer Jones, who worked at Blackburne and had a record."

I nodded. "I remember that. He was a cook. But you interviewed him and let him go, right?"

Briggs snorted. "Tofer couldn't catch a cow, much less kidnap a rich white kid and keep him hidden somewhere. When he was nineteen, he tried to walk out of a mall in Richmond with some clothes in a backpack, said he wanted to get his mother a Christmas present but didn't have any money. Few years later, a rape victim in Mechanicsville ID'd Tofer in a photo lineup, but he was visiting family in D.C. at the time and even had a job interview an hour before the rape occurred, so all charges were dropped, and rightfully so. It was a no-brainer that he wasn't involved in Fritz Davenport's disappearance. But Tofer got hotheaded when Ricky and I interviewed him, pushed Ricky's buttons, and Ricky thought Tofer was a good suspect. Ricky and I got kind of heated. Sheriff Baines had to cut both of us off." Briggs sat back. "Didn't matter in the end, anyway."

"Why not?"

"State police got involved, for one thing. Sheriff called them in the day after Fritz went missing. They've got more manpower and expertise for this kind of thing than we do. They interviewed Tofer themselves, realized pretty quick that he wasn't a viable suspect, and cut him loose. Interviewed a few other Blackburne employees, too."

Like Pelham Greer, I thought. "Some folks were upset," I said.

"You might be, too, if you were being interrogated about something you had nothing to do with," Briggs said. "Happens a lot. Most folks are cooperative, some are nervous, and then you've got the ones full of righteous indignation who take it personally. That's not unusual. But we had to ask everyone. How did Fritz walk down off that hill in the middle of a rural county, at night, and vanish? We had dogs track him as far as the main entrance, but then the trail went cold. Wind and cold played hell with the scent. Folks figured he had to have gotten in a vehicle. And we needed to know if someone at Blackburne had helped him leave. But then the feds got involved, and that changed everything real quick."

I had been thinking of the main entrance to Blackburne, the two lions on their pedestals. Fritz would have passed by them if he had left campus that way. If the lions could talk, what would they report they had seen? Had Fritz walked out confidently, knowing where he was going? Or had he been scared to death of leaving everything behind? Or—and this was the worst thought—had someone abducted him? Then I realized that Briggs was waiting for me to respond, and I recalled with a start what he had said. "Did you say . . . the feds? You mean the FBI?"

Briggs sighed. For a moment he looked weary, as if the story were tiring to tell. Then he shrugged it off. "A special agent from D.C. He showed up the following week, wanted to go back over the whole investigation. The Davenports had connections."

This was new information, but not all that surprising. At Blackburne, we had all thought that the Davenports would call the FBI or a private investigator. Some classmates, like Fletcher Dupree, had said the local cops were too incompetent to handle something like Fritz vanishing into thin air.

Briggs gestured with his hand as if discarding an unpleasant thought. "I don't have a problem with the FBI in general. But it just muddied the water when they came in. Who's in charge? Who has jurisdiction? Who makes decisions, and who carries them out? Those are all the sorts of things you don't want to have to deal with in the middle of an investigation. The feds wanted to review everything we'd done so far, which slowed us all down. They did their own interviews. They were thinking kidnapping and ransom. Mr. Davenport's company did a lot of business with the military, which meant money and national security issues." He paused to sip his coffee.

Listening to Briggs was surreal, like eavesdropping on a movie set. *Kidnapping, ransom, national security.* "Are you telling me," I began, and then lowered my voice. "Are you telling me that Fritz disappearing might have had something to do with national security?"

Briggs put down his coffee. "No," he said. "I'm not. I'm saying what some theories were at the time. Thousands of people go missing every year, for all sorts of reasons. They get lost, they run away with someone, maybe *from* someone. They're mad at their parents, or at their girlfriends, and want to give them a scare. Someone wants to step out of his life and into another one. A kid running off to the city to make it big, that kind of thing."

And this got at the crux of the issue—*why* Fritz had run away. Guilt flushed through me. At a remove of almost ten years, it seemed ridiculous and even self-centered to think that Fritz had run away solely because I had lied to him, even though at the time I had thought it was true. Yet I still felt guilty. "If the FBI hasn't found him by now," I said tentatively, feeling my way around the idea even as I spoke it aloud, "then all those scenarios you just listed don't make a lot of sense."

Briggs looked at me with something like resignation. "The FBI hasn't found him because they're not looking for him," he said.

I blinked. His words didn't fully register. "Excuse me?" I said. "What, they—did they *find* something, or . . . Wait, is this because of the legally dead thing, or—"

Briggs shook his head. "The feds stopped looking for him a week after they showed up," he said.

I stared at him. He looked back at me impassively, patient as a clock. "Why the fuck would they do that?" I said, my voice rising. In her corner, the waitress stirred.

Briggs didn't blink. "Somebody had them stop looking," he said. He wasn't being playful or coy, just relaying facts. "One morning the special agent in charge went to Sheriff Baines's office, and after he left, the sheriff told us that the feds were out and it was our case again, along with the state police."

I realized that somewhere in the conversation I had taken hold of my coffee spoon and was now gripping it hard enough to leave a welt in my palm. I put it down on the table. "Why—why would they do that? What would make them just *stop looking* without some sort of . . ." I trailed off, uncertain how to end that thought and not sure I wanted to.

Briggs hesitated. "It was more like they realized they'd made some sort of mistake and pulled out," he said. "I don't know for sure. The official word was that the FBI had found no reason for its involvement. And to be honest, there didn't seem to be. There wasn't ever any ransom demand, for one thing, and no real clues about anyone being involved in any sort of kidnapping or abduction or any other federal crime. But once the feds get out of their chairs, they don't tend to just sit back down and call it a day without having done something first. All they did was get updated on the case, run down a few leads, and then head back to D.C." Briggs looked at his coffee cup, as if considering whether to take another sip. "Ricky Townsend must've been thanking his lucky stars when that happened."

Incredulous, I asked, "Why, do you . . . Do you think the *sheriff* had something to do with Fritz's disappearance?"

Briggs frowned, causing an ugly wrinkling of his face. "God, no," he said with a trace of disgust. "No. He's a lot of things, but . . . just no." He ran a hand over his forehead, which was probably his equivalent of extreme agitation. "That's not what I'm suggesting. I'm talking about *perception*. Spin. Ricky's theory about Tofer Jones was shot full of holes by the state police, but all that got forgotten when the feds showed up. And by the time they left, folks half thought the feds had come up with that theory and got egg on their faces. Meanwhile, Ricky was around to talk to the media again, standing beside the state police and nodding at press conferences. He dropped the abduction story and started quoting statistics about runaways." Briggs stopped abruptly, as if he felt he had said too much.

I thought I understood. "You're saying Townsend did some sort of verbal jujitsu and made the FBI look stupid instead of him," I said. "And then he took your theory about Fritz running away and made it his."

Briggs hesitated and then gave me a resigned shrug. "And now he's sheriff and I'm a retired deputy," he said. "He didn't like how I'd argued with him, and Ricky Townsend doesn't forget. When he got elected sheriff last year, I knew it was just a matter of time before I found myself at a desk job, so I retired early. Got my pension and health benefits, so it's okay." He sounded like a man working to convince himself.

"So why are you telling me all this?" I asked. "You thought I had an agenda. What's yours? Is this just about some beef you have with Sheriff Townsend?" I was a bit surprised by my own words. A knot tightened in my gut.

But Briggs just considered the top of the table, as if looking there for an answer. Then he looked back up at me, and his face expressed sorrow and a kind of pain. "It was when I heard about that boy who shot himself," he said quietly. "For a school to lose two boys . . . Well, it brought up a lot of old memories. I thought you deserved to know."

I shook my head. "I appreciate it, honestly. But I'm not sure exactly what you think I should know."

Briggs leaned forward in the booth, his plain brown eyes fixed on me. "When somebody runs away, sometimes the key isn't where they're running to, but what they're running from. I remember you felt bad about having an argument with Fritz the day he vanished. Maybe that upset him, but not enough for him to disappear off the face of the earth. If he took all that money out of the bank the week before, he was planning this long before your argument." I felt hot tears at the back of my eyes, a curious mix of shame and exoneration. Briggs continued speaking quietly and intently. "Take that along with the FBI dropping the case like a hot pan, and it all points to someone with connections, power. Influence. Someone who frightened Fritz enough for him to run away from everything he had, including his best friend."

I looked up at him and spoke in a cracked, harsh whisper. "What are you saying?"

Briggs leaned back in the booth so the vinyl squeaked. "If you want to find your friend," he said, "I suggest you start looking at his family."

CHAPTER FIFTEEN

W ith an echoing roar that rose like a wave and swept across the stadium, Blackburne and Manassas students greeted their football teams as they streamed onto the Manassas Prep field, arms raised and spirits high. Crimson-and-gold Blackburne banners were thrust into the sky in defiance of the home team's blue and white. A concussive noise of air horns and kazoos blasted the air, including the awful beehive sound of vuvuzelas that some students had snuck past the faculty in defiance of a clearly stated ban. Posters belittling each team's mascot hung on the stadium walls. One showed a Manassas knight cracking a whip at a cowering Blackburne lion, while another showed a nightmarish lion chasing a fleeing Manassas knight who had dropped his sword. "Burn Blackburne" was a popular sign among the Manassas students, as was "Tame the Lions." For our part, I saw a number of signs that read "Beat ManAsses Prep," which I thought rather unimaginative until I realized that the overlarge A and the misspelling were calculated, and had to grin at the silly audacity of it. Soon the crowds of students began hurling chants at the other side like catapults unloading onto besieged castles. "We've got spirit, yes we do, we've got spirit, how 'bout you?" Almost two thousand students, alumni, faculty, and parents were whipped into a frenzy of adulation and glorious hatred.

I stood in the visitors' stands among the Blackburne students, cheering and yelling along with them, lost in the primal will of the crowd. For the past week, I had brooded over my meeting with Lester Briggs and what he had said about Fritz and the Davenports: *I suggest you start looking at his family.* While grading papers and eating in the dining hall, while covering Gray's dorm duties as payback for covering mine, and even when I was trying to fall asleep, Briggs's words nagged at me, unraveling any other thoughts in my head. I was nearly sick from lack of sleep Monday night after meeting with Briggs, and it was something of a shock on Tuesday morning to realize that the Game was only four days away. Part of me felt that it would be wrong to attend a football game just days after Terence's death. Now, shouting a Lion cheer at the faceless mass of blue-and-white Manassas fans, I embraced the whole idea of the Game, welcomed it with all my heart, even if it granted me only a temporary respite from my thoughts.

The football captains walked to the center of the field to shake hands before the coin toss. All eyes were on them. Henry "the Duke" Duquesne was a Manassas linebacker, with an action-hero jaw and a chest and shoulders that Michelangelo would have immortalized in marble. The Duke was the most dangerous defensive football player in the Old Virginia League. I'd heard Coach Gristina describe the Duke's ability to evade blockers and tackle runners as a kind of lethal ballet.

At midfield, the Duke lined up across from Blackburne's hero, Jamal "Bull" Bullock, our star running back. Bull was broad as an ox and would explode out of formation, battering his way through a defensive line. No matter what happened, Bull almost always carried the ball at least three yards on every run. I'd seen him run for nearly ten yards, carrying on his back two defensive linemen, who would be hanging on to him like so many koala bears, before a third player finally tackled him and brought him down. Diamond, who was Blackburne's football demigod when I had been in school, had danced between linemen; Bull plowed straight through them.

On the Manassas field, the Duke and Bull gazed at each other stoically, like gunfighters at high noon, while in the stands hundreds of students went berserk.

"Duuuuuuuuke," the Manassas side called, waving blue-and-white flags.

"Bull! Bull!" retorted the Blackburne side, speeding up the chant like a locomotive. "Bull! Bull! Bull!-Bull! Bull!-Bull!-Bull!-Bull!"

Blackburne won the toss and elected to receive the kickoff. Both teams huddled on the sidelines, getting final instructions from their coaches, before lining up in formation on the field. The referee consulted his watch, blew the whistle, and the Manassas kicker began his slow-motion trot toward the football, accelerating forward. Then *snap!* The ball was kicked and flew into the air to deafening cheers and a chorus of vuvuzelas.

I had been so intent on watching the action on the football field that it took me a moment to realize someone in the aisle was tugging on my sleeve and shouting my name. I turned, and there stood my classmate Trip Alexander, in a Blackburne tie and tweed overcoat, grinning in my face. His hair was a bit shorter but still threatened to spill into his eyes, which now sat behind rimless glasses. "Hey, Matthias," he said casually, as if we were passing each other on the way to class.

"Trip! Jesus!" I had not seen Trip Alexander since graduating from Blackburne, but seeing his unexpected, smiling face lifted my heart so that only now I realized how low it had been. I gave him a bear hug by way of greeting, nearly knocking him down along with the poor Blackburne student in the row in front of me, and I started laughing so hard, it was close to sobbing. For his part, Trip pounded me on the back and told me to calm down before somebody made us get a room.

Since no one was sitting in their seats, we stood half in the aisle and briefly exchanged information in between plays on the field. Trip said he was a financial reporter for the *Washington Post*. I had always figured Trip would become a lawyer, but I could see how his shrewd analytical skills would be a great asset for a journalist. Trip had read *The Unforgiving* and made me promise to sign a copy for him. I sidestepped his questions about any new novel I might be writing and instead spoke generally about teaching and working at Blackburne. As perceptive as he had always been when we were in school, he understood that I was avoiding the topic of writing, and he turned our attention to the field. While we had been talking, Blackburne had converted our initial possession into a field goal, but Manassas was now marching downfield, looking to score a touchdown.

Watching the game, I found myself following the progress of a Manassas wide receiver. Most high school football games rely heavily on running plays, but this Manassas player had already made one difficult catch and evaded two Blackburne tackles before finally being brought down inside our forty-yard line. He was tall and rangy and could cut around the Blackburne cornerback like a basketball player heading for the hoop. I wasn't sure at first why this player, whose name I didn't know, captured my attention. Then it struck me, just as the Manassas quarterback passed to him and he stretched out his hands and snatched the ball out of the air before being tackled. He looked like Fritz, the way he moved and ran, even the way he wiped his hands on his hips before the ball was snapped. The similarity was so strong that I stood silent for a moment among the screaming Blackburne fans as the wide receiver executed another play, drawing the cornerback and a safety after him, which opened a hole in the defensive line that a Manassas halfback took advantage of. As the fans around me groaned and shouted in disappointment—the Manassas halfback had made it to our twenty-yard line—the earlier, raw joy I had felt while immersed in the crowd began to withdraw like a tide, leaving behind a cold stone bank of resentment. I had wanted to ignore this growing obsession with Fritz, with what had happened to him, for one day. I glared murderously at the Manassas wide receiver as he lined up for another play, as if it were all his fault.

"You okay, Matthias?" Trip said. He was looking at me with concern. I clenched my jaw, put on a smile, and said I was fine.

Manassas scored a touchdown on a sideline pass to the wide receiver, who skipped untouched into the end zone to great rejoicing from the Manassas side. The extra point was good, and then Blackburne's offense took the field as we cheered with a hint of desperation now, as if we were watching soldiers go over the top in a WWI movie. On our first play, the Duke waltzed through the offensive line and clobbered our quarterback, a senior named Bobby Craw. I could feel the impact from my seat in the stands. The referees' whistles signaling the end of the play sounded like a dismayed alarm. But the quarterback rose to his feet to cheers from the Blackburne side and went on with the game. On the next play, Craw handed the ball to Bull, who ran straight up the middle, making up the lost yards from the sack and more. The following play, he again handed it to Bull. First down. A Blackburne student gleefully set off a deafening air horn in the row behind us. Craw threw a pass, which bulleted past the receiver and out of bounds. Then Bull again, for six more yards. The Duke was clawing to get through the offensive line for another sack. Once again a handoff to Bull, who ran with Manassas defenders clinging to him for five yards and another first down.

"He's good!" Trip said, and I nodded, beginning to feel buoyed up again by the crowd's energy.

Then on the next play, Bull took the ball around the right end, where he found the Duke waiting for him. The Duke spread his arms wide as he lunged toward Bull, who lowered a shoulder and plowed forward, the ball cradled in one arm. For an instant I thought about the hypothetical meeting of an immovable object with an irresistible force. Then the two players collided, Bull rearing upward as the Duke hit him square in the chest. Their feet scrabbled for purchase in the torn earth, each perfectly balanced against the other. Both the Blackburne and Manassas sides hollered and blew their horns. Then players from both teams leapt onto the two boys, burying them in a blur of thrashing arms and legs as the referees blew their whistles. After hauling players off the pile, the refs discovered the ball still in Bull's arm, but he had not advanced one inch. Mayhem erupted, especially on the Manassas side. Duke had stopped Bull! "Duuuuuke!" they crowed. "Duuuuuke!"

"That fucking sucks," Hal Starr said, two seats down. I didn't have the heart to reprimand him.

On the next play, Craw took the snap and handed the ball to his fullback, who ran to the left end. The Manassas defense shifted to cover him and then seemed to stall. We gaped: the fullback had handed the ball to Bull, who was running in the opposite direction. A reverse play! The Duke, having been pulled away by the feint, sprinted to catch up, but the Bull was gone. He didn't slow down for the entire eighty yards, shrugging off two ineffective tackles and crossing the goal line to ecstatic gyrations and cheers from the Blackburne side. Someone threw their Coke up into the air, drenching a couple of third formers. Trip let out a rebel yell and thrust his arms into the air in victory. I high-fived him and bellowed with joy along with the crowd.

With two minutes left in the half, Blackburne had the ball on Manassas's forty-two-yard line. Craw faked a pass up the middle, then pitched it to Bull, who had built up a head of steam and shot around the right end. The Duke loomed, arms wide again, and Bull crashed into him. Again the two struggled, throwing up clots of mud and grass around them. Then their teammates fell on top of them to a shrieking of whistles. Again a referee began hauling players off the heap. Then he suddenly blew his whistle, crossed his hands over his head, and placed a hand on top of his cap.

"What is that?" I said. "Ref time-out?"

Trip craned his neck to try to see the field better. The referee was waving frantically at the Manassas sideline. "Somebody got hurt."

The last players scrambled up from the ground to reveal the Duke lying in the mud, writhing in pain. A moan rose from the crowd. The Duke's right leg bent sharply outward below the knee.

"Oh shit," a Blackburne student said behind me. A lone voice in the Manassas stands screamed in anguish.

A pair of trainers with a stretcher hustled onto the field, followed by two coaches. The Manassas players, heads bowed, stood around their fallen comrade. Alabama, Michigan, and North Carolina had been courting the Duke. Now he wouldn't play anywhere next year, if ever. I could imagine football scouts in the audience shutting their notebooks and looking for the exits. We stared at the field, stunned at witnessing a dream cut down before our eyes. The Blackburne players milled around uncomfortably. I saw Bull pull off his helmet and stare at the Duke, who was now lying very still as the stretcher was put down next to him. Bull was crying. Then he was among his teammates, grabbing them by their shoulder pads and elbows and hustling them to the side where they knelt in a ragged circle, Bull leading them in prayer. In silence, the crowd watched as an ambulance, lights revolving, backed onto the field. When the paramedics lifted the stretcher and aimed for the open doors of the ambulance, the crowd stirred as if waking and began clapping solemnly. Someone blew a vuvuzela and was almost immediately silenced. The Manassas players all knelt now, heads bowed as the ambulance slowly drove off, taking the Duke with it. The clapping tapered off and then died, the crowd murmuring ominously in its wake. Rising to their feet, the Blackburne and Manassas players were awkwardly slapping one another's shoulders in an attempt at encouragement, while Coach Gristina conferred with his Manassas counterpart before both nodded their heads and trotted back to their sidelines. The Game would continue.

Trip let out a low whistle. "Poor kid," he said bleakly. "What a goddamn shame."

I pictured Terence Jarrar lying on the river rock, blood running into the water from his shattered head. The image was like being plunged into ice water, and I almost gasped at the force of the memory. Something close to rage was building in my chest. "He's alive," I said brusquely.

I could feel Trip tense next to me, uncertain. "Yeah, but his scholarship chances—"

"Fuck his scholarship chances!" I shouted. Students jerked their heads around toward me. Trip blinked in shock, too startled to even step back. "He broke his leg—it's not like his life's *over*. He didn't *die* or—"

Trip's mouth dropped open. The student to my left shrank away from me as if I had sprouted bat wings and a pair of horns. I closed my eyes to shut them all out. Then I pushed past Trip and walked up the concrete steps of the aisle to an exit tunnel. Behind me, the referees blew their whistles to signal the start of play again, although to my ears it sounded as if the whistles were directed at me, calling foul.

I MADE MY WAY outside of the stadium and looked around for the red Blackburne alumni tent I knew would be somewhere nearby, thinking mean-spiritedly that Blackburne would never miss an opportunity to suck up to its alumni. I found the tent sitting off to the side on a grassy lawn between the parking lot and a brick Manassas classroom building. Few people were under the tent at that point—most were still in the stadium, commiserating over the Duke's broken leg or impatiently waiting for the game to start again. Platters of cold cuts and bread and fruit-and-cheese trays lay waiting to be consumed, while a scattering of small circular tables and folding chairs gave the sense of an abandoned wedding reception.

I found the cash bar and paid for two whiskey sours, drinking the first in one long gulp and then wandering off with the second. My plan was to remain in the alumni tent for the rest of the game and get drunk, and then take a cab to some dump of a motel and sleep it off. *Fuck this school*, I thought, taking a sip of my drink. *Fuck football, fuck the Game, fuck Ren Middleton. And fuck Fritz, too.* I swallowed the rest of my drink to drown the protest my conscience made at that last thought.

This was what being with Michele had been like near the end, a long,

deliberate war against my conscience, with my sobriety as occasional col-
lateral damage. Early on I had stopped trying to keep up with Michele's
cocaine use and just drank when we went out. Regardless, at least once
every couple of weeks I had woken up with my mouth tasting like the
bottom drawer in my fridge and my head feeling as if it had been used as
an anvil. Finally, after one all-night party, Michele collapsed on a fashion
runway, her heart misfiring from arrhythmia, while I was throwing up in
a nearby toilet. Her agency sent her to the hospital and then to rehab. Our
relationship ended when she finished her thirty-day program and told me
I had to move out of the apartment. Since then, I had avoided getting truly
drunk. Right now, I wanted to do nothing else.

I had just bought my third whiskey sour, and the bartender was eye-
ing me dubiously, when someone called my name. I turned around to see
Abby Davenport, standing in dark pants and a green sweater set and looking at me with a raised eyebrow.

"Hel*lo*," I said, trying to cover my surprise. "What are you doing here?"

She brushed a strand of hair back over an ear. "I took the weekend off,
came back home. My uncle's visiting." She glanced at the whiskey sour in
my hand. "Celebrating early?"

"It's five o'clock somewhere," I said. "Can I get you a drink?"

She held up a Diet Coke can.

"Ah," I said, as if she had satisfactorily answered a question, and because
I couldn't think of anything else to say, I took a sip of my whiskey sour.
The sour mix coated my tongue unpleasantly. "So Uncle Wat's come to
town?" I said.

She shrugged. "He lives in Georgetown now. But he's coming over to
dinner." Her expression suggested that this required her attendance at the
family manor.

Seeing her now in the sunshine instead of in the dim light of a school
dance, I was surprised to realize that she had aged. Not any more than I

had, and probably less, but there were worry lines around her mouth and the first faint indication of crow's-feet by her blue eyes. For some reason, this softened me a bit.

Unbidden, Lester Briggs's words rose to mind. *If you want to find your friend, I suggest you start looking at his family.* I took another drink as if swallowing the thought.

Abby said, "I also thought you might be here." She said it almost as a challenge, as though defying me to take it personally.

I stared at her. "You wanted to find me?" I said.

She nodded. "I heard . . . about the boy last week. At Blackburne. I wanted to see if you were okay."

We stood looking at each other. Abby was one of the only people who might appreciate how Terence's death had upset me, how it had shaken the wall I'd constructed around the memories of Fritz's disappearance. *No, I wanted to say. I'm not okay.*

"I'm fine," I said. "But thanks. Thank you for asking." I took another drink. "So, teaching," I said, gesturing to include both of us. "Who knew?"

Abby smiled. A tired smile, granted, but a smile nonetheless. "Yeah," she said. "All that studying in France finally paid off."

"You studied in France?"

She nodded. "In college. I spent two summers in Paris, and then a semester in Lyon."

The whiskey sours had begun to rise to my head, creating a warm glow. "They let you do that at Juilliard? I didn't know they let you all out of the music hall."

Abby's expression was still. "I didn't go to Juilliard," she said.

A bit too late, I recalled the dance at Saint Margaret's, me asking Abby if she still played the cello and her redheaded friend—Kelly? Kerry?— laughing in disbelief. *Music? Abby hates music.* Embarrassed, I rubbed my eyes. "Sorry," I said.

Abby shrugged. "Things change. How's the writing going?"

I shrugged back. "Things change," I said, smiling. It wasn't convincing. Abby looked disappointed, as if I'd failed to live up to her expectations. Which I probably had. "Did you read my book?" I asked, and then immediately regretted the question. I never, ever asked people if they had read my book.

Abby shifted on her feet, gazing somewhere off my shoulder, and then looked me square in the face. "No."

I nodded. "Thanks for the honesty."

"Are you sure you're okay?" Abby asked.

I sipped my drink, stalling, and realized my cup now held only ice cubes. How to answer that question? My choice was, as usual, avoidance. "Why did you all declare Fritz dead?" I asked. My voice was hard, callous. It wasn't me speaking, I thought.

Abby stared at me. I crunched an ice cube in my mouth, waiting for an answer. The moment yawned before us, as if I had just taken a step and only now understood that I was falling.

"Wow," she finally said. "That's amazing. We're having a nice . . . *moment*, or whatever this is, and you just kill it off with a handful of words." She was furious, tears filling her eyes, although she looked as if she were refusing to cry.

"Do you think he's dead?" I asked. "Because I don't."

"Go to hell," she said. She threw her can of Diet Coke at me. I ducked late, and the can skipped off my shoulder. Coke fizzed down the back of my coat, although most of it splashed on the ground. When I looked up, Abby was stalking out of the tent into a crowd of people who had suddenly appeared from the stadium. Halftime.

I gathered a handful of napkins and was wiping off my coat when Trip appeared. "Was that Abby Davenport who just walked out of here?" he asked.

"Yeah," I said. "We said hello."

Trip took in my coat and the napkins in my hand, and then apparently decided not to ask. "Look," he said. "About . . . in there. I'm sorry. I heard about the boy who died at school. That must have been rough."

I sighed. "No, man, I'm sorry. I was a complete asshole. No excuse for it."

Trip raised his hands in appeasement. "We're good, then."

I continued to wipe off my coat, not looking at Trip. "Did we score before the half?" I asked.

"Yeah, touchdown. Our guys looked like they were about to apologize for it, too." He hesitated. "You want to get out of here?"

I wadded up the napkins and threw them into a nearby trash can. "Absolutely," I said.

WE FOUND AN APPLEBEE'S two blocks away, and Trip ordered a burger and a beer while I prudently ordered iced tea and a club sandwich. We avoided talking about Blackburne. Instead, I asked Trip more about his life since graduation. He told me about going to school in Missouri, switching from political science to journalism, meeting his fiancée, Mary, and then moving with her to D.C. where she took a job as a nurse anesthetist and he started writing a financial blog for a nonprofit. He'd been among the first professional bloggers to write about the subprime mortgage crisis and the ensuing tsunami that wrecked the financial world, and he'd been able to parlay that into a job as a staff reporter at the *Post*. It sounded both extraordinary and normal, a life with a person he loved and marriage and kids on the horizon, and as I bit into my club sandwich, I felt a pang of jealousy.

"I thought newspapers were dying," I said. "Print journalism is a dinosaur, and all that."

"You mean like book publishing?" Trip said.

"Touché." The third whiskey sour had turned my earlier warm glow into an angry burn behind my eyes. I scanned the restaurant for the waiter to order more tea.

Trip smiled. "It's bad, and it's changing. Newspapers can't keep up the old business model. People get their news off the Internet for free."

I finally caught our waiter's eye and held up my empty glass. He scurried away. "So you did this sort of backward?" I asked. "Starting as a blogger and then moving to print?"

Trip picked up his burger in both hands. "Oh, I still write a blog," he said. "On the side. The *Post* might eventually pay me to write one for them. Although what'll probably happen is I'll get an offer from somewhere else, maybe an online magazine." He took a bite of his burger, savoring it the way a man who is pleased with his life can enjoy little things like his lunch.

I shoved some fries into my mouth. "I can't balance my checkbook, let alone figure out Wall Street," I said around the mouthful of fries. "Nice to know they've got somebody with brains writing about finance so the rest of us know what the hell to do."

Trip wiped his mouth with a napkin. "You must have done all right with your novel," he said. "I heard film rights can sell for good money. If you like, I could set you up with a financial planning guy I know. He could talk to you about investments."

"You're about a year too late, my friend," I said, trying to sound non-chalant but unable to keep a bitter note from creeping in. The burn be-hind my eyes refused to die down. "Which is why you now see me as a humble teacher of English at our alma mater."

Trip looked at me quietly as the waiter came back and dropped off another glass of iced tea, whisking the empty one away. As I took a bite of my sandwich, Trip said, "It must be hard, teaching at Blackburne." The quiet way he said it made it clear he wasn't talking about classroom management.

Slowly, I nodded. An idea had been forming in the back of my mind, although I hadn't been sure how to broach it with Trip. His comment pro-vided an opening. The bite of club sandwich had turned to sawdust in my mouth, and I concentrated on chewing. When I'd swallowed, I said, "I've learned some things. About Fritz."

Trip didn't move other than to blink, but I could sense the excitement and dread stirred in him by my words. Fritz was a taboo subject, and therefore talking about him, crossing that boundary, had caused a thrill to run up Trip's spine, the same thrill I was feeling. It was a little like we were teenagers again, both eager and frightened as we talked behind the closed doors of our rooms about sex or drugs, hoping the teachers wouldn't overhear us.

"What do you mean?" he asked after a long pause.

"Last Sunday I talked with the sheriff's deputy who came out the night Fritz disappeared. Guy named Lester Briggs. Briggs told me some things about the investigation into Fritz's disappearance. Like how the FBI showed up and then a week later suddenly left, like they'd been called off."

Trip frowned, causing his glasses to wobble slightly. "What do you mean, 'called off'?"

"That's just it. They came in, interviewed some people—like Tofer, remember him, the cook?—and then just left, said they hadn't found any reason for their involvement."

"So why'd they show up in the first place?" Trip asked. Then he answered his own question. "The Davenports."

"Exactly. But Briggs said it seemed too abrupt the way the feds dropped the case, like someone had ordered them to stop."

"Someone? You mean like a supervisor or something?"

I paused. "Briggs said I ought to take a look at the Davenports."

Trip looked blankly at me. "Why?"

I knew how Trip would react, and how he might even be right, but I couldn't let it go. "He wondered if Fritz's family might have something to do with him running away. If they didn't want the FBI to find out what had really happened."

Trip took a long sip of his beer and then carefully put down the glass. "You know how that sounds," he said. "Why would they do that?"

"I don't know. But Briggs said the FBI doesn't usually back out like that once it gets involved in a case."

Trip sat back in his chair. "Has he had a lot of experience with the FBI, this Deputy Briggs guy?"

I shrugged. "Sounded like he had."

"But maybe not," Trip said, not unkindly. "So maybe he's misreading it. The feds didn't find any reason to be involved, so after doing a favor or whatever for the Davenports, they backed out."

I hesitated, but Trip was an old friend, and if I was committing to this, I might as well go all in. "There's more," I said. I reached into my pocket and pulled out Fritz's Saint Christopher medal. It sat dully in my palm, the chain coiled around it. "It's Fritz's. I found it underneath my pillow the night he disappeared."

As Trip stared at me in astonishment, I told him about how I'd found the medal, about my encounter with Mr. Davenport the next day, about talking with Pelham Greer and then Sheriff Townsend a few weeks ago. He listened intently, his hamburger lying half-eaten on his plate. When I finished, he looked down at the table, gathering his thoughts. "So you're trying to find Fritz?" he asked. "Actually find him?"

"Yeah. I guess I am."

He ran a hand through his hair. "Did you talk with Abby about this?"

The sense of optimism I'd felt now sank a bit, like a leaking life raft. "Sort of." Trip raised his eyebrows. Irritably I said, "I asked her why her family had Fritz declared dead."

Trip looked at me with compassion. "That was *her* drink you were wiping off your coat, then. You dumbass."

I leaned forward. "Listen, I need a favor. Two, actually. I want to take a look at whatever news there was about Fritz's disappearance. The actual articles. I found some stuff online, in the Richmond paper archives, but I thought maybe you could find something more useful."

I paused, waiting. Trip gave no sign of agreement; in fact, he had the look of a man with doubts. "You said you needed two favors," he said.

"I need you to dig around and find out what you can about the Davenports," I said. Trip's eyes widened in alarm, and I hurried on. "See if they have any secrets, any kind of—"

Trip's voice rose sharply. "Are you fucking insane?"

"Just hear me out—"

"What the hell do you think I *do*? I'm not a *cop* or some—"

"*Listen.* Davenport's company does lots of work with the government, the military. Briggs said—no, *listen*—he said that the feds had a theory that maybe Fritz was kidnapped because of NorthPoint. They handled contracts that had to do with national security—"

"According to Briggs, an ex-deputy from rural Virginia."

"These were contracts worth hundreds of millions of dollars, Trip. Maybe billions. That's what you write about, isn't it? Maybe someone grabbed Fritz to get at some of that money."

Trip shook his head, like someone shaking off a punch. "Okay, first, I write about *finance*, Matthias, not criminal investigations. Second, there wasn't ever a ransom demand. Even your deputy said that, right?"

"No demand that we *know* of," I persisted. "Maybe the Davenports got one and called the feds off, settled with the kidnappers."

Trip tried to follow my reasoning. "If they paid a ransom, then where's Fritz?"

"I don't *know.* That's why I want your help."

Trip ran both hands through his hair and settled his glasses on his nose as if regrouping. "Have you thought that maybe you're seeing conspiracies that aren't there?" he asked. "This boy at Blackburne, the one who shot himself. That has to be upsetting to you." I saw where this was going and opened my mouth, but Trip stilled me with a raised hand. "It would upset me, too. And so you've got this boy who died, and it reminds you of Fritz, and how we were all afraid that he was dead, too."

"He's not dead," I said. "I don't believe it. I refuse to believe it."

"That doesn't mean it's not true. But regardless, this boy last week, he *is* dead. And you can't do anything about that. But you think maybe you *can* do something about Fritz." He sat forward, eager on making his point. "Let's say for argument's sake that Fritz isn't dead, that he's alive. He took all that money out of the ATM the weekend before. Maybe he *was* planning to run away, Matthias. He was going to use that money to get away from school. If he did, then he doesn't want to be found. Or maybe he was picked up by some wackjob. We don't know."

"That's the point, Trip. I don't know. Look, I just want to know what the fuck happened to my friend, all right? Is that so wrong? He was your friend, too."

Trip's eyes flashed with anger. "That's not fair. Of *course* he was my friend! We were all devastated when he disappeared. You weren't the only one."

I placed my palms on the table, forcing myself to calm down. "I never said I was the only one hurt by Fritz disappearing. We all were, I know that. But that doesn't make how I felt any better. How I *feel*. It's . . ." I took a deep breath. "Look, I cut myself off from everyone at Blackburne. You, Diamond, everybody. I tried to move on like it was just a—a bad *accident*, some car wreck I had to get over. And I fucked up everything in my life. My relationships. My friends. I wrote a novel, but now I can't write anything anymore. It just—doesn't *come*. My agent dropped me, my girlfriend and I imploded . . ." I paused. "Nothing's good," I said. "Except I think I might actually be good at teaching. I took the job because I was a fucking mess and had nothing else, but I *like* it. I like the kids. I like talking about *poetry* with them, for God's sake." I paused and closed my eyes. "But everywhere I turn, I see Fritz, or something that reminds me of him. Christ, the fucking Manassas *wide receiver* reminded me of him." I opened my eyes. Trip sat stricken across from me, but I plowed on. "The night Fritz vanished, when I talked with you in the library?" Trip barely nodded. "The night before, I cheated on a take-home test." Trip's eyes grew wide. A heavy, crushing weight sat on my heart, and I kept talking, hoping I could dispel it. "I had to go in front of the J-Board, with Fritz right there, and I lied and said I didn't do it, and they found me not guilty. I walked around all that day feeling like such a liar, a *fraud*. And when I ran into Fritz that afternoon, down at the lions, I was *drowning* in it, in my own guilt. He—he told me he knew I hadn't cheated, and I couldn't fake it. He took one look at my face and he knew. He looked so *hurt*, like I'd stabbed him in the back. Which I guess I had." I took another deep breath, this one shuddering a bit, but I held it together. "We fought about it. And then he turned and ran away. He ran away from me. That was the last time I saw him. I don't want that to be the last time I see him. The last thing he remembers about me. If I don't . . . put him to *rest*, I'm going to fail at this, too. I've fucked up almost everything else, and I can't fuck this up. I have to find out what happened to him. I have to." I sat back in my chair, suddenly exhausted, emptied.

After a minute, I realized Trip had stood up and was laying cash down next to his plate. I looked up at him.

"I'll get those articles for you," he said. He kept his voice neutral, calm. "But the Davenports . . ." He shook his head, clapped me once, hard, on the shoulder, and left.

I didn't feel especially relieved about disclosing everything to Trip. What I felt was a certainty that Trip would help me, and while the heavy weight on my heart was not gone, it was a bit lighter nonetheless.

CHAPTER SIXTEEN

O n Sunday, my head pounding after three hours of grading papers, I threw on my barn coat and headed out into the chill air for a walk. The windows of the Brickhouse were steamy from the students gathered inside for fries and Cokes, and a couple of new boys were halfheartedly throwing a Frisbee on the Lawn, but otherwise a kind of limp exhaustion had settled over the Hill, as if even the few leaves left on the trees were too tired to let go and sail to the grass below. Sundays were for doing laundry, catching up on homework, or watching an old movie for the fourth time in the A/V center. Students were bored and already mourning the weekend that was not yet over, watching with dread the hours tick by toward Sunday dinner, chapel, and study hall.

I didn't want to just take a short stroll around the Lawn and head back to the dorm, so I walked past the chapel and Sam Hodges's house, thinking I might stop by the infirmary and see if Porter was in. But the porch was empty and Betty Yowell's kitchen window was dark, so I decided to wander down the drive to at least the start of the trees. It was brisk, a light wind cooling my breath. Low gray clouds hid the sun, although you knew it was there, like a lamp held up behind a shade. If it had been colder, I would have thought of snow, although we were a few weeks away from that at least. In that strange, soft light, I cast no shadow as I walked down off the Hill, the drive a ribbon of asphalt at my feet.

I reached the grove of hickory, oak, and poplar that were older than the trees by the lions at the other end of campus. Rather than a manicured green lawn, the ground underneath these trees was blanketed in dead leaves. This drive was used more as a service entrance, a back door that did not require the same attention to appearances that the lions' entrance did. As a result, the woods here were more like an actual forest, wilder, more real. The light dimmed around me as I continued to walk down the drive that led to the bridge and the river, where Porter and I had spotted Terence's body. Looking back over my shoulder, I saw the gentle slope that rose to Saint Matthew's Chapel and the rest of the brick-and-columned Hill. Then I turned my back on it and walked on into the trees.

When I had been a student, this had been a favorite run of mine in the spring, when flowers bloomed in the undergrowth and the oak trees rose like gray columns wreathed at their crowns by golden-green leaves. Now in mid-November, the leaves scorched and the bushes bare, the branches were more skeletal and angular, like the naked limbs of an older woman stripped of her finery. Still, there was a melancholy beauty in the fading gold leaves and the stark branches, and the trees still held a sense of majesty, if less splendid than in early fall or spring.

Such thoughts on the relative beauty of the woods vanished when the bridge came into view. It lay across the river like something abandoned, a graceless span of metal and wood. Beyond it, around another curve, were the skeet range and a couple of faculty houses tucked away among the trees, and then the back entrance to Blackburne. I walked out onto the bridge. Leaning against the rail, I looked down at the flat rock a football field away where Porter and I had found Terence's body. There was no visible mark left on the rock, no bloodstain or other sign that a boy had died there. Still, the place seemed marked, somehow, the air itself haunted by what had happened. But Terence Jarrar was not a ghost wandering the banks of the Shenandoah. His body was in the ground by now, far away. It was sad how little I knew of him. And now I wouldn't have the chance to know him any more.

Sick with such thoughts, I almost missed the sound. It was low but distinct, the sound of a flat piece of wood striking another. It reverberated through the trees and then faded to nothing, all within a second or so. I looked around, puzzled. There was no one on the bridge, nor on the road in either direction. I glanced one more time downriver, seeing nothing on either bank, and then walked across to the other side of the bridge and looked upstream. That was when I saw, among a stand of poplars on the school side of the river, the heavy outline of the outing cabin. The cabin had a screened-in porch that looked out over the river, and I realized that what I had heard was the slam of a wooden screen door, as if someone had opened it and it had swung back on its spring, shutting with a bang. There was a breeze, but not enough to blow open a screen door. I kept my eyes on the cabin. There was a flicker of movement behind the screen door. Or had it been my imagination?

There was the faintest hint of a path from the bridge to the cabin. No one was nearby as far as I could see, no faculty member walking a dog, no student lurking behind a tree. I walked up the path to the cabin, which was roughly built but looked sound. It was at least sixty years old, with small dusty windows and a steep roof, a few tiles from which lay on the ground under the eaves. I took the steps up to the screen door, one board popping beneath my feet. The door was unlatched, the porch beyond in shadow. I opened the door, which made no sound whatsoever. Part of me was disappointed that it hadn't made an eerie screech. I smiled at the thought and then froze in the act of stepping through the doorway. On the bare wooden floor of the porch, not two steps ahead of me, lay a thick brass disc. It looked for all the world like a miniature hockey puck. I might have stepped on it had I not happened to glance down. I knelt and picked it up. It was heavier than I would have thought. On the surface was the engraved inscription PLS. Someone's initials? The disc had a hinge at one end, and I swung the lid open to see the round white face, elegant script letters, and hovering needle of a compass. The needle seemed to work, as far as I could tell. It wasn't all that surprising to find a compass in a cabin used by the outing club, I reflected. Then again, this compass looked clean, without any dust or leaves covering it to indicate that it had been there for a long time. As if it had been dropped on the porch recently.

I looked across the porch at the door to the cabin. It was painted a shade of green that might have once been bright. About a foot above the doorknob were a steel hasp, firmly bolted into the door, and a staple on the door frame over which the hasp would fit. A padlock hung from the staple, but the hasp was not fitted over the staple—it swung freely from the door.

There were windows to either side of the door, both dark and cobwebby. I couldn't see anything through either of them. The hairs on the back of my neck stood on end as I reached for the door. I grasped the knob and silently stood there, listening. I heard nothing. Yet I was sure someone was inside. It wasn't just the unsecured hasp. It was almost a physical perception, like sound or sight, except it wasn't either of those. I just knew. Knowing didn't make me feel any more at ease as I opened the door.

It creaked as it swung inside, and I stepped into a large common room with crate furniture—a sofa and three blocky chairs with ancient foam cushions—and an old brick fireplace. The fireplace held a few ancient cigarette butts, but nothing that had been smoked in recent history. There was nowhere to hide in the main room, no space underneath the crate furniture. Two doors sat in the back wall, seeming to lead into separate rooms. The right-hand door was opened inward about a foot.

I stood in the center of the room, weighing the compass in my hand. Was there a door between these two rooms? Or was there a rear entrance? No sound came from behind either door.

"*Hey!*" I shouted, suddenly, hoping for a reaction. The word rang off the walls. Then, when the sound had dissipated, it was as if the earlier silence had grown denser, withdrawing into itself. Nobody had yelped in panic or stumbled, revealing his hiding place. "I've got your compass," I said. "I just want to talk." Now I felt like a cop in a bad movie, trying to negotiate with a fugitive. Next I would demand that someone come out with his hands up. A steady silence was my only answer. Swearing, I strode toward the open door on the right, pushed it open, and stepped into the room. Two sets of heavy bunk beds, a window through which milky light hovered, and dust. There was also another door that connected the two back rooms, a fact I became aware of only after someone on the other side of that door shoved it open, hard.

I turned toward the noise, and the door caught me like a well-timed punch to the face. Lights sparked in my vision. I fell backward, grabbing at the door, which seemed impossibly tall. Then something smashed against the back of my head, and the world shut down around me like an electrical cord yanked out of a socket—a brief flicker and then nothing.

I OPENED MY EYES and immediately winced. Pain shot through my left cheek. I sat up on a dusty wooden floor. I was in the room with the bunk beds. The back of my head throbbed where it had hit something. Dazed, I looked at the window. The milky light was still there. I looked at my watch and figured I'd been out for only a couple of minutes, max.

The door. Someone had opened it into my face—on purpose. I got to one knee, ignoring the flares of pain in my head, and then stood, my hand on a bunk bed frame. My cheek stung, and when I touched it, my fingers came away with a drop of blood. Whoever had pole-axed me with the door was gone—I could see through the open doorway that the third room held more bunk beds, no hiding places. It did, however, have a back door. I hurried to it and tried to push it open, but the door stayed firmly closed. My guess was it had its own padlock, this one properly locked on the other side.

The front door. I turned and hurried back to the front common room.

If whoever had been in here had secured the hasp on the front door, I could be locked in. Panic began tickling my throat, but when I reached the front door, it opened under the pressure of both my hands so that I almost stumbled outside onto the porch. A crow, startled, cawed at me from a nearby bush and beat its way into the sky.

I looked around through the trees and then back toward the drive. Someone was running up the drive, more than a hundred yards away, back toward school. He was wearing a dark jacket, maybe a fleece, and jeans, and a dark skullcap. I took all three of the porch steps in a single leap, nearly stumbling again when I landed, and then started running through the woods toward the drive. My feet thudded on the ground as I ran, my breath rasping in my ears. Pain flickered in my head like a dying lightbulb, threatening one final blaze before burning out. I stepped on a fallen branch, causing it to snap with a loud *crack* as if I'd broken it over my knee. Ahead, the runner turned his head to look back—a pale face but nothing else I could make out—and then he ran faster.

It seemed to take me several long minutes to finally reach the drive, and when I finally ran out of the woods and onto the asphalt, the runner was gone. I continued running up the drive, pumping my arms, drawing breath through my nose, and blowing out my mouth. No matter how fast I sprinted, I wouldn't catch him before the trees ended, but if he was heading back to the Hill, I just needed to be able to see where he went. I settled into a steady, loping run. Why I thought he was heading for the Hill, I'm not sure—probably because I assumed he was a student and would want to get to his dorm and hide in anonymity as soon as possible. But if the letters on the compass I had found were his initials, they would point to his name. At that thought, I realized I was no longer holding the compass. My heart sank. He must have taken it after bashing me in the face with the door. There was an S, I remembered, but the other two letters blurred in my memory. The cold air burned my bruised cheek, and my legs began to protest. I ran harder.

By the time I reached the edge of the trees, I had a stitch in my side and was beginning to breathe more rapidly through my open mouth, still shy of gasping for air but well on my way. Up ahead, more than halfway up the Hill, someone in a black fleece was running past the infirmary. I ignored the stitch in my side and kept going.

At the top of the drive, by Saint Matthew's, I had to stop and bend over, palms on my knees. Ten years ago I'd been able to run two miles without breaking into a heavy sweat. Now I was wheezing like an asthmatic smoker, sweat dripping off my nose, my legs burning and threatening to cramp. Still bent over, I raised my head to scan the Hill. Empty. No one moved under the trees or on the walkways. The Frisbee throwers from earlier were gone. I tried to slow my breathing, letting the stitch in my side work its way out. He could have run across the Lawn to the gym, or ducked into the library or Huber Hall or maybe even into one of the dorms. I'd lost him. "Dumbass," I said aloud in between breaths.

On the far side of Saint Matthew's, to the left across the Lawn, someone walked into view, heading down the road away from me toward Stilwell Hall. He wasn't wearing a skullcap, but he had on a black fleece. I stood up. "Hey!" I managed to shout. The person turned and then began running. From that brief glance, I could tell he was young, with dark hair, but he was still too far away for me to get a good look. I lurched after him. He sprinted down the road that circled the Hill, passing the gym and some of the other dormitory buildings—Raleigh Hall, Rhoads Hall. I cut across the Lawn, trying to keep him in sight. If he got to Stilwell, he'd lose me easily in that massive building with all its twisting corridors and stairwells.

I ran harder, my heart pounding at my ribs. Then I saw the runner turn suddenly and dash inside Vinton Hall, the senior dorm. Ten seconds behind him, I ran up the steps and through the front entrance, nearly colliding with someone just inside the door. "Hey—" the person shouted, and I almost grabbed him by the arm, thinking I'd caught the boy I'd been chasing. Then I realized this boy was wearing gray sweats and was much darker in skin tone. It was Jamal Bullock.

"Mr. Glass?" he asked, puzzled. "You all right, sir?"

"Somebody ran in here . . . a second ago," I said, in between catching my breath.

Bull nodded. "Yeah. Ran upstairs."

"Who was it?"

He shook his head. "When I came out of my room, he was already halfway up the stairs." He leaned forward to get a better look at me, and his eyes widened. "What happened to your face?"

I ran past Bull. "Get the faculty resident," I called to him, and then took the stairs two at a time.

The stairs came out in the middle of the upstairs hallway, which ran from the front of the dorm to the back, with rooms on either side. By instinct I turned left, toward the back. There were fire escapes on the rear wall of Vinton. But the window at the end of the hall was closed, the windowsill crusted with old paint and dust, a dead fly on its back by the latch. No one had gone out this way. Which meant that he was still on the second floor somewhere. Two rooms I barged into had no one in them, while in a third, a blond-haired boy, lying on his bed and listening to his iPod, glared at me. Realizing I was a teacher, he began to apologize as I let the door swing shut. In the bathroom, I startled a senior in the shower but saw no one else, either in the shower or the stalls. Back out in the hallway, I heard a strange scraping sound, wood rasping against wood, coming from behind another door. When I opened it, I saw someone across the room in the act of stepping through an open window and onto a gabled roof below, one leg and arm still inside. He got his other leg through the window, but I grabbed his arm before he could withdraw it, too. He put up a mighty struggle, trying to yank his arm out of my grasp, but I dug my fingers in, nearly wrenching the boy's arm out of his shoulder as I yelled for Bull. "No!" he started yelping as I braced a foot against the wall and began pulling him back through the window. "I didn't do it! I swear! I didn't do it! No! I swear I didn't do it!" By the time Bull came running down the hall with the faculty resident, I had managed to pull the boy back through the window and into the room, where he lay sobbing in a heap on the floor. He covered his head with his arms, but not before I recognized him.

"What the hell is going on?" demanded the faculty resident, a young, sandy-haired teacher named Matt McGuire.

"Mr. McGuire," I said far more calmly than I felt, "would you please call Mr. Middleton and ask him to meet us in his office?"

McGuire looked at me, opened his mouth, seemed to think better of it, and then nodded before heading off to call Ren Middleton. Bull stayed in the room, his wide shoulders blocking the doorway so that other students, drawn out of their rooms by the commotion, had to peek around him to see Paul Simmons, the headmaster's son, lying on the floor and crying as if his heart were breaking right before our eyes.

MCGUIRE CAME BACK A little later, sent the gawking students away, and said Ren Middleton would meet us in fifteen minutes. He said this a bit accusingly, as if I'd dragged him into trouble, but he also looked interested despite himself. I told him that I'd found Paul in the outing cabin, which was strictly off-limits to students. This was enough to satisfy McGuire, although he kept glancing at my face. I knew my eye and cheek had swollen, could feel the skin tightening, but I said nothing about it and McGuire didn't ask. We walked downstairs, and I asked McGuire to escort Paul, who was now limp and silent, to Ren's office while I stopped by my apartment. McGuire hesitated, but then walked off with Paul as I cut across the Lawn to Lawson-Parker.

On my dorm, students were stirring to life. A few were in the showers, while others were folding laundry or blaring music in their rooms, a final defiant act against the ending of the weekend. I shut my apartment door on all of it and went up to my bedroom, opened the top drawer of my dresser, and retrieved the plastic bag of marijuana, which I stuffed into the outside pocket of my coat. Then I thought about why I'd been able to catch up with Paul on the Hill, why he hadn't run to any of a half-dozen other places. He'd walked out from behind Saint Matthew's, trying to look casual. He'd also ditched his skullcap. After deliberating for a moment, I shut the dresser drawer and headed for Saint Matthew's, figuring that Ren Middleton could wait for five more minutes.

REN WASN'T HAPPY. HE sat behind his desk, in a dark blue suit and white shirt but no tie, as though I had disturbed him in the act of getting dressed for Sunday dinner, and glowered at me as if I were the one being hauled in for questioning. Paul Simmons sat in front of Ren's desk, looking at no one, slumped in his chair. An uncomfortable-looking Matt McGuire sat next to Paul.

"Mr. Glass," Ren said. "Thank you for finally coming. Mr. McGuire tells me you chased Mr. Simmons here through Vinton Hall and dragged him back through a second-story window." He made it sound as if I'd been vandalizing the dormitory. "Can you tell me why, precisely?"

I sat without waiting to be asked to do so—in the same chair that Terence Jarrar's mother had sat in, just over a week ago—and told him about walking down to the river, seeing someone in the outing cabin, going inside to investigate and being clobbered by the door, and then chasing Paul, without yet knowing who he was, up the Hill and into Vinton. I could sense McGuire alternating between rapt attention and disappointment, as if Paul's injuring me with a door in the face were somehow unsatisfactory. Paul continued to stare at the floor, picking absently at his thumbnail, and said nothing. At the conclusion of my story, Ren nodded once and then turned his attention to Paul. "Mr. Simmons," he said, "why were you in the outing cabin?"

Paul continued to stare at the floor.

"Mr. Simmons," Ren said, his voice laced with threat, and despite himself, Paul looked up, his blank expression now tinged with fear, "why were you in the outing cabin?"

Paul opened his mouth, closed it, looked down at his lap, and let out a short, strangled sigh. "I was thinking about Terence," he said in a low voice. He glanced up. Ren's face was impassive. "I was . . . sad. About what— what happened to him." He shivered as if cold. "I wanted to go down to the river, to where he . . . And I couldn't, I couldn't do it. I made it to the cabin. We'd gone there once, this fall. With the outing club. We'd had fun. And . . ." He fell silent and looked at his lap again.

Ren grunted. "What about injuring Mr. Glass, here?"

Paul shot a fearful look at me and then looked back at Ren. "I didn't mean to do it, sir. I swear. I just—I was scared, I thought I would get caught and in trouble, and so I just shoved the door open to—"

"Why?" I asked, interrupting. Ren bristled, but Paul turned to me, a worried frown on his face. I spoke gently, without accusation. "Why did you think you'd get in trouble?"

"Because we're not supposed to be there," Paul said. He sounded confused.

"If you'd just told me what you were doing there—"

"Mr. Glass makes a good point," Ren said, leaning forward and regaining control of the interrogation. "If you had simply spoken with him, you might be facing a detention. As it is, you made things much worse. Much worse."

It was the wrong way to go. Underneath the apologetic exterior, Paul seemed deeply shaken. I recalled him on the floor in Vinton, crying and saying, "No, I didn't do it! I swear!" over and over. He needed coaxing, not threats.

Paul shrank back into his chair under Ren's words. "I didn't mean to," he mumbled.

Ren sighed, whether from weariness or annoyance, I couldn't tell. "Mr. Simmons, would you please wait in the room next door. I need to speak with Mr. Glass for a moment."

Paul began to get up, but my words stopped him. "Actually, Mr. Middleton, there's something else. I . . ." I glanced at Matt McGuire. "I'd like to speak with both you and Paul, if I could."

Paul sank back reluctantly into his chair. Ren looked at me for an uncomfortable three seconds and then said abruptly, "Mr. McGuire, thank you for your assistance."

McGuire's face fell, but he stood. "Thank you, sir." He nodded at me and then, with a glance at Paul, he walked out of the office, closing the door behind him.

I reached into my coat pocket and pulled out the plastic bag I had found in Terence's lava lamp and placed it on Ren's desk. He looked at it and then at me. "Where did you get that?" he asked evenly.

"I found it in Terence Jarrar's room."

Ren's eyes widened slightly, and he tilted his head to the left, as if it had been momentarily imbalanced by the news. "When?" he asked, his voice sharper.

"Last weekend, when I cleaned out his room." So far Paul Simmons had done nothing but flick a glance at the bag of pot. His face showed no emotion other than a clear desire to be somewhere else.

Ren raised his chin and looked at me as if sighting down the barrel of a gun. "Last weekend," he said softly. He was livid—his lips were pressed together, and his face was flushed, accentuating his round, staring eyes.

I turned to Paul. "Do you have anything you want to say, Paul?" I asked.

Startled, Paul looked at me. I could sense the calculations going on behind that blank stare. "I—what?" he asked.

"Do you have anything you want to say? About that?"

Paul looked at the bag of pot on the desk and then back at me, then at Ren and back to me, a roving searchlight looking for answers in the dark. "I don't . . . I don't know what you mean."

I reached into the inside pocket of my coat and pulled out a skullcap, which I also placed on Ren's desk. Inside the skullcap was another plastic bag. It, too, contained marijuana buds, two of them, along with a handful of white oval pills. I looked at Paul, who had gone very still.

"I found this outside of Saint Matthew's," I said, still looking at Paul.

"In a planter off to the side of the entrance. Where you put it before I caught you in Vinton." I had thought saying this, making a big *J'accuse!* statement, uncovering a truth, would give me a small rush of triumph. Instead, I felt resentful and a little sad.

Ren stared at Paul. "Is this true?" he asked.

Paul worried at his thumbnail for a moment and then said, "I want to talk to my father."

There was a pause. Ren set his jaw. "In due time," he said. "First, I want to know if what Mr. Glass said is true. Did you put this bag in the planter by Saint Matthew's?"

Paul looked at him, malevolence now rolling off him like heat from pavement. "No," he said. I thought this is what the police must feel like after interrogating someone they know is guilty and the suspect smiles, sits back, and says he wants a lawyer.

Ren looked at me. "Did you see him do it?"

I shook my head. "I didn't. But he did get to the chapel before I did, and instead of running away and hiding somewhere before I came up the Hill, he made sure he'd gotten rid of it. Probably thought he could pick it up tonight after chapel. Be pretty easy to do in the dark."

"I didn't do it," Paul muttered.

"You said that in Vinton," I said. "Several times. 'No! I didn't do it! I swear!' But you weren't talking about that," I said, pointing at the bag. "Or about opening a door into my face. You were talking about Terence, weren't you?" Paul stared at the floor, picking incessantly at his thumbnail. "Did you go down to the river with him last weekend? Did you take the shotgun out of the locker?"

Paul shot me a look of such loathing, I almost stopped. Ren was sitting forward. "Mr. Glass—"

"Did you smoke with him down at the river?" I said hurriedly. "Is that what happened, Terence was stoned and the gun slipped—"

"That's enough!" This time Ren's voice was a whiplash. "Paul, go across the hall and sit outside your father's office, next to Mrs. Robinson's desk. Do not move from there, not an inch. Go."

After a moment, Paul got to his feet and went to the door, not without another poisonous look at me. Then he was gone.

As soon as the door shut, Ren said, "I don't know what the *hell* is going through your mind, but it will stop, right now."

"Look, I'm sorry that I interrupted you—" I began.

"Interrupted me? Sweet Jesus, man, you all but accused Travis Simmons's son of *manslaughter*."

"I made an inference based on a gut feeling—"

"A *gut feeling*?" Ren looked incredulous. "You shouldn't be listening to your gut. From where I sit, your judgment is seriously clouded. You find marijuana hidden in a student's room, and you hold on to it for over a *week*, without telling me or anyone else. Then you make this baseless accusation—"

"It's not baseless."

"This *baseless* accusation about Paul Simmons somehow being involved in Terence Jarrar's death."

I took a breath. "That boy knows something about Terence's death," I said. "He was panicked when I grabbed him, Ren. Not angry, or scared of me. He was panicked."

"You pulled him out of a *window*. I'm not surprised he was panicked."

"I pulled him back *in through* a window because he was trying to climb out onto the roof! You can't tell me he did that because he was scared of detention."

Ren sat back in his chair and gave a disgusted sigh.

I continued. "I think he feels guilty over Terence's death. He *knows* something, Ren. I think he and Terence got stoned, and Terence shot himself, accidentally or otherwise. The marijuana in that bag I found outside Saint Matthew's looks an awful lot like the marijuana I found in Terence's room. I'm no botanist or pot expert, but I know there are different kinds, like different brands of beer. Both of these look the same. That means they might have gotten it from the same place. And those pills? They're Vicodin. Look, you can see it stamped into the pills."

Ren looked at me through narrowed eyelids. "You still haven't explained the marijuana you supposedly found in Terence's room."

Now it was my turn to be incredulous. "*Supposedly* found?"

"You didn't bring it up until now. According to you, you've held on to it for a week."

I shut my eyes briefly, trying to regain my equilibrium, and then opened them again to look evenly at Ren. "I tried to bring the bag to you when I brought that box of Terence's stuff over to your office. I wanted to give it to you then, but his parents were here. I couldn't tell you what I'd found in front of them."

"And what kept you from telling me later?" His voice was withering. "Is your schedule so busy you couldn't stop by my office once this entire week to let me know that you had found drugs on campus?"

I thought of meeting Deputy Briggs at the Fir Tree, listening to what he had to say about Fritz's disappearance and his suspicions about the Davenports. If I offered this up as an excuse to Ren, he would think I was even crazier than he did now. "I just . . . Other things came up," I said lamely. "I made a mistake, clearly. And I'm sorry."

Ren reached forward and jabbed at a key on the laptop computer on his desk, bringing it out of sleep. "Let me tell you about the consequences of your mistake," he said. "On Wednesday afternoon, I received an e-mail from Mrs. Jarrar. She was quite upset. She had been looking through her son's things, including his composition notebook. A notebook he had for *your* English class." Ren looked at his computer, seeming to search for something, and then turned the laptop around so I could see the screen. "Read this," he said.

Reluctantly, I leaned forward. On the screen was an e-mail exchange between Mrs. Jarrar and Ren. Ren had scrolled down to the bottom of the screen so I could read the first e-mail, from Mrs. Jarrar.

From: Samah Jarrar <samah-jarrar@gmail.com>
Date: Friday, November 19, 2010, 8:52 p.m.
To: Ren Middleton <ren.middleton@blackburne.org>
Subject: Terence

Dear Mr. Middleton,

I needed to contact you regarding something I found in one of Terence's notebooks. It was his composition notebook for English class, and apparently he had been writing in it as a sort of journal. Terence was fond of writing poetry, and it was in his poems that I discovered something disturbing. In two different entries, Terence makes references to smoking and one reference to "grass." As you can imagine, this greatly upset my husband and me. We are trying to come to terms with our son's death, and while we have no desire to disrupt the Blackburne community, which has been so gracious and supportive as we deal with our grief, we wish to understand as much as we can how this tragedy came to pass. Do you or anyone else at Blackburne have any idea if Terence could have been involved with smoking marijuana? Or how he could have had access to that shotgun? I apologize for being direct, but we must know the truth, or otherwise we shall be haunted by uncertainty. The police have conducted an autopsy, including a drug test, but the results will not be available for at least another week.

Of course, we wish for this to be investigated as discreetly as possible. These poems of Terence's may simply have been creative exercises rather than evidence of any hidden truths, and we do not

wish our son's name to be blackened, nor do we want to do anything that could harm Blackburne's reputation.

Any assistance you could give us would be most appreciated,
as always. Thank you for your help, and I look forward to your
response.

Sincerely,
Samah Jarrar

From: Ren Middleton
To: Samah Jarrar <samah-jarrar@gmail.com>
Date: Sunday, November 21, 2010, 12:38 p.m.
Subject: Re: Terence

Dear Mrs. Jarrar,

First, my deepest apologies for not responding earlier. I was away
from campus and without Internet access for most of Saturday and
did not return to Blackburne until a few minutes ago, when I read
your e-mail.

I completely understand your need to know the circumstances,
and the school and I shall do everything we can to assist you. I can
tell you that, given the structure and amount of faculty supervision here, it is extremely unlikely that students could engage in
such behavior. We have, as you know, a zero-tolerance policy for
the possession of drugs or drug paraphernalia, which has been an
effective deterrent for many years. I will speak with Terence's English teacher, Mr. Matthias Glass, about the composition notebook,
although I am sure that if Mr. Glass had had any concerns, he
would have forwarded them on to me or his department chair. You
are probably correct that the entries you read were of a creative

nature. I will be back in touch with you by Monday afternoon at the latest.

Again, please accept my deepest sympathies. The entire school community stands ready to support you and your husband in any way we can.

Sincerely,
Ren Middleton
Associate Headmaster
The Blackburne School

I looked up at Ren, beginning to feel squeezed by a sense of dread. I tried to shake it off. "Seems like my theory isn't so ridiculous."

Ren ignored me. "This notebook," he said. "Did you read it?"

I felt comforted for a moment, on familiar ground. "It's a journal I ask them to write in occasionally—free writes, personal reflection, creative exercises, that sort of thing. I take them up every few weeks. I haven't read them this month so far. I don't recall reading anything like that in Terence's notebook, or anyone else's for that matter. Maybe if I could see the notebook again, I could—"

"No." It was blunt as a hammer stroke. "You said yourself that students wrote creative exercises in these notebooks. We leave it at that."

I blinked. "But—if he was stoned, and if Paul Simmons was with him, we ought to find out how they got the drugs in the first place so we don't have another accident."

"We won't," Ren said. "I learned today how they got the shotgun."

"What?"

Ren leaned forward, putting his elbows on his desk. "Porter Deems came here today after lunch, to my office," he said. "He confessed to being careless with his master key. He would let his advisees use it if they had to get back into the library for their backpacks or if they wanted extra toilet paper out of the supply closet. His advisees knew he kept it in his desk drawer. Two weeks ago, just before Porter took Terence and his other advisees to Charlottesville for a movie and dinner, Porter couldn't find his key in his drawer. The next day, it reappeared in the drawer. He said he keeps nothing else in that drawer other than a legal pad and a few pens, so he's positive the key had been missing. Porter now suspects that Terence took the key, had a copy made in Charlottesville, and then brought the original key back the next day when he stopped by Porter's apartment with a question about his history homework."

I sat back in my chair, floored. Porter? It seemed incredible. And yet he could be reckless in just this sort of way. "What's going to happen?" I managed. "To Porter?"

Ren turned his laptop back around and shut the screen. "Porter resigned. Effective immediately."

"That's not . . . This isn't all *Porter's* fault."

"He took responsibility for his actions. He is the one who suggested resigning."

I shook my head, unwilling to let it go. "We have to talk to Paul. His father could get him to talk, maybe."

"That will be between Paul and his father," Ren said.

Then I remembered the shotgun cabinet. "What about the combination lock on the gun cabinet? Did Porter open that up for Terence, too?"

It was the only time I saw Ren look uncomfortable during that entire conversation. He blinked and glanced away from me for a moment before saying, "Terence must have found out the combination. Perhaps he watched Porter open it once and remembered the numbers."

He was bullshitting. I knew it, and he did, too. Terence had gotten the combination from someone else. Maybe it was written down somewhere and he'd copied it. Or someone else knew it—someone like Paul Simmons, the headmaster's son. "We need to talk to Paul," I said.

"No."

"Ren, I get that you want to protect the school. But—"

"I said no."

"If you would just listen to me for—"

"I don't need to listen to you!" Ren stood behind his desk, his outrage palpable. I found myself on my feet, as if ready to physically defend myself. A vein forked in his forehead, thick and dark under the skin. "You deceived me, Matthias," he continued angrily. "You made me look like a fool. And we are *not* telling the Jarrars about any of this. A faculty member was negligent, and a boy stole his key, resulting in a tragic accident. That is what happened."

So this was why the school would say nothing: aside from the threat of a potential lawsuit, this was about Ren's anger over looking foolish to the Jarrars. If I hadn't been horrified by the whole thing, I would have laughed at the absurdity of it. "So we just ignore it?" I said. "We don't even look at the possibility that Paul Simmons has some sort of responsibility?"

"Travis Simmons will take care of his son," Ren said. "I suspect he will withdraw and continue his education elsewhere."

"It's a lie."

Ren didn't blink. "It's an omission."

I couldn't believe I was hearing this. Ren came around the side of his desk and stood a few feet from me, the fingertips of one hand balanced on the desktop. "Some truths are best left uncovered," he said quietly. "All of us face that fact at some point."

"Lying, omitting the truth, whatever you want to call it, it's just wrong."

Ren nodded slowly, in consideration. "And what about you, Matthias?" he asked. "What about that physics test your sixth form year?"

I stared at him, stunned. *How in the hell did he know about that?* After a moment, I said, in an utterly unconvincing voice, "I don't know what you're talking about."

"All of us keep things hidden," Ren continued. "Not because we want to lie, but because it's necessary in order to function in society. Otherwise we have messy stories to tell, uncomfortable truths about ourselves we would rather not share with others. Colleagues, for instance. Or future employers."

I managed to find my voice. "Are you threatening me?"

Ren looked disappointed. "No, Matthias," he said. "I'm simply pointing out that all of us do such things, so you can better understand why the school will do so as well. For the greater good." Ren reached over and picked up the two bags of pot, opened a drawer in his desk, dropped the bags in, and shut the drawer. "Your contract, as you know, is for one year," he said. "I can't say if we'll continue to have the same position available next year. But should you decide to seek employment elsewhere, I would write you an excellent letter of recommendation." The look on his face was inscrutable, tight as a closed fist.

After a moment or two of silence, I realized I had been dismissed. Without protest, I walked out of the office and shut the door behind me. Going down the hall in a daze, I felt as if I had suddenly woken from a dream and found myself alone, in unfamiliar country, with no idea of how to get home.

CHAPTER SEVENTEEN

P orter Deems packed his bags the same Sunday night I had my conversation with Ren. A grad student from UVA who was working on his dissertation took over Porter's classes. Paul Simmons transferred to a school out in Utah, the official rumor being that he had struggled academically at Blackburne and needed to attend a school where his father was not the headmaster. I soon learned that "out in Utah" was code for residential treatment or therapeutic boarding school.

The same week that Paul Simmons left for whatever educational experience awaited him in Utah, I ran into his father outside the dining hall before dinner. He and Ren Middleton were walking together, engaged in deep discussion, when I came upon them from the stairwell by the doors to the dining hall. Dr. Simmons came to an abrupt halt so as not to run into me, and as I stammered an apology, he gave me a look that stopped my words in my throat. His expression was a mixture of sorrow, disdain, and fear. At that moment, he looked old and worn. The look vanished, and he smiled and asked how I was getting along, and then passed into the dining hall. Ren Middleton followed him after giving me a warning glance. I turned away, my appetite gone. The message Ren had given me in his office the day I had brought Paul Simmons in had been very clear: *Keep your nose clean and I'll help you find another job—just not here.*

Ren's comments about my J-Board hearing had been a way for him to show he owned me. Telling people outside the confines of Blackburne that I had once been suspected of cheating on a test would mean little, but Ren knew he had shaken me. More important, one negative recommendation from him and I could forget about teaching anywhere. The irony was, as I had said to Trip, I thought I was actually a good teacher. And my career as a writer still seemed on hold, if not comatose. Every time I opened my laptop to try to write—which, admittedly, was not often—I found myself staring at the winking cursor on the screen, or I spent up to an hour playing Internet solitaire, promising that if I won this round, I would write; by the time I had won, it was nearly midnight and I would fall into bed, exhausted. At least I wasn't going to coach winter track with Ren, which I found out just before Thanksgiving break. Instead, I'd been assigned extra dorm duties, proctoring study halls, and so forth. So I just focused on my teaching and worked very hard not to give Ren Middleton any reason to notice me except as a productive, happy drone.

FOR THE FIVE-DAY THANKSGIVING break I stayed at Blackburne. To see the school empty in November, with dead leaves whirling in eddies by the stairs to Stilwell Hall and the dormitories dark at night save for the entrance lights, was eerie. But Sam Hodges and his wife, Laura, invited me for Thanksgiving, and we had a merry holiday together. It was nice to have almost a week to sleep late and finish grading work in preparation for fall exams, which students would take just before Christmas vacation. I avoided running into Ren and Dr. Simmons by either staying in my apartment to work or visiting with Sam.

Sam brought up Terence only once. We were sitting in his study one afternoon, talking about exams, though it would be more accurate to say that Sam, who had taught English for three decades, was talking while I listened. He glanced out his window at the falling light and then removed his glasses, absently polishing them with a handkerchief. "You doing okay,

Matthias?" he asked, looking at me with that strange, almost vulnerable look people have when they normally wear glasses but aren't.

I hesitated. I had thought about confiding in Sam, telling him about the marijuana and the Vicodin and Paul Simmons, but I was still shaken by the look Dr. Simmons had given me and by Ren's implicit threat. I didn't know if Sam could help, and I feared that if I asked him to try, I would just drag him down with me. So I smiled. "Yeah," I said. "I am. Thanks." Sam glanced at me once more, his eyes as perceptive as ever, but he tapped his desk once with his fingers, put his glasses back on, and we continued talking about essay questions.

While I enjoyed the brief holiday, I dreaded the idea of spending the forthcoming two and a half weeks of Christmas vacation at Blackburne. So, reluctantly and not without a fair amount of guilt, I called my parents to ask if I could come visit. I had not been home, for Christmas or for any vacation, for almost three years, ever since I'd been with Michele. Her mother had died in a car crash when she was in high school, and she had a rich father somewhere in New Jersey, but he was busy doting on wife number three and their twin sons, so Michele had written him off. She'd balked at the idea of going home to Asheville with me for our first Thanksgiving together. Instead, she wanted the two of us to start our own tradition, cozying together in the big city. I'd had just enough of a taste of an elite Manhattan lifestyle that the idea of going home to see Mom wearing an apron and pulling a turkey out of an oven seemed ridiculously clichéd. When I called to tell my parents we were staying in New York, my father told me they understood, although Mom, when she got on the line, sounded almost shrill in her happy denial of disappointment. "You kids stay up there and enjoy each other!" she said. "Dad and I will be just fine! Don't worry!" Michele ended up burning the turkey, and we found ourselves ordering General Tso's chicken to accompany the sides of green bean casserole and mashed potatoes that I had managed to make, which tasted just enough like Mom's to make me wish I were eating the real thing. After that Thanksgiving, my parents had flown up to New York three times, each visit more stressful than the last. Nothing horrible had happened, although Michele had been brittle and tense, and I felt I was being too loud when regaling my parents with stories of famous people we had met. My parents were nothing but kind to me and Michele, which somehow made me feel worse.

I had not seen my parents since their last visit the previous February, and while I had told them about losing my agent—to which my mother especially had responded with sympathy and outrage—I had said nothing about Michele's rehab, or that we had broken up. Anxiety coursed through me as I made the call—I almost hung up as I listened to the phone ring. But then I heard my mother's warm voice on the other end and, despite myself, I was suffused with something like relief. She was delighted to hear from me and said in her no-nonsense way that of course they would love to have me come for Christmas. "It'll save us the postage for mailing your present to you," she said with a laugh.

The days between Thanksgiving and Christmas break came and went like so many hours. My students clamored for study packets and review sheets and asked questions that I pointed out they should have been asking all semester. I had to force myself to remember that I had most likely done the same thing when I was a fourth former.

When they weren't stressing over exams, my students were anticipating Christmas vacation like submariners looking forward to shore leave in some exotic port. Rusty Scarwood's family was going to the Bahamas, Hal Starr's to Disney World. Christmas music blared from dorm rooms, the cornier the better—"Grandma Got Run Over by a Reindeer" was a favorite. Stephen Watterson was almost purple with embarrassment as he dropped off a gift at my door: a jar of strawberry preserves his mother had made. "She makes them for all my teachers," he said, as if by way of apology.

Ben Sipple still looked pale and haunted, but he had moved in with

Brian Schue, Terence's old roommate. Ben would acknowledge me with only a brief nod or a simple yes or no, and I figured he was embarrassed at how he'd broken down in front of me that night in the chapel. However, on the last page of his exam responses—which students still composed in Blue Books—Ben had written, "Have a good break, Mr. Glass." That lifted my heart a little.

THE DAY AFTER THE students departed, I graded the last of my exams, and then I packed a bag and drove south. It was a gorgeous day, the sky a deep, clear blue with large white clouds passing overhead, backlit by a bright sun. The mountains marched by on either flank as I drove down the highway, and when I came out of the Shenandoah Valley and began the long, sweeping descent out of the Virginia mountains to the North Carolina border, I could see the cloud shadows racing over the plains a thousand feet below.

Late that afternoon, I turned westward toward Asheville and was again climbing the Blue Ridge. The sun was going down, and by the time I drove into the valley and past Black Mountain and Swannanoa, night covered the hills.

Mom and Dad lived in Biltmore Forest, a small community of winding roads and tall pines, rhododendrons, and boxwoods, just south of Asheville proper. As I turned into the Forest, I could see the Christmas lights and wreaths adorning doors and windows, red ribbons on green foliage.

Finally, I pulled into the driveway, the white gravel shining under the distant stars, and gazed at the modest, two-story brick Colonial Revival house where I had grown up. I hadn't even gotten out of my car before the front door opened and Dad came out onto the porch, arm raised in greeting.

We hugged briefly, and then Dad looked appraisingly at my Porsche. "Very nice!" he said.

This saddened me, since my father seemed to be forcing himself to compliment something he didn't actually approve of. At that moment I was embarrassed by my car, which suddenly seemed to represent everything shallow and failed about my life. "My only indulgence," I said, trying to wave the feeling off with a joke, and then opened the tiny trunk and wrestled my bag out. "How's Mom?"

"Making dinner," he said. "A feast for a king."

We good-naturedly argued over who would carry my bag, with Dad winning and leading the way, wobbling slightly under the bag's weight. He looked different than the last time I had seen him, a bit more worn, and with a pang I realized he was sixty. How many more times would I walk into this house behind him? Then my mother was in the front hall, wiping her hands on a flowered apron before flinging her arms around me. "Matthias! Oh, it's so good to see you! Let's get you inside. I've got a roast in the oven. Thomas," she called to my father, "just put his bag down and let's get Matthias a glass of wine. How was your trip?"

I tried to smother a smile, but failed. "Good," I said. "Good trip." I was grinning at my mother, at her busyness and her orchestration of everything, from dinner to where my father put my bag. She realized what I was doing and made a face at me. Then she hugged me again, fiercely this time. "It's so good to have you home," she said in my ear. Then she hurried back to the kitchen, saying she had to get the roast out before it was burned and yelling again for Dad to get me a glass of wine. I stood in the front hall, listening to them call to each other from separate parts of the house, and closed my eyes for a moment, soaking in everything familiar, awash with contentment.

CHRISTMAS WAS A BIG deal in my house when I was growing up, the one time of year my parents indulged themselves. As I was an only child, my parents actively worked against spoiling me, except at Christmas. I remember many Christmas mornings when I would sneak down the stairs at dawn, the wooden risers cold and hard beneath my feet, and peek into the living room, where the tree, decorated to perfection by my mother, rose over a spreading pile of brightly wrapped presents. Each of us had at least one big gift that sat unwrapped by the fireplace. My mother excelled at finding small, personal stocking gifts—a tee shirt, a bottle opener, a book of poetry—which she bought throughout the year and stored up for this one extravagance.

This year was no different. On Christmas Eve, we went to All Saints Episcopal in Biltmore Village for the Lessons and Carols service, which I had always loved. Mercifully, the church was packed, and we didn't see many neighbors to whom my mother could show me off, or who would ask questions about what I was doing now. After the service, we drove home and solemnly put out a plate of cookies and a glass of milk for Santa Claus before heading to bed. As I laid my head on my pillow in my old room, which seemed far too small with its dormer windows and the ceiling slanted along the roofline, I could hear Mom and Dad moving around downstairs, putting something together quietly, almost furtively, as if I were five and still in the grip of the Santa myth. In my darkened room, I rolled my eyes and smiled.

The next morning, Mom had to wake me up, which was a definite change from my childhood when I had always been awake at dawn on Christmas morning. She went off to brew coffee and bake sweet rolls while I waited at the top of the stairs for my father, who came out in his bathrobe, yawning. "Merry Christmas," he managed.

"Merry Christmas, Dad."

We went downstairs and walked into the living room, and then stopped. In the middle of the room, like a pagan altar, sat an enormous silver gas grill. "Wow," I said.

Dad nodded, a smile on his face. "Just imagine what I could cook on that," he said.

"You plan on grilling in the living room?"

Dad gave a slight smile. "Your mother insisted we put it together inside so you could see it when you came down," he murmured. "Surprise and all. Help me carry it outside later?"

"Coffee's making," Mom said, coming in behind us. She looked at me, her face alight with glee. "Did you see the grill?"

Once we had coffee, we commenced the opening of the presents. Mom laughed as she unfolded a gift from me, a red apron with a gold Blackburne lion's head on it. I'd gotten Dad a nice bottle of Shiraz and a Blackburne baseball cap, which he promptly put on his head and wore for the rest of the morning. Then Mom found another present from me and opened it. Inside was an elegant tablet with raised keyboard buttons like blister packs on pill sheets. My mother glanced at me, a strange look on her face.

"It's a Kindle, Mom," I explained. "See, you can download books to it in like sixty seconds. You can carry a whole digital library with you in that one device. Isn't that cool? I know how you and Dad like to go on trips, and you both read, so I thought—"

Mom exchanged a look with Dad.

"What?" I asked.

Dad reached under the tree and wordlessly handed me a present. *To Matthias*, the gift tag read, *With All Our Love, Mom and Dad*. Puzzled, I ripped open the wrapping. Inside, I found an identical Kindle. We all looked at one another and then burst into laughter. When we'd finally settled down, wiping away tears and catching our breath, my mother said, in a reasonable imitation of my voice, "See, you can download books to it," and we were all howling again.

LATER, AFTER WE HAD cleared away all the wrapping paper, Mom began preparing Christmas dinner while Dad went outside to get some more firewood, and I sat alone in the living room. Someone had turned on the stereo, and Frank Sinatra was crooning "Have Yourself a Merry Little

Christmas." I used to hate this part of Christmas morning, with its inevitable sense of anticlimax after the excitement of opening presents. But now I bathed in the post-gift-giving letdown, welcoming it. I couldn't believe I hadn't been home in three years. Neither of my parents had said anything about it, other than Mom repeating almost hourly how glad she was that I was home. I knew this wouldn't last, that my parents would at some point gently broach the topic, would ask how I liked teaching, how my writing was going, what I would do next. I had been dreading that conversation, but now I was resigned to it. Let be, as Hamlet said to Horatio. I closed my eyes, listening to Sinatra sing about how we'd always be together if the Fates allowed.

Dad came in, and I opened my eyes to see he was still wearing his Blackburne cap. "Ready to help me move this thing outside?" he said, gesturing to the grill.

"Dad," I said.

He paused, waiting. Sinatra crooned in the background: "Here we are as in olden days, happy golden days of yore . . ."

I took a breath. "I'm sorry," I said. "I'm sorry that I didn't come home sooner." Something hard and hot was in my throat, and then I was weeping. *Good job*, I thought as I sat there on the couch and cried. I hadn't cried in front of my father since I was seven and had fallen off my bike, scraping my arm and leg.

My father was never very affectionate, not physically. He would smile and talk and listen, but he wasn't a hugger like Mom. Now he came over and sat next to me on the couch, and then awkwardly patted me on the back. "Are you all right, Son?" he asked quietly. I nodded, and then cleared my throat and wiped at my eyes. Dad handed me a tissue, and I blew my nose. "Thanks," I said, my voice thick. "Let's get that grill outside, huh?"

Dad nodded, and we rolled the grill through the living room and out the back doors of the den onto the stone patio. We didn't speak about it any more, as if we'd rolled the incident outside, too, and left it in the cold.

AS I EXPECTED, IT was Mom who brought everything up. I suspect Dad may have told her that I had apologized, in tears, about not
coming home, because she stopped making a big deal about how glad she
was that I was there. But the day after Christmas, when Dad went back
to work, Mom stayed home "to clean the house down," which meant taking down all the Christmas decorations. Once Christmas was over, the
ornaments had to be boxed up, the crèche on the sideboard put away, and
the tree taken to the curb for recycling—all immediately, as if we were
committing an act of hubris by continuing to celebrate a holiday that had
already passed. "The office can manage for one day without me looking
over their shoulders," Mom said, shooing Dad out the door. Still, I knew
why she was staying home when she told Dad that I would help her clean
the house.

We started with the tree, carefully removing every ornament and laying
it in its box or compartment. "Remember this?" she said, holding up a
plastic ball ornament with a lumpy handprint in glitter paint. "You made
this for me."

"Yeah, when I was four."

"It was sweet. Things like this are important, you know. Good memories."

I glanced at her, wondering whether she was using this as an opportunity
to open a discussion, but she was looking at the ornament, smiling, and
then she laid it carefully in its box. Occasionally she would comment on
one or another of the ornaments: a reproduction in gold filigree of Monti-
cello, which we had visited the summer before I started at Blackburne; a
wool-knit Santa Claus that my grandmother had made; a cornhusk angel
with delicate, dragonfly wings. I unwrapped the strings of lights from the
tree, coiled them up, and put them in a Macy's shopping bag where they
had lived for as long as I could remember. Then Mom helped me shove
the tree through the front door, and I dragged it down to the street while
she vacuumed up the pine needles.

I was beginning to think that I would escape unscathed, when Mom, who was now packing up the crèche, said, "So, what's it like, teaching at Blackburne?"

"Hard," I said, and then quickly followed up with, "I mean, teaching is hard. Figuring out what to say to students in class, grading, living on dorm."

She nodded, wrapping one of the wise men figurines in tissue. "Must be strange, being on the other side of the desk," she said. "Seeing the school in a whole different light."

An image of Terence Jarrar, dead and lying on the rock in the river, was so startling that I flinched. I looked quickly at my mother, but she was putting the wise man into a box and hadn't noticed. "Uh, yeah," I said, trying not to sound shaken. "I've definitely seen the school differently." I picked up another figurine, a shepherd, and grabbed some tissue paper to keep busy.

"How's your writing going?" Mom now held the Joseph figurine in her hand. As always, Joseph looked a bit bewildered, trying to figure out where exactly he fit in with Mary, God, and baby Jesus.

I twisted the tissue around the shepherd. "I'm actually taking a break from it. It's insane how busy it is at school, with grading papers and dorm duty, weekend duty. But I'll get back to it."

Mom began wrapping Joseph. "Well, I hope they let you make some time to write next semester. You've got a gift, Matthias. You don't want to lose it."

I stopped wrapping the shepherd. "I haven't lost it, Mom."

Mom looked at me, eyebrows raised. "Honey, I'm not suggesting you have. I just don't want you to waste it. That's all."

"I'm not. I'm just busy."

"Okay."

"Fine." I finished wrapping the shepherd and shoved him into a box.

A brittle silence descended, and we packed up the rest of the crèche without saying anything else. When we next spoke to each other, it was about taking down the wreath on the front door and the electric candles Mom had placed in every window at the front of the house. Mom fussed at me about how to pack up the candles. When I took the wreath down from the front door, I told her she should get an artificial wreath she could use year after year. She retorted that artificial wreaths looked tacky and she and Dad liked the real thing. Later, I stood on the pull-down stairs to the attic and made Mom hand the ornament boxes up to me rather than allow her to climb up herself. In passive-aggressive skirmishes like this, we spent the rest of the morning.

At noon, Mom called for a lunch break. "We could go to the Grill Room at the club," she said.

The Grill Room would be full of more neighbors who would want to know how I was doing, how teaching was, et cetera. "Not the Grill Room," I said.

She made a face. "You used to love the Grill Room."

"I used to love *Sesame Street*."

Mom put her hands on her hips. "Matthias Duncan Glass, are you going to be a pain in the ass all day, or are you going to have a nice lunch with your mother?"

I'm not sure which was more effective, her use of my full name or her calling me a pain in the ass. I stared at her, openmouthed. She scowled at me. Then she suddenly chortled and put a hand over her mouth. "You look like a trout that just got pulled out of a pond," she said, still smiling, and then took me by the arm. "Let's eat here. Come on."

Mom made hot tomato soup and tuna fish sandwiches with homemade mayonnaise. When we sat down in the dining room to eat, I started to apologize, and Mom shushed me. "We eat first," she said. Food for my mother was the basis of all social contracts. If people sat down and had a good meal together, she had always asserted, they could solve almost anything. Dutifully I ate while Mom talked about the various Christmas cards she and Dad had received, the old friends who still kept in touch and the ones who didn't, who had gotten married and who had given birth. "How's Michele doing?" she asked in the middle of all this. "You two still together?"

I managed not to choke on my soup. "We broke up."

"Oh, honey, I'm sorry," she said sincerely, although I could see the relief in her face.

I did not want to talk about Michele or our sordid, dysfunctional relationship, and so I asked the first question that popped into my head. "Did you get a Christmas card from the Davenports?"

My mother was as surprised as I was by my question. "No," she said, shaking her head. "They haven't sent us cards since—since you graduated."

There was an unspoken question in her voice, and I shrugged. "I ran into Abby Davenport. At a mixer at Saint Margaret's. She's a teacher there now."

Mom wiped her mouth with her napkin and pushed her chair back from the table. "I almost forgot," she said. "Just a minute." She stood up and walked into the kitchen, the door swinging shut behind her. I could hear her open and close a drawer in her desk. Then she came back through the door, holding something. "I found this in your room when I was cleaning it," she said. "Last week before you came down."

It was a jewel case for a compact disc. I took it from her and opened it, even though I already knew what was inside. It was the recording of the Bach cello suite that Abby had made for me ten years ago. I stared at it, hearing the melancholy strains in my head. *To Matthias. Christmas 2000. Love, Abby.*

"Matthias?" my mother said.

I closed the case. My heart swelled with something like grief. "Thanks," I said, my voice squeezed in my throat. "Thanks for finding this." I took a breath, exhaled. "There was a boy, at Blackburne. His name was Terence Jarrar. He died, at school. Right before Thanksgiving." Mom gasped, her face pained. "There's more," I said. "I found drugs in his room. And—and I don't know what to do about it."

She reached over and took my arm above the wrist, squeezing hard. "Do you want to wait for Dad to get home?" she asked. "Tell us both about it all at once?"

Despite everything I smiled a little. My mother was ever the practical one. "No," I said. "I think I'd better tell you now. Before I change my mind."

IN THE END I had to tell it all twice, the second time over dinner that night in order to bring my father up to speed. Oddly enough, it wasn't any easier to talk about Terence the second time around. I said nothing to either of my parents about Fritz or what I'd learned from Lester Briggs. Instead, I told them about Terence's death, about hearing the gunshot and finding Terence's body in the river. I told them about later discovering the marijuana in his room and arguing with Ren Middleton, who was going to sweep it all under the rug and get me to help him do it. Still, it felt like less than half a confession, as if by telling them about Terence, I was trying, and failing, to balance out everything I wasn't telling them about Fritz.

Dad listened intently the entire time, occasionally taking a bite of his dinner. Mom picked at her food and looked back and forth between Dad and me. I ate almost nothing, although I did drink from my glass of very good Pinot Noir.

When I finished, I realized I was starving, and in the hush that had fallen, I began shoveling food into my mouth. "Sorry," I said, glancing at Mom. She shook her head and gestured at me to keep eating.

Dad sat back in his chair and took a reflective sip from his wineglass. "So, what do you want to do?" he asked mildly.

I shrugged. "I don't know if there's anything *to* do," I said around a mouthful of mashed potatoes.

"Don't talk with your mouth full, Matthias," Mom said.

I rolled my eyes, but I swallowed my potatoes. "It's stupid, anyway. I don't know why this bothers me so much."

"That boy *died*, Matthias," Mom said gently. "I can't imagine what it must have been like to find him."

"It's not that," I said reluctantly. "I mean, yes, that was horrible. Finding him in the river. But it's the whole thing with the drugs and Ren Middleton that's nagging me, which seems stupid. I can't let it *go*. I mean, what do I care if the kid was smoking pot, or popping Vicodin, or whatever? I'm not the morality police."

Dad stirred. "No," he said, "you're not. But this Ren Middleton is manipulating you, number one. And number two, the whole thing doesn't sit right with you. You don't like lying."

I almost laughed, bitterly, and instead drank the rest of my wine in one draft and reached for the bottle to refill my glass. "Funny thing to say about a guy who writes made-up stories," I said. "I tell lies for a living." *Or used to*, I thought.

"You write stories, Matthias," Mom said. "You're not lying. You're telling a different kind of truth. Your novel wasn't a *lie*. It's not like you were trying to deceive anyone by writing it."

I thought about saying something like writing was an escape, that creating stories was a way to shape the world into a nicer, neater version of itself—in other words, a kind of lying—but instead I turned to my father. "I don't have the luxury of being morally outraged at what Ren Middleton does," I said. "No, I don't like how he's holding a reference letter over my head, but what choice do I have? I screwed up by holding on to that pot I found in Terence's room. If I were Ren, I'd be pissed, too. And Paul Simmons gets to walk away from it. Why shouldn't *I* walk away from it?"

My father looked at me over the dinner table. "So that's it?" he asked. "That's how you're going to let it be?"

I couldn't believe what he was saying. "Are you . . . You're *criticizing* me?" I said, hearing my voice rise. I'd had too much Pinot and too little food. "You're always telling me, 'Most things in moderation' and 'Safe is boring, but it works,' and now you're telling me you think I'm a *coward*? What the hell is that?"

"Matthias," my mother said.

"You are no coward," my father said evenly. "But you're giving up too easily." I opened my mouth to argue, but his words plowed over me. "Ever since you graduated from high school, ever since Fritz disappeared"—at this I sat stock-still, my mother inhaling sharply—"you've been eaten up by guilt, like it was your fault. I know you felt that, and I think you still do, and it hurts me to see you do that to yourself. It changed you, Matthias. Just as surely as falling in love, or having a child, can change someone for the better. I know—" Here he glanced at my mother before continuing. "I know your mother and I blamed Michele for keeping you in New York City, but you left home long before you met her."

"I went to boarding school, Dad," I said. "Of course I left home a long time ago."

"Yes, and Blackburne was your home for four years. It's where you grew up. And you left that, too, but not because of graduation. Because of Fritz. You went off to college and never really came back. And then you moved to New York City and still didn't come back. And now you go *back* to Blackburne for a teaching job, when you never really showed much interest in teaching before, so I'm guessing either your writing isn't going so well or you've got other reasons for returning there." I couldn't say anything, just stared at him. "And then one of your students dies, in what the school says is a horrible shooting accident, and you find evidence suggesting it might be more complicated than that, and the school wants to whitewash it. And you wonder why you don't want to let it go? It's because it's like Fritz all over again—"

"Terence Jarrar is *not* like Fritz, Dad," I said.

"It's like Fritz all over again because somebody was lost, except you think you might know why *this* boy was lost, and you feel like maybe you could do something about it, but Ren Middleton is standing in your way." My father looked at me compassionately. "Matthias, I'm not trying to win an argument. I just want you to see what I'm seeing."

My mother had tears in her eyes. My own eyes were blurry, and I wiped my arm across them, but I didn't cry this time. I just stared down at my dinner plate, trying to calm the storm in my head. "I'm stuck," I said. Saying the words was like lifting heavy rocks from a riverbank, but I managed it. "I think I've been stuck since he disappeared." And then, slowly, the frustration and the anger of the moment began to seep away, as if everything I had said had loosened a plug in a drain. I exhaled and leaned back in my chair. "Nice work, Dad," I said, conjuring up a smile, although it must have looked a bit sickly. "You'd have made a good psychologist."

At that my father gave his own little smile. "I'm a pediatrician, Matthias," he reminded me. "I have to get two-year-olds to tell me what hurts. After a while, you either figure other people out, or you have a very empty waiting room."

THAT NIGHT IN MY room, I opened up my laptop and sent two e-mails. The first was to Trip Alexander, asking if he'd managed to find out anything yet. The second, after visiting Saint Margaret's website and finding the e-mail addresses for faculty and staff, was an e-card to Abby Davenport, wishing her happy holidays and, in a postscript, apologizing for acting like a fool at the Game.

The next morning, I found a reply in my in-box. It was from Trip, a single word: Patience.

CHAPTER EIGHTEEN

I had been afraid that after a day or two with my parents, I'd be climbing the walls. Now, as the end of Christmas break approached, I didn't want to leave. On New Year's Eve, we stayed up, yawning, to watch the ball drop in Times Square. I looked at my parents' tired but happy faces and felt a pang at the thought of departing home for Blackburne and Ren Middleton. But Trip's e-mail suggested that he was, indeed, looking for information on the Davenports, which encouraged me. And I realized that I was looking forward to seeing my students again, to hearing their stories about break, to getting back into the classroom.

On the day I left, Mom managed not to cry when I hugged her in the driveway, although her voice trembled a little. "Take care and drive safely," she said. Then she said, her words tumbling over one another in her rush to speak, "Maybe you could come visit again for spring break? Only if you want to and aren't too busy."

"Sure," I said, smiling. "That'd be great."

Dad hugged me briefly but firmly. "I'm proud of you, Matthias," he said, and although I rolled my eyes self-deprecatingly, my heart was buoyed by his words. As I drove away, Dad had his arm around Mom's waist, both of them waving good-bye and shrinking in my rearview mirror until I turned at the end of our street and they slipped out of my vision.

TWO WEEKS AFTER I returned to Blackburne, I got a most unexpected response to my e-mail to Abby. One Saturday night, Blackburne hosted a "Midwinter Mixer" with a few girls' schools and a DJ. In the spirit of my new desire to be a model employee, I had agreed to chaperone in place of Gray Smith, who was surprised but grateful for my offer. But an hour into the dance, I was on my third Sprite and feeling sluggish and waterlogged. It was hot and humid in the gym, and the shrieking music, jump-dancing bodies, and dim light finally drove me outside onto the front steps of Farquhar. The chill night air was like a refreshingly cold pool on a summer's day. Stars hung overhead in the deep black. Small knots of students stood huddled here and there on the steps. I leaned against one of the massive white columns and breathed in and out, trying to ignore the thudding presence of Kesha from inside the gym.

"Well, *hello*," said a female voice, and I opened my eyes to see the red-haired woman from Saint Margaret's, Abby's friend. She wore a puffy black down jacket and a pixie grin, and given her height and roundness, she looked for all the world like an adorable female version of the old Michelin Man. "Figured we'd run into you, Matthias," she said. "I'm Kerry, Abby's friend?"

"Of course," I said, grinning. "How are you?"

"Freezing my ass off," she said cheerfully. "But it's this or the dance sauna. I'm trying to decide if our high school dances were that loud, or if I've just gotten snobbier in my musical taste."

"Little bit of both, probably," I said, trying surreptitiously to glance behind her.

"She's not here," Kerry said, still smiling, though with an *I know what you're doing* look in her eyes. The disappointment must have been all over my face, because she laughed aloud. "God, you're like a puppy," she said. "I meant she's not *here*. As in not on these steps. She ran inside to get a Coke."

"Oh," I said. "Good. I mean, I'm not trying to be rude, or . . . anything. I just . . ."

She shook her head and smiled. "You're still in love with her," she said.

Now I shook my head. "No," I said, and then, as Kerry raised her eyebrows in disbelief, "It's complicated."

Kerry made a wry face. "'Complicated.' That's what Abby said. Name something worthwhile that isn't."

I was unable to keep from asking. "What else did she say?"

Kerry nodded at something over my left shoulder. "Ask her yourself."

I turned. Abby was standing about seven or eight steps above us, wrapped in a navy peacoat with a red beret on her head. She was holding a plastic cup in each hand and looking down at us. I could see her calculations in her face—stay there, come down, or go back inside—and then she walked down the steps toward us. "What are you doing here?" she asked.

"He works here," Kerry said before I could speak. "Where else should he be? Can I have my Coke?" She took it out of Abby's hand. "This isn't Diet, or Coke Zero, is it? Because I specifically ordered a plain Coke."

"How are you?" I asked Abby.

"Good," she said, nodding. "I'm good."

We stood there, nodding at each other for a few more seconds, Kerry watching us. "Oh Jesus Christ," she said. "Look, go patrol the golf course. Seriously." Abby and I stared at her. "Go," Kerry said. "I just saw Jenny Wysocki walking over there with some boy. Do your duty as chaperones and go save her virtue. Go, go, go." She waved her hands at us as if she were shooing pigeons.

Bemused, Abby said, "You're a chaperone, too."

Kerry's eyes widened in mock outrage. "Do I look like I can chase teenagers across a golf course? No, you flush them out, and I'll tackle them on the steps. It'll be like a safari. Go! Jenny needs you, trust me—her virtue's easily compromised."

Abby and I looked at each other. I shrugged. "We can't let her virtue be compromised," I said.

Abby snorted. "Jenny Wysocki's a slut," she said, and as Kerry laughed, Abby and I headed down the stairs together.

WE WALKED ACROSS THE parking lot toward the boxwood hedges that demarcated the beginning of the first tee, behind Saint Matthew's. Sodium lamps hung on poles at the corners of the parking lot, casting a pale orange glow over us. Halfheartedly we poked in the bushes and kept an eye out for movement among the cars and buses in the lot, even though we both knew no one was there. I let Abby lead while I followed behind her.

"Kerry seems nice," I said innocuously.

"She's manipulative," said Abby, peering through the dark windows of an Oldfields bus. "Trying to get us together so we could talk."

"Is that so bad?" I said, stopping behind her. Abby hesitated, and before she could speak, I rushed in. "It gives me a chance to apologize. I'm sorry for acting like an asshole at the Game, Abby. I—maybe part of it was because of . . . what happened, the weekend before, but that's no excuse. You don't deserve that. It was wrong and I'm sorry."

Abby turned around, and her eyes fixed on me so that I was conscious of my own breathing. Her face was pale, though her cheeks were tinged with red, whether from the cold or something else, I wasn't sure. "Apology accepted," she said, a bit stiffly. Then she moved off to the edge of the parking lot, head swiveling from left to right like a sentry. I hesitated. Should I go ahead and apologize for what I had said years ago when she wouldn't come with me to look for Fritz, when I had said she must not love her own twin? I kept quiet and followed her.

Abby walked through a gap in the hedge and onto the first tee. I came through the gap and stood beside her, an arm's length away, looking up at the night sky and the stars in their fixed orbits.

"I'm sorry about Juilliard," I said carefully, not looking at Abby. "I know how much you wanted to go."

I heard Abby draw in a breath, release it. "I did go," she said flatly. "To Juilliard."

"What? But you said—"

"I know what I said." She wasn't angry, just matter-of-fact. "After we . . .

broke up, I went. And I was back home by Christmas." She stood stiffly as if holding her breath; then she looked at me with a tight, sad look. "I couldn't do it. I couldn't *play*. It just didn't—work. I practiced more, even hired a tutor outside of school, but it wasn't any good. My professors were nice about it, but I was a failure. It was like being the one kid in the choir who can't sing. People started avoiding me, not wanting me to rub off on them. So I quit." She shrugged, tried a smile. "Things change."

Quietly, I said, "I'm sorry about that, too."

We both stood there, looking up into the night. It struck me that we were standing in the same place where Ren Middleton had talked with me about killing off the inertness of the fourth formers. I was annoyed that whatever rapprochement I might gain with Abby was taking place on the same spot.

Abby spoke quietly. "It was terrible, at first. Not going to Juilliard. I just . . . I couldn't leave home again, not right then. My mother was happy to have me home, and . . . I told myself it would be a semester, maybe a year, there were other schools and conservatories I could apply to. I took classes at American, part-time, and, long story short, I never left." She paused. "It used to be you went to a place like Saint Margaret's, or Blackburne, and then you could do anything. Anything."

I risked a glance at her. She was looking down the fairway, toward the bank of trees at the edge of campus where I'd last seen her brother. They lay in utter darkness beyond the lit security booth and gate.

"I'm sorry," I said, struck—not for the first time—at how empty, how unhelpful that phrase sounds.

"It's all right," she said bracingly. "I got my degree in French, which I've always enjoyed, and now I'm teaching near home and can see my mother whenever I want."

I didn't ask about her father; I assumed he was still chained to his office at NorthPoint. "So, do you play at all anymore?" I asked, thinking about my own writing, or lack thereof.

Abby stiffened, and I cursed myself for my blunt stupidity. But calmly she said, "No, I don't. Simple as that. I once played cello and now I don't. Like I once had a brother and now I don't."

Her words stung me. "You have a brother," I said unsteadily.

She looked at me with a pained expression. "It's been almost ten years, Matthias. *Ten years.* Fritz is gone. He's been gone for a long time."

"You're talking about him like he's in the past," I said, my voice rising. For a moment I was furious, ready to shout at her. *What the fuck is wrong with you,* I thought. With difficulty I restrained myself. "He's not in the past. He's right now."

"Who are you to decide that?" Abby said, and the unvarnished pain in her voice put my anger in check. "You can't imagine what it was like to have him declared dead. It was like closing the lid on his coffin. I had to convince my mother it was the right thing to do. My father cried when the court issued Fritz's certificate of death. So don't tell me he's not in the past."

I stood there, transfixed, Abby before me in her grief and anger like some terrible divinity, beautiful and remote as one of the stars overhead. I could barely breathe. And then tears welled in her eyes and spilled over, and before I knew it, I had stepped toward her and opened my arms, and then I was hugging her, the scent of her hair like lavender and some undercurrent of peppery spice. She trembled slightly, resisting. Then she sighed as if releasing her grief and quietly cried into my shoulder as I stroked her back and murmured into her ear, telling her it was okay. We stood there, holding each other on that freezing hillside, and about the time I felt her breath on my neck, my hands had found the small of her back. She tilted her face up to mine, her eyes a gray-blue through a wash of tears. Then, somehow—did I move first or did she?—I was kissing her. Her lips were soft and insistent, her scent wrapped around me like a lover, and my God, I had no idea how much I'd wanted this, wanted her. Desire rose in me with the force of a sun, my heart and breath thrumming to it. My tongue met hers, and I pressed her body to mine. Even through our coats I could feel the curves of her buttocks, her breasts against my chest, the heat of my lust burning so fiercely that I thought I might combust and consume us both.

She broke off and took two steps back, staggering slightly. Her beret slipped off and fell to the ground, and she bent with a jerk to pick it up, her black hair mussed, her eyes wide, lips parted as if she had just witnessed something shocking. I stood there, tranquilized, her scent still hovering in the air, tantalizingly close.

"That," Abby said thickly. She swallowed. Her eyes were huge and all-encompassing. "That can't happen again," she said.

"Abby," I managed to say. My brain was like the overhead light in my classroom—it had been turned off for a few moments, and now it was taking an inordinately long time to flicker back on.

Abby turned and hurried away, walking to the gap in the hedges. Stepping through it, she vanished from sight.

MAYBE IT WAS THIS frustrating encounter with Abby Davenport that led to my inane behavior the following week. Lucky at cards, unlucky in love, they say, and as I'd proven pretty unlucky in love, I thought I'd test the other half of the expression. Which, of course, proved foolish.

The Monday after the mixer, I went to talk to Brian Schue, Terence's old roommate who now roomed with Ben Sipple. It was on the pretext of morning inspection, which I did infrequently enough as the prefects usually handled this, and I asked Ben to leave the room and give us a minute. Brian sat down at his desk and looked a bit apprehensively at me as I considered what to say. He was a slight boy with dark eyes and wavy brown hair. In a couple of years, girls would probably find him a romantic loner. I liked him. "How are you doing, Brian?" I asked.

He shrugged. "Okay, I guess."

"Any difficulty with . . . your new roommate?"

He shook his head. "No, Mr. Glass, he's okay. *I'm* okay. Thank you."

I nodded and picked up a plastic Blackburne cup from Ben's dresser, put it down again. "Brian, I feel that I need to tell you about something. Something that I found in your old room." I glanced at Brian, who was alert but out of curiosity, not fear. "In the lava lamp, actually," I added.

Brian blinked. "The lava lamp? That was Terence's. I thought you packed all that stuff up for his family."

"When I was doing that, the bottom of the lava lamp fell to the floor." I fixed Brian with a firm gaze. "Do you want to tell me anything, Brian? Because it would be better to tell me now than later."

I thought I could detect fear in his eyes. He cleared his throat. "What . . . I mean, I don't know of anything—" He looked around the room, as if he would find what I seemed to be looking for hidden in plain sight, on his bed or hanging on the wall. He was upset by what I was asking; that was clear. It seemed equally clear that he had no idea what I was talking about.

"Dip," I said. If Ren Middleton would lie by omission to hide the truth, I would lie outright to try to uncover it. "I found dip inside the lava lamp."

Brian frowned, his hair inching down so it almost fell over his eyes. "That's weird," he said. "Terence hated dip. He hated the smell and thought it looked stupid."

I continued to look straight at him. "So it wasn't yours?"

Brian shook his head. "No, sir. Honest. I just . . . It's weird he would have it, you know?"

I nodded. "Sometimes it's hard to know what people really think, or who they are." I let this silly and rather ominous-sounding piece of wisdom sink in. Then I thanked him and stepped out into the hallway, nearly colliding with Ben, who had been listening by the door.

I'm not sure what I had hoped for as a result of that meeting, although I knew that with Ben listening in, the conversation might as well have been broadcast to the entire student body. Which was what I wanted to happen. An indirect message to whoever might have been involved with Terence and his stash: *Somebody knows.* Maybe someone would come talk to me, confess to selling pot to Terence, tell me where the Vicodin had come from. Maybe someone would try to figure out what else I knew, and thereby reveal who else was involved. Half-baked at best, I know. I wasn't all that worried about Ren finding out—the students would hardly be likely to talk with him or any other faculty member.

Nobody came to my apartment door for a late-night confession. Two days after my talk with Brian, however, I walked past one of the large trash cans outside the dorm entrance and got a whiff of something violently pine scented. Looking in the bin, I could see three round cans of dip, Copenhagen Long Cut Wintergreen, half-covered by some wadded paper towels and an empty box of laundry detergent.

CHAPTER NINETEEN

Forget what T. S. Eliot said about April—February is the cruelest month. Christmas vacation is long past, and spring break seems like a mirage in the distance. The weather is cold and sodden, snow melts in your shoes, your nose runs constantly, and every classroom and dormitory smells like wet dog. Students' faces grow longer and grimmer with each passing week. The only good thing about February is that it's also the shortest month, although this fact did not bring me much comfort in my first week of February as a teacher. My students were struggling through *Macbeth*, which I had loved as a fourth former, particularly the Roman Polanski film version. With cold winds and occasional sleet buffeting the windows of the classroom, I would circle up the class to read Shakespeare aloud, trying to instill in them a love of language and a sense of the passion and the evil in the play. In response, they ducked their heads and spoke into their books, as if mortified to hear their own voices.

Listening to Stephen Watterson attempt to read Lady Macbeth's "unsex me here" speech aloud, I looked out the window at the gray morning sky and the snow on the ground and wondered how much longer I could continue being the responsible English teacher. I was much more interested in my newer role of detective.

Fate must have been listening, like a jaded old gambler who sees a fresh mark he can play, because he dealt me an early win. My laptop pinged quietly, and I turned away from the window and glanced at my screen. I had a new e-mail, two words from Trip Alexander: Call me.

TRIP WOULDN'T JUST TELL me over the phone what he'd learned but insisted that we meet in person. This aspect of detective work hadn't occurred to me—I'd envisioned an exchange of information via e-mail or a phone call, not driving across northern Virginia to meet Trip in a hotel room off the highway. But I had asked for his help, so on my free Saturday that month, I drove for two hours through sleet and bad traffic to a hotel outside of Culpeper. It was not a cheerful trip. Grimy snow and slush lined the roadside. Houses sat back from the road with a closed, brooding look. Knots of trees stood bare against a freezing rain that fell from a sky the color of iron. At one point, I passed a tow truck, its amber lights revolving, as it labored to pull a crumpled car out of a ditch.

By the time I got to Culpeper, I was in a foul mood. My shoulders ached from the stress of being hunched over my steering wheel and peering at the road through the frozen rain. I wondered why Trip was being so cloak-and-dagger. I'd asked him to find out all he could about Fritz's disappearance, but I thought it must be the second request I'd made of Trip— to find out what he could about the Davenports and NorthPoint—that was behind this clandestine rendezvous. I glanced at the small duffel I had tossed in the front seat. At the last minute, I had packed the bag, not wanting to get stuck overnight in bad weather without a change of clothes.

The Hancock Inn was a graceless stucco box. Dark stains ran down the walls by the downspouts. If possible, an overnight visit was now even less appealing. The parking lot was half-empty. I pulled into a space near the front entrance and called Trip on my cell. "I'm here," I said when he picked up.

"Room two-twelve," he said, and hung up.

I stared at my phone, trying to formulate an appropriate response to this

Mickey Mouse bullshit. Then I stuffed the phone into my coat pocket and got out of the car. I passed through the glass front doors and into the lobby with its heavy wooden furniture upholstered in a shocking maroon-and-green floral pattern. The desk clerk glanced up at me with a painted-on smile and then went back to her magazine when it was clear I wasn't there to book a room.

When I found Trip's room on the second floor, I knocked on the door, and after a moment, Trip opened it. He looked as if he had slept in his clothes, but he was grinning. "Hey," he said, grasping me by the shoulder and drawing me into the room. "Thanks for coming. Bad drive?"

"Bad enough," I said. "What's with all this sneaking-around crap, anyway? We meeting with Deep Throat or something?"

I took a few steps into the room and froze. It was a typical hotel room—two queen-sized beds facing a long dresser with a built-in TV, and two chairs flanking a small table at the far end of the room. What was atypical was the man in a khaki-and-green uniform who stood up from one of the chairs. "Deep Throat, my ass," he said. It was Diamond.

I stood gaping at him for a few seconds. I hadn't seen Diamond since graduation. Now he was standing in front of me in a military uniform, rows of multicolored ribbons over his left breast pocket. His cornrows were gone, his hair shorn so close he was nearly bald. "Diamond," I said. "What the fuck?"

He grinned. "Still haven't cleaned up your language, have you, Fuck-head?" he said, and the sound of his rich, deep voice suddenly made it true—Daryl Cooper was standing in front of me. I held out my hand, which Diamond took and squeezed, and then he pulled me to him. Startled, I leaned back, resisting for half a second, until I realized he was trying to hug me. I relented, awkwardly clapping him on the back.

"So what the hell, man?" I asked, pulling back. "You're in the army?"

Diamond punched me in the arm—it was playful punch, but it still felt like someone had whacked me in the arm with a baseball bat. "Marines, fool," he said. "I'm no army doggie."

Trip said, "This here is Captain Cooper, Matthias. Marine adjutant at the Pentagon."

I stared at Trip and then at Diamond. "But . . . you were going to Duke," I said. "On a football scholarship."

"Still did," Diamond said. "Then Nine/Eleven happened, and I talked to a recruiter and joined ROTC by December. When I graduated, the Corps sent me to Iraq."

"You fought in Iraq?"

Diamond nodded. "Anbar Province, Ramadi, Haditha. Lots of places."

Trip smiled faintly. "You really ought to read the alumni magazine, Matthias."

I dimly recalled reading somewhere about Anbar being one of the more difficult areas of Iraq for American troops and their allies—the insurgents had been based there, or something. I'd shaken my head when I'd read in the papers about casualties from suicide bombers and the like in Iraq, but I'd had no idea Diamond was there. It made sense—if Diamond was going to be a marine, he'd want to be right in the thick of it.

"So," I said, making an effort to be lighthearted, "you got moved stateside to a desk job. How'd you manage that?"

Diamond plucked at his right pant leg and lifted it up to reveal a metallic, skeletal limb. "Lost my leg below the knee from an RPG outside Ramadi," he said. "Not exactly suitable for running across the desert after al-Qaeda."

I stared at Diamond's leg, or what was left of it. The rest of him looked fine—hell, he still looked like a bronzed Perseus come to life—and he'd spoken of losing his leg matter-of-factly, without a hint of regret or self-pity, but I was stunned. I couldn't wrap my head around all of this. The indelible image I had always had of Diamond was of him running effortlessly on the football field, the ball cradled safely in one arm. Now he stood before me on a prosthetic leg. I had a sudden unpleasant image of Diamond and Pelham Greer, the Blackburne groundskeeper, comparing stumps. Diamond had been my roommate and my friend, and I hadn't even bothered to try to see him after we graduated.

"Matthias, you okay?" Trip asked.

I nodded. "Just need to sit down," I said. The room shimmered for a moment, like heat waves off summer-hot asphalt, and then I was sitting on the edge of a bed, blinking dazedly. "Water," I managed to say. Trip ducked into the bathroom. I heard water running, and then he reemerged with a plastic cup, which he almost spilled in his haste.

Diamond looked at me and gave a short grunt of a laugh. "He's all right," he said to Trip. "Just smiled at something. Probably laughing at you running over here like his mother with a glass of water."

"Drink this," Trip said to me. "Ignore the marine. Come on, drink it."

I took the cup and waved Trip off. "I can drink it all by myself, honest," I said. "I just . . . got dizzy for a second. Lot to take in." I took a sip of water and concentrated on breathing. "I guess I almost fainted," I said after a few moments. "Never happened to me before."

"Well," Diamond said, "I have been known to have that effect on people. Though typically they look much better than you."

Trip and Diamond pulled up chairs and sat across from me, perched on the edge of the bed. "So," I said, feeling on the cusp of something momentous—a feeling that, at the same time, I found ludicrous. "Don't take this the wrong way, guys, but why the surprise reunion? And why meet in some hotel outside of Culpeper? Why not in D.C.?"

"Because D.C.'s wired six ways to Sunday with surveillance," Trip said.

I smiled. "What, Big Brother is watching us?"

Diamond's mouth quirked. "You have no idea," he said.

Trip said, "I called Diamond and asked if he would help me with a little research."

"About Fritz?" I asked.

Trip looked at Diamond and then back at me. "About his father's company, NorthPoint."

I turned to Diamond, whose face was expressionless. "What do you know about NorthPoint?" I asked. I think I kept my voice relatively calm.

Trip and Diamond glanced at each other. "Just so we're clear," Diamond said, "I am saying and doing nothing that compromises national security."

"Um, okay," I said. "Do I need to take some kind of oath or something?"

In a low voice, Trip said, "He's serious, Matthias."

I raised my hands in mock surrender. "Okay, I get it. I'm not asking anybody to compromise national security, for Christ's sake. I just want to know what happened to Fritz. Do you know something, Diamond? Trip?"

A few moments passed in taut silence. Then Trip and Diamond both leaned forward to talk, and then stopped, unwilling to interrupt each other. Curiously, it was Diamond who leaned back and gestured to Trip to start.

"Okay," Trip said, running his hands through his hair as if slicking it back. "NorthPoint's been contracting with the government for years, ever since Fritz's father started it back in the eighties. But since Nine/Eleven, it's mushroomed. More office buildings, more employees, lots of new areas of interest."

"What does that have to do with Fritz?"

"I'll get there," Trip said. "Just follow me. NorthPoint was a privately owned company until 1997 when they went public. They needed investor money, and they got it. Allowed them to push through R and D in several areas, get more contracts with Uncle Sam, and become a major player. I couldn't find any financials on NorthPoint before 'ninety-seven—one of the privileges of being a privately owned company up to that point—but I was able to find budget info for them after they went public. And in 2000, they had one curious item: a three-hundred-thousand-dollar increase in payment to Alliance, a private detective firm in Reston, Virginia."

I tamped down my irritation and played along. "So they hired private detectives," I said. "What's the big deal?"

"Why would a security company earning millions of dollars a year hire private detectives?" Trip asked. "They'd have their own guys. Why hire outside people?" He looked at me encouragingly, but I shrugged, not getting it. "Corporate espionage," Trip said. "Companies spying on companies, stealing trade secrets, research, technology. This isn't like Pepsi trying to steal Coke's formula, though. This is one IT company trying to steal another IT company's latest project so they can develop it. Problem is, the latest project is a government contract, which means money and power and—if the wrong people get their hands on the project—maybe even a threat to national security. So companies like these will hire private detectives to dig up dirt on competitors, or find out who leaked details about the new gizmo to another company. In December of 2000, NorthPoint's budget for private detective services spiked."

"Why?" I asked.

"Don't know. Which is why I called Captain Cooper." Trip turned to Diamond with a light flourish. For his part, Diamond just sat in his chair, shoulders back, feet flat on the floor, hands resting on his knees. "He's involved in military intel," Trip continued. "Which is why he's very clear about what he will and will not share."

I shook my head. "The Marines are involved in . . . spying? I thought that was the CIA."

Diamond snorted. "Every service branch has an intelligence service," he said. "Army, navy, air force, coast guard. And most definitely the Corps."

Trip leaned forward. "Matthias, this goes beyond the military or organizations like the CIA. There's an entire community in America that thrives on top-secret work. And when I say community, I'm not talking about some secret town in the desert. I'm talking about more than a thousand government organizations, two thousand private companies."

I took this in for a second. "Private companies like NorthPoint," I said.

Diamond and Trip both nodded. It was Diamond's turn to sit forward. "NorthPoint works with the Corps, the navy, NSA, DIA," he said. "Cyber ops is one area they're involved in."

"Cyber ops?"

"Cyber operations," Diamond said. "Digital espionage and warfare. Imagine attacking an enemy through his computer network, crippling his communications, his logistics. Or stealing intel by hacking into his database. Designing defenses to keep others from doing the same to your computer systems. That's one area NorthPoint is into, big-time. Add in surveillance technology, satellite imagery, technical intelligence of all kinds, and North-Point is a player. Upward of a billion dollars in revenue a year."

Stubbornly, I said, "I still don't see what this has to do with Fritz."

Diamond held up a finger, as if shushing me. "Three months before Fritz disappeared, NorthPoint dropped a lot of cash on private detectives. More than twice what they'd ever spent before."

"That doesn't mean the two are connected."

"True," Diamond said. "It's simply a point of reference." Now he held up two fingers. "Point number two," he said. "After Fritz goes missing, the feds get involved. Then one week later, they drop it. That didn't make sense to me. Your deputy friend was right—the FBI doesn't get involved and then just walk away. So I talked to a buddy of mine at Justice, ex-marine. He did some digging and told me that the Davenports called an old friend of theirs at the FBI, two days after Fritz went missing. Friend's name is Jeff Jacobsen. He was assistant director of the FBI's cyber division. Soon after that, the FBI shows up at Blackburne."

I was growing frustrated. "Diamond, we already *know* they called the FBI."

Diamond shook his head. "Not *they*, Matthias. It was Mary Davenport who called."

I frowned. "Mrs. Davenport? Fritz's mother?"

Now Trip spoke. "Jacobsen wasn't just an old family friend. He dated a girl named Mary Gillespie in college. She broke up with Jacobsen to go out with another classmate, Frank Davenport. And now she's Fritz's mother."

I stared at him. "Exactly how much did you find out about the Davenports?"

Trip shrugged. "You asked me to dig. I dug."

I got up off the bed and started pacing around. I'd discovered while teaching that I liked to do this when I thought, especially out loud. "Okay, so what? Mrs. Davenport calls up an old boyfriend at the FBI. Makes sense. Her son's missing. I'd do the same thing."

Diamond looked at me. "It was Fritz's dad who called Jacobsen back and told him to drop it."

I stopped pacing and sat down on the bed again. I felt I needed something solid underneath me. "Mrs. Davenport calls an old boyfriend to ask for help in finding her son," I said slowly, "and within a week her husband calls the same guy and tells him to stop looking. Why the fuck would he do that?"

"Had to be difficult for both of them," Trip said. "Mary Davenport calls up Jacobsen, who she dumped in college, and asks him for help finding her son, and then Frank Davenport calls Jacobsen and tells him to quit helping."

"Why would Jacobsen listen to Davenport?" I asked.

"Money," Diamond said. "NorthPoint had a contract with the FBI to help them upgrade their IT systems, which sucked, frankly. Jacobsen ran the cyber division, so he was in charge of managing the contract on the FBI's end."

"So, what, Davenport threatened to break the contract?"

Trip gave a wry grin. "Nothing like blackmailing the FBI," he said. "And it worked. Would've cost millions if NorthPoint had walked away and the FBI had to start over. Jacobsen would've been demoted or fired."

I stared. "You have proof of all this, I'm assuming."

Trip snorted. "*Legal* proof, as in court of law? Not a chance. But it's what happened, or something close to it. I've got my own sources at Justice that confirm what Diamond found out."

I sat on the bed, rubbing my hands on my knees and trying to comprehend all of this. "This is the point where you tell me what this has to do with Fritz," I said.

"Let's assume," Trip said, "that the Davenports really wanted to find out what happened to their son. Calling in the FBI makes sense. But when the feds start poking around—and they are nothing if not thorough, these guys—who knows what they might find."

I stared at them both. "Something big enough to keep the Davenports from wanting to find their son?"

"Big enough to want them to get rid of the FBI, anyway," Diamond said.

I shook my head, remembering Mr. Davenport's anger and frustration almost boiling off him. "You didn't see Fritz's dad," I said. "After Fritz vanished, he came to our room. He wanted . . ." I paused, searching my memory. "He wanted to know where Fritz was," I said slowly, still thinking. "But he asked me—he asked me something else. Before he screamed at me, he asked me . . ." Various scenes cycled through my brain, and suddenly I was watching the right one. "He asked me what Fritz *said*. He wanted to know what Fritz and I had talked about."

Trip frowned. "I don't get it."

"What if Fritz knew something, something about NorthPoint? And his dad wanted to know if he'd said something—something to me?"

Trip shook his head, still frowning. "Why would Fritz say something to you about his father's business?"

I ignored him. "Three months earlier, NorthPoint hired private detectives and paid them for a lot of work. What if they were up to something illegal? Or they were helping cover up something illegal that NorthPoint had done?"

"And two months after Nine/Eleven," Diamond said, nodding slowly in agreement, "NorthPoint wins a contract with CENTCOM. Had to do with miniaturizing electromagnetic spectrum sensors. The kind of thing used on Predator drones. You can guess how much that was worth. If that had fallen through, NorthPoint might have stalled and missed out on all that government cash."

Trip raised his arms, palms up and spread apart. "Are you suggesting what I think you're suggesting?"

"I'm looking for a motive," I said.

"You think *Davenport* had his son disappear?"

"I don't *know*, Trip. That's why we're meeting."

"We're *meeting* because you asked me to dig into the Davenports. And I found some evidence to suggest that Davenport called off the feds because they might find out something that would ruin his company, not that he . . . *offed* his own kid."

I thought again about Mr. Davenport in my room, surging up in my face and screaming at me. Was this the behavior of a concerned parent at the breaking point? Or of someone desperate to hide something?

"Does Mrs. Davenport have anything to do with NorthPoint?" I asked.

Trip blinked, clearly not expecting this. "No," he said. "She helps raise money for charities, organizes flower shows, things like that. Nothing to do with NorthPoint."

"Okay," I said, "so Mrs. Davenport just wants her son back, which is why she calls the FBI. But Mr. Davenport quietly arranges for the FBI to get off the case. He knows something his wife doesn't. Another point in favor of NorthPoint being involved somehow."

Trip shook his head again. "I don't think Frank Davenport had his son . . . *erased.* I don't buy it."

"You're telling me the thought didn't cross your mind?"

"For about a second before it died a righteous death. The parents are the *first* people the cops look at. And Frank Davenport isn't a fool. He could convince the feds not to look into NorthPoint, but he couldn't keep them away if there was even a hint that he murdered his own son. There's no way, Matthias. Diamond, help me out here."

I looked at Diamond. His military uniform was crisp, his shoes polished so they shone like dark mirrors. *He's killed people,* I thought suddenly. My old roommate had probably shot and killed insurgents in Iraq. The thought seemed to blow a fuse in my brain; for a moment, I couldn't comprehend anything but the idea that Diamond had taken someone else's life. Slowly, Diamond shook his head. "I'm with Trip on this one, Matthias. It's not impossible, but I don't think it's likely. I've met Davenport a couple of times. He's ruthless, and maybe he did something that he didn't want exposed, but I don't see him hiring someone to kill Fritz. Too risky, makes him too vulnerable." He eyed me. "That doesn't answer your question, though."

"Question?"

He shrugged, almost sadly. "What happened to Fritz?" he said.

I glanced at Trip, who sat back as if my glance had pushed him back into his seat. "Don't even think about asking me to look into that," he said. "I've used up a lot of favors to get this info. No way am I going to start asking people whether or not they think Frank Davenport could have had his own son disappear."

"I get that," I said. "And thanks for what you've found. But you think Fritz's disappearance might somehow be tied into NorthPoint?"

Trip shrugged. "Looks possible. Although we don't know how."

Slowly, I nodded. "Okay," I said. "No worries. I've got another idea."

A FEW HOURS LATER, evening fell as I drove into Washington. I'd been to D.C. several times, mostly on day trips from Blackburne when I was a student, and my view of the nation's capital was complicated, a blend of postcard images of the White House and the Capitol with a kind of nausea of the soul, an inherent distaste for political machinations. Overlying all of this was a thin but bright layer of romantic idealism, like a coat of varnish on a moldering but beloved oil painting. No matter how cynical I could be, there was something about driving over the Potomac on the

Teddy Roosevelt Bridge and seeing the crystalline blaze of the Kennedy Center reflected in the water, or the white columns of the Lincoln Memorial, or the obelisk of the Washington Monument thrust into the indigo sky—these sights gladdened and quickened something within me. It was not without regret that as soon as I crossed the river, I curved to the left, leaving the familiar sight of the Kennedy Center behind as I headed for K Street and Georgetown.

Soon I found my destination, an impressive brick town house near Twenty-Sixth and P Street. By a stroke of luck, I found a parking spot only two blocks away and walked through the bitter night air, my feet crunching on road salt and the icy remnants of the storm that had tapered off that afternoon. I felt as if a cold block of marble were lying against the exposed skin on the back of my neck. But the view of the town house was almost as salutary as a good fire. The structure was in the Federal style, neatly proportioned but clearly renovated and painted a dark terra-cotta. The windows gave off a warm glow, while the black shutters gleamed in the soft light thrown by the streetlamps. The brass knocker on the front door was the size of a ship's anchor. After foregoing the knocker for the doorbell, I heard the muffled chimes of the opening passage of Mozart's *Marriage of Figaro* ring inside.

Footsteps, then a murmured exchange followed by laughter. The doorknob turned with a solid *chunk*, and the door swung open to reveal Wat Davenport in a charcoal-gray flannel suit, a highball glass in one hand. His smooth, tanned face creased in a smile. "Matthias, there you are. Get in here out of the cold." He stepped aside, ushering me in.

In the foyer, which was flanked by white built-ins and mantled with a coffered ceiling, stood another man, shorter, less commanding than Wat. He wore the navy-blue suit of someone in government. Wat turned to the man and said, "Bob, this is Matthias Glass, an old family friend."

Bob's handshake and greeting were polite and perfunctory, and as he stepped past me for the door, he turned his head and said, "Thanks again, Wat. I'm forever grateful."

Wat beamed. "A fact I shall surely remind you of," he said. "Say hi to Doris for me."

After the door shut behind Bob, I turned to Wat. "I didn't interrupt anything, did I?"

Wat waved his hand, the gesture both a dismissal and a benediction. "Business. What else?"

"Is he a client?"

"Oh, no. A congressman." Wat took me by the arm. "Let me show you around."

The town house was a series of bright, open spaces anchored by neutral-toned couches and armchairs, with strategically placed throw pillows of vibrant orange. Modern, abstract artwork hung on the walls, creating the sense of a place that was somewhere between a gallery and a home. A stacked pile of logs burned cheerfully in a massive white fireplace. Classical music played from hidden speakers—Beethoven, maybe, or Tchaikovsky. We passed through a formal dining room with heavy drapes and slipcovered chairs and walked into the kitchen, a sleek affair of wood and chrome and marble countertops. Here, Wat topped off his whiskey and poured me a glass of wine. "Abby told me she'd seen you," he said, corking the bottle. "At the Game."

I took a rather large sip of excellent Shiraz, stalling. I had no intention of talking about how that meeting with Abby had gone. "Um-hmm," I managed. "Yes, I did. See her."

Wat chuckled and tucked the bottle into a cupboard. "Obviously it was a warm reunion," he said. "All right, I won't torture you about it, although I confess I am sad that you and Abby didn't work out." He gestured to the living room. "Shall we?"

We ensconced ourselves in a pair of armchairs by the fire. "So," Wat said with the air of a man who has had a good meal and a good drink and is prepared to grant favors. "What can I do for you? Your call sounded urgent."

Now that I was here, I hesitated. I had called him that afternoon because I needed to talk to somebody involved with NorthPoint, somebody who, I hoped, would be willing to talk to me and confirm what Trip and Diamond had told me. But now I felt like this was not the wisest course of action. I was about to invoke the Davenport family ghost, not to mention inquire about NorthPoint. Was this a patently stupid idea?

As if reading my mind, Wat smiled. "You can trust me, Matthias," he said. "You were a good friend to my nephew, and no matter what my brother might think, you are my friend as well."

"What your brother might think?" I couldn't help it—the comment bothered me.

Wat glanced down at his glass, took a sip. "Frank is a difficult man," he said. "Of course, Fritz's disappearance took its toll on him. He sees enemies that don't exist, plots that aren't there."

I saw Frank Davenport looming in front of me in my dorm room at Blackburne, screaming in my face. This from the man who had gotten the FBI to drop its investigation into his own son's disappearance. I found I was clutching the stem of my wineglass so hard, I thought it might snap, so I set it down on the coffee table in front of me. *Fuck him*, I thought. "Actually, I need to talk to you about Fritz," I said. "About his disappearance."

Wat's eyebrows rose, but only a millimeter or so, and he sat patiently as I told him the condensed version of Fritz's disappearance and what I had recently learned: Fritz's leaving his medal under my pillow, his father's screaming at me in our dorm room, my interview with Pelham Greer and subsequent realization that Fritz had left campus much later than anybody had thought, Deputy Briggs's story of the FBI. I left out Trip's and Diamond's contributions. Wat said nothing as I talked, just kept his gaze leveled at me and paid attention. When I finished, he got up, went into the kitchen, and came back with the wine and the whiskey and filled our glasses. Then he sat down. When he spoke, his voice sounded worn. "My nephew has been missing for nearly ten years," he said. "An entire decade. And now you suspect that my brother may have kept him from being found."

"I'm not saying it was intentional—" I started, but Wat cut me off with a sharp sweep of his arm.

"You want to know if I know anything," he said. "If I can shed any light." He took a good swallow of his drink and then looked at me. For the first time all evening, he seemed to be really seeing me. "I loved Fritz. I don't have any children of my own, but he and Abby always filled that role. The day he disappeared . . ." He paused, blinking. The pain in his eyes was hard to bear, and I dropped my gaze before it.

After a moment, Wat continued, his voice under control. "You know that I no longer work for NorthPoint," he said. He must have seen the surprise on my face. "I consult from time to time, but I'm not involved with day-to-day operations. I haven't been for years. Not since—since Fritz disappeared." He paused, seeming to gather himself like a diver at the top of a tower. "In 2000," he continued, "I was chief operating officer at NorthPoint. That December, we found evidence that someone was trying to steal some of our research. Encryption software, mostly, although we also learned some work we'd done on miniaturization was at risk. My brother and I hired a private detective firm, as we weren't sure we could trust our own security. Long story short, they found one of our technicians and a security officer were on a Chinese payroll. We fired them before they did any serious damage. But Frank was livid. We were negotiating contracts with the Pentagon right then, and if word had gotten out about these two NorthPoint employees passing secrets to China . . . well, in all likelihood I would be living in a split-level outside of Richmond right now instead of here in Georgetown. Those were our first real contracts, Matthias. They *made* NorthPoint." He smiled wanly. "This all came to a head a month before Fritz vanished. You can imagine how that shook Frank and Mary, and Abby. And then when the FBI wanted to poke around . . ." He shrugged and finished his drink.

"You didn't want them finding out about the private detectives and the Chinese spies," I said.

Wat laughed, a short, bitter sound. "It sounds like a bad movie, doesn't it? Chinese spies!" He sighed. "In my brother's defense, he thought Fritz would turn up in a matter of days. The FBI didn't seem necessary. Of course, he was wrong. I argued that we should let the authorities investigate, tell them everything. But Frank was scared. NorthPoint had gone public three years earlier, and we'd spent a lot of investor money to get to where we were in 2000. If we had lost those Pentagon contracts, North-Point wouldn't even be a memory today. So Frank got the FBI to drop it." He looked at me, and something in his stare—a cold certitude—made me catch my breath. "And because of that, I resigned. I left within the month, long enough for Frank to assure the Pentagon that he could cover for me." Wat smiled acidly. "Mustn't let anything happen to NorthPoint. Frank's golden goose. Which he didn't want cooked."

I sat back in my chair, deflated. Wat's story explained what Trip and Diamond had found, and it did so in a way that didn't make Frank Davenport into some sort of a monster who would kill his own child. But I was still no closer to finding Fritz. Disillusionment washed over me. I realized I was actually disappointed that Frank Davenport probably had nothing to do with his son's disappearance.

Wat leaned forward. "I'm sorry I don't have anything more for you. Something that could help you find Fritz. That's what you're doing, isn't it? Looking for him?"

I gave a resentful snort of laughter. "I'm beginning to think that's all I've been doing since he disappeared," I said. "Even when I didn't know I was doing it, when I was actively trying *not* to do that. I've been waiting for

him all these years like he'll walk back in through the door. And he hasn't."
I looked at Wat. "What do *you* think happened to him?"

Wat blinked in surprise. "I don't know," he said simply. "I've thought
about it ever since. He *must* have had his reasons for leaving. I know . . .
I know that my brother can be a hard man, and that he and Fritz did not
always see eye to eye, but I don't see Frank as capable of murdering his
own son." I stared at him, and he laughed weakly. "That's what you were
wondering, isn't it?" he asked. "It's all right. I've wondered it myself, lying
awake at night. But . . . no. I can see him driving his child away. Not killing him."

"Could the two guys you fired, the ones passing secrets to the Chinese—
could they have had anything to do with Fritz's disappearance?"

Wat shook his head. "Frank hired another firm to investigate them.
They didn't find anything. Frank made them look again, and they did.
Still nothing. Just a couple of employees who got greedy. They weren't
kidnappers or anything like that." He sighed. "Frank really wanted it to
have been them," he said softly.

Wat fell silent after that, but he sat with me while I stared into the burning logs, as if I'd find some augury there.

CHAPTER TWENTY

I spent the night in Wat's guest room at his insistence—he wouldn't hear of my going to a hotel. So much had happened that day that I thought I might be up all night, my brain spinning away as it tried to process everything. But after retrieving my duffel from the car and walking upstairs to my room, I felt exhausted, limbs heavy as marble, and when I fell into bed, I slept a gray, dreamless sleep. The next morning, I woke and sat up bleary-eyed in a strange room, struggling for several seconds to understand where I was. I took a quick shower, trying to slough off the night's sleep and largely succeeding. Once dressed, I padded downstairs in my socks to find, in the kitchen, a smiling Korean woman who was evidently the housekeeper. She directed me toward a pot of hot coffee, a plate of muffins, and an elegantly handwritten note from Wat:

Matthias,

    My apologies for not being at home when you wake up, but I have an early meeting.

    I'd cancel, but it's with someone from the vice president's office. Far duller than it sounds, trust me.

    Thank you for calling on me. I appreciate it far more than you know.

Keep in touch and let me know if I can ever be of service—my cell phone number is on the card I left with this note.

Sun Hi will take care of you if you need anything. Safe journey back to Blackburne.

Wat

I looked at Wat's business card—bold serif script on cream-colored paper heavy and stiff as a credit card—and put it in my wallet.

After breakfast I wrote Wat a short thank-you note and left. The storm was completely gone, leaving a clear blue sky behind. It took more than three hours to get back to Blackburne, a long time to ponder what I had learned from Trip and Diamond and Wat, which was both a lot and not much. Mrs. Davenport had called the FBI to help find her son. Mr. Davenport had called them off for fear of uncovering some unflattering truths about NorthPoint. Wat Davenport had resigned in protest. None of this helped me find Fritz.

I should have taken my time getting back, because when I finally turned into Blackburne's drive and drove past the lions and up the Hill, and then circled around behind Lawson-Parker, I found a sheriff's patrol car parked by the rear entrance. Something cold and hard formed in my gut. Had there been another accident? Another student death? I went inside the dorm and ducked into the commons room, but no one was there, so I hurried down the hall to my apartment, opened the door, and stepped inside.

The first person I saw was Sam Hodges, sitting on my futon. He looked startled, as if I had woken him up. Behind him, putting a magazine down on a side table, was Deputy Smalls.

"Sam?" I said.

Sam stood up, slowly. "Matthias," he said.

Ren Middleton walked around the corner from my kitchen. "Mr. Glass," he said.

"What's going on?" I said.

Deputy Smalls stepped around the futon toward me. "Mr. Glass, I have to inform you that you are under arrest."

I blinked—it was as if he had slapped me across the face. "What?"

"How could you," Ren said.

"How could I *what?*" I said, growing angry. "Sam, what's going on?"

"Mr. Glass, you are under arrest for possession and intent to distribute illegal narcotics," Deputy Smalls said. He took a pair of handcuffs from his belt. "Please turn around, sir."

Whatever anger had risen in me vanished in the face of Smalls and his handcuffs, and, numbly, I complied. Smalls snapped one of the cuffs over my right wrist, brought it up to the small of my back, and then brought my left hand up, snapping the second bracelet over my left wrist. As he was cuffing me, Smalls went through the Miranda litany: "You have the right to an attorney, anything you say can and will be used against you." The entire time, incredulous, I watched Sam's face. I had to look over my shoulder to do this. His expression ran the gamut from uncertainty to disbelief to sadness. It was this last image of Sam's sad face that lingered long after Smalls turned me around and swiftly and professionally escorted me out of my apartment to the parking lot and into his cruiser, placing his hand on my head to steer me into the backseat. Stunned as I was, I did manage to feel thankful that no students appeared to have seen me led in handcuffs to a police car. Just then, I saw Stephen Watterson, standing, mouth open, in the glassed-in second-floor walkway. He stared at me as I was placed in the backseat of the cruiser.

THE MIDDLE RIVER REGIONAL Jail had two large holding cells. One was empty and dark. They put me in the second one. A dozen people eyed me lazily when another deputy escorted me in and closed the cell door behind me with a hollow clang. I found a spot on a bench and sat down, rubbing my hands over my head. *This would be funny,* I thought, *if I weren't sitting in a jail cell with an open toilet in the corner.* As if he could hear my thoughts, one of the other prisoners stood, ambled over to the toilet, dropped trou, and squatted on it.

For hours, it seemed, I just sat there, staring at the mottled concrete floor and the drain in its center. I tried to get a hold on what was happening. Deputy Smalls had told me that a student had found a plastic bag with three buds and a handful of Oxycontin pills in my classroom desk and told Ren Middleton, who had called Sheriff Townsend. Smalls had been dispatched to my apartment, where he had found traces of marijuana. My stating emphatically that the marijuana in the classroom desk wasn't mine didn't seem to make an impression on Smalls, or perhaps his carefully neutral expression was simply a professional necessity. Or maybe he was used to people protesting their innocence when they were hauled to jail. Staring at the cross-hatching of the metal drain in the floor, I wondered about my students, about who would teach them now. Would someone pass them back their papers, which I had graded and were in my workbag next to the futon in what had been my apartment? Would my students want to read my comments, or would they just talk about how I'd been arrested? What would happen to the boys who lived on my dorm? The look on Stephen Watterson's face as he stared at me in handcuffs floated in my head like a hangover.

Sitting in that cell, I considered my prospects, which weren't cheerful. My job was gone, for one thing—that was certain. One didn't remain a teacher for long if one was handcuffed and marched out of school in front of students. I was apparently going to need a lawyer, but while a female deputy had said something about public defenders and arraignment hearings, I'd been unable to process what she said. I did know that if I wanted to get out of jail, I would need bail money, but as that would likely involve calling my parents, I balked and refrained from asking the guard for my phone call. I felt I would rather have my teeth pulled out of my mouth without the benefit of anesthesia than call my mother and father and ask them to bail me out of jail. Whom else could I call? Sam Hodges's face had been like a closing door. Gray Smith, who for the past several months had covered for me on dorm duty after I had gently harassed him, would probably hang up, and I was pretty sure he didn't have much in the way of available cash. I briefly considered calling Wat Davenport but buried that thought out of a mixture of shame and pride. That morning I had been eating blueberry muffins in Wat's Georgetown home; it seemed indecent, somehow, to call him that afternoon from jail. Trip was a possibility, but I held back for the same reasons I wouldn't call Wat. Abby? Right. It was like some sort of Kafkaesque test of friendship: Whom could you call if you were incarcerated? Maybe I could call Diamond and have the Marines bust me out. Or I could pull a Jason Bourne, disarm the one overweight deputy, who appeared to be endlessly reading the same magazine at his station across the hall, climb up the wall to the window at the top, and wriggle out.

The dinner they served us was on a heavy cardboard tray with corn, carrots, applesauce, and some sort of mystery meat. Two deputies passed out the trays in the cell, along with grade-school-sized cartons of milk. I ate mechanically, not because I was hungry but because it was something to do.

After dinner, I was thinking about calling Wat Davenport, and my pride be damned, when the fat deputy got a call on his cell phone, grunted into it, and folded it shut. "Glass!" he called out. I raised my hand, like a kid answering roll call in class. "Step up," he said. "You've got a visitor."

THE JAIL'S VISITING ROOM followed Hollywood conventions to the letter—the camera mounted in a corner of the ceiling, the uniformed deputy scanning the room, even down to the rows of booths and the glass barriers between prisoners and visitors.

Out of eighteen booths, only one, at the far left, was occupied—a thin, bearded prisoner was talking to a tired-looking woman with graying hair. Someone could have taken a photograph of the two and titled it *Despair* and sold it in a gallery. The fat deputy steered me to the middle booth, where I saw Lester Briggs waiting for me. He was wearing the same plaid shirt he'd worn when we'd met in the Fir Tree.

I pulled out my chair and sat down across from Briggs, who leaned forward to talk at me through the glass. "You okay?" he asked.

"I'm incarcerated, Lloyd," I said. Briggs blinked. "It's from a movie," I said. "Forget it." I wanted to giggle. No—I wanted to laugh out loud, guffaw in the face of the deputy in the corner at the absurdity of all of it: *this is just too fucking funny!*

Briggs moved his jaw a bit as if mulling over his words. "Your arraignment won't be until tomorrow at the earliest," he said. "You'll want to make bail then."

I chose to continue ignoring reality and smiled. "And how much would bail be?" I asked lightly.

Briggs thought for a moment. "First-time offender with possession of drugs on school grounds, you're looking at twenty thousand, give or take."

My attempt at lighthearted indifference evaporated. "Twenty thousand *dollars?*"

"Maybe more with the charge of intent to distribute."

All the air in my lungs seemed to have been sucked away, leaving behind an empty void. *This isn't happening*, I thought. Twenty thousand dollars? My stomach curled into a fist. "I'm a high school English teacher," I managed to say. *Was*, I realized, but tamped down the thought and kept going. "I don't have that kind of money."

Briggs raised his eyebrows slightly. "Aren't you going to protest your innocence?"

"You know I didn't sell any fucking drugs," I said, my voice rising. To my left, the bearded prisoner leaned back out of his booth to look at me.

Briggs looked at me for a good ten seconds, long enough for me to shift in my chair, but I didn't break eye contact with him. "No," he said slowly. "I don't think you did."

For some reason, this made me feel slightly better.

The comfort didn't last long. "So, do you smoke?" Briggs asked. "Or pop oxy?" He didn't think I was selling drugs to Blackburne students, just that I might be getting high in my apartment.

"I—no," I said. "No. I mean, I have before—I've smoked pot—but not now. And not at Blackburne." I took a breath and made a quick decision. "Somebody put that in my desk to set me up." And I told him about finding the pot in Terence Jarrar's lava lamp, about holding on to it instead of turning it in immediately, and about my half-assed plan to let whoever was selling at Blackburne know that I knew. Briggs's eyebrows rose fractionally higher.

"That was stupid," he said.

"Obviously."

He tilted his head to the side, like a bird considering whether to stay or fly off. "You haven't asked me why I'm here," he said.

"My apologies. Why are you here?"

"I wanted to ask you if you'd learned anything about the series of events we discussed last fall."

My heart gave an odd squeeze. "You want to know if I've learned anything about the Davenports," I said.

Briggs glanced at the couple at the far end, who had quit looking at us and were back to droning quietly at each other. The fat deputy in the corner was pointedly looking away from us. Briggs leaned forward. "Have you? Found out anything?"

"Can you get me out of here?" I asked. "I'll tell you what I've found out."

Briggs twisted his mouth—it could have been the beginnings of a smile—and then put his hands together briefly so that he appeared ready to fall on his knees and pray. "First things first," he said. "You need to get a lawyer. Then you need to call somebody about making bail. Family, friends, a bail bondsman, whatever. Then you'll need to go to your arraignment."

As he continued outlining the steps I needed to take, something lifted in my chest. The shame and humiliation of having been arrested, of finding myself removed from society and placed in a jail cell, were astounding. A sodden darkness had fallen on me, momentarily extinguishing any thoughts about how I had ended up in here, or what I would do once I got out. But Briggs was a lantern in a coal mine. His gruff, businesslike manner, plus the fact that he understood the criminal justice system far better than I did and apparently knew all the deputies in the jail, rekindled something in me. It was less like hope and more like anger.

"Someone planted that stuff in my classroom," I said aloud, cutting across whatever Briggs was saying. "Someone at Blackburne."

Briggs watched me patiently. I found myself wanting to pace back and forth, but instead I sat in the chair in front of the window and drummed my fingers on the countertop.

"It's got to be whoever's behind selling drugs at Blackburne," I continued. I had two ideas about this, too. Either some of Paul Simmons's friends were in on the drugs and were pissed that he'd been sent to Utah, or Ren Middleton was involved in more than wanting to avoid a lawsuit and had decided that waiting until the end of the school year to get rid of me was no longer an option.

Briggs nodded slowly. "Makes sense," he said. "Getting you arrested gets you out of the way. Although my guess is whoever did this won't stick around."

I frowned. "Why not?" I asked. "I mean, he's winning, right? I'm in here."

Briggs snorted. "You won't be in here for long," he said, shaking his head. "They arrested you because of what they found in a desk in the classroom where you teach. They didn't find it under your pillow or in your underwear. It's a weak bust."

"But it's my classroom."

"You the only one who teaches in there?"

I had to think for a minute. Matt McGuire taught a Spanish class in there—classroom space was tight in Huber Hall due to ongoing renovations. "No, there's another teacher who has a class in there. But I'm not gonna say that he—"

"You're not going to say anything—your lawyer is. Have you got one yet?"

"Kinda hoped you might have a suggestion."

He actually grinned at this, and again I saw the sudden warmth of his smile, banishing at least for the moment whatever dark clouds had still been hanging over my head. "I've got a cousin who's a lawyer. He's not cheap, but he won't cheat you. Now, this classroom where you teach. You said someone else teaches in there, too. There a lock on the desk?"

"No."

"Classroom door locked?"

"No."

Briggs held out his hands, palms up, as if presenting me with an answer. "Like I said, it's a weak bust. I'm almost surprised they arrested you."

"They found traces of pot in my apartment."

Briggs waved a hand. "From last fall. You turned those buds in to Middleton, right? So we get him to testify." He must have seen the look on my face, because he sat forward, serious again. "Look, whoever got you stuck in here, he'll have had time to think about it by tomorrow. It's a questionable bust. That classroom is open to anyone who wants to stash something in that desk. You didn't murder anyone or run a cartel, so you'll make bail. And if it goes to trial, it's likely a judge would see that you didn't do anything." I opened my mouth after that last comment, feeling especially troubled by the *likely* part, but Briggs ignored me and plowed straight on. "If our perp is smart, he'll figure all this out, which means he'll probably do one of two things. He'll try to ride off into the night in case anyone takes a second look at whoever might be selling dope to the Blackburne boys. Or he'll try to get rid of any evidence linking him to selling dope."

"So what do we do?"

"We get you the hell out of here." Briggs smiled grimly. "And then you'll tell me what you've learned about Davenport." He stood up and, after a moment, so did I.

"Why do you care about Davenport?" I asked quickly—the deputy behind me had stirred and was coming forward to escort me back to the cell.

"I've got my reasons," he said. "I'll see you tomorrow. By the way," he added suddenly, the shadow of a smile on his lips as he looked over his shoulder on the way to the door, "you're a little too young to be quoting *Say Anything*."

BRIGGS'S LAWYER COUSIN TURNED out to be a tall, reed-thin man named Clarence Stuart who wore a brown three-piece suit and blew his nose delicately and continuously into a white handkerchief. As Stuart sat across from me the next morning in a separate room for lawyers and their clients and had me repeat my story to him, I caught him peeking into his handkerchief before he folded it and put it back into his jacket pocket. He carefully went over what would happen at the arraignment later that morning and how I was to arrange bail, assuming that the judge would allow bail in this case. "Which he will," Stuart said, punctuating this by removing his handkerchief and blowing his nose again. He saw me glance at the handkerchief. "Allergies," he said, tucking it away again. He suggested that if I needed help arranging bail, I should tell him whom to call; then he folded his hands on top of the table and looked placidly at me. I gritted my teeth and gave him my parents' names and phone numbers, which he jotted down on a notepad.

The hearing itself was anticlimactic. I was escorted upstairs from the jail to a courtroom, where Stuart was waiting for me. Lester Briggs sat in the back of the court and nodded as I passed him. The judge sat in black robes at a dais, presiding over a series of arraignments. I was third in line. Stuart and another lawyer, who must have been an assistant district attorney, discussed my case in clipped legalese as if negotiating a car sale. The ADA spoke about my possession of marijuana and Oxycontin with a clear intent to sell, and Stuart calmly described my lack of criminal record and the "tenuous" nature of the evidence against me. I stood there with the odd, disembodied feeling you have when people are talking about you as if you are not standing right in front of them. I said nothing until prompted to enter a plea, and my "not guilty" seemed to fall flat in the air. The ADA and Stuart haggled over bail, which the judge set at twenty thousand dollars before he perfunctorily rapped his gavel and the bailiff announced the next case in line. The entire hearing took three minutes and was both boring and oddly reassuring.

Within an hour, I was walking out of jail with Briggs and Stuart, my bail having been secured by my father. That was a conversation I was not looking forward to, but for now it felt good to draw breath outside of a jail cell and feel the sunshine, even if the air was chilly and snow still covered the ground. Stuart shook my hand on the courthouse steps, saying he would be in touch, and hurried back inside. I turned to Briggs. "That's it?" I said.

"That's it until your court date next month," he said.

I hesitated to bring the next point up but had little choice. "I don't know where to go," I said. "I mean, all my stuff is at Blackburne. My clothes, my car—"

"Your car's in a parking lot in town," Briggs said. "And your stuff. Sam Hodges and Grayden Smith drove it out here." When I stared at him, he added, "Officially the school doesn't want you back on campus. But I think Sam and Grayden don't feel too good about it."

As I struggled to take this in, someone called my name. We both turned, looking back up the steps. Sheriff Townsend bore down on us, a flat expression on his face.

"Shit," Briggs muttered.

Townsend stopped two steps above us. Ignoring Briggs, he said to me, "You got lucky, Mr. Glass."

I looked up at him, trying not to be intimidated by his bulk and his sheriff's star. "I was set up, Sheriff. I've lost my job, and I'm being charged with drug dealing. I'd hardly call that lucky."

Townsend spread his hands as if revealing a banquet of riches. "You're out, though. Got representation, bail, et cetera. I'd call that lucky for someone selling drugs to children."

Anger rose in me like a quick tide. "I didn't sell—"

"Shut up, Matthias," Briggs said.

"I know what you did," Townsend said. "Ren Middleton told me all about it."

I laughed bitterly. "I'm sure he did. He tell you he's covering up Terence Jarrar's death, too?"

"*Matthias*," Briggs said. "Let's go."

Townsend gave a hard smile. "I'd be careful about making wild accusations," he said softly. "And I'd be careful who you're friends with." He nodded toward Briggs while his gaze remained focused on me. "Corrupt ex-cops don't usually do the Good Samaritan bit for nothing."

I looked at Briggs. His face turned gray and then flushed brick red. I thought he was either going to have an aneurysm or take a swing at Townsend. Instead, he took me by the elbow. "Let's go," he repeated more forcibly, and we walked down the steps, leaving Townsend behind, watching us walk away.

WE GOT MY CAR out of a parking lot downtown, after making sure my meager belongings were in the trunk—I felt both disturbed and grateful that Sam and Gray had packed my things into boxes for me—and I followed Briggs in his truck to the Fir Tree to get lunch. The diner seemed an appropriate place to regroup. I realized I was starving, so I ordered a hamburger and fries while Briggs got a Cobb salad, which he picked at with his fork as if grudgingly searching for something in it worth eating.

"So what was that about?" I asked him finally. "With the sheriff?"

Briggs sat back, an ugly look on his face as if he were revolted by his lunch. "He wanted to piss me off, that's all," he said.

I took a bite of hamburger, chewed, and swallowed. "Come on," I said. "He didn't just make some random comment. So what did you do?"

And then Briggs seemed to slowly deflate. He stared down at his salad. "My wife," he began, and then grimaced, picked up his glass of iced tea, drank, put it back down. "Emma was sick," he said. "Breast cancer. It got into her bones. Ate her up, along with all our savings. She was a nurse, but she had to quit when she got sick, and we had other bills . . ." He shifted in his seat, still looking down at his salad. "By the time . . . that night, when Fritz Davenport disappeared . . . she was at home in bed, down to about ninety pounds. I couldn't stand to see her like that. We had talked about hospice, but I was stubborn at first about . . . letting strangers in to help. I didn't want her in a hospital. *She* didn't want to be in a hospital. I thought having her home would be better." He looked up at me then, a world of anguish and shame in his eyes that made me sit back. "When I got the call to go out to Blackburne, I was glad to get out of the house. Emma's sister was over, so she could watch her. I just—needed a break." He laughed then, a hard, bleak sound. *Stop*, I wanted to say, but I sat there unable to speak, drawn along in Briggs's story. He glanced out the window, his eyes restless. Then with a force of will, he turned his gaze on me and held it there. "Doing my job was something I could control, something I could direct. So I focused on Fritz and argued with Ricky Townsend and followed leads and just—turned my life over to it, almost. Because I was scared to sit at home and watch my wife die."

He stopped. Dimly I could hear forks clink on plates in the diner, other customers enjoying their lunches and having their own conversations.

Briggs paused for so long that I said, "How does that . . . I mean, I'm so sorry, but . . . what does that have to do with—"

Briggs took a deep breath. "Frank Davenport came to me after the FBI quit. Met me at the station. Said he wanted to thank me for everything I'd done to help find his son. I told him that wasn't necessary and that we were still looking. He could tell I had my suspicions about him. But he just thanked me again and left." Briggs took another breath. "The next morning, two nurses from a hospice agency were on my doorstep. They said they'd been hired to help take care of my wife. I told them there must be a mistake, but they said no, it was an anonymous gesture, everything was paid for privately, wouldn't even be on my insurance. I almost said no, but they insisted. They had already been paid, they said, so it would be a waste. While I stood there trying to figure out what to do, Emma called out from the bedroom. She was frightened. I . . . The hospice folks came in with me, and I let them. Emma was—she was in a diaper at that point, couldn't get to the bathroom, and she needed it changed. The hospice people started cleaning her and talking to her and Emma just—she just looked at them so gratefully, and then at me.

"Then the phone rang. It was the bank calling, saying they had approved the refinance on our mortgage. I'd called about that three months earlier and no dice, and now someone was calling and said no problem, it's all taken care of. Meanwhile the hospice people are in my bedroom, cleaning up Emma and talking to her and . . . It was like a dream, like a lottery or a fairy godmother. I knew what it was, *who* it was who had done it all, but I stood there in my kitchen holding the phone and listening to the banker on the other end talk about papers to sign, and I just—I gave in. I let it happen and just . . . pretended it wasn't happening."

He stopped and closed his eyes, a man in need of benediction, and I stared at him for a long moment. "But," I said, "did you ever—I mean, it was Davenport? You're sure?"

Briggs opened his eyes, which looked dull, clouded over. "A week later, I called someone at NorthPoint, following up a lead about some new contracts they had, couple of people who got fired a few months earlier. Thought there might be a kidnapping angle." Startled, I remembered what Wat had told me about the two NorthPoint employees selling secrets to the Chinese. Briggs continued, not noticing my reaction. "The assistant I'd spoken with had been very helpful up until then, but that day she said she'd have to check with Mr. Davenport before getting back to me. An hour later, the bank called me. There might be problems with the refinance after all, they said. I argued with them, and then hung up and went home for lunch to see Emma like I usually did, intending to head over to the bank right afterward. When I got home, the hospice worker who was there was all upset and wringing her hands because her boss had called and said that they might have to terminate services immediately due to lack of funding." Briggs took another drink from his iced tea. "So I called Davenport's assistant back and told her never mind. Next day, everything with hospice and the bank was fine again. Emma lived another couple of weeks, comfortably. Died with a smile on her face while I lay next to her in the bed, holding her." Briggs set his glass down deliberately and gave me a wasted, haunted look.

"You lied to me," I said, thinking it and uttering it aloud at the same moment.

"I told you to look at Fritz's family."

"You told me this wasn't personal."

Briggs considered this. "True. Score one for you. Now tell me what you learned about Davenport."

I stared at him. "This is—what? Revenge?" He said nothing. A new thought struck me. "How does Sheriff Townsend know about this?"

Briggs actually smirked. "You think Davenport didn't do the same with him?"

I sat in the booth, trying to take all this in. Davenport had paid off two officers, probably more besides, to keep them from investigating his son's disappearance. Or was it to keep them from investigating NorthPoint? Everything kept coming back to that. It was like a locked door in my own house that I couldn't open, couldn't find the key to.

Briggs was saying something, pulling me out of my thoughts. "What?" I said.

"You ever read *Moby-Dick?*"

"What? Yes, I've read it. A long time ago, in college. Why?"

"Melville wrote that Ahab chose the white whale as his enemy and swore vengeance on it. Everything evil, everything wrong in the universe, Ahab puts on that whale, and he seeks it out to destroy it." Briggs took another sip from his glass of tea. He seemed calmer now, focused, as if telling his story had strengthened him somehow.

"You're telling me Davenport is your white whale?"

Briggs leaned forward. "Everything I understood about honor I compromised because of what he offered me. I know you can understand that—they teach you about honor up at that school. I've dealt with my own faults and lived with them for ten years, and I will take whatever punishment comes to me. But he did something wrong and needs to take responsibility for it. Not for bribing me—that's my fault for accepting it. He kept people from finding his son. How can that be justified?"

I sat back in my seat, staring at him. "You know Ahab was insane, right? Melville wrote that, too."

Briggs picked up his fork and speared a slice of hard-boiled egg. "Everybody searches for something, Matthias," he said. "You telling me Fritz isn't your white whale?"

He chewed his food, watching me as I sat across from him at a loss for words. "So," he said, swallowing, "what did you find out about Davenport?"

WE SPENT ANOTHER TWO hours talking in the diner. It's probably more accurate to say that Briggs interrogated me and I answered his questions. He wasn't satisfied with what Wat Davenport had told me about the two NorthPoint employees selling secrets to Chinese clients. Frank Davenport might not have had the two investigated, he argued—he may have lied to his brother. Or he may have sat on whatever information he'd learned from private detectives. "You need to go back to Wat Davenport, see what else he knows," Briggs said.

"I'm not doing anything until I solve my problems here," I said, a bit heatedly. "We need to find out who tried to frame me at Blackburne."

Briggs grunted and pulled a small worn notepad from his hip pocket. "So we make a list," he said.

It was a short list. Ren Middleton was at the top, then Travis Simmons, followed by his son, Paul, and then the hypothetical "Paul's friends/customers."

"I don't buy that a kid did that," Briggs said. "Got drugs into your desk and apartment. They'd need access to keys, for one thing."

"Blackburne's got an honor code," I pointed out. "People are trusting. Makes it pretty easy to lie and steal things." Briggs raised his eyebrows. "Well, it does," I said stubbornly.

"It'd still be easier for an adult," he insisted.

"Like Ren Middleton."

"I get that you want it to be him. Guy throws you out on your ass, you'd like him to get what's coming to him. But all he had to do was just wait another month or two, tell you he wasn't going to offer you a contract, and send you on your way."

"Maybe he feels threatened. He tried to get me to lie about Paul Simmons and the drugs."

"He's not threatened by you in any way that firing you doesn't take care of. What about Travis Simmons? He'd be pissed about his son—maybe he blames you."

"And he gets me by planting drugs?" I shrugged. "I don't see it, but it's possible. Maybe he'd see it as ironically fitting. Which brings us to Paul."

"Who's 'out in Utah,' according to you."

"His friends at Blackburne, then. He gets them to set me up out of revenge. If Paul Simmons knew how to get that shotgun out of that locked cabinet, he could get into my apartment and classroom without a problem."

"His father's the headmaster, for Christ's sake."

"Exactly. His son could get access to anything at Blackburne if he wanted to."

"Which comes back to my problem with a kid doing this. I mean, the oxy they could steal from a parent or relative, but where'd they get that much pot? Most kids would smoke it instead of holding on to it."

"Okay," I said, rubbing my eyes, "let's go over it again."

"You'd make a decent cop," Briggs said, using the back of his hand to stifle a yawn.

"I'll take that as a compliment."

"You know," Briggs said, "what about Terence? Maybe *he* has friends who were pissed about what happened to him. Or they're pissed that you could mess things up for them with your half-assed drug investigation. Who did Terence hang out with?"

I shrugged. "Ben Sipple, although I don't see him doing this. We . . . have a history, but we worked it out." When Briggs gave me a significant look, I added, "Trust me," thinking about Ben in Saint Matthew's, where he had ripped off the altar sheet and then sobbed against my shoulder. "Paul Simmons, obviously. Other than that, I don't know. Terence was kind of a loner." I thought about Terence's journals, the odd, fragmented poems. His mother's face rose out of my memory, beautiful and sad. Lost in thought, I stared out the window, my eyes wandering over Briggs's truck. It had oversized wheels. *Wheels . . .*

> *The steel wheels*
> *Turn and turn and turn*

In the night
Shining with light
As if they burn . . .

burning wheels light up the bricks
as fate rolls down the path toward me

"Son of a bitch," I said aloud.

"Excuse me?"

I turned to Briggs. "I need to get to Blackburne. Tonight."

CHAPTER TWENTY-ONE

Briggs dropped me off by the lions at a quarter past ten. It was dark, a heavy shield of clouds raised against the moon and stars. The road was deserted, patches of snow scattered over the fields on one side, the woods looming on the other. There wasn't a sound, not a car or an owl or even the low keen of the wind. Briggs and I could have been the only two people left on Earth.

"You sure about this?" Briggs asked for the tenth time.

"Positive," I said, making sure my iPhone was in my outside coat pocket.

"Trespassing is a serious crime, Matthias."

"They won't let me back on campus." Saying it aloud, hearing the words in my mouth, stoked my anger. "I can't just walk back up there in the open. They'd call Sheriff Townsend in a second."

"And if they see you tonight, they'll do the same thing," Briggs said. "You could end up back in jail. You willing to risk that?"

I pulled on my gloves. "Yes," I said. I wasn't being cocky or brave—it was simply a statement of fact. "Just stick to the plan and I'll be fine."

Briggs's face was in shadow, but I was pretty sure he was frowning. "All right," he said finally. "But don't be stupid. Just get what you need and come back."

I opened the car door and went out into the night. It was like stepping into icy water. I shut the door, and Briggs drove away slowly, past the entrance. He would pull off the road about a hundred yards away or so. I checked my boots to make sure they were laced, more out of nervousness than anything else, pulled my wool hat a bit lower on my head, and set off up the drive. I passed the stone lions without a glance. Inside the gate, I left the pavement and moved about five yards into the trees on the left-hand side, in case there was a bus returning late.

It was slow going. I didn't want to risk using a flashlight because of the guard at the security booth just beyond the tree line, so I made my way through the dark carefully, not wanting to run into a tree trunk or poke my eye out with a branch. It occurred to me that I was making the reverse journey that Fritz had made all those years ago—he had escaped Blackburne, while I was sneaking in. My earlier anger about being banned from campus still burned in my gut. It was as if I had been expelled, only worse—this was karma for cheating all those years ago. Was I a victim, or an offender finally getting my due?

Eventually I reached the edge of the playing fields, the trees a wall at my back. The Hill and its lights lay ahead of me, a beacon in the dark. Much closer, about thirty yards away, stood the security booth, soft yellow light illuminating its window and revealing a single person, one of the Slater brothers, seated inside. He looked like he was reading a magazine. Even if the light would ruin whatever night vision he might have, I needed to be careful. Snow glimmered on the ground, but otherwise the fields were covered in shadow. I gingerly stepped out from the trees and began walking slowly but steadily across the fields.

By this time, I was breathing somewhat heavily, the air rasping in my throat. My legs were heavy, and the Hill had never seemed so far away. I crossed a soccer field and glanced back—no one had stirred in the security booth—and then started up a sloping fairway that led straight to the base of Farquhar Gym.

When I finally reached the gym, I could see, by the ground at the bottom of the wall, a row of skylights ablaze with light. This was what I had been looking for. Crouching, I crept over to the skylights, a dogwood hedge shielding me from view of anyone, and peered through the glass.

Below me was Pelham Greer's gym apartment. Greer was home. He was in his wheelchair, his back to me, emptying something into a tall garbage can by the door that led to the inside stairwell, the door through which I had first entered his apartment last fall. Then he turned. I leaned back automatically from the skylight, afraid he might catch a glimpse of me, and then slowly leaned forward again. He had rolled over to his kitchenette, where he opened a cabinet and retrieved a spray can. He then sprayed his apartment for a good thirty seconds or so, thoroughly spraying into every corner. When he seemed satisfied, he put the spray can back into the cabinet, rolled his head to stretch his neck, and then wheeled over to his bed. As he started to swing himself out of his chair and onto his bed, I backed away from the windows and glanced behind me down the hill to make sure no one was around. The golf course remained empty. I glanced at my watch: eleven o'clock, lights-out.

I made my way to the right, heading toward the front of the gym, until I reached a Dumpster. Behind the Dumpster was a half-hidden set of double doors. Reaching into my pocket, I withdrew the set of keys I still had, including the one gym key all faculty had so they could use the gym and other amenities. I'd had these in my pocket when I had been arrested, and I had received them along with my other personal possessions when I had been released that afternoon—Blackburne had forgotten to request their return. I could have gone into Greer's apartment through the door I had entered all those weeks ago last fall, but that would have meant entering the gym another way and possibly encountering someone else. Besides, Greer's bed faced that door.

I inserted the key into the lock very slowly, then pulled out my phone, opened an app, and put the phone back in my pocket. Then I turned the key. The lock moved smoothly and quietly. Quickly I turned the knob and opened the door, stepping inside and then closing it behind me.

I was at the top of the shallow ramp that led down to the floor of Greer's apartment. To my left, Greer jerked his head up toward me, a magazine forgotten on his lap and his mouth open in surprise. "Jesus, you scared the hell out of me!" he said.

"Good," I said, turning the dead bolt in the door.

Greer was momentarily shocked by my appearance—I was counting on that. But he had been a soldier, and as I walked down the ramp to the floor, his training and instincts kicked in. He moved with uncanny agility for his wheelchair, parked right next to his bed. But before he could do anything other than get into the chair, I walked to the kitchenette cabinet and opened it, retrieving the spray can I had seen him use earlier. The label on the can read *Ozium*. I turned and held it up to him as he rolled out from behind his bed, scowling.

"What the fuck do you think—" Greer began.

"Citrus scent," I said, cutting him off. I waved the can in the air. "Sort of a potpourri smell. Gets rid of smoke odors. Guy I knew in college swore by this stuff."

I couldn't tell if I imagined Greer glancing at the trash can or not. "You aren't even supposed to be here," he said. "You got arrested. Fired. You—"

"Because of you," I said. "Because of what you put in my desk."

Greer blinked. "I don't—"

I headed for the trash can. Instantly Greer was wheeling forward to intercept me, but as I passed the card table, I reached out and grabbed the one chair at the table, pulling it over onto the floor in Greer's path. He stopped short, and then reversed and maneuvered around the chair easily enough, but it bought me enough time to reach the trash can and open the lid.

"Get out of my shit!" he yelled.

With my free hand—I was still holding the can of Ozium—I reached into the trash can and pulled out the wilted end of what must have been a rather large joint. My hand was flecked with ash, no doubt from the ashtray I'd seen Greer emptying into his garbage can not two minutes earlier.

There was a quiet *snick* behind me, and I turned to see Greer right behind me, moving his arm back. A long black stick had magically appeared in his hand. I ducked to the side, just in time for the stick to miss me on the downswing. It smashed into the plastic trash can, cutting a deep gouge into its side. Greer yanked it back, freeing it from the trash can, while I backed up, a spray can in one hand and the butt-end of a joint in the other. Then the baton slashed through the air, its tip just catching the back of my left hand. A burst of white-hot pain seared my hand, and the joint I had been holding sailed across the room. I backpedaled, holding my hand to my stomach. It felt as if it had been sliced open. Greer was working his wheelchair with both hands, the baton in his lap, but before I thought to rush him or do anything else, he stopped pushing the wheels and picked up the baton in his right hand. Instinctively, I stepped to my right, away from the baton—he'd have a harder time hitting me across his body. But Greer's left hand reached down to the wheel and palmed it back, and he spun to his left like a kid on a skateboard, bringing his baton arm around to me. I avoided being hit in the face only by leaping backward, striking a wall as I did so. Greer wheeled forward and raised the baton again, his face taut with anger. There was no furniture I could throw down in front of him this time. I dove to the left, the baton striking the wall behind me hard enough to chip the paint.

I got to one knee as Greer whirled around and advanced, the baton raised again. I threw the Ozium can at him as hard as I could, and when he raised his baton arm instinctively to deflect it, I got to my feet, ran forward, and leapt at him. I didn't think about it beforehand, just acted—I was as surprised as Greer was. I crashed into him, pinning the baton between our bodies. The momentum carried him back and tipped his wheelchair over, and both of us fell to the floor. He struck his head on the floor, while some part of his chair hit me in the ribs like a solid kick, and I bounced off the chair and rolled over, gasping, a sharp pain in my side now joining the pain in my hand. Groaning, I turned my head toward Greer in time to see him on his back, the wheelchair on its side like an overturned vehicle, one wheel spinning in the air. He was groping for the baton, which lay next to me on the floor just beyond his fingers. I snatched the baton and flung it away so that it hit the card table with a loud *smack* before falling back to the floor, well out of reach.

Greer blinked at the ceiling and let out a moan. I got to my feet, shakily, my ribs and hand both complaining about it. "Are you all right?" I asked, a bit harshly.

"How'd you know?" he managed to say.

"Terence Jarrar," I said. Greer turned his head to stare at me. "Or his poems," I continued. "He wrote about you. 'The steel wheels / Turn and turn and turn / In the night, / Shining with light / As if they burn.' There was more, about burning wheels on the bricks and fate rolling toward him. Took me a while to get it."

Greer closed his eyes, a look of disgust on his face. "Fucking chair," he said. He opened his eyes and looked venomously, not at me, but at the wheelchair toppled over onto its side, a wheel still turning.

"So, when did you start selling to him?" I said. "He wrote about getting stoned, too. That part I got. I just didn't connect it with you until later."

Greer shut his eyes again.

"He was stoned the night he died," I continued. "He and Paul Simmons. They were high, on pot or oxy or Vicodin, and they were fucking around with a shotgun by the river, and Terence shot himself. You were the one who sold to him. And when you got scared that I might figure that out, you planted those drugs in my desk. How'd you get a student to find them? You suggest that they look in there? Ask them to get you a piece of paper or something?"

Greer remained silent. Then, his eyes still closed, he said, "It was detention. I had a kid helping me clean desks, getting gum off the undersides. He ran out of paper towels, and I told him to look in your desk— sometimes teachers keep some in there." He opened his eyes. "It was easy." He said this without pride or scorn.

"And Terence?" I prodded him.

"Help me," he said, struggling to sit up.

"What about Terence?"

He gave up and lay back, breathing hard. "Help me," he spat.

"Tell me about Terence," I said, insistent. "Did you sell to him?"

He lay there, staring at the ceiling. "Fuck you," he rasped. "You have no idea."

"Enlighten me."

He turned his head to look at me, anger and disgust mingled in his face. "*Enlighten* you?" he said. "You see my legs?" He jabbed a hand toward them. "I got shot, in Kuwait. Sniper got me in the spine. Instant paraplegic." His eyes burned into mine, furious. "Doctors saved my life, but they wouldn't save my legs. I could have spinal surgery and get prosthetics. I could walk again, like a real man. But it costs fifty grand to get the surgery, and the VA won't cover it. Instead, they gave me that fucking chair. Meanwhile, I get headaches like someone's in my skull with a jackhammer trying to get out. And nothing touches the pain unless I take enough meds to start drooling on myself."

"So you started smoking to manage the pain," I said. Suddenly I felt very tired. "And then, what, you figured you'd start dealing to make a little money on the side? Save up for your surgery?"

He stared at me. "Except for the army, I've worked here my entire life," he said. "Even when I was a kid, I worked here summers. And now people like you look at me like I'm some sort of sad, weird fucker who's just good enough to pick up your trash. Grads come back and high-five me and shit, want to have a beer with the cripple to show *they* weren't like that, *they* were decent human beings. You think one of them's gonna pay for me to have surgery? You think I'd ask?"

In spite of everything, I burned with shame at the truth in his words. I recalled Porter Deems's initial reaction to Greer at the faculty party back in August: *Creepy dude in a wheelchair.* I looked at Greer, lying on the floor with his useless legs splayed out in front of him. He would never walk again without a surgery he couldn't afford. It was almost enough to make me reconsider everything. But then I thought of the Jarrars in Ren's office, Mr. Jarrar's sorrow so great he could not speak, Mrs. Jarrar's grief so intense it broke my heart, and their son lying dead on a rock in the middle of the river. And if that sounds too noble, I admit I also thought about my own neck, about the county jail and the charges against me.

I pulled his wheelchair upright and pushed it over to him. "Come on," I said.

Greer looked up at me. His eyes narrowed in suspicion, and for some reason this pissed me off. "You practically begged me to help you a few seconds ago," I said. "So get up. You've got something to do for me."

Greer hesitated, his hand already outstretched toward his chair. "Help you how?"

"Clear my name. By telling the cops what you did."

Greer sneered. "I don't need to tell them shit," he said.

I reached into my coat pocket and pulled out my iPhone. "That's true," I said. I touched the Play button on the sole recording in the Voice Memos app. "*Jesus, you scared the hell out of me!*" Greer said from my iPhone.

"*Good,*" my voice replied.

Greer's eyes had widened. I fast forwarded and touched Play again.

"*You were the one who sold to him. And when you got scared that I might figure that out, you planted those drugs in my desk. How'd you get a student to find them? You suggest that they look in there? Ask them to get you a piece of paper or something?*"

There was a pause, and then Greer's voice, sounding tired, came out of my iPhone. *"It was detention. I had a kid helping me clean desks—"*

I paused it. Greer looked like he had forgotten how to breathe. Then his eyes flicked over toward the baton lying on the floor more than ten feet away.

"Not happening," I said, stepping between him and the baton. He remained on the floor, watching me tap the screen on my phone. A few moments later, I finished e-mailing a copy of the recording to Briggs and then looked at Greer. "I'm thinking the cops might treat you a little better if you go ahead and confess."

Greer looked up at me, loathing and despair warring in his face. Then something closed in his eyes—or maybe opened; I couldn't tell. Greer raised himself slowly onto one elbow. "What if," he said, "I could tell you something? Something you'd want to know?"

"Like what?" I said, putting my phone back into my pocket.

He lowered his head slightly, as if ashamed to say what he had to say. "Like I know where your friend Fritz is," he said.

I froze, my hand in my pocket. Greer was looking up at me with a small, ingratiating smile.

"You son of a bitch," I said.

Greer's smile fell from his face.

I walked over to the baton and bent to pick it up, ignoring the sharp jab of pain in my side, and walked back toward Greer. He was looking at the baton, then at my face, then at the baton again. "Hey," he began.

"Don't you *ever*," I said, my voice shaking, "*ever* try to . . . *use* my friend like that, you *fuck*." I grasped the baton hard enough to whiten my knuckles, hard enough to hurt, because I was afraid that if I didn't, if I wasn't fully paying attention to what I was doing, I might find myself beating Pelham Greer to a bloody pulp in his own apartment. Rage, a deep red vein of it, pulsed in my brain.

"Hey, look," Greer said. There was a wariness in his face now, a look like *I'm dealing with a lunatic here.* "I'm not trying to use anyone, okay? I'm just, I just know something. Something about Fritz."

I stared down at him as I continued to grip the baton. "Bullshit," I said.

"I'm not lying," he said.

"Prove it."

Greer touched his lips with the tip of his tongue. He started to say something and then swallowed the words.

"Uh-huh," I said, trying to sound dismissive. Instead, my voice was a husky croak. Deliberately I relaxed my grip on the baton and switched it to my left hand so I could reach into my pocket for my phone. It was time to call Briggs.

"Kevin Kelly," Greer blurted out. "Kevin Kelly knows."

I looked down at Greer, incredulous, the phone forgotten in my hand. "What the hell are you talking about?"

"Kelly knows. He knows where Fritz is."

I slowly replaced my phone in my pocket. "Kevin Kelly who used to go here?"

Greer nodded. "That's him."

The Nazis. That's what Kevin Kelly had called me and Fritz when we were fourth formers and he was a year behind us. I stared down at Greer, who was looking both desperate and hopeful. "How do you know him?"

A pause. I could practically hear the wheels spinning in Greer's head. "He gets me the stuff," he finally said.

"Stuff? He's your . . . supplier?"

Greer nodded.

"Okay," I said. "Okay. What the hell does that have to do with Fritz?"

"Last fall, we met to—to handle a delivery," Greer said, awkwardly. "This was after you came by my apartment. Kelly asked about you. He remembered you from when he was here. I told him you had asked about Fritz, and how we had talked about him disappearing. He laughed and said he knew where Fritz was. Saw him last spring. He was keeping that as insurance, he said. He was all pleased with himself about it. Like he got a bang out of knowing something other people didn't."

He stopped, looking up at me like a student hoping that his excuse was being bought. For my part, I wanted to sit and catch my breath. Actually I wanted to lie down, to be inert for a while. *Kevin Kelly knows where Fritz is* kept going through my head. *He knows where Fritz is.* It was as if my sense of hope had been lost deep in a cave and had just lit a match.

"Where is Kevin Kelly?" I asked. "Where does he live?"

"Outside Charlottesville," Greer said. "I always meet him at a house outside of town, anyway."

"You drive?"

Greer nodded. "In my van. I've got hand controls. One thing Blackburne did for me, I'll say that for them. Got me that van." He narrowed his eyes. "Why?"

"Because you're going to take me to him."

CHAPTER TWENTY-TWO

Watching Greer drive was a bit like watching a pilot at the helm of a spaceship in a low-budget sci-fi flick. Chunky plastic boxes with red-and-green lights and dials surrounded the steering wheel, turning it into a cockpit area. The driver's seat had been removed, allowing Greer in his wheelchair to enter the van in the back via a lift and then roll straight forward to the steering wheel. On either side of the wheel, mounted on small posts that rose from the floor, sprouted a trio of vertical handles, each wrapped in black foam, arranged in a triangle with the point facing forward. Now, as we pulled out of the parking lot by the gym, each of Greer's hands grasped the foremost handle, the other two handles surrounding his wrists. He glanced once at me as we drove down the Hill toward the lions. "Freaks people out, first time they see me drive," he said conversationally.

"I like being able to see your hands," I said. "Make sure you don't have any other batons."

He turned his head to look at me. "Yeah, 'cause I'd be trying to bash you in the face with one while I'm driving." He smirked and turned back to the road. "Thought you were supposed to be smart."

It had taken a bit of doing to convince Greer to take me to Kevin Kelly, but when I pointed out that the police would be very interested in his taped confession of selling drugs to students, he agreed to drive me. The trick was that I needed to tell Briggs, but I didn't want to call and have a conversation Greer could overhear. So when Greer rolled into his van and was out of sight, I texted Briggs and told him that Greer was taking me to his supplier, who apparently knew something about Fritz. Briggs immediately texted back that I should just go ahead with what we had planned: make a citizen's arrest on Greer so he and I could take Greer to a state police station. I replied by texting Briggs to follow us and shoved my phone into my pocket before climbing into Greer's van. The phone had buzzed three times since then, but I didn't answer. I didn't want Greer to know Briggs would be following us—I'm not sure why, other than some half-assed idea of keeping an ace up my sleeve.

We rolled past the lions, Greer applying the brakes with a squeeze of a handle to bring the van to a stop at the road. I purposely did not look to our right, where I knew Briggs was in his truck about a hundred yards away.

Greer turned right onto the state road. "So where are we going?" I asked.

"Like I said, a place outside Charlottesville." He glanced at me. "It's not far, don't worry."

And then we were driving on, past empty fields and stands of trees, a distant yellow square indicating the lit window of a house. We were easily half a mile from the lions, but I saw no sign of Briggs's truck. I wondered if he had driven off, fed up with me ignoring his calls and deviating from the plan. A knot of anxiety tightened in my chest. *This is not a good idea,* said a voice inside my head, but I shut it off as best I could. I thought about taking out my phone to text Briggs, but Greer kept glancing at me.

"He's not going to want to talk to you, you know," Greer said.

I shifted in my seat. "I'll worry about that," I said. "Just drive."

"Not going to be happy with me bringing you to his house, either."

"I think he'll like me coming up there better than the state police."

Greer snorted. "So, what, you'll just go up and ask him where Fritz is?"
I had no reply, mostly because this was essentially my plan.

Sometime in the past half hour the cloud cover had begun to fray and tatter, revealing the silver-white coin of the moon. Beyond the headlights, I could see snowy fields and hillsides glow with a milky translucence. Trees forked up from the ground, black claws tearing at the sky. Suddenly I remembered one February night in college, riding in a car out to a party at a country house, and as a joke the driver had turned off the headlights, plunging us into an eerie darkness. A girl in the backseat beside me had shrieked in my ear, and for a moment I had been terrified we would crash into a tree or another car. But there had also been something ghostly and beautiful about driving down the road with only the moon and stars to guide us, almost as if we were flying through the night sky. I felt an echo of that as Pelham Greer drove through the dark countryside toward Kevin Kelly and whatever he knew about Fritz. It felt strangely reassuring, but also ominous.

Soon, however, a sodium glow appeared on the horizon ahead, the lights of I-64. Greer took the on-ramp and headed east through the foothills toward Charlottesville.

I HAD BEEN GLANCING in the side mirrors to see if anyone was following us. I still hadn't seen Briggs, but he'd been a cop—he was probably good at following people without their knowing it. *Or maybe he went home*, a voice nagged me in my head. Once I thought I'd seen a pair of headlights behind us before we had gotten on the highway, but no one had followed us onto the on-ramp, and then we were driving through light traffic. I broke down and pulled out my phone to read Briggs's texts, but as I swiped the screen to unlock it, Greer said, "What the hell you doing?"

"Checking my messages."

"You're not calling anybody out here," he said coldly. "This is you and me going up to his house, no one else. You call anyone and I stop the car right here and you don't ever find out about your friend."

I raised a hand, palm out as if warding him off. "Fine, okay," I said. "Jesus." But I'd had enough of a chance to see that Briggs had in fact texted me back only once—Where r u—and then the other two times were phone calls, no voice mail messages. I put my phone in my pocket and stared out the window at the passing mile markers. I was alone.

"How'd you hook up with Kelly?" I asked, more to keep my mind occupied than anything else.

Greer screwed up his face, as if tasting something unpleasant. "Showed up out of the blue one weekend about two years ago. Looking for me. I thought he just wanted to feel better about himself, have a beer with the cripple. But it wasn't like that at all. He had a 'business proposition' for me. That's what he called it. We went outside to the Lawn, away from everybody, and he told me he'd heard I was having problems, headaches and all. He said he was in contact with some medical marijuana groups, could help me out. Gave me a bag right there. I figured out pretty quickly he wasn't just being generous. Turned out he wanted me to sell for him, on campus. Said I could make a lot of money toward that operation I wanted." Greer's lip twitched, and he sucked in a breath through his teeth. "Dude had me figured out to the ground. Don't know how he learned all that about me."

I stirred in my seat. "He was like that in school," I said. "Obnoxious little fucker."

"He's more than that," Greer said. "He's smart. Acts like this is some sort of chess game, and he's five moves ahead of everybody else. Pretty soon it wasn't just pot but oxy, Vicodin, E, even ADD meds. I don't think I'm the only guy he has out there selling, either. But he seemed to really want me to sell for him."

Or he wanted someone to sell at Blackburne, I thought. Kelly had been kicked out of Blackburne, I'd heard. If Kelly had been expelled, then I could see why selling drugs to Blackburne students would be particularly appealing to him.

"So, you just . . . pick up drugs from him and then sell them?" I asked.

Greer shrugged. "Basically."

"And you don't care that you're selling to teenagers?"

He glanced at me and then turned his eyes back to the road—he seemed to be looking for an exit sign. "How naive are you, man? They don't buy from me, they'll buy from someone else. They all smoke, man. I give them really good product, and I get a cut toward my surgery."

"So Terence Jarrar was, what, just one of those things that happen?" I asked, unable to stop myself. Part of me marveled at my self-righteousness.

Greer's jaw tightened, and he opened his mouth as if to reply, but all he said was, "There she is." I looked ahead and saw an exit sign for Highway 29, and then we were curving off to the right, off the interstate. Orange light hung in the air ahead, a night glow reflecting off the bellies of the overhanging clouds—Charlottesville proper. But Greer was heading south, away from town, and we passed a new subdivision on the left, its inhabitants slumbering peacefully as we drove past into the dark, the hills rising on either side of us cutting off the glow behind.

After several minutes—we had passed a few isolated clusters of older homes and a pair of battered churches—Greer slowed and pulled over to the right shoulder. "Are we here?" I asked, surprised.

"Not yet," Greer said, leaving the engine idling. He turned to me. "Give me your phone," he said.

"What? No."

"You want me to take you to Kelly, I want that phone with the voice recording on it. That's the deal."

I hesitated. A car approached from behind us, the headlights shining through the windows on the rear door and washing over Greer's face so it looked like a skull. The car passed us, and Greer's face returned to shadow. He held out his hand. "You want to see your friend again?" he said. "Give me the phone."

I took the phone out of my pocket, making sure to thumb the power button on the top so it turned off. At least the pass code would keep Greer from swiping open the phone. I handed it to him. He dropped it into a chest pocket on his shirt, nodded once, put the van in drive, and pulled back out onto the road.

"How much farther?" I asked.

"He's off a side road up here somewhere," Greer said, leaning forward slightly and squinting through the windshield. "Never come up here after dark." He made a little sighing grunt of recognition and swung the van to the right, onto a narrow road that wound uphill. We passed a field on our left, a few tufts of grass poking up out of the snow, and then we were among trees, the road getting bumpy and the light from the van's head-lights wobbling in and out of the tree trunks.

"How much farther?" I asked again.

"Maybe a quarter of a mile."

"Stop the van."

Greer looked at me but then manipulated the hand controls, pulling the van over to the left and bringing it to a gentle stop, the engine idling.

"Turn it off."

"Why?"

"I'm going for a walk. Turn it off."

Greer turned the key, leaving it in the ignition, and the idling engine cut off abruptly, the van seeming to settle down as if resting on its haunches.

I held my hand out. "Give me the keys."

"The hell for?"

"So you don't leave me alone out here."

"I'm not—"

I leaned forward and jerked the keys out of the ignition. Greer grabbed at my hand, and I leaned back away from him. "Fucking *dick*," he sputtered, pawing at me. "Piece of *shit*." Fending him off with my left arm, I awkwardly grabbed the door handle with my right hand, still holding the keys, and swung the door open. Then I gracelessly half slid, half fell out of the van to the ground. "Give me my keys, you asshole!" Greer screamed. Instead, I stood up and slammed the door shut. "Fuck you!" Greer shouted, his voice muffled by the door. I held up the keys so he could see them and gave them a jingle. My well-developed sense of guilt kicked in for a moment—*you're taunting a man in a wheelchair*—but only for a moment. The guy had sold drugs to students and then tried to frame me for it, after all. So I pocketed the keys, turned my back on Greer, and began to head up the heavily rutted road.

Leaving Pelham Greer in the van was actually smart, I told myself as I trudged up the dirt road in the dark. Driving up to Kelly's front door didn't seem like a good idea—if he was selling drugs, he might not appreciate a car pulling into his driveway in the middle of the night. I figured walking around a bit to scope out the area was a good idea.

Behind me, the van's engine turned over and then roared. Headlights flared on, pinning me to the dark background of trees. I looked over my shoulder to see the van lurch forward. For a second I just stood there, mouth slightly open. *He has a spare set of keys*, I thought. Then I moved, stepping quickly off the road and behind a large oak. The van jerked to a stop ten feet away, the engine rumbling. I looked around the tree to see Greer's face through the windshield, his lips curled back in a snarl. The trees were too big and too close together for him to drive between them and run me down. He raised a middle finger, and then the van was moving backward, turning tightly to the left before jerking again to a stop and then moving forward. It completed the turn and drove away from me into the night. "Damn it," I said, staring at the red taillights winking at me. Greer had left me in the middle of nowhere, and he had my phone. At least the phone was locked, so he couldn't call Kelly to warn him. Unless he had his own phone. Sighing, I turned and resumed my walk down the road toward whatever was waiting for me at the end of it. Snow crunched beneath my feet, and my face stung with the cold.

I was just beginning to think that Greer's estimate of a quarter mile was off—I had walked more than that, I was sure of it—when the road hooked to the right, snaked between a pair of pines, and then opened into a snow-covered yard backed by a long ranch house. The house was trim and neat without being fussy, white siding on a brick foundation, a small covered porch shading the front door. A light shone on the porch, revealing a pair of empty wooden rocking chairs flanking the closed door.

Staring at the house, I walked right into a waist-high sign planted to the left of the driveway. It was oval with curled black text on a white background: "Ollie's Orchids."

I stepped to the side of the sign and moved behind a smaller pine tree, peering at the house. There were no other lights on besides the porch light, no cars in the yard. But I could see where tire tracks ate into the snow around the left-hand side of the house, so I sidled that way, trying to keep behind the trees as I went, my eyes on the house the whole time as I made my way around the back.

A small floodlight mounted over the back door of the house illuminated a cluttered backyard. A pickup truck, dark and empty, was parked beside a stack of firewood. Beyond the firewood stretched a long glass building—a greenhouse. I could hear a fan running over there—probably a heater. I could see nothing through any of the house's back windows. The truck made me cautious, though, and Greer had assured me that Kevin Kelly would be home.

Unbidden, the memory of my father's words from years earlier surfaced. *In times of crisis, a man's instinct is to do one of two things: retreat to a place of safety, or gather up his strength and hurl himself headlong into the fray.* I walked back around to the front of the house, stepped up onto the porch, and knocked loudly on the front door.

I didn't hear footsteps or any other indication that someone was inside, but suddenly the door was pulled open. Startled, I stepped back.

Kevin Kelly was standing before me. He was taller than I remembered. He had a mop of curly hair and a week-old beard ringing his round face. He was wearing jeans, a dirty long-sleeved tee shirt, and a pair of wire-framed specs. "Matthias," he said. "Come in." He turned and walked into the house, leaving the door open behind him. I hesitated, and Kevin was swallowed in the shadows past the foyer. His voice floated out of the darkness. "Close the door behind you. I'm not paying to heat the front yard."

I walked into the house and pulled the door shut behind me. Inside it was dim, the air still and close. At the back of the foyer, Kevin turned left down an unlit hall, and after a moment I followed. As I passed a closed door, I could both hear and feel a steady, muffled hum, as if a large piece of machinery were throbbing nearby behind thick walls. Then I entered a well-lit kitchen, a room with low wooden beams overhead, the stove and refrigerator, and what I presumed was the back door on the wall to my right. To the left was a heap of broken furniture, half covering a door that presumably led to one of the front rooms off the foyer. In the middle of the kitchen, Kevin stood by a square wooden table. I now noticed his tee shirt had a picture of a cartoon moose with skis, under which was the caption "Chase the Moose." He was scratching his right arm. "Rash," he said. "Occupational hazard. Don't know if it's from the plants or the nutrients. Anyway." He indicated one of two straight-backed chairs. "Have a seat." His voice was just as I had remembered—slightly nasal, assured, the voice of a man who knows exactly what he is doing.

I sat in the chair, facing him across the table, and he settled into the other chair, still scratching his arm. A light fixture overhead shone in tight white circles on his spectacles, giving him the look of a benevolent, other-worldly creature, eyes ablaze with silver light. Then he leaned forward, and I could see behind his specs a pair of dark eyes that gazed curiously at me, in the way someone might watch a strange new animal in a zoo.

"So," I said. My lips were dry, and when I licked them, they stung. "Kevin. Good to see you."

Kevin smiled and leaned his elbows on the table, bringing his hands together as if in prayer, and regarded me through his specs. I realized that

Kevin had maneuvered me to sit with my back against a wall while he sat between me and the only two exits: the back door and the hall we had walked down. Sweat prickled in my armpits. Then I recalled Greer's baton in my coat pocket, and I drew some comfort from that.

"You don't seem surprised to see me," I said.

"Security cameras," Kevin said. "Front and back doors. Saw you tiptoe across my front lawn and peek around back." He cracked his knuckles and continued to regard me.

"Okay," I said after a long pause. "Now what?"

Kevin scratched his arm again in a preoccupied sort of way. "Now you tell me why you're here," he said.

I realized belatedly how stupid this was. I was alone, in an isolated house somewhere outside of Charlottesville, with no cell phone. With a casual bravado I didn't feel, I said, "This how you treat all your visitors?"

Kevin was grinning now. "Just the ones who are trespassing in the middle of the night. Or were you interested in buying some orchids?"

I looked blankly at him. He seemed disappointed.

"Ollie's Orchids?" he said. "The sign out front?"

"Missed that," I managed to say. "Who's Ollie?"

"Olivia. Woman I bought the business from."

"Which business?" I asked without thinking. *Shit.*

Kevin's grin slowly drained off his face, and he now appraised me like a puzzle he needed to work out. He looked like a graduate student in his tee shirt and jeans, specs, and scruffy beard. "Ah," he said. "Well, there it is. Which business. I bought the *orchid* business from Olivia. She wanted to retire, move to Florida. Her father built this place back in the fifties."

I said nothing. Kelly scratched his arm again, noticed it, stopped.

"But you're not growing orchids," I said.

He considered me. "No, I'm not growing orchids. And *you*, you're teaching at Blackburne." The way he said "Blackburne" suggested a sense of loathing that had not been in his voice before.

I took a minute to process this. "Why?" I managed.

He frowned slightly. "Why grow what I grow?" he said. "I'm good at it. It's lucrative."

"No, I mean why sell at Blackburne?"

Kevin's eyebrows went up. "Why? Why the hell not?"

"Just seems like a lot of effort," I said, keeping my voice at a casual register. "I mean, you'd get better sales in cities, at colleges. Blackburne's isolated. It's—"

"Do you ski, Matthias?"

I stared. "What?"

"Ski. It's a beautiful sport. Trying to go as fast as you can without falling down or running into anything. There's a kind of purity to it. A contest between you and the slope."

I looked at the cartoon moose on his tee shirt—it was grinning madly as it apparently zoomed down a snowy hill—and tried to formulate a response.

"People ski for lots of reasons," Kevin was saying. "Because other people do it and they're like lemmings. Or because they think it makes them cool."

"Or they like the clothes," I said, trying to keep up my end of the conversation. "All that neon."

Kevin smiled appreciatively, a parent indulging a wayward child. "Or they like the sport of it, the contest," he said. "The rush as you fly down the side of a mountain fast enough to bash your brains out if you scrape a tree or hit a rock. And every time, something's different. The snow pack is thicker, or the moguls icier, or the wind is blowing in your face instead of at your back."

"It's a game," I offered.

Kevin nodded. "Exactly," he said. "That's it. A game." He waved a hand around him. "Which is what this is. A game with a nice payout. But instead of a mountain, I'm playing against people."

"I don't—"

"People," he said louder, "with their weaknesses and addictions and their need to take anything to make themselves feel better. People with their bullshit rules and narrow minds. But I provide a service that people want. You know how many customers I have who smoke because they're sick and nothing else works? Cancer patients, people in constant pain."

"Like Pelham Greer," I said. I wondered how quickly I could get the baton out of my pocket if I needed to.

Kevin jabbed a finger at me. "My point exactly. Pelham Greer. There's a guy who got injured in the service of his country, a country whose government won't pay for a surgery that could make his life infinitely better. And that same government deems illegal the one thing that makes him feel better, that gets rid of his headaches. Back-ass-ward. Medical marijuana, my friend. It's the future. Hell, it's here now."

A slow-building emotion turned over sluggishly in my chest. It took me a moment to realize what it was: anger at Kelly's self-justification. "It's not just pot," I said. "What about the oxy, the Vicodin? And you aren't selling to cancer patients at Blackburne."

Kevin narrowed his eyes. He reached below the table for his waist—I thought he was scratching his stomach—and when he brought his hand back above the top of the table, I saw that he was holding a knife. It was broad, with a serrated edge like a shark's mouth, the other edge polished and gleaming so I could see, even in the weak light, the sweep of the blade curve upward to a point. It looked like something you could use to kill and butcher a wild hog.

"No," Kevin said softly. "I'm not. Which makes me a bona fide drug dealer to children. But there are reasons to do something other than altruism, or profit. Do you know what Blackburne kicked me out for, Matthias? I was caught having sex with a girl from Chatham Hall. We were on the golf course, and Mr. Downing comes around the hedges with a flashlight and sees us just fucking away on the ninth hole. I didn't lie or get drunk on campus or get in a fight. I was getting laid. It was consensual, we were both eighteen, but her parents had a shit fit. Nothing they could do, legally. But Blackburne kicked me out. Said I'd 'crossed the line' one too many times. I was going premed to Richmond, but when I was expelled, they rescinded my acceptance. I had to repeat senior year at another school, apply to college all over again." Kevin's voice grew even quieter. "I begged them. *Begged* them to let me stay at Blackburne. And they told me to fuck off with six weeks left to graduation." His eyes gleamed with cold fury. "I was *wronged*, Matthias. And you should understand that. We were both wronged. Blackburne laid down a black mark on each of us."

I stared at him, unable to speak. He leaned forward. "You know what I mean, don't you," he said. "You ever feel that if things were just a little different, you'd be set? If just one thing were different, your problems would be gone?" He smiled grimly. "Course you do. Your life has never been the same since your roomie disappeared. That's your one thing. Well, Blackburne is that one thing for me. 'Prep school.' Prepping for what? Go to college, get a degree, become successful? How many Blackburne grads went to college and now sleep on their parents' sofa? All that crap about honor, work ethic, achievement? Horseshit. So fuck 'em."

As I sat in that kitchen and continued to stare at Kevin Kelly, I realized, with a sickening drop of the soul, that this infuriated, bespectacled drug dealer across the table was not so different from me, that with a few twists and turns in my own life, or perhaps only one—like being kicked out of Blackburne—I could easily have turned into what he was: self-indulgent, cruel, and vindictive, a damaged man who took out his fear and pain on others. What was even worse was the realization that perhaps I had been that man, could still be.

Then Kevin leaned closer, so that I could see the pores on his cheeks, his eyes behind his specs wide and intense. He raised the knife in his hand, blowing away every other thought in my head except for a bright yellow fear. "Now tell me," he said, "why you are here."

"Fritz," I said.

He seemed taken aback. "Fritz?" Then he suddenly laughed. "The *clown*," he said. "Ah, fuck. You talked to Greer, didn't you?"

"What . . . clown?"

He shook his head dismissively. "He told you how to get up here? Greer?"

"I made him drive me up here. He said—"

"Hold on," he said. "Hold the fuck on. You had *Greer* drive you up here?"

Maybe I could shove the table at him, give myself an extra second or two to get out the baton. "He brought me in his van," I said. "I made him stop and let me out a little ways down the road so I could walk up here. He drove off and left me, I don't know—"

"Why would Greer drive you up here?" he asked.

"Do you know where Fritz is?"

"Why the fuck would Greer—"

"Do you know—"

"Shut up!"

"—where Fritz is?"

"Did you bring the cops? *Did you call the fucking police?*"

"No! I didn't—"

He was so fast, I didn't have a chance. One second he was shouting at me from across the table, and the next he was on his feet and right next to me, the knife pointing down at my face. My fingers twitched for the baton, but he put the point of his knife right up to my nose and with his other hand batted my fingers away from my pocket. As he reached into my pocket with his left hand and fished around, all I could see was the knife a couple of centimeters from my eyes. Bizarrely, I thought of teaching *Oedipus Rex* last fall, and how my students had been gruesomely fascinated by how the proud Greek king had stabbed out his own eyes. *Jesus God, don't blind me*, I thought. Then Kevin pulled the baton out from my pocket, glanced at it, and threw it onto the floor behind him, where it fell with a loud clatter and rolled underneath the refrigerator.

"Do you think I'm stupid?" he asked. "Because I will cut you up and bury you alive where animals will find you and snack on your balls."

"No, *listen*," I said, desperation in my voice. "They fucked me, Kevin. Greer fucked me. He set me up, and the school believed him. They didn't even try to listen to me. But I've got proof that Greer did it. Then he said you knew where Fritz was, and I told him to bring me here, or I'd call the cops. I—"

"What proof?"

"I . . . He talked about planting drugs in my desk, selling to students. I recorded him saying it. It's on my iPhone." Then a thought shone in my mind, a bright warm light that drew me to it like a moth. "You could listen to it. It's on the Memos app. He doesn't say anything about you on it—he told me that later, after I'd stopped recording. You could use that. We could send him to jail."

He raised an eyebrow. "*We?*"

I drew a shaky breath. "I want in," I said. "On selling. At Blackburne."

He laughed, incredulous. "You *do* think I'm stupid."

"No! Look, Blackburne tried to ruin my life, Kevin. I went to jail. They took me out of my dorm in handcuffs, in front of students. But if they realize I didn't do it, that it was Greer, then he'll get fired and I'll be *set*. I'll be pure as fucking snow, Kevin. The school will freak out about lawsuits, or, or they'll be scared I'll write a book. That'd *terrify* them. They hate anything that could hurt their reputation. They'd practically *beg* me to come back and teach. And once I'm there, fuck *them*. I want in. I'll help you. You can have my phone, do whatever you want with it."

Kevin looked at me as if I were raving. But he wasn't telling me to shut up or doing anything with the knife. He had even pulled it back a few inches from my face.

"Listen to the recording I made," I insisted. "Greer said that you know where Fritz is. And . . . I want to know. I want to know where Fritz is. Just . . . please—"

"Shut up." Kevin stood there, calculating. Abruptly he held out his left hand, his right still holding the knife. "Give me your phone," he said.

"I—" Then I remembered. "I don't have it. Greer took it. He made me give it to him before he drove me here. Call him and ask. Call my phone if you want. Or his. Whatever. He'll tell you—"

"Shut up," Kevin said again. I could almost see things moving into place in his head, facts and perceptions rearranging themselves like so much furniture. Then he pulled out a cell from his jeans. "What's your number?"

I told him, and he dialed it into his phone with one hand, the other still holding up the knife. Maybe I could rush him . . . and get stabbed in the gut, or the face.

"Stay here," Kevin said, holding the phone up to his ear. "Don't fucking move." He turned and walked out of the kitchen and into the back hall. Clearly he wanted to talk to Greer in private. I let out a long, shaky breath. My hopes didn't exactly rise once Kevin left, but they lifted a bit. I figured Kevin would talk to Greer to corroborate my story with the voice recording. What Greer would have to say, I didn't know. And I didn't think for a second that Kevin would truly consider my insane offer. But it gave me time. The problem was, I had no idea what to do next. Maybe I could reach the baton under the refrigerator, or find a knife of my own in a drawer? Or I could run out the back door. I recalled Kevin saying he had security cameras, but I could hide in the woods.

I stood up and started for the back door, and then nearly cried aloud. Lester Briggs was peering in through the back door window. I darted a glance at the back hall, but I didn't see Kevin. Now Briggs gestured at me to open the door. I looked again at the back hall, the thought of that knife causing my skin to crawl. I got up and went as quietly as I could to the back door and turned the bolt to unlock it, letting Briggs in. He wore a heavy red-and-black-checked wool coat and a black knit cap, and his nose was red with cold, although he grinned at me.

"How the hell did you find me?" I whispered.

He actually chuckled. "Think I don't know how to follow a car?"

"There's a man in here, Kevin Kelly. He's got a knife. He's on the phone with Pelham Greer and coming back any second."

Briggs shook his head. "I doubt he's talking to Greer. State police should have him in custody. I called in a favor." He peered around the kitchen. "You say he's got a knife?"

"A big one." I looked back down the hall but still didn't see Kevin. I could still hear that low, throbbing hum from somewhere in the house. When I looked back at Briggs, I saw he had a revolver in his hand.

"Did he have a gun on him?" Briggs murmured.

I shook my head. "Don't know. Didn't see one."

Kevin had to have heard us by now. Where was he? The rest of the house was silent, dark.

"Let's go," Briggs was saying.

I shook my head again. Kevin hadn't said anything about where Fritz was. Now that Briggs was here, I felt together we could persuade him to talk.

"Matthias," Briggs said.

"He's in here somewhere," I said, stepping into the back hall. I could barely make out something in the hall—a slightly open door. The throbbing sound was louder. Behind me I could hear Briggs bite back a curse. I reached the door, looked down the hall again, and still saw no sign of Kevin. I pulled the door all the way open. That hum grew louder— definitely some kind of machinery—and I saw a set of stairs leading down to a basement lit by a dim light. Quickly I went down the steps, keeping an eye out for any hands reaching for my feet.

The room at the bottom was small, about fifteen by fifteen, with a concrete floor and a bare lightbulb hanging from the ceiling. A set of metal shelves lined one wall and reached to the ceiling. The shelves held plastic containers with labels I couldn't read. There was a closed door across the room—the throbbing hum I heard was coming from behind it. Between me and the door were a pile of junk and bric-a-brac, moldering boxes, and more broken furniture.

"Anything down there?" Briggs said from the top of the stairs.

"There's another door," I said. "Maybe—"

I heard a sharp scuffling on the stairs. I turned to see Briggs seem to launch himself down the stairwell, arms out in front of him as if he were diving. He hit the floor like a sack of wet cement, and there was a muffled *crack*, like an old tree branch snapping in two.

Kevin Kelly came down the stairs, the knife in his hand. Backpedaling away from him, I stumbled over the pile of garbage in the center of the room. Frantically I looked around me for something I could use as a weapon. Damp boxes of magazines, blooming with mold. A disintegrating rattan side table. An empty, rusted paint can. Broken pieces of terra-cotta pots. A sagging leather golf bag, stained and worn through at the bottom. Groping inside, I grasped and then withdrew a golf club, its head a flat-faced wedge. Kevin had nearly reached the bottom of the stairs. I continued backing away from him, holding the golf club up in front of me like a sword. Then I bumped into the door on the wall opposite the stairs. As Kevin stepped over Briggs, a snarl on his face, I threw open the door and ran over the threshold.

The sound and the dank heat hit me simultaneously. That throbbing hum I had been hearing was now sharper but still muffled, like the sound from a lawn mower encased in bales of cotton. In front of me was a long room full of brightly lit bulbs hung over a small forest of spiky green plants. The marijuana seemed to be growing out of large trays of water arranged neatly in rows down the length of the room. At the far end of the room, on the left, was another doorway, this one with no door, and the hum seemed to emanate from there. A generator. There were no other doors or exits.

Kevin Kelly came through the doorway behind me, knife raised with the tip up. The golf club forgotten in my hands, I ran down the middle aisle away from him, knocking marijuana plants over to try to slow Kevin down. He gave an angry cry as I threw down an entire tray of plants, leaves thrashing and liquid spilling onto the floor. He kicked the tray out of the way as I continued to run down the aisle. "Where you going?" he asked, waggling the knife at me. With my left hand, I grasped the top of another plant and flung it backward at him. He ducked and batted it away with a forearm. He was laughing. *Fuck this*, I thought, and I raised the golf club and swung at him. Kevin spun to the side, and my club smashed another tray of plants. There was a searing pain on my right arm just above my elbow. I stepped back and saw blood welling through my sleeve.

"That's for the damages," Kevin said. The tip of his knife was wet, and although he was smiling at me, his eyes were furious. "I'm going to hurt you down here. No one will find you. You'll just disappear like your precious roommate."

I swung the club again, backhanded, and struck his left knee. He cried and stumbled, but didn't fall. Instead, he jabbed at my face with his knife. I backpedaled and swung at him again. He bobbed out of the way, and instead of hitting his forehead, my club smashed a low-hanging lightbulb with a spectacular pop of light, showering him with glass. Raising his hands to protect his face, Kevin staggered back and tripped over another tray. I tried to angle around him for the door, but he scrambled to his feet and swung his knife in a vicious arc, forcing me to leap back. Gripping the club, I swung hard and up, as if hitting down the fairway, and he sidestepped, the club missing his chin by inches. The follow-through of my swing made me lose my balance, and I planted a foot to regain it, but my foot splashed down into a puddle of liquid from the overturned grow trays. Something hit the back of that foot near the heel, and pain flared up my calf, my ankle suddenly numb. My leg crumpled beneath me and I fell, crushing yet another tray of marijuana, the heavy, pungent smell of the plant, like citrus and skunk, filling my nostrils. I lay on my back on the floor, the club gone from my hands and my foot aching—I could already feel the swelling. Kevin Kelly stepped forward, looming over me, the blade of his knife now reversed and pointing down at my chest.

"This will hurt," he said.

There was a loud *bang* like a detonation—I thought something had happened to the generator until Kevin, who had frozen in the act of plunging his knife down into me, opened his mouth. Blood stained his lips. He fell forward onto his face just beside me, his body no longer obstructing my view of the doorway, where I saw Briggs leaning against the door frame. A revolver was in his hand, smoke curling lazily from the barrel.

CHAPTER TWENTY-THREE

As it turned out, Kevin Kelly had had more than five hundred plants growing in his basement. Had he lived, he could have easily earned a million a year on the pot alone—that wasn't counting all the oxy and the E and the Vicodin. I was a key witness for the police investigation into Kevin Kelly and Lester Briggs's shooting of him, but I had asked to be allowed to convalesce at my parents' house in North Carolina. I had ruptured my Achilles tendon when I stepped down into that puddle in Kevin's underground grow room, and surgery was required. I turned over my passport to the court and agreed to commute back for the trial.

Briggs, in the UVA hospital for a broken arm and ribs and a herniated disc, said the DA was making a circus out of it because he had his eyes on a bigger desk. "Big bust, lots of press, why wouldn't the DA make hay out of it?" Briggs said to me as I stood on crutches beside his hospital bed. "Probably run for office one day. They all do." He assured me that everything would be fine, especially as Pelham Greer was cooperating.

THE SURGERY ON MY Achilles was amazingly quick, only about an hour and a half long, for something that was so debilitating. One ruptured tendon and I was on crutches, banging off the walls of my parents' house, unable to carry anything unless it was in a backpack, unable to drive to the store to buy milk, unable to do much of anything except sit and prop my foot up and think, which I did not want to do. I had had enough intrigue and adventure, thanks—I didn't want to relive it in my head. I was having occasional nightmares in which Kevin Kelly chased me with a knife that sometimes became a machete, sometimes a broadsword. The dream always ended with me on the ground looking up at him as he raised the blade and swung down. That was when I would wake up.

Seeing someone killed in front of me had undoubtedly taken a toll. Briggs had even suggested I talk to someone about it. But I didn't want to see a therapist—that would mean I would end up having to talk about Fritz, and I wanted to brood on him a little while, keep him to myself a little longer. The fact that Briggs had shot and killed Kevin in order to save my life meant a lot to me, but it also meant that now Kevin could not tell me where Fritz was. His "clown" comment stayed with me. Did he mean Fritz had become a clown? Was he in a circus? The idea just seemed utterly ridiculous. But Kevin had said the word in a mocking sort of way, too, so maybe he had just been calling Fritz a fool.

Blackburne reached out to me in their official sort of way. I received a letter on their trademark red-and-gold stationery, the envelope unmistakable. I opened it and saw with some surprise that it was from Travis Simmons. He did not offer me my old job back, but he did offer his apologies for my being let go due to charges that seemed to be "erroneous," although "the circumstances at that point had warranted the school's action," and he concluded by saying that, if I were found not guilty of those charges, the school would deposit the remainder of my year's salary as stipulated by my contract into my bank account. My heart actually rose at this gesture until I realized that in all likelihood Blackburne was trying to head off a potential lawsuit. My speech to Kevin Kelly about Blackburne being scared of me turned out to have been a bit prophetic.

The same day the letter from Travis Simmons arrived, I got an e-mail from Sam Hodges. It was from a Gmail account, not his school one. It consisted entirely of a short block of verse:

> *Sir, in this audience,*
> *Let my disclaiming from a purposed evil*
> *Free me so far in your most generous thoughts,*
> *That I have shot my arrow o'er the house*
> *And hurt my brother.*

It was from the last scene in *Hamlet*, when Hamlet asks Laertes for forgiveness for the pain he has caused him. I stared at the screen. Sam was apologizing. But he hadn't done anything with regard to the drugs in my room—which, I realized after a moment, was his point: he hadn't done anything, said anything, until now. For a moment, I recalled sitting in jail, no one other than Briggs coming to see me, and resentment stirred. Then I remembered that Sam and Gray Smith had packed up my belongings and brought them and my car to Staunton for me, and my resentment vanished. Sam had, after all, done something, although he clearly felt it hadn't been enough. I sat in front of my laptop, thinking, and then composed and sent the following response, quoting from the point in the play when Hamlet is dying and speaks to his friend:

> *But let it be. Horatio, I am dead,*
> *Thou livest; report me and my cause aright*
> *To the unsatisfied.*

I figured Sam could help restore whatever reputation I had left at Blackburne.

Of course, I heard nothing from Ren Middleton, which suited me just fine.

I'M NOT SURE WHAT led me to e-mail Abby. Boredom would be the easy response, and it's true I was getting rather tired of staring out the window and watching *Matlock* reruns. But it's hardly a satisfactory answer. Love? A need for sympathy? A desire to reconnect after our kiss at the winter dance?

I typed: Hey. So, I got arrested, fired, and crippled since I last saw you.

Less than two hours later, while trying to reread a favorite Tim Gautreaux story, I got her response: Is that supposed to be funny?

Hardly, I typed. Then I attached a picture of the scar from my Achilles surgery, an ugly two-inch pink centipede behind my ankle, and sent the e-mail.

Three minutes later: Oh my God. Are you okay? What happened?

Former classmate chased me with a knife.

And he cut your foot?

I tore my Achilles tendon trying to get away from him.

You must have pissed him off?

I found out he was growing pot and selling it to students at Blackburne. Tried to frame me for it.

After sending this last e-mail, I sat with my fingers touching my keyboard, uncertain what to type next. I hoped what I had already written wouldn't make Abby want to close her laptop. Then I received another e-mail from her: Message me on Facebook. She included a link to her Facebook page, abbydabby1983.

Her page consisted of a blank profile pic, bare-bones info (Lives in Fairfax, Virginia), and nothing else. I saw I had a new friend request—Abby. I accepted, and then messaged her: abbydabby?

Shut it [she said], you're lucky I have a Facebook page.

Is that what this is? Looks like the Internet equivalent of an abandoned condo.

I just set it up, okay? Easiest way to IM. E-mail too slow.

You set up an FB page for me? I'm touched.

Says the prep school pot dealer. Tell me again—were you framed, arrested, or crippled? Oh, right, all three. Do tell.

Somehow, telling Abby via Facebook messaging was cathartic, almost therapeutic. I could cast events in a brighter light, gliding past the dark horror of the basement and the wild stink of fear from Pelham Greer as he tried to fight me for the keys. But behind the snarky joking lay the fact that, once we had exhausted my adventures in drug busting, I would have to find something else to talk about, something that wouldn't drive Abby away again. For the moment, though, it was enough to message her about the joys of being on crutches and having her reply by calling me Gimp.

IN APRIL, AS FLOWERS began to bloom from the spring rains, my cast was removed, and I began walking around in what looked like a space-age ski boot, complete with inflatable balloons on the inside to support my ankle. I handed my crutches to my mother and asked her to throw them in a Dumpster. Tutting, she placed them in a coat closet, saying you never know when they might be needed. I reveled in my newfound freedom of movement, in my ability to walk from the kitchen to the dining room carrying my own dinner plate.

In the midst of congratulating myself on recovering the ability to walk, I received another letter from Blackburne. This one was a reminder of my tenth class reunion in June. I almost tossed it in the trash before I noticed that Trip Alexander was one of the reunion cochairs. I stood in the foyer, the glow of the late-morning sun falling through the sidelights by the front door, and thought of Trip and Diamond and the rest of my classmates whom I had cut off like someone going deep undercover. I hadn't even called Trip or Diamond since I'd last seen them in that hotel room in Culpeper. Before I could change my mind, I ticked the "Yes" box that I would attend, shoved the invitation into the return envelope, and stuck it in the mail.

That spring rolled on, sometimes swiftly and sometimes like watching ice melt. Rehabilitating my Achilles, and my calf muscle, which was ridiculously atrophied, took only a couple of hours a week with a physical therapist. The rest of the time I spent lounging around on my parents' couch, reading old issues of the *New Yorker* and goofing around on the Internet. Lester Briggs and I started e-mailing, mostly comparing hospital stories and empathizing with each other on the indignities of recovery. But no official business. Neither of us was in the mood for it. Abby and I still exchanged e-mails and messaged on Facebook, usually about her classes at Saint Margaret's or how her mother was doing better. We avoided talking on the phone altogether, although there were times I wanted very much to hear her voice. The closest I got to it was taking out the CD she had sent me and listening to it, her voice announcing what she was about to play.

Eventually, my father, ever the pragmatist, made a pointed reference to my seeking gainful employment. Truth to tell, I had found myself gazing at online job postings in the Asheville area. UNC-Asheville wanted a creative writing teacher for two summer sections. Abby, thinking it was a great idea, messaged me: You're too good a writer not to do something with it.

I replied: Says the girl who never read my novel. (Boom!)

Actually, not true now.

What?

I read it.

You did?

There was a brief pause, two minutes that felt like an hour as I stared at the laptop screen. Finally, she typed: Like I said, you're too good a writer not to do something with it.

The phone rang. I looked away from my laptop and stared at the phone. It rang again. My palms suddenly moist, I picked up the phone and nearly dropped it. "Hello?" I said. "Abby?"

"Next guess," Lester Briggs said in his honey-graveled voice. "Got some news for you—an update on Kevin Kelly's business deals. You busy?"

I looked back at my laptop screen. Abby had signed off Facebook. I hesitated, and then said, "No, I'm good. What's up?"

"They keep finding more on Kelly. He had dealers in other private schools in Virginia. Manassas Prep was one of them, if you can believe that. Spent a fair amount of time out west, too, in the past year or so. California, Colorado, Nevada."

"What was he doing out west?"

"The DA thinks he was meeting with other pot growers, maybe planning to branch out."

"He said something about medical marijuana being the future. That was before he threw you down the stairs. How are you doing, by the way?"

I could picture Briggs shrugging. "Finally out of the cast," he said. "Arm's all shrunk, looks like a twelve-year-old's. Back hurts every time I have to sit on the john. Don't get old, Matthias."

"So you shouldn't have come rescue me, is that what you're saying? You should've just let him gut me in his basement, save me the agony of getting older?"

There was a pause.

"I'm joking, Deputy," I said. "Ha-ha, a little laugh in the face of death."

"Everyone's a comedian," Briggs grumbled.

"Seriously, I'm glad you didn't let a guy in a moose shirt kill me. Never would have lived that down."

Briggs uttered something between a snort and a chuckle. "The DA's in seventh heaven," he said. "He's like a bull in a field of cows, trying to figure out which one he's gonna screw first."

I laughed, but it was automatic. My joke had inadvertently rung a bell deep in my own head—a moose shirt . . .

I pulled my laptop over to me, opened a new tab, and started a Google search. Briggs was going on about the DA when I interrupted him. "Where all did you say Kelly had been out west?"

"Why?" Briggs's voice was sharp, interested.

"What about Jackson Hole?"

"Wait a minute. Where?"

"Wyoming," I said. On my laptop was one result of my search: an image of the same tee shirt Kevin Kelly had been wearing, with a cartoon moose on skis. I clicked it, and a new page loaded. I scanned it quickly. "Chase the Moose," I said. "It's a ski race near Jackson Hole. Was Kelly out there?"

"Hold on," Briggs said. I could hear him typing on a keyboard. "Yeah, he was, last May. What's going on?"

"He said something about a *clown* . . ."

"Matthias, what the hell are you talking about?"

"Pelham Greer told me that Kelly knew where Fritz was, that he'd seen him last spring. And when I mentioned it to Kelly, he said, 'The *clown*.' Just like that, all . . . derisive."

"I was wondering when you were going to finally tell me about Fritz," he said. "That's the whole reason you went up to Kelly's house, isn't it? Unless you *wanted* to get stabbed and snap your Achilles tendon—"

"Are you still online? Can you help me look up circuses around Jackson Hole?"

"You think Fritz is a clown?"

I had already started typing. "Got any better ideas?"

Five minutes later we had hit a wall. There were no circuses based in or around Jackson Hole, not ones with clowns and tents at any rate. Of course, clowns could be hired for children's parties. But somehow I didn't see Kevin Kelly flying out to Jackson Hole to build his drug empire and making the time to stop by some kid's birthday party and running into Fritz wearing an orange wig and gigantic shoes. It was beginning to feel a bit ludicrous. "Can you find out who Kelly met with in Wyoming?" I asked Briggs. "Maybe they could tell us where Kelly could have seen Fritz?"

"It'll take time," Briggs said. "DA might not want to share."

"You're resourceful."

"He didn't just go to Wyoming, Matthias. There's California, Nevada, Oregon, Colorado. You want to look at all the circuses in those places, too?"

"If I have to, yes," I said, though I felt deflated. Jackson Hole had felt so right, somehow.

After a pause, Briggs said, "Maybe we're thinking about the wrong kind of clowns."

"What do you mean?"

"There's the kind of clowns with the face paint and the rubber noses who honk horns at kids in a big top. Then there's the kind who keep bulls from stomping all over their riders once they throw them off."

"A rodeo clown," I said, sitting up. I leaned forward and started typing again. "When was Kelly out in Jackson Hole, specifically?" I asked, looking at my laptop screen.

"Last May," Briggs said. "Memorial Day weekend, actually. Why?"

"Because," I said, my voice trembling with excitement as I stared at the screen, "the Jackson Hole Rodeo starts on Memorial Day weekend."

CHAPTER TWENTY-FOUR

The Jackson Hole Airport is in the middle of a wide valley, a flat scrubland underneath a dome of sky, ringed by sharp mountains. From a distance, the Blue Ridge Mountains around Asheville look like rising folds in a bedsheet; as you approach, they gather you in slowly until you realize all at once that you are among them. In Jackson Hole, the Tetons thrust themselves into view, giant rocks dropped from space by a Titan. As I stepped out of the plane and walked down a wheeled set of steps to the tarmac, I stared at the Teton Range jutting out of the scrublands. Although a couple of miles distant, they seemed within arm's reach. It was a cloudless, sunny day in late May, and yet I was shivering in the breeze—I was well over a mile above sea level and freezing when I passed through shade. I had difficulty grasping that I was still on the same planet, let alone the same country.

I found a cheap hotel called the Lucky Dollar that seemed to have little familiarity with dollars and even less with luck, but it had a forlorn room with a king-sized bed waiting for me. I threw my suitcase onto the floor of the tiny closet and lay on top of a hideous saffron-colored bedspread that felt like it was made of oven mitts. I was exhausted but too keyed up to sleep, so I stared at the ceiling and waited for evening, when the rodeo would start.

THE RODEO WAS LOCATED in a fairgrounds lot backed up against Snow King Mountain, which rose steeply at the southern end of Jackson as if barring passage beyond. At half past six, I parked my rental car in the rodeo lot and crossed a dirt-and-gravel yard, my Achilles tendon stiff but not complaining yet. I passed several parked semis with transport rigs for horses and bulls and eventually stopped at a ticket booth, where I gained entrance through a swinging gate to the arena itself, a mud-churned space with stands on one side and chutes on the other. The stands were filling slowly with families, small groups of men in cowboy hats, grandmothers, and teenagers in denim and boots. I bought a cup of hot chocolate and cupped my hands around it, grateful for the warmth, and then found a seat near the front with a clear view.

Bright white floodlights shone down on the arena below. The parking lot was to the right beyond sheets of plywood hung over the fence. Off to the left, fenced-in pens extended from a large warehouse-like stable. Across from me stood the chutes, behind which milled several men in chaps and cowboy hats—I assumed they were the riders. I couldn't see them well, but I knew that eventually they would come close enough for me to get a better view. Breath misted out of everyone's mouth as the sun fell toward the western peaks and the sky began to shade toward a deeper blue.

A flat, metallic voice came out of the speakers, informing us that the rodeo was about to begin. A young woman with a sheet of shimmering brown hair and a white cowboy hat stepped up to a microphone at the far edge of the muddied field below, and everyone stood and removed his or her hat as the woman sang "The Star-Spangled Banner," and we cheered politely. A crew of men in jeans and work gloves brought out a series of barrels that they placed around the arena before hurrying off into the shadows of the stable. The same flat voice as earlier announced the barrel-racing contestants, who rode one by one out of the stable, their tall, clean Stetsons and bright shirts contrasting sharply with their horses, who took dignified steps as they entered the arena, mud up to their fetlocks, heads carried high as if suffering their riders for only the moment. They raced around the barrels, the riders leaning into their mounts and coming within a hairbreadth of grazing the barrels with their knees as they rounded them tightly and then galloped for the finish line. After the adults competed, there was another race for children. A tiny girl on a huge brown horse, her hat almost as big as she was, won easily and waved a petite hand at the audience.

The men in work gloves ran out and removed the barrels, and the flat speaker voice announced the calf-roping competition. A young cowboy, barely out of his teens, rode down a bawling calf and flicked his lasso so it caught the calf's rear legs and the animal crashed to its side. The cowboy dismounted, ran to the calf, and tied the rope around its hooves in less than five seconds to general applause. The second cowboy, older and gaunter, was even faster—one moment he was on his horse, lasso secured to a calf's hind legs, and the next he was standing in the mud, the calf trussed up and helpless. A third cowboy made a great show of twirling his lasso overhead, but when he popped it at his calf, the animal spooked and dodged, the lasso missing it by several feet. The cowboy's horse tossed its head as if in disgust, trotting off to the stable with the rider's expression hard and set.

In the pause after the calf roping, I could see lots of activity by the chutes across the way. One or two gates shuddered as the bulls behind them vented their frustration at being penned in. Two men in bright red chaps, plaid shirts, and face paint came out onto the field to cheers. I squeezed my empty Styrofoam cup and leaned forward, peering through the white haze of the spotlights. One was balding with a bad comb-over, although I couldn't tell if that was real or part of his makeup. The other was tall and lean, younger, but with more of a stoic face behind the white-and-black greasepaint. I followed him as he strode around the muddy arena, working the crowd, waving at kids in the stands, pretending to lasso them and then dropping his hat, bending over to pick up the hat and then standing up as his red chaps fell to the mud. I couldn't tell if it was Fritz.

The two clowns met up at the gate to one of the middle chutes, the balding one grasping a rope. The announcer read off the name of the first bull rider in his flat voice. A bell rang and the balding clown threw open the gate, the bull within bursting forth, heaving and plunging, and the rider clutching the rope lashed around the bull's chest. The rider's free hand whipped about through the air like a pennant in the thick of battle. I had thought the horses were big, but the bull was the size of a small car. Still plunging up and down, the bull began to rotate in a circle. The rider slipped, his face banging against the back of the bull's neck; then he fell off to the side and hit the mud, one of the stomping hooves landing on his arm. The two clowns rushed forward, the balding one waving in the bull's face, the tall one grabbing the fallen rider and leading him away. The bull danced madly in the center of the arena until two riders with lassos approached, driving the animal back toward the pens.

The next rider had a bit more luck, his bull merely whirling around and around as if trying to bite its own tail. He lasted the full eight seconds, and then leapt off the bull, landing clumsily in the mud and falling to his knees, but he scampered to the wall and climbed over it before the bull could charge him. The tall clown had been shouting at the bull, and I strained to hear his voice, but unsuccessfully. I realized I had shredded the empty Styrofoam cup in my hands and let the pieces drop to my feet.

The third rider looked to be in trouble before his chute even opened. I caught a glimpse of his eyes, wide with fright. The gate rattled on its hinges as the bull, dark with a barrel-sized hump, struck it with its flank. I could see the wicked curve of a horn shine like an ivory tooth in the floodlight. Then the bell rang and the chute opened. Immediately the bull tore out of the chute, bucking and kicking out its hind legs, leaping and spinning in a circle, the rider's hat blown through the air. The rider seemed to hunch over the bull, as if trying to hide from its rage by lying prone on its back, and then with a jerk he fell to one side. Even from the stands I could feel the impact of the bull's hooves striking the ground, mud spraying as if from a mortar shell. The rider clutched at the rope, hanging on to the side of the heaving bull. His feet were dragged through the mud, and were then thrown up in the air as he was tossed like a proverbial rag doll. *Just let go,* I thought, and then I saw that his left hand was caught in the rope. The bull continued to carry him along as it plunged and spun. "Oh, mercy," an older woman said behind me.

The two clowns ran up to the bull, the balding one again in the bull's face while the taller one dashed to help untangle the rider. But the bull ignored the balding clown and, with almost casual violence, turned and lowered its head, hooking the tall clown around the back of the legs with its horns and tossing him aside in a backward somersault. Meanwhile, the rider flailed uselessly at his trapped hand. My breath caught as I watched the tall clown hit the mud facedown. He scrambled to his feet.

The two men on horseback approached, lassoes in hand, but they hesitated, clearly unwilling to do anything that could harm the rider, who looked like a man being slowly churned to death. The balding clown was waving a green hat at the bull, trying to distract the animal, but the tall one couldn't get to the rider and was holding a hand to his ribs. Meanwhile the bull continued to spin around and around, tossing its head angrily, its horns stabbing the air.

Two men in jeans and flannel shirts ran into the arena, part of the work crew that had moved the barrels earlier. They still had their work gloves on. One, Hispanic with a brush of a mustache, went to the tall clown to see if he was all right. The second, with short blond hair, made straight for the bull, his arms wide as if rushing to embrace it. The bull stomped and began to run at the man, lowering its head, the rider being dragged helplessly along. At the last moment, the bull's horns thrusting toward his navel, the blond brought his arms in, pivoted off his right foot, and spun once around, the bull charging through empty air. It was like watching a dancer pirouette around a rhino. The man ended up next to the bull's shoulder, his hands on the rope binding the rider. Then the rider was free, leaning heavily on the blond man. The balding clown helped drag them to the wall as the men on horseback moved in, crying out at the bull, their lassoes whirling and moving the beast off to the side. After a stunned second or two, those in the audience clapped and cheered, some waving their hats.

I found myself on my feet with the rest of them, but I wasn't clapping. I stared down into the arena at the blond man in work gloves, sweat running down his face. The hair was completely different, but I had seen that pivot and spin before, the same fast shuffle of feet, the angle of the shoulders as the man had turned into his tight spin. He had done that before in a game against Norfolk Academy on a lateral pass, where he had pivoted around the end of the line, dodged a cornerback, and run into the end zone. I stood in the chill night and watched Fritz Davenport climb up onto the fence and straddle it as the other cowboys led the bull away.

I FORCED MY WAY through the standing crowd, people still talking about that last bull and the man who had rescued the rider, and made my way toward the stairs that led down to the ground by the pens and the stable. But a church youth group, all its members in matching purple tee shirts underneath their coats, was clogging the aisle, a score or more of boys and girls apparently heading for the porta potties standing next to the pens. I turned and went back through the crowd the other way, toward the parking lot, ignoring a shout as I stepped on someone's foot. My own foot was beginning to clamor for attention, the dull ache in my heel that I felt at the end of every day now upgraded to a burn, but I just craned my neck to see whether Fritz was still by the chutes. All the cowboys seemed to have exited the arena. Limping, I made my way down the stairs at the far end, hurried out the gate and past the ticket booth, the gravel crunching beneath my sneakers. There was a closed gate, against which leaned a fat, bearded man in a red plaid shirt and a dirty cowboy hat. Despite my sense of urgency, I hesitated. Just walking up and asking about Fritz didn't seem like the right play. It might scare Fritz off, and I hadn't come this far to lose him. He might not even be using his real name. Then a man farther down the fence, pulling bales of hay off a flatbed, called to the fat cowboy, who pushed himself off the gate and ambled over to help. As soon as he left, I quickly pushed the gate open and stepped through, letting it swing shut behind me. I didn't look back.

Here stood a handful of trailers, all backlit by the bright lights of the arena and crossed in shadow. Knots of men stood around smoking and chatting. The flat voice of the announcer came out of the speakers again, talking about bronc riding. A medic in a blue uniform knelt down in front of the last bull rider, who was sitting in a folding chair, his shoulders trembling, head down in defeat. Beside him were the two clowns, their face paint now ludicrous, even bizarre. The balding one had a slightly affronted air about him, as if embarrassed by the rider's behavior. The tall one was closer to me, and I caught his eye. "You know where I could find the guy who saved him?" I said, indicating the bull rider with a nod.

The clown looked at me, the sweat that was running through his grease-paint making his face seem half-melted. "Might be over there, getting a cup of coffee." He pointed off to the right, toward the stable. "Why?"

I waved and moved off, not wanting to engage with anyone else until I found Fritz. Pausing to let a man carrying a pail of water cross my path, I glanced back and saw that the tall clown had left the bull rider and was dogging my steps. I hurried on, stepping around the end of a trailer and moving toward the stable as I tried not to let my limp slow me down. To my left, I could hear the crowd gasp; turning my head, I saw in the arena someone attempting to ride a bronco. The horse was kicking frantically, its rear hooves bucking into the night sky and its rider leaning back as if riding a barrel down a waterfall.

Ahead, by the pens, I saw a table with a stainless steel urn and stacks of coffee cups, and a group of men standing around and talking. "Hey," someone said behind me. I ignored the voice and strode forward, trying to get a good look at the men around the coffee. A hand touched my shoulder. "What do you think you're doing?" came the slow voice of the tall clown.

"I'm looking for somebody," I said, turning around and tearing my arm out of his grasp as I glared at him. His face looked like an overheated wax impression of a panda, black circles smudged around his eyes.

"There's nobody back here don't work here, boss," he said calmly. "You need to move on."

"No, I just need to—I'm looking for a friend of mine—"

The men around the coffee looked up.

"You need to get out," said the clown, "or you'll be escorted out, your choice."

I wanted to laugh aloud at the absurdity, the man in the melting clown face demanding that I leave while Fritz was back here somewhere. But the laugh died in my throat as the blond man who had rescued the bull rider looked around from the coffee and stepped slowly forward. His hair was short and thatched, his face tanned and roughened and slack with surprise, but I knew him.

"Pete?" the clown said, addressing the blond man. "You know this guy?"

I looked at the man the clown had called Pete. "Ho," I said.

"Ho," said Fritz.

WE STOOD IN A trailer that served as a changing room for the rodeo clowns—bullfighters, Fritz had called them. The trailer held a rack of various colored shirts and overalls. A heap of straw hats lay on a counter next to a small round mirror and a flat box containing what I guessed was greasepaint. A shabby green sofa sat propped against the wall at this end of the trailer. The room smelled of sweat and mildew and the sharp tang of dipping tobacco.

"Sorry about George," Fritz said. He was referring to the tall clown. "He's protective. Thought you might be trying to serve a warrant or something."

"A warrant?"

"Happens sometimes. Last week a stable hand got served divorce papers." Fritz leaned back against the counter with the hats. "We try to take care of one another."

The pause after this stretched on, the tension taut in the air. I felt that if I spoke a moment too soon, something would irrecoverably break. All those years since that March day in the trees at Blackburne, all the choices I had made or avoided—it all seemed reduced to this moment in a trailer, standing across from Fritz. I found myself looking at a *Far Side* calendar on the wall, the picture of a cow standing at a microphone reading something. The calendar was too far away for me to read what the cow was saying.

"So, what's with the 'Pete'?" I said. Some distant part of me registered the anger in my voice but elected not to do anything about it. It was beyond unimaginable to find Fritz here, with blond hair and a new name and identity, with friends.

Fritz shrugged. "It's simple. Easy to remember."

"So, what, you've got a driver's license, Social Security number? Whole new life?"

"How'd you find me?" he asked. He placed his hands down on the counter he was leaning against and looked at me. "Did my family send you?"

I stared back. "Your family had you declared dead," I said. "Last year."

I am not proud to admit that I took some small pleasure in seeing his reaction. His face drew into itself, and he dropped his head slightly. I noticed a smudge of dirt on his forehead, just above his left eye. He took in a breath. "Are they okay?" he asked, looking at his boots.

"Sure. Great," I said, pacing in the narrow space. There wasn't much room—I had to turn around after two steps. "Your sister quit Juilliard and can't listen to classical music anymore, let alone play it. Your mom doesn't want to stick her head in the oven anymore. Your dad lives at his goddamn company. Your uncle—well, shit, at least he's got something going on in his life."

"You've seen my uncle?" Fritz said, still looking down at the floor.

"Yeah. He's pretty torn up about . . ." I waved a hand vaguely at the trailer, unable at the moment to conceive of an appropriate word.

Fritz stood up off the table and lifted his gaze. "Did he send you here? Does he know where I am?"

"No, he didn't send me—"

"Please don't lie to me, Matthias." It was the first time he'd called me by my name.

I gave a sharp bark of laughter. "Lie to you," I said. I wanted to shout, to rage. Anger and bitterness and sorrow flowed through me like separate dark rivers, a flood of emotion carrying me off to whatever happened next. "I'm not lying to you, Fritz," I said. "Your family has no idea where you are. Honest to God. They think you're *dead*, remember?"

Fritz picked up a straw hat and toyed with the brim, turning the hat slowly round and round in his hands. "I'm sorry I hurt you," he said. "I know how upset you must be."

I wanted to snatch his hat and throw it out of the trailer, watch it sail across the lot and fall into the mud. As if reading my mood, he laid the hat back down on the counter. "So how *did* you find me?" he asked.

It was startling to look at my friend after all these years, to see his old face, which had always been on the edge of a lopsided smile, half-hidden within the face in front of me now, which was weathered and keen and sad. The same, but different. I wondered how he saw me, if my face was as changed from what it had been, and for a piercing moment I had a glimpse of what it might be like to grow old. "It's a long story," I said. Suddenly, I was bone-tired. "Remember Kevin Kelly, from school?"

Fritz frowned, remembering. "That kid who called us Nazis?"

I nodded. "He saw you out here, last year. I figured, what the hell, it was worth a shot."

"He told you? Are you guys friends?"

I laughed at that, an ugly sound. "He was selling drugs at school. At Blackburne. I'm teaching there—well, I was, anyway. I found out about it, the drugs, and heard he knew where you were, so I went to try to get him to tell me. Didn't quite work out the way I had planned."

Fritz considered this. "Is he here with you?"

"No. He's dead. A cop shot him when he tried to stab me in his grow room. Ex-cop, actually."

Fritz stared at me. "Oh-*kay*," he said, and his guarded look of confusion actually made me smile.

"Needs some more explanation, I know," I said.

Fritz spread his hands out. "I'm not exactly in a position to demand explanations," he said. For the first time, a small, lopsided smile hovered on his face.

That look, that acknowledgment of debts unpaid, dislodged my anger enough to make me sit down and tell him, from start to finish, the story of the past year, from getting the job at Blackburne to confronting Kevin Kelly. I left out nothing, including what I'd learned from Trip and Diamond. He leaned against the counter, listening, his face intense and hard. Twice he raised his hand halfway to his neck and then put it down. The second time he did it, when I was explaining how Briggs had helped me realize what Kevin had meant by *clown*, I stopped talking and waited expectantly for him to look at me, and then I slowly drew out from my pocket the Saint Christopher medal on its chain.

"I thought you might want this," I said.

Fritz stared at it, and for the first time since I'd begun my story, something shifted over his face, a look of longing. He reached for the medal, but I closed my hand around it.

"I've told you my story," I said. "Now tell me why I should give this to you. You left it under my pillow, Fritz. Before you walked off the map. Tell me why."

He looked at my closed hand, and then at me, but before he could speak, there were two short knocks on the trailer door, and it opened to reveal George, still wearing his greasepaint. "Show's over, Pete," he said, ignoring me. "You okay? Tommy's asking for you."

His eyes on me, Fritz said to George, "Tell Tommy I'll be there in a minute."

George hesitated, glancing at me. "Need me to cover for you?"

I'll admit George and I had not gotten off on the right foot, but my patience was worn thin. I was on the verge of getting answers to a mystery that had shadowed my life, and George was acting like a jealous prom date. "Who's Tommy?" I asked, interjecting myself into the conversation like a dog lifting a leg on a rival's rosebush.

George's sour look was replaced by alarm as a commotion broke out behind him. He turned toward the door. "You can't—" he started, and then a small dark-haired boy, three or four years old, ran past him into the trailer. He was wearing jeans and a sweater. A frayed straw cowboy hat on a string around his neck bounced against his shoulders. He grinned and ran up to Fritz, ignoring both me and George.

"The show's over," the boy announced to Fritz.

"Yes, it is," Fritz said. A slow smile spread across his face.

The boy turned to look at me like a curious bird. "What's in your hand?" he asked.

I looked down at my closed hand, the Saint Christopher medal in it and a loop of the chain hanging from my fist. "Something that belongs to my friend," I said.

The boy's eyes widened. "Can I see it?" he asked.

Fritz stirred. "Can I see it, please," he said. He nodded at George, who, with a final suspicious glance at me, withdrew and closed the door to the trailer behind him.

"Please," the boy said.

I opened my hand, and the boy looked at the medal, his mouth slightly open. "Oh," he said.

Fritz put his hand on top of the boy's head. "This is an old friend of mine. His name's Matthias."

The boy tore his eyes from the medal and looked up at me, smiling. "That's a funny name," he said delightedly.

I smiled back. "It is." I looked at Fritz.

"This is Tommy," Fritz said. "My son."

CHAPTER TWENTY-FIVE

The next morning, I returned to the rodeo lot with two coffees. Tommy sat at one end of Fritz's trailer, armed with a stack of coloring books and waiting for *Sesame Street* to come on. I sipped my coffee gratefully, and Fritz looked tired, but he just cupped his hands around his coffee and let it slowly grow cold as he told me about Tommy's mother, Shanna.

There were a few other things I wanted to know besides the story of Tommy's mother—why Fritz had run away and was now a rodeo bull-fighter, for instance—but it was clear that Fritz needed to tell me the story his own way. And I was here to listen.

He had met Shanna five years ago when he'd been working as a stable hand outside of Houston and a horse had reared up and clipped Fritz in the head with its hooves. "Shanna was an EMT at the hospital," Fritz said. "I come into the ER, blood running down my face, and this little girl on the bench sees me and asks her mom in this loud whisper, 'Is he gonna die?' But Shanna just took me off and stitched me up. Got a great scar just above my hairline. I asked for her number, right there in the ER, and she just laughed and said that horse must've hit me harder than she thought. But I went back and asked her out. We dated for a while, and then she told me she was pregnant." He turned the cup around in his hands. "Thing is, I liked the idea of having a family," Fritz continued. "I'd been alone for a long time." He glanced at me, but I just sipped my coffee, refusing to take the bait. "I was half in love with her, so I asked her to marry me. She said no, but she stayed with me through the pregnancy. Or might be more accurate to say she let me stay with her. Right after Tommy was born, I started working the rodeo, so we traveled a lot. Shanna thought it would be a big adventure, and they need EMTs everywhere. For a while she worked for the rodeo, too. But it was hard with a newborn baby—crying, feeding, diapers, all that and you get no sleep. Everything is twenty-four-seven about your kid. Once I held that baby, though . . ." He looked across the room at Tommy, who was talking to his coloring book as he scribbled in it. "It's a cliché, maybe, but I didn't know how much I could love someone else until I had him."

When he had paused for a good while, I said, "Shanna didn't feel the same way?"

He shook his head, glancing at Tommy, who was now playing with his stuffed animals. Fritz lowered his voice. "She liked to go out, have fun. Not a party girl, not like that, but staying at home with a baby wasn't what she wanted out of life."

"But she *had* a baby."

Fritz sighed. "She could've had an abortion, but she was a little nervous about it, and I convinced her to keep him. I thought she'd change her mind once he was born. But we started fighting instead." He glanced at Tommy again, but Tommy was engrossed with his animals—they were all apparently pirates because he was having them say things like "Argh, matey, walk the plank!" and then marching them off the edge of the television. Fritz lowered his voice even more. "When Tommy was about a year old, she talked about giving him up for adoption. I knew that was it. I kept Tommy and she left. She's back in Houston, sends him cards, calls every few months. It's okay."

I watched Tommy show one of his coloring books to a teddy bear, pretending to read him a story. "No, it's not," I said quietly.

Fritz sagged a little in acknowledgment. "No," he said. "Dammit."

"Daddy," Tommy said solemnly, not looking up from his teddy bear, "that's a bad word."

"Sorry, buddy," Fritz said. He hesitated, and then said, "Tommy, I'm gonna turn on *Sesame Street*—"

"Yes!"

"Hold on—Mr. Matthias and I are going to step outside and leave you here to watch TV. We'll be right outside if you need us."

"Okay, Daddy," Tommy said.

It was cold and clear outside, the sky an immense brilliant blue. The Tetons ranged along the horizon. I stretched, enjoying the sun on my face after being closed up in the trailer, but Fritz hunched his shoulders in his jacket. We walked slowly around in the cold mud and gravel of the lot, keeping the trailer in sight. A man in a shearling jacket and skullcap walked past and nodded a greeting, though Fritz barely noticed. He seemed to be deciding something. I held my breath, waiting and walking in silence.

"The day I left," Fritz said. He turned to face me and stopped, and so did I. "I didn't want you to think I was leaving because of you. I wasn't. That was why I left that medal under your pillow. Sort of a . . . good-bye, a sign of friendship. I don't know. Maybe I should have kept it."

An invisible hand tightened its hold around my lungs and heart. And then slowly, slowly, it released. Just as slowly, I took my hand out of my jacket pocket and held the Saint Christopher medal out to him. Fritz looked at me, then at it, and held out his hand. I placed the medal into his palm.

"Take it back," I said. "Just tell me why you left. Please."

Fritz considered the medal in his hand, hefted it, and then raised his head to look across the yard at the door of his trailer, then at the single window, the blinds to which were shut. "I was . . ." He cleared his throat and then grimaced. His hand clenched around the Saint Christopher medal. "When I was eleven," he said, talking to his clenched hand, "my father started working a lot. He'd always worked a lot, but now he was coming home at nine, ten o'clock at night, driving to work at five the next morning. Some nights he just stayed at the office, slept on the couch. I remember wondering if he was having an affair. I even said something like that to my mother. She just looked at me with a sad smile and said the only affair my father was having was with his work."

He glanced up at me, as if to make sure I was listening. I nodded in encouragement, though I wasn't sure where Fritz was going with this.

He coughed, once, and continued. "This went on for a while, and Abby kept asking Mother why Father didn't come to her recital, why Father never took us out to dinner anymore. When he was home on the weekends— and he was even busy working then, bringing home a big briefcase stuffed with papers—he would throw a ball with me or listen to Abby on her cello, something he said he loved. But he still wasn't always there—part of him was always back at the office. So one day—it was June and we weren't in school—the doorbell rings and I go to answer it and it's Uncle Wat, beaming down at me like Santa Claus without a beard. That's how I remember him that day. Abby came running downstairs when she heard his voice, and he swept us both into a big bear hug and said he was coming to stay with us for a while if that was okay. We thought it was fantastic. We loved Uncle Wat—Mother didn't have any brothers or sisters, so he was our only uncle. He always gave us great Christmas presents and told stories about hunting trips he'd gone on or how he'd once seen a live sperm whale. Wat told us that his town house had to be renovated, so he was going to stay in our guest room until it was finished." Fritz started walking again—it was still chilly if you didn't move around—and I kept pace with him as we slowly walked round the yard again.

"Even then, I figured there was something else going on," Fritz said. "I think my parents had decided that if Father couldn't be home much, then Uncle Wat could sort of step in as a replacement dad, someone to help

Mother with us. Wat worked hard and spent a lot of time at NorthPoint, too, but he always seemed to have time to do something with us, whether it was attending one of Abby's recitals or coming to one of my swim meets or just having dinner together, laughing and eating more than anyone else.

"I could tell Mother liked having him around, too. You know Wat—he's bigger than life. When he'd walk into a room, it was like someone had turned on extra lights, and you hadn't even realized until then that it had been kind of dark earlier. Mother craved the company of another adult. She'd been an art history major at Vassar and probably would have ended up curating at a museum, except that she married my father and stayed home to raise us. With Father being gone so much, she'd started reading a lot, hours at a time stretched out on the couch. Sometimes she wore her dressing gown all morning. She was smoking, too, every once in a while going out onto the deck out back for a cigarette. Abby actually yelled at her about it once, and Mother told her that she wasn't doing it in the house, she wasn't flaunting it in front of us, and that it was her business.

"With Wat home, though, Mother changed. She was . . . cautious, at first, protective of what had been her run of the house. That vanished inside of a week. She laughed more, for one thing. Wat told outrageous stories and jokes, and he was always very gallant with Mother, pulling out her seat for her at dinner, complimenting her food, all that. She started wearing lipstick again, too. Abby teased her about it at dinner one night, and Wat told her that beauty was something to be admired, not ridiculed. He was being the dashing gentleman, you know, even gave a little wink to Mother, like she was in on the joke, but she blushed a little.

"When Father came home one night, a bit earlier than usual, we were all eating dinner and listening to Wat tell a story about a hot air balloon ride and his beauty pageant date, who was getting airsick. It was hysterical. Abby was snorting, and my stomach hurt from laughing. Mother was holding her hand to her mouth, saying, 'Wat, now stop,' but clearly not wanting him to stop. I was the first one to see my father. He was standing in the kitchen doorway, right across from me, watching us. I stopped laughing immediately. His expression was pretty blank, but my first thought on seeing him was that I was doing something wrong. Then I realized that he was watching what our family was supposed to be like, but wasn't. It was one of the few times I felt like I understood my father, empathized with him, even. After a minute, Mother saw him and stood up. He waved her down and pulled up another chair, and Wat finished his story, although what we had thought was hysterically funny now only seemed amusing. I remember feeling a little embarrassed and wondering why we'd all been laughing so hard.

"It was maybe a week later, I guess. It was pouring rain outside, had been all day. Abby was at another cello lesson, and Wat and Mother and I were stuck in the house. Father was at work, of course. I was in a funk. I didn't want to listen to any of my music, read a book, watch TV, any of that. I was just *bored*, you know? The way we'd get sometimes at Blackburne on Sundays, sick of the day and wanting it to end but dreading Monday at the same time? Well, that was me that day.

"Mother tried to play Scrabble with me, but we ended up fighting about words and spelling. Wat was sitting in a corner, reading Shakespeare of all things, *Much Ado about Nothing*, but he would look over the top of his book to watch us play. Mother kept building really good words off mine. I'd play *help* and she'd build *epoxy* off that, and get a double-word score. She was getting a kick out of it, too, I could tell. Now I look back and think she wasn't thinking about beating me as much as winning a game, if that makes sense. But all I saw was that my mother seemed to enjoy making me look stupid. Then she played *jovial* for something like sixty points, and I was so irritated, I shoved the board away from me. Next thing I knew, she got up out of her seat and slapped me. She'd never done that before. I was being an asshole, I know, but then she just . . . *cracked* me across my face. She was pissed, but it all drained out of her face as soon as she realized what she'd done, and then she looked . . . I don't know, *old*, I guess, and scared. I stormed upstairs, ignoring her as she called to me, and I heard Wat say something to her before I slammed my bedroom door and fell on the bed. I cried, man. Bawled into my pillow. My own mother had *hit* me, you know?

"After a while, there was a knock on my door. It was Wat. He came in and closed the door behind him and came over and sat down on my bed, his hand on my back. He didn't say anything. I felt . . . like I was *safe*. Like he was on my side. 'It's all right to cry,' he said. 'There's nothing embarrassing about crying.' I sat up and wiped my arm across my face, trying to get the snot off. He handed me a handkerchief, and I wiped my eyes and blew my nose and all."

Fritz stopped walking and looked again at the Saint Christopher medal in his hand, although I got the sense that he was no longer seeing the medal, or anything else other than his memory. We had walked around to the far side of the yard across from his trailer by a stack of hay bales. Somewhere beyond the trailer, I could hear men calling to one another, and a bull lowing. Fritz continued to stare at nothing. I was about to say something, his name maybe, when he sighed and looked at me, his eyes sad and weary.

"He kissed me," he said.

I had no idea how to reply, so I simply parroted his words back at him. "He kissed you?"

"I turned to give him his handkerchief back, and he leaned over and kissed me, full on the mouth." Fritz said this clearly and without obvious emotion in his voice, although the bleak look in his eyes was awful to see. "I was shocked, you know? Like I didn't know what to do. I just sat there and let my uncle kiss me."

"Fritz—"

"Worst part was, I think I probably kissed him back. More reflex than anything, I guess. It's . . ." His voice trailed off, and something hard shone in his eyes then. "He pulled away, looking at me. I couldn't tell what he was thinking. He put his hand on my cheek for a moment and then got up and walked out and closed the door behind him." Fritz took a breath, exhaled. "You know the weirdest part? All I could think was that he would get in so much trouble if anyone found out. That was my biggest fear. Everyone loved Wat. *I* loved him. So I went to the bathroom and washed my face and then went downstairs and told my mother I was sorry, and she hugged me and cried and said she was sorry, too. And Wat sat in the corner behind his Shakespeare, smiling."

The silence after Fritz stopped speaking was too horrible, so I rushed to fill it. "But you told someone, right? Tell me you told someone."

Fritz shrugged, the movement a pitiful rising of his shoulders. "Who could I tell, Matthias?" he asked. "I was afraid. Not so much for me, but for Wat. I was afraid my father would kill him. And it didn't feel like he was molesting me."

"You were, what, twelve? He's your *uncle.*"

"Thanks for clearing that up," he said dryly.

"Jesus, Fritz!"

Fritz actually smiled a little, the old lopsided grin. "I don't think Jesus had an awful lot to do with it."

His calmness and that smile disarmed me so that I simply stood there. "So," I said, my voice a bit strained, as if I were having to speak around something in my throat, "did this happen—I mean, was this a one-time event, or . . ." I didn't know how to continue.

Fritz raised an eyebrow. "Have you ever known Wat to restrain himself?" he said.

I managed to sit down on a hay bale. If there hadn't been a hay bale, I would have had to sit on the ground.

Fritz stood there, considering me. He sighed and then rubbed his face again. "This sounds bizarre, I know," he said. "But it felt like . . . something *special* with him. A connection, something private. Everyone wanted a piece of Wat. Women especially, even my mother. Men wanted to be seen with him, shake his hand, get into conversations with him. And here he was paying all this attention to me." I must have made a noise or grimace, because he raised a hand out to me, as if in supplication. "I know, it's crazy. And sick. It's sick, Matthias, I know that. I didn't have sex with him. Not *intercourse*. God, what a horrible word." He took a breath as if about to dive underwater. "When Wat moved back into his town house about a week afterward, he would invite me to visit. Wanted to show me Washington, he'd say to my parents. He'd invite Abby, too, but she had lessons and recitals all the time. Now I see he planned it that way. So I'd go visit for a night, and Wat would show me D.C.—the Washington Monument, the Mall, the Capitol building. He tried to get me into the White House once, but it didn't happen. And then we'd go back to his town house and have dinner, maybe watch baseball. And maybe Wat's hands would wander, or he'd kiss me again. He'd be sitting next to me on the couch, and it would just sort of . . . happen. Not every time I visited." He peered down at the Saint Christopher medal in his hand. "My God, once when he just kissed the top of my head after dinner and went upstairs to bed, I was almost *hurt*." He shook his head, bemused by his own reaction.

In a low voice, and making an effort to keep my voice from shaking, I said, "Is that why you ran away?"

Fritz put the medal in his pocket. "No," he said. "Not entirely. I'd thought about it before—what kid doesn't think of running away from home, right? I guess I had more reason to run than most. The whole thing with Wat was—*confusing*. Was he gay? Was *I* gay? Women loved Wat, so why was he doing the things he did with me?

"I've had a lot of time to think about this, obviously. And I think, sexually, he was immature. He loved women, but somehow they frightened him at the same time. I wouldn't be surprised if he's never had sex with a woman. Or if he has, I'm positive it wasn't a great experience. And it wasn't like he was trolling school playgrounds, picking up kids from bus stops or anything. He knew me. I was *family*, which in a perverted kind of way makes sense. He could trust me. I wasn't threatening.

"But that started changing. I'd see Wat maybe once a month, but then NorthPoint started making inroads with the government and the Pentagon, and both Wat and Father would be gone for weeks. The longer I was away from him, the more I could look at what he was doing—what *we* were doing—objectively. And by the time I was fourteen and about to head to Blackburne, I was beginning to freak out. Can you imagine what our classmates would have thought about what I'd been doing with my uncle?"

I shook my head in protest. "Look, there's nothing wrong with *you*. You were the victim. Wat—"

"Wat is a pervert and a lech, but I was perfectly willing to let him be that," Fritz said. "And you know I'm right. What would Diamond have said? Or Trip? Would you have roomed with me for three years, knowing what I'd done with Wat?" He appraised me for a few moments as I sat there on that pile of hay, shamefully unable to reply. "It's okay," he said. "I understand. Keeping that secret ate at me, though. You know when a battery is old and the acid leaks out, it gets all corroded? That's what I felt like.

"I did some research, too. Looked up sexual abuse on the Internet, read articles about pedophiles. Something like half of all child molesters were molested themselves. I remember sitting in the library, staring at the computer screen after reading this, and thinking that I might grow up to be a child molester."

Something cold and hard seized me, a half-acknowledged and dreadful thought. Unable to stop myself, I glanced past Fritz to the trailer door. Tommy was in there, playing alone. *He wouldn't do that*, I thought. *He wouldn't.* Then, horrified, I realized Fritz saw where I was looking. "No, Fritz," I said, "I don't—I'm not—" I felt my face flush and panic rise in my throat, threatening to squeeze it shut. I stood up, waving my hands as if to blot out what I had just done.

"I know," he said, reassuringly, but I had seen the look of pain on his face when he had realized what I was thinking. "I fucking *know*. That's why . . ." He closed his eyes and then seemed to force them open again. "I haven't—*talked* about this, ever. Not to Shanna, not to anyone. It's this *thing*, a—a *shame* . . ."

I shook my head vehemently. "You would *never* . . . I mean, come *on*, Fritz, you—you wouldn't do that. Not to anyone."

To my great relief, Fritz let out a long breath and smiled weakly. "I don't think I would, either. But then, after everything that happened with Wat, all I saw was the possibility that I *might* end up doing that. I was fucking freaked out. Every time sex came up, I'd freak out. Fletcher Dupree or someone else would say, 'Blow me,' and I'd start sweating. I'd go to the A/V center on Saturdays, sit in the dark with everyone, and watch R-rated movies . . . Remember *Dracula*, the Coppola one with Keanu? That vampire chick rises up between his legs?"

"Monica Bellucci," I said unsteadily. "Goren loved that flick, watched it every weekend."

Fritz nodded. "I'd watch it, and I'd wonder if I was turned on *enough*. I couldn't keep a girlfriend—"

"You always had a girlfriend."

"Never kept the same one for long, though," he said. "Sort of like running away, I guess. First sign of trouble or stress over sex, I'd dump her and move on." He closed his eyes. "I almost killed Wat once."

Silence for a beat. "Okay," I said.

He opened his eyes. "I mean it. He was at our house one night over Christmas break our senior year, and Mother had to run to the store. My father was at the office, as usual. Abby was upstairs writing a letter or something. Wat decided to watch *The Searchers* on cable while waiting for Mother to come home and have dinner. He just sat there on the couch, watching John Wayne, and I went to the hall closet and found a pistol my father had always kept there, tucked under an old blanket on the top shelf.

It was a .45, big ugly thing. I'd never fired it before, but I walked quietly down the hall to the den where Wat was watching the movie, his back to me, and I pushed the safety off and pointed it at his head." He paused and then exhaled heavily. "Didn't do it. Couldn't."

"Why not?" I murmured.

"Abby," he said simply. "I didn't want to shoot him and have her see him that way, see me with the gun in my hand. It was a near thing. I pushed the safety back on and put the pistol back into the closet and went outside and threw up behind the garage. There's got to be something wrong when the only reason you don't shoot your uncle to death is because you're worried how your sister will react. Later, of course, I was horrified at the idea. I almost went to pieces. I didn't come back to school until later, remember?"

With a shudder, I did remember. "Yeah, your mom said you were sick—flu, I think."

"On the verge of a nervous breakdown, more like it. And then spring break . . ." Fritz grimaced.

"What?"

"My father found pictures on Wat's computer. He was doing a security sweep to pave the way for some government contracts or something, every NorthPoint computer account got the once-over, and his IT guys flagged something buried in Wat's hard drive. A file with hundreds of pictures. All porn. All boys."

"Jesus."

"Wat was at our house that night when Father came home. I'd never seen my father so angry. He told Wat he needed to talk with him, and Wat raised his eyebrows and went into Father's office and closed the door. I stood outside Father's office and listened to him shouting at Wat, asking how he could download porn of all things, accusing him of setting the company up for ruin. I couldn't hear what Wat said, but suddenly he opened the door, trying to leave, and I nearly fell into the room. Father looked livid, just white with anger, but Wat stared at me as if I were a ghost. Then Father looked from him to me."

I said, "He knew?"

Fritz shrugged. "It was all over our faces. I was scared—terrified, even— but at some level I was relieved. We could deal with it, get it out in the open." He said these last words with such bitterness that I nearly rocked back on my heels.

"What happened?" I said.

Fritz clenched his jaw as if afraid to speak. "He buried it," he said. "My father buried it. Had Wat's laptop wiped clean and fired the IT guy who had called him. Made up something about the guy selling NorthPoint secrets to the Koreans or something, I don't know."

"The Chinese," I said hoarsely. I saw in my mind's eye Wat Davenport in his townhome, sitting in front of the fire, his laughter brief and harsh. *It sounds like a bad movie, doesn't it?* Wat had said. *Chinese spies!*

Fritz frowned. "Yeah, maybe it was the Chinese. Anyway, he fired the guy to keep my uncle from getting in trouble. And he wouldn't even talk to me the rest of vacation. He just . . . looked at me, like I was offensive." Fritz's voice wavered slightly before hardening again. "Then he sent me back to Blackburne. That was when I knew I had to leave. My own father didn't want to know what had happened to me, or how I felt, or anything. He just wanted me gone because he thought it would hurt his fucking company." He stabbed a finger toward his trailer. "And now I'm a father, and I have a son, and I swear to God I won't *ever* abandon him the way my own father just . . . left me. He *left* me." His voice dropped, though his tone was no less harsh and insistent. "He left me. When I needed him, he wanted me gone. I just obliged him. I got as much cash together as I could and planned to take off after spring break."

I heard myself ask, in a small voice, "How did you do that? I mean, you didn't 'take off'—you *disappeared*. You walked off the edge of the fucking earth."

Fritz looked weary now, resigned, as if he revisited his history every day. Which, I realized with a shock, he probably did. "I stole a bicycle," he said. "Earlier that year. One of the older faculty kids left it out in a field near his house, and one day during cross country practice, I ran by and saw it and realized that was how I could get away from my family. I pretended my laces were untied and let my teammates run past. Then I went and got the bike and rode it into a stand of trees about a quarter mile away. I felt bad for the kid who owned the bike, but I just saw it as something I needed. The night before I left, during study hall, I ran back to that stand of trees and found it still lying there, a little rust on it but nothing terrible. I think I told you I was studying in the library." He shrugged in apology. "The next night I went back and got on the bike and just rode down the Hill and down the driveway out past the lions. Made it to Staunton in an hour and bought a bus ticket to West Virginia, and then kept going west." He made a halfhearted gesture at the trailer. "Ended up out here, eventually. Finally got to be a cowboy, I guess. Dodging a bull's not much different than dodging tackles. George is training me."

"I thought," I started to say, and then had to clear my throat. "I always thought you left because—we had that argument. About college and . . . how I lied to you." My voice sounded pitiful in my own ears. *Your uncle molested you and you almost killed him, and when your father found out, he covered it up and then you ran away, but the important thing is that I need to apologize.*

Fritz gave me a strange look. Then he reached into his back pocket and pulled out a worn leather wallet, from which he extracted a much-folded piece of paper. He held the paper out to me, and I took it from his hand and unfolded it. It was a letter from UVA addressed to Francis McHugh Davenport. "Dear Fritz," it began. "Congratulations! You have been accepted . . ." I looked up from the letter and stared at Fritz, who gave another small, lopsided grin.

"Got that the day I left," he said.

My head was whirling. I'd heard that description before, about one's head whirling, but this was the first time I had fully experienced it—a sense of vertigo, the ground seeming to lift and rotate beneath me, the air itself thin and hard to breathe. "Wait," I said. "Wait a minute. You told me you hadn't gotten any mail that day. We were by the lions. You said you'd gone and looked in your mailbox and there was nothing."

"There wasn't anything when I looked at first," he said. "Mail came late that day. I was literally about to walk down the Hill and leave that night when I had to check one more time. And there it was."

I stared down at the acceptance letter, and then back at Fritz. "You weren't stressed about getting into college, were you?" I said slowly. "You were planning to leave the whole time."

Fritz closed his eyes as if in prayer. "You have to understand, it didn't seem real, running away," he said. "It was like a game I played with myself, seeing how far I could plan. I didn't *want* to leave, but I didn't feel like I had a choice. I couldn't tell anyone." He opened his eyes to look at me. "I couldn't tell you." He shook his head, sighed. "You knew I was upset, that I couldn't sleep. Everyone else was freaking out about college, so it was easy to let everyone think that I was, too."

"But you *could* have gone to college," I said. I held up his acceptance letter. "You . . . We could have gone together. You'd have been out of your father's house. You wouldn't have had to see your uncle again . . ."

Gently, Fritz took the letter out of my hand, refolded it, and replaced it in his wallet. "I keep it to remind me of that," he said. "But I couldn't have gone, Matthias. Not without them. They both went to UVA, they would have come to visit, professors would have said, 'Oh, aren't you Wat Davenport's nephew?' I just—I needed to get *away*. In fact, you helped me do it." He looked at me, the honesty and pain in his face so raw, I was transfixed. "When you told me you had cheated, I—I felt betrayed. It hurt. But it was the final push I needed to go. And I had to go. I almost shot my uncle. If I hadn't run away, I guarantee I would have gone to get that gun again. And I might have shot myself, too. So I *had* to leave. And the only way to do that was to leave you and my sister and my mother and . . . everything. I'm sorry."

You think sadness is a feeling that you experience on a continuum, that even though it can be slight or strong, it is essentially a fixed emotional state. But what I felt then was a grief that swelled around me, isolating me from the rest of the world even as it seemed to encompass me, Fritz, that rodeo lot, the sky itself, and the distant stars beyond. I felt caught in a tidal grip of loss and despair almost too great for tears, and all I could do was bow my head before it.

"Me, too," I muttered, wiping my eyes. "I'm sorry, Fritz."

We sat there in the awkward silence.

"So," Fritz said, as if we had just discovered that we were standing in a chilly rodeo lot in Wyoming. "Now what?"

CHAPTER TWENTY-SIX

NorthPoint's headquarters in Arlington was a sleek, black chrome-and-glass structure that looked as if an award-winning architect had mated a bunker with a modern art museum. The glass entrance doors were massive and yet opened at a touch, swinging silently inward. The atrium was an immense, open space—even the sound of my shoes striking the marble floor was swallowed up in the emptiness. I approached a curved information desk that looked like a bridge console from *Star Trek*. A corporate blond fembot behind the desk smiled. "May I help you?" she asked politely.

"Frank Davenport," I said.

Not a flicker of doubt. "Do you have an appointment?"

"He'll want to see me." As she drew breath to speak, undoubtedly to deny me access, I said, "It's about his son, Fritz."

A security guard in blazer and gray flannels, standing impassively behind the fembot's shoulder, gave me his full attention. I ignored him.

"Your name, sir?" the fembot asked, touching two screens on her console.

I told her and then looked across the atrium at a waterfall, its sound somewhere between a gentle rain and a rushing brook. The security guard continued to gaze at me. I winked at him, considered winking at the fembot, and then decided against it—she was pressing two fingertips to her jaw and talking quietly into an earphone, her glance flickering over me once.

Presently, two more security guards arrived. "This way, sir," said one of them, gesturing to a nearby wall of elevators. They escorted me into an open elevator and remained with me as we rode up. Then the elevator came to a stop, and the door opened to reveal a semicircular waiting room with another fembot—this one a redhead—behind a round leather-paneled reception desk. "Mr. Glass," she said, and she stood, tall and elegant as a porcelain vase. "Right this way." She led me past the desk and into a short corridor with muted lighting and oil paintings—probably the originals—that I knew I could find in an art history textbook. The two security guards continued to flank us like an honor guard. At the end was a set of doors that towered over us, like the gates to some corporate Valhalla. The redhead turned the handle on one door, opened it inward, and extended her hand toward the doorway, palm turned upward as if serving something exquisite. "Please, go in," she said. I glanced behind me at the two security guards, who clearly were following me no farther. I nodded to them and stepped through the doorway, the redhead pulling the door shut behind me.

The office was the size of an aircraft hangar. Fully half the back wall, which curved outward, seemed to be glass, although it was dimmed somehow to a smoky color that filtered the sunlight. The floor was dark, polished wood. Before me were various armchairs, side tables, a couch, and a desk that anchored an enormous oriental rug. To the left was a conference table with leather-backed chairs, the wall behind it taken up by what looked like the world's largest flatscreen. Behind me on either side of the massive doors were built-in mahogany shelves holding thick red and blue binders. The ceiling was high, and recessed lights washed the room in a soft glow.

Mr. Davenport was seated at his desk, writing. A lamp cast a brighter circle of light upon his desk, and he bent over his writing as if to shield it from the light. I stood there, watching him hunched over his papers, his pen moving as if it were a blade with which he was parrying an unseen foe.

"One minute, Matthias," he said without looking up.

I reached for the pen I had in my shirt pocket, unclipped it, and with an underhand motion tossed it onto his desk. It landed with a satisfyingly noisy clatter, right on the piece of paper on which Davenport was writing. Then it rolled toward the edge of the desk, stopped only by Davenport's free hand. He put down his own pen and picked mine up, examined it, and then looked at me. The bags under his eyes were dark as charcoal.

"I gave you this pen," he said, a rasp in his voice. "For Christmas, when you were in school."

"I know about your brother," I said. Bitterly I heard the slight tremble in my own voice, but I kept going. "I know what he did to Fritz. He molested his own nephew. Your son. And you buried it when you found out. Your own goddamn son."

I expected Davenport to react with a wide-eyed look of shock, or indignation, in any event something contemptuous and loud and threatening. Instead, he placed the Montblanc on the desktop in front of him and looked at me out of those dark, unsettling eyes. "Whom did you speak to, my brother or Fritz?" he asked calmly.

A bit unnerved by his poise, I pushed on. "Both of them, actually," I said. "But it was Fritz who told me what Wat had done. What you did."

"What I did," Davenport echoed. He continued to stare at me. I was struck by how much older he looked than when I had last seen him, in my dorm room ten years ago. His face was thinner, the skin worn and blotched like pages in a dog-eared paperback, notes inked in the margins, passages of text underlined. "You have no idea what I have done."

Anger rose in my head like blood. "I know you drove your son away, that you—"

He cut across my words. "Why are you here, Matthias?"

The blunt query stopped me in my tracks. I contemplated the question and then said, "Because I wanted you to know that I know. I wanted you to know that I spoke to Fritz. I saw him. And he told me why he left, why he ran away from Blackburne, from me, everything. Because you put your fucking company ahead of your own child. You got the FBI to back off, you bribed policemen, all because of *this*." I waved my arm to encompass his office and NorthPoint in general. "It's pathetic."

Annoyingly, Davenport looked unmoved by my self-righteous rant. "You want me to be evil, the cruel, uncaring father," he said. "A monster. That would be easier to understand." He stood up, walked around the desk until he was facing me. I almost took a step back but held my ground. "I've done things you could call monstrous," he said. "I've designed and made things that were used to kill other people in the name of peace and security. I've helped to stop wars and to start them. I've aided the United States government in protecting our country from terrorist attacks. What I didn't do was protect my own family."

I stared at him. If he was going to play the pity card, I might hit him in the face. "I just told you I spoke to your son who's been missing for ten years," I said. "Don't you even want to know if he's all right?"

Davenport picked up a tablet from the conference table next to us. "I know he's all right," he said. He woke up the tablet, tapped it. On the wall behind the conference table, the flatscreen flickered briefly and then displayed a digital outline of the United States. Red dots lay scattered across the map, principally in the western half in a ragged line from Texas to Montana, a few dots farther west in Utah and Nevada, some to the east in Nebraska and Minnesota. An arrow pointer appeared on the screen, glided over top of a red dot in Wichita, Kansas. A window popped up to the side of the red dot: September 2009. The arrow moved south to Houston: December 2009, November 2010. Fort Morgan, Colorado: February 2011. More cities, more dates, a month or so in between cities and towns. Several had multiple dates going back to 2006. Then I noticed that one dot on the map was bright green: Jackson Hole. I stared at Davenport. He moved the arrow onto Jackson Hole, clicked it. May 2009, May 2010, May 2011. He clicked the most recent date, and a photograph blossomed like a digital flower: a blond-haired Fritz leaning against a fence post, hands in the pockets of his jeans, along with two other men, one wearing a dark cowboy hat. The man in the hat was George, the rodeo clown who'd had the melting makeup face. In the photograph, George was laughing, and Fritz was looking at him with that slight, lopsided smile that was so familiar it hurt, a sharp pang of loss and remorse.

"I know where my son is," Davenport said. "I've known for a long time." He put the tablet down on the conference table and looked directly at me. "My father fought in World War Two. He came back from the Pacific a bona fide war hero. He saved thirteen crewmen from burning to death on his destroyer after a kamikaze hit it. That was his moment in the sun. When he came back home, the sun went behind a cloud. For the rest of his life, he felt he was owed something for his service, more than the already significant amount that was due to him. People grew tired of buying him drinks, tired of hearing his war stories. He never had a steady career after the navy. He failed to provide a steady home for me and my brother. I swore that I would never do that to my own family, and so I built NorthPoint." Davenport turned away from me and looked at the photograph of Fritz on the flatscreen. "And because I was afraid of losing my company, because I lost sight of the reason for which I worked all my life, which is so ironic it's obscene, I drove my own son away, possibly for good, and I have lived with that ever since. I will live with it for the rest of my life. So I am reduced to spying on him. It's what I have instead of a relationship with him."

Somehow I was able to find my voice. "But you could . . . You could go to him, you could talk—"

"It's been ten years, Matthias," he said quietly, still looking at the picture on the flatscreen, a digitized Fritz hovering over the conference table with his sideways smile. "He knows where I am. If he can bring himself to forgive, he'll come to me." He glanced at me, saw my look of incredulity. "If I went to him," he said, "tracked him down to whatever backwater motel or rodeo lot he was living in this month and showed up on his doorstep, what do you think he would do? He's been running from me and my brother for a decade. In time he'll come back. On his own terms."

"Does Abby know?" I managed. "Or his mother?"

"No," he said. "They believe he is dead. Which, for all intents and purposes, he is."

"Legally declared dead," I said.

He inclined his head. "It allowed my wife and daughter to mourn him so they could achieve some kind of closure."

"That's not the only reason," I said. Davenport looked at me with his dark eyes. "There was a trust, wasn't there? From Fritz's other grandfather, your wife's father. All in Fritz's name. Your son told me. How much did you get? Six, seven million?"

Davenport continued to look at me like a snake sizing up a boy with a stick. "Enough to cover some . . . indiscretions that my brother made," he finally said.

"NorthPoint cleared a billion dollars last year," I said. "Your pocket change could pay off any 'indiscretions' of Wat's. You had to rob your own son?"

"My family lives comfortably," Davenport continued in that same calm, even tone. "But most of my personal wealth is tied up with this company. Using monies from the trust fund was more discreet than cutting a corporate check."

"And Wat? What does he know about . . . this?" I indicated the map.

Davenport's face revealed no hint of what he felt. "Nothing," he said. "And I intend to keep it that way." He reached over and touched the tablet, causing the photograph to vanish.

I looked at him and then at the trail of dots on the flatscreen, the chart of his son's wanderings. He had followed Fritz for years, keeping him under a watchful eye while letting the rest of his family believe Fritz was dead. I had thought Ren Middleton was Machiavellian, but this was a whole different order of magnitude.

"Why are you telling me this?" I said. "I could go tell people what happened, what you did."

Davenport frowned. "That would be foolish, considering that Fritz doesn't want to be found. That, as well as the fact that I could bury you if I wished. Really, Matthias, such a crude threat is disappointing."

Before I could think of a response, Davenport raised a hand toward me as if he were offering something. "I know that you've suffered from this. That day in your dorm room, right after Fritz ran away, when I . . . confronted you. Shouted at you. I apologize. I shouldn't have done that."

"You shouldn't have done that," I repeated. I wanted to laugh, to scream. "Wow," I managed. "You abandon your son and lie to your family, but you're apologizing for shouting at me."

Davenport gave a pained, aching smile. "One must start somewhere," he said. "A lifetime of secrets and subterfuge renders you rather unsusceptible to regret. It's a luxury I cannot afford. Do you remember what Polonius says to his son? 'To thine own self be true.' As I am—true to my own nature. But I am . . . trying."

Feeling slightly sickened, I remembered why I was there, the promise I had made to Fritz. I reached my hand into my pocket, pulled out a jump drive, and laid it on the table next to Davenport's tablet.

Davenport looked at it for several seconds. "What's on it?" he finally said.

"A video from Fritz," I said. "For you and your brother."

Davenport's eyes were wide. "What does he say?" he asked, and for the first time his voice betrayed the slightest hint of doubt.

"Why don't you watch it, Mr. Davenport?" I said. "I'll let you do that in peace." I turned and walked toward the doors. When I reached them, I glanced back. Davenport was turning the jump drive over in his hands, his expression a blend of eagerness and dread. I walked through the doorway and pulled it shut behind me.

I didn't need to see the video. I already knew what was on it: a three-minute message from Fritz that included a series of instructions. Now I just needed to wait and see if Frank and Wat Davenport followed them.

CHAPTER TWENTY-SEVEN

A n enormous Welcome Alumni sign hung above the lions, which sat atop columns now bedecked with red and gold streamers. The decorations seemed both festive and foolish, like putting a leather jacket on a wolf. The snarling lion looked ready to rip the streamers to shreds; the other gazed coldly at me, the missing eye conferring a sense of dignity unsullied by the crepe paper looped around its base. "Keep the faith, brother," I said aloud, and as I drove slowly past the lions, I offered them a casual salute.

It was the end of a cloudless June day, the sunlight softly playing over the green leaves, birds flitting from shadow to shadow. I found myself once again wending my way through those trees, although now the sunlight and recent events made the way less haunted, less freighted by the ghosts of memory.

Just past the trees and the security gate, the athletic fields now served as parking lots, and though it was early yet, several cars sat in rows in front of the soccer goals. A police officer in uniform was directing traffic, his gaze lingering on me as I rolled past him, and I recognized Deputy Smalls. I drove down a short aisle, pulled into a spot, and killed the engine. I supposed that I could just sit there in my car until he was distracted, but this was my alma mater, my class reunion, and so I got out of the car, closed the door, and walked toward him.

"Mr. Glass," he said, nodding affably as I approached.

"Deputy," I said, nodding back at him. I felt a little like a cowboy who had been run out of town and was now riding back in, daring the lawman to do something about it. That feeling evaporated in the heat of my embarrassment when Smalls stuck out his hand to shake mine. "Glad to see you made it," he said.

"You referring to my reunion or the whole drug-dealer misunderstanding?" I said. I was still holding his hand.

Smalls smiled. It wasn't as radiant as Briggs's smile, but it was nice. "Yes," he said.

I smiled back, and we dropped our hands. "Okay," I said. "Um, thanks."

He nodded. "Someone's looking for you," he said, glancing over my shoulder.

Feeling uneasy, I turned, expecting to see Sheriff Townsend. Instead, I saw a uniformed Lester Briggs sitting in an old ladder-back chair. He waved me over impatiently, and I made my way down the aisle of parked cars to him. He looked thinner without looking feebler, as if he had burned away any superfluous weight, distilling his intensity. He had in his hand a clipboard of license plate numbers, which I presumed belonged to the cars parked all around us.

"I like the uniform," I said. "All law enforcement-y. How's the sheriff feel about it?"

Briggs snorted, like he was throttling a laugh in his throat. "He brought it to me personally," he said. "We're best friends now. The DA loves me, so Ricky Townsend loves me. DA's not the only one looking to move into a bigger office. I got injured trying to make a citizen's arrest and prevented a drug dealer from committing a murder. I'm a hero."

"I'll buy you a cape, maybe some boots. Your back doing okay?"

"Keep the cape. I'll take a new pair of boots. And my back is fine." Briggs eyed me. "You found him, didn't you," he said.

"Didn't pan out," I said lightly. "You were right. Kevin Kelly went to too many places out west. It'll take me a long time to check them all out."

Now he did laugh. "I've got a grandnephew just turned four. He lies better than you do."

"Let's say I had a talk with Frank Davenport and delivered a message to him. Justice was served, et cetera."

He looked at me, and I looked back. "You're not going to tell me anything else, are you?" he said.

I shrugged. "Nothing else I *can* tell you."

Slowly, he nodded, and then stood up just as slowly, wincing. "Well," he said, a whole raft of conflicting emotions behind that one word. He slapped the clipboard against the side of his leg. "You enjoy the rest of your weekend."

"Will do. You watch your back."

He began to nod, did the briefest of double takes, and then shook his head. "Everyone's a goddamn comedian," he said. I walked away, a smile on my face. When I glanced back, he had sat down in the chair and was looking over the clipboard.

I walked up the drive to the Hill. Here and there, I saw small knots of adults, men in slacks and khakis, some in blazers, some with wives, all talking and gazing around with contented looks of nostalgia. Suddenly I felt exposed, walking alone past the broad steps of Farquhar Gym. Running into Lester Briggs had been a surprise, but a relatively easy one to navigate. I now had the irrational fear that Fletcher Dupree would step out from behind a hedge, a smirk on his face and a "water buffalo!" joke at the ready. The administration wouldn't want me here. My classmates were strangers to me. Why had I come back?

"Mr. Glass?" a voice said. I started and turned to see a boy in shorts and a red-and-gold Blackburne polo coming down the gym steps, a tennis racket in a bag slung over his shoulder. It took me a moment to realize it was Ben Sipple.

"Ben!" I said. "Hi. What are you doing here? Isn't school out?"

He shook his head. "Sixth formers are still here—exams next week. The tennis team made it to the state championship."

"Didn't know you played tennis. Congrats. You must be good."

"I guess," he said. "Thanks. Uh, weren't you fired?"

For a second I stared at him. Then I laughed. He frowned, puzzled.

"Yeah, I was," I said. "But it was a mistake. What they fired me for."

"Oh, okay," he said. It was the verbal equivalent of a shrug, as if he were thinking adults were strange but didn't want to say it out loud. Then he added, "I heard something like that. That someone was selling drugs and tried to put it on you."

So Sam Hodges had understood my e-mail. This buoyed me up considerably. "Yeah, well," I said, unwilling to enter into specifics. "I'm here for a class reunion, though. Alumni weekend and all that. You doing okay, Ben?"

He considered this for a moment. "Yeah," he said. "I'm going to go visit my dad this summer, in Boston. He broke up with his girlfriend, so it'll just be the two of us for a couple of weeks."

"That sounds good," I said.

"Yeah, well." He hesitated and then suddenly stuck his hand out. "Thanks, Mr. Glass, for . . . everything."

I shook his hand. "Sure thing, Ben. You take care, okay?"

He nodded. "Okay." He waved and then ran up the gym steps two at a time, disappearing through the doors as I stood at the foot of the steps, watching him go.

REGISTRATION WAS IN THE front hall of Stilwell, printed name tags lined up by graduating class on a long table. I signed in with a woman I didn't recognize from the alumni office, smiled through her polite greeting, and looked for my name tag. I found myself looking for other names, too—Trip Alexander, Daryl Cooper, Miles Camak. And Fritz Davenport. Even though I now knew Fritz was okay and safely on the other side of the country, it felt wrong that his name wasn't included.

"Matthias?" A tall, prematurely balding man in a crimson polo beamed at me. It took me a second to recognize him, and when I did, I remembered him playing the Beastie Boys at full volume on dorm and endlessly watching *Dracula* in the A/V center.

"Max?"

Max Goren laughed and gave me a bear hug, which, startled, I returned as best I could. "Knew it was you!" Max was saying. "God, what's it been, since graduation? Come on, the alumni tent's behind Stilwell. Cash bar, but what the hell." He steered me past the table and on into the dining hall. There were only a couple tables of sixth formers in there, and they all looked up at me and Max, the same look on all their faces: *What are those older guys doing here?* I knew what they were thinking; I'd thought it myself when I'd been a student. I grinned at them. A few politely smiled back.

Max was chattering about real estate in Richmond, where he lived with his wife. "Expecting a daughter end of next week," he said proudly. "Kristie's at home fit to bust, didn't want to ride in the car over here, but she told me to go on, give her the last peace and quiet she'll get for a long time."

As he went on, I nodded and made inquisitive noises at the appropriate moments, but mostly I was wondering when Max Goren had grown up. He'd always been a nice guy but a bit of a clown, and now here he was a bona fide adult, a real estate agent, married with a kid on the way. When had that happened?

At the back of the dining hall were double doors that led outside to a set of steps down to a brick patio, behind which was a little-used lawn ringed by boxwood hedges. The alumni tent was pitched here, bigger than the one at the Game this past fall but with the same fold-out chairs and tables, the same cash bar. This time there were other people scattered in groups, talking, laughing, telling stories. Three wrinkled gentlemen in sweaters despite the warm evening wore name tags declaring them members of the class of 1946. Another group of what looked like college students clutched bottles of beer and looked around a bit confusedly, as if unsure of how to act. I guessed they were here for their fifth-year reunion. I understood how they felt.

Then Max was saying, "Hey, look who I found!" and I saw, in a corner of the tent, a table of beaming faces turned my way. I registered Miles Camak and Roger Bloom and Tom Dodrill among the small crowd before they were all on their feet, shaking my hand and slapping me on the back, someone putting a cold beer in my hand. I was so flustered with all the greetings and questions and smiles that I couldn't speak for a few moments, just grin bashfully and exchange high fives and drink my beer. Miles introduced me to his wife, a petite blonde with a big smile. Roger had apparently been in the middle of telling the story about the fake list of football players' numbers he'd been given for Third Form Night, and as he continued, I laughed along with the others, joined with them by both the memory and the ability to laugh at what had seemed so terrifying all those years ago.

Then I saw Fletcher Dupree sitting across the table from me. He looked stouter, something about him a bit blunted. He gazed at me, and I raised my beer in his direction. "Fletcher," I said, and my classmates grew a bit quieter, sensing a different kind of reunion.

Fletcher nodded. Deliberately he said, "Matthias, what's going on?"

I shook my head. "Not much," I said. "You?"

"Heard you were teaching," he said, and I heard in his voice a hint of goading. I saw Roger Bloom and Tom Dodrill glance back to me.

"Was," I said. "I was teaching. Here."

"Didn't like it?" Fletcher asked. "Kinda different from writing novels."

I took a deep breath. "I liked it okay up until the point some kid stashed drugs in my desk and tried to frame me for selling to students," I said evenly.

Silence. Fletcher looked like a dog that had just found a fresh bone to gnaw. "You were *framed* for selling drugs?" he asked.

"I read about that," Tom Dodrill interrupted. "It was in the Charlottesville paper. Wasn't it Kevin Kelly?"

"Kevin Kelly?" Miles said. "That kid a couple of years behind us?"

"Yeah," Tom said. "He had a grow house outside of Charlottesville. Sold to lots of schools, I read."

"What, here?"

"Yeah. Heard Pelham Greer was helping him."

"Greer? No shit?"

Fletcher cut across the questions. "So you were framed?" he asked me.

"Yeah," I said. "All charges were dropped."

"But that's pretty serious," Fletcher continued innocently. "I mean, did they fire you or anything?"

I felt as much as saw all eyes turn to me. Anger and embarrassment rose to my face. I'd had no interest in hashing this out with Fletcher, or with anyone else, and yet here I was doing it. Then a familiar voice behind me said, "Mistakenly, Mr. Dupree. The issue has been settled."

I glanced up to see Sam Hodges in his trademark suspenders and bow tie. Startled, I put my beer down and got to my feet. Several of my classmates did the same. "Keep your seats, fellas," he said genially, waving his hands down, but now everyone stood up to greet our former dean, Fletcher among them, although he looked peeved. "Turns out Matthias here discovered a staff member was involved in criminal activity," Sam continued, putting a hand on my shoulder. "Unfortunately, we were fooled into thinking Matthias was the criminal. We were wrong, and all has been forgiven." He looked at me ruefully. "On our side, at any rate. I wouldn't blame you if you felt differently."

"Not at all, Sam," I said. "Thank you." Sam squeezed my shoulder and then moved among the crowd, shaking hands, laughing, exchanging with everyone a brief word or story. I saw, with a dark kind of glee, that Sam managed to ignore Fletcher entirely as he greeted the rest of my classmates.

The evening sky grew deeper, and lights glowed under the tent. A band began setting up near a dance floor that had been set down on the grass. I sat back in my chair, sipping my second beer and watching my old classmates rather than engaging in conversation. I noticed without rancor that after the initial greetings, everyone was reverting to old behavior. Julian Pumphrey, our class valedictorian, was talking rather didactically about the perils of investment banking to a bored-looking Max. Fletcher, having recovered from his failure to bait me, had gathered Miles and Roger around him and was telling stories about other classmates, smirking and laughing throughout. Tom Dodrill and Jeb Tanner were arguing about SEC football. I realized that Fritz and I had usually joked privately about this sort of thing, the cliques our class had formed, and although I felt a slight melancholy, I was content to sit back and observe. Occasionally I chatted with Max or Tom or Miles's wife, but mostly I just nibbled at my plate of shrimp and listened to everyone else talk. No one had asked about Fritz, which was both fine and, illogically, just a little disappointing.

Just as the band began playing "Only the Good Die Young," Sam appeared again at my side, and I stood up. "So, how are you, really?" Sam asked, hooking his left thumb under one suspender in a familiar gesture.

"I'm doing fine, Sam, thanks. And thanks for what you said back there."

He winked. "I figured Fletcher Dupree needed to shut his hole," he said.

I looked around at the alums, a few of them taking to the dance floor. "Is Dr. Simmons here?" I asked.

Sam shook his head. "Asked me to come in his place," he said. "Travis is out in Utah, with Paul. Some family bonding time."

My estimation of Travis Simmons rose a bit. Maybe he and Paul would turn out okay. "Does Ren Middleton come to these things?" I asked. "Can't imagine he'd be happy to see me here tonight."

"No," Sam said. "He's not big on these." He looked at me shrewdly. "You have every right to be here, Matthias, if that's what you're suggesting. Travis and even Ren would agree."

I shook my head. "No worries." And I meant it.

"So," Sam said, "what will you do next?"

"Thought I might take a teaching job in Asheville," I said. "Creative writing instructor. It's not much, but it's a start."

Sam grinned. "Put me down as a reference." He looked past my shoulder. "You've got some more friends just came in," he said.

I turned. Trip and Diamond had entered the tent. With a roar of welcome, my classmates swarmed forward, nearly pummeling them both on the back, especially Diamond, who got both Miles and Max into a headlock under each arm to shouts of laughter. Before I could reach Diamond, however, Trip saw me and walked over. "Come with me," he said, touching my arm and guiding me off to the side. Puzzled, I followed Trip, who moved past a few tables until he reached a relatively quiet corner of the tent.

"What's going on?" I asked.

"Wat Davenport's dead," he said.

A sickening void formed in my gut. "What?"

"He drove off the Arlington Memorial Bridge into the Potomac. Happened this afternoon."

Hope trembling slightly in my voice, I said, "An accident?"

"He was in some sort of souped-up Hummer. Two witnesses say he floored it going onto the bridge, swerved around a delivery truck, and then swung hard right and punched through the railing. You might do one of those things if you're having a heart attack, but not all three."

"But maybe—"

"The Hummer was something NorthPoint was working on for the military. Had a reinforced chassis made specifically for ramming. It went through a reinforced concrete parapet like it was a split-rail fence."

I had to lean back against a table. "Jesus, Trip," I said. This had not been the plan. At all.

"Frank Davenport just announced he's resigning as CEO of North-Point," Trip went on. "Saw it on my phone a few minutes ago. Says he was already considering retirement with the tenth anniversary of Fritz's disappearance coming up, and now with his brother's death, he's done."

"Makes sense, I guess," I said weakly.

"Bullshit," Trip said. "It makes *no* sense. When his son disappeared, he missed four days and then went right back to work. He *is* NorthPoint. Guys like him don't retire—they die at their desks. This is the kind of thing congressmen do when they're about to be indicted."

"Trip—"

"Did you have anything to do with this?" he asked.

"Did I—did I have anything to do with Wat Davenport *killing himself*?" I didn't have to fake the outrage, although guilt crested like a mounting wave, threatening to swamp me. I felt like I might vomit right there.

"No, *listen*," Trip continued, relentlessly. "Diamond and I stuck our necks out for you. We dug up dirt on Frank Davenport, and we tell you and you go off to D.C. to talk to his brother. Then you don't tell us jack—"

"I went to *jail*, Trip. And then I was almost killed. Kinda threw me off."

"And a couple of months later," Trip said, ignoring me, "Wat Davenport kills himself and Frank Davenport retires. I met Wat once—everyone in D.C. does sooner or later. Full of life, full of himself. I don't see him driving off a bridge. So either he was dying of cancer or AIDS or something and couldn't face it, or somebody had something on him so bad, it was enough to make him want to kill himself rather than deal with it."

"Trip," I managed to get out, "you're being *paranoid*. I don't know why—"

"Matthias," he said, "look me in the eye and tell me you didn't have anything to do with this."

In Jackson Hole, Fritz had insisted on making the video. I'd thought it was risky, but he'd been adamant. *If Kevin Kelly found me and you could find me, then it's only a matter of time*, he'd said. Fritz had gotten a hand-held video camera and had me film him in my hotel room, a blank wall behind him as he talked into the camera. It was all of three minutes long, and it wasn't Scorsese by a long shot, but it had obviously worked, albeit not in the way we had planned. Fritz's demands were simple. Of his father Fritz required that, within a week of seeing the video, he deposit the same amount of money he had withdrawn from Fritz's trust into a new, separate trust for Tommy. Fritz could access the interest but could not touch the principal, which would go to Tommy when he turned twenty-five or when Fritz predeceased him, whichever came first. *Something good out of all that corruption*, Fritz had said. Of his uncle, Fritz had said only that Wat was never to seek him out, or Tommy. If his father and uncle didn't abide by these conditions, Fritz would send another video, addressed not to them but to the world, in which Fritz talked about how and why he had run away ten years ago and spoke in explicit detail about what Wat had done to him. That second video had taken far longer to film, and it had been excruciating to watch Fritz recount his story again. Fritz had included an excerpt from it on the jump drive I'd given to his father. *This stays a secret*, Fritz had told me. *They'll leave me alone if they think they can keep this covered up. I'll keep it covered up if they pay the price.* But we hadn't figured on the price Wat Davenport would be willing to pay.

I looked at Trip, who was waiting for my reply.

"I had nothing to do with this," I said.

He held me in a long gaze. Just when it was becoming unbearable, he closed his eyes and sighed. "Okay," he said. "Sorry. I just . . . I got freaked out. These are powerful men, and it looks like somebody got to them, and I—"

"Hey, no," I said. "I understand. Seriously. It's all right. And I'm sorry I didn't tell you what happened with Wat. It was a bust, actually." I briefly outlined Wat's story about the Chinese spies and Frank Davenport's fears about losing the Pentagon contracts. As I was telling this to Trip, I was thinking about how I didn't even have to make this part up—Wat Davenport had done that for me.

My phone started ringing. "Hang on," I said to Trip, fishing my phone out of my pocket. He shook his head and waved, and headed across the tent for the bar. I looked at the phone display, which showed an unfamiliar number with a Virginia area code. I answered. "Hello?"

"Matthias?"

"Abby," I said. *Oh shit.* "Hi."

"What the hell is going on?" she demanded.

The band chose this moment to begin playing "Brown Eyed Girl," and I had to hold my free hand over my other ear and shout at Abby to hold on while I made my way to the exit. Outside the tent, I welcomed the cooler air and walked off a little ways, phone to my ear, a boxwood hedge on my left. The back of Stilwell Hall loomed before me. "Sorry," I said into the phone. "I'm at Blackburne, my reunion. There's a band—"

"Do you know why my uncle killed himself?" she said.

"I . . . Trip just told me, Trip Alexander, he—"

"Does this have to do with Fritz?"

I stopped walking. "Fritz . . . What?"

"Does it have anything to do with Fritz?"

I looked up at the sky. The sun had set a while ago and was just a dull crimson smear in the west, but above the sky was a deep indigo and the first stars were shining, cold and remote and beautiful.

"Matthias?" Abby's voice was insistent.

You can't tell anyone else, Fritz had said. *No one. Not my sister, my mother, our friends, anyone.*

I drew a breath. "Abby, Fritz is gone," I said. "Like you told me. He's been gone for a long time."

Silence on the other end. "I don't believe you," she said.

Jesus. Had her father told her something? Had he sought forgiveness by showing her the map tracing Fritz's progress across the United States like some bizarre connect-the-dots puzzle? "You don't believe that Fritz is gone?" I said.

"My father came home last night and announced that he was resigning from NorthPoint, and then he locked himself in his office," Abby said. I couldn't tell if she was angry or on the verge of tears. Probably both. "He wouldn't talk to me or Mother. Then my uncle came over and went right into my father's office. I thought they were going to kill each other. The last time I heard them like this was just before Fritz . . . disappeared." There was a hitch in her voice, and she paused for a moment before resuming, in control but brittle. "I listened outside the office door. My father said something about being exposed, and then—then Wat said Fritz's name. I couldn't hear the rest of it, but Wat stormed out a while later, didn't even say good-bye. And today they found him dead. They're saying he drove off the bridge on purpose, Matthias." Her voice wavered under the threat of tears, but she still held them in. "Why would he do that? My father won't say anything. Do you know? Wat always liked you, Matthias. He respected you. Did—did you talk to him, about Fritz?" Ragged breathing, a sniff. "Please."

I ground my teeth. Not telling Briggs or Trip the truth about Fritz had been simple; not telling Abby was something else entirely. Should I betray my friend, or the girl I once loved—still loved? My throat seemed to swell with the pressure of keeping this lie bottled up, another lie.

"Matthias?"

The Davenport family secret had festered and spread in the dark—it was sending out roots and tendrils like some nightmarish vine, clinging to everything and everyone involved, choking us all.

"Matthias, please."

Don't tell my sister.

"He had secrets, Abby," I said. "Your uncle. They were awful, and he had to live with them."

"What do you—?"

"I . . . Abby, I can't explain. You'll have to talk to your father."

Pause. Now, ridiculously, the band was playing "Gimme Some Loving" by the Spencer Davis Group.

"Matthias—"

I stared at my phone, a faint glow in the oncoming night, and then with my forefinger I pressed End, cutting off the call. I could only imagine Abby's reaction right now, wherever she was. But she knew something wasn't right. My hanging up on her would only confirm her suspicions. And so I'd kept my promise to Fritz while indirectly goading Abby toward the truth. Yet I hesitated in the dark outside of the tent. Was this how I was going to leave things with her? Some cryptic clues, a hang-up, and a vague hope that all would be well?

"Fuck it," I said aloud, and I opened up Facebook on my phone. Then I typed and sent Abby a message—Hamlet's letter to Ophelia:

> *Doubt thou the stars are fire,*
> *Doubt that the sun doth move,*
> *Doubt truth to be a liar,*
> *But never doubt I love.*

Then I shut off my phone and stuck it back in my pocket.

I wandered back into the tent out of an essential need for light and company, and the first person I ran into was Diamond. Unable to help myself, I glanced down at his leg, but all I could see was a khaki pant leg with a bayonet-sharp crease. I looked up to see Diamond smiling. "Yeah, it's still fake," he said. "Wanna race?"

"I need a drink first. And a head start. And a new Achilles."

Diamond held up two beers and then took one step back. "Two out of three ain't bad."

The crowd around my classmates' table had grown a bit, but Diamond managed to wrangle two empty seats next to Trip, who looked at me, concerned. "Everything okay?" he asked.

"Abby called," I said. "Her uncle."

Max Goren leaned forward. "Hey, I just heard about that—Trip was telling us." He shook his head. "That poor family. I guess you never . . . heard anything else, about Fritz?"

Others leaned in now, too, lured by the fateful name, the tragic story of our class. I hesitated. Then I shook my head. "No," I said, glancing at Trip, who said nothing. "No, I didn't."

A hush settled on us, each seeming to bow his head before the unlaid ghost. Then Trip raised his beer. "To Fritz Davenport," he said, "wherever he may be. I wish he were here."

"To Fritz," Diamond said.

Two dozen drinks were raised up, mine included. "To Fritz," we echoed, and we drank. It was a balm, an acknowledgment of a missing comrade. My eyes stung, and I was surprised to see one or two other classmates wipe a finger across their eyes, too.

"So," Roger Bloom said after a few moments, "are you writing anything new, Matthias?"

Fletcher Dupree smiled. "Drug dealers, arrests, guess you have a lot to write about, huh?" he said.

"Yeah, but not that," I said. "I've got a new novel in mind." It was true, inasmuch as I had just that moment thought of it.

"No shit," Max Goren said. "What's it about?"

"A cowboy," I heard myself say. "Modern day, though, not the Wild West."

There were several *oh*s and *hmm*s of polite acknowledgment. Fletcher, though, looked disappointed. "How did you pick *that?*" he asked. "You know a lot about cowboys?"

I paused in my reply, letting the moment spin out. Someone coughed nervously. Slowly, Fletcher began to smile in anticipation. I grinned back at him. *The hell with it.* "Oh, I don't know, Fletcher," I said good-naturedly, looking him dead-on. "I'm a novelist. It interests me, and what I don't know I'll make up as I go along. Good enough for you?"

There was an awkward moment or two, the tension coiled around us. Fletcher frowned, and then Diamond grinned and said, "Yippee ki-yay, motherfucker!" and everyone laughed, the world righted again. Then we all drank and proposed other toasts: to Blackburne, to Sam Hodges, to the lions. As we laughed and remembered, I thought of Kevin Kelly and his angry rant against the school, how Blackburne held out a false promise of success. But as I looked around at my classmates, I saw that each of them had made his own way—Trip to the *Washington Post*, Diamond to the Marines, Max to real estate. Even Fritz, I realized. And me, too. I had found my way back to this group, these guys I had thought were lost to me, only to find they had been here all along. I had avoided them for so long because I'd felt damaged, sullied, not deserving of a place at the table. But Fritz had felt that way, too, through no fault of his own. And no matter what we had done, or what had happened to us, our places at this table had been set long ago, waiting for us to return.

I sat there among my classmates, my friends, and let their talk flow over me like clear water, this charmed circle of men with its missing brother who was not forgotten—who might yet be returned to us. Until then, we would go on, his absence a ghostly echo in our hearts that would cease when he appeared and we could welcome him back into the fold, letting the lion's share of loss and grief slip away.

ACKNOWLEDGMENTS

For the teachers who encouraged me and taught me the craft: Ted Blain at Woodberry Forest School; Marshall Boswell, Cathryn Hankla, Dabney Stuart, and Jim Warren at Washington and Lee University; Trudy Lewis, Michael Pritchett, and Carol Anshaw at the University of Missouri–Columbia; and Pam Durban, David Bottoms, and John Holman at Georgia State University;

For the authors who read my early attempts at fiction and offered their time and wisdom: Peter Carey, Deborah Eisenberg, and Richard Ford;

For my fellow students and writers who helped me get here: Scott Howe, Lyrae Van Clief-Stefanon, Traci Lazenby, Mike Land, Pam Johnston, Bernadette Murphy McConville, Alison Umminger, and Tina May Hall;

For the encouragement, advice, and friendship of Jonathan Evison, and for everyone in the Fiction Files;

For Sarah Smith Chapman, for reading an early draft and making invaluable suggestions;

For Mollie Glick, Joy Fowlkes, Emily Brown, Jane Steele, Peter Steinberg, and the rest of the amazing folks at Foundry Literary + Media;

For the patience, talent, and eagle eye of my editor, Andra Miller, who took a chance on me, and to Betsy Gleick, Elisabeth Scharlatt, and everyone else at Algonquin Books for making a lifelong dream come true;

For Patti Callahan Henry, Emily Giffin, Mira Jacob, David Liss, Amanda Kyle Williams, and Ed Tarkington, whose kindness is matched only by their talent:

The only way I can thank you all and repay your generosity is to write true lines.

Thanks also to David Simpson, for answering my questions about the legal system; to John Holman (again), Tom McHaney, and Josh Russell, who served as my dissertation committee and suffered through my first novel; to my parents, David and Nancy Swann, who never once asked me if I should think about doing something else other than writing; to my graduating class at Woodberry Forest School (hope you like the Easter eggs, fellas); to Holy Innocents' Episcopal School—particularly the English faculty and the department chairs—for cheering me on and helping to support my writing habit; and to Ronit Wagman, Wes Miller, Laura Regan, Margee Durand, Andrew and Autumn Swann, and Croom and Meriwether Beatty.

Above all, thanks to Kathy Ferrell-Swann, my first reader, editor, critic, cheerleader, and wife. I love you.